THE KISS PLOT

BOOK TWO OF THE QUICKSILVER TRILOGY

NICOLE FRENCH

To every queen.

PRELUDE

In his head, it wasn't quite an onomatopoeia, but it was close. Repetitive and grating, like the worst kind of figurative language. Like a nursery rhyme someone had composed on the spot, or a fingernail tapping on a window. Innocuous at first, but eventually you thought it might break your brain completely.

Something was leaking in the corner. A broken pipe, maybe, or a crack in the ceiling. Eric had no idea because the room was pitch-black. Cold and damp, it also reeked of sweat and mildew mixed with clumps of dirt on the floor, and whatever the liquid was had been slapping in a steady, sloppy pool interminably since he'd been tossed in here like a dog.

Eric pressed his head into the wall, hoping the chill might quiet the sounds. It didn't work. How long had he been lying on the dusty concrete? Hours? Days? His stomach rumbled. He had barely been able to eat lunch in his suite at the Waldorf, and that had been hours before he was due at the church along with half of New York. Even after he'd gone down to deliver his vows to Jane's room and hear her voice before the ceremony, his nerves had been too jittery to stomach much more than a salad and some nuts. There would be food at the reception, after all. After the deed was done, and he and Jane were finally married.

Of course, things hadn't exactly gone as planned, but they never did with Jane. Fucking hell, she'd looked stunning, though, standing there at the crossing, a white, lethal combination of fury and beauty, like one of the carved archangels in the church come to life. She had been so angry, so betrayed, even after their shouts had echoed around the small chapel while the wedding guests murmured in the main hall.

For a bit, he'd honestly thought she was going to leave him there. That poetic justice would finally be served, and he'd be the jerk left at the altar.

Still, in the end, Jane had chosen the vows, hadn't she? Gritted through her teeth, sure, but she'd still said them. Eric had to believe a part of her had meant them. He certainly had.

But before he could tell her, everything had gone to hell.

He twisted on the floor, which was difficult, considering his hands were duct-taped behind his back.

Was anyone looking for him? He had barely heard the commotion of Grandmother collapsing as Carson and his thugs shuttled him away. The cathedral doors were still open when the words "she's dead!" echoed off the high stone walls of St. John the Divine. And if that were true—if the cantankerous, stubborn, pearl-dripping matriarch of the de Vries clan had finally met her maker—well, it wasn't likely that many others would care if Eric was alive or dead either.

His cousin Nina, for instance, and her husband, Calvin. Nina wasn't a bad egg, but both were undoubtedly relieved that he might be out of the picture, unable to take what even Eric had to admit should rightfully belong to his cousin, considering she was the one who stuck around for the last ten years.

Or his aunt Violet, who made no secret of her anger that the family's holdings were to be transferred to a prodigal son like Eric rather than her own dutiful daughter.

His mother, to whom he had barely spoken in a decade, was more likely diving into a bottle of gin while she survived her second marriage to a hedge fund owner.

Would any of them care that Eric had vanished?

Doubtful.

And Jane.

Jane.

Jane.

Eric slumped to the floor, suddenly light-headed. Jane's face, so perfect and imperfect at the same time, flashed again through his mind. She had looked almost alien in the white dress, simple but for the train that seemed to stretch miles. Her black-brown hair pinned back into a demure bun, except for the bright streak of red in the back she'd kept just for him. Her glasses were gone, the black nail polish replaced with clear, the dark makeup, the wild jewelry...all of it traded for the almost doll-like woman standing there, waiting for him.

Except her lips. They had still been a bright, garish red. Taunting him even as her mouth twisted with hurt and rage.

Eric pressed his forehead into the concrete, willing the vision of her face, contorted in anger, to disappear. God, it hurt. His chest was like a twisted sponge and throbbed with an endless ache.

And it was his fault, too. Not because of what he'd done—in the grand scheme of things, did it really matter that he'd slept with Caitlyn Calvert, a family friend, five years ago? After he and Jane had done equal damage to each other's hearts anyway?

No, it wasn't that. It was the fact that he'd concealed it. That he'd kept it to himself with every dinner party, every event, every moment they'd shared with Caitlyn over the past six months. He'd known, and he'd never told her.

Just like he'd never told her about so many other things that filled him with regret. Like Janus.

Deorum vocas.

He had never hated Virgil so fucking much.

The door to the room slammed open, and a light was flipped on, revealing to Eric for the first time something of his surroundings. Not that it did him much good. After hours in darkness, the harsh glare of the single fluorescent bulb dangling from the ceiling was blinding. Eric felt rather like the men in Plato's cave, squinting with the pain of sudden sight. Except, of course, he hadn't escaped at all. He was still trapped.

"In the chair."

A deep voice Eric recognized as Carson's sounded behind him, and Eric's eyes adjusted just in time to register two others: Jude, Carson's right-hand man, and an enormous bodyguard who had retrieved Eric from the church with Carson. The two lugged him roughly off the floor by his bound wrists and shoved him onto a seat in the middle of the room. It was an odd chair, with a stiff metal back and a large circle cut out of the seat. Rather like sitting on a toilet. Not uncomfortable—especially compared to hours on the floor—but still odd.

"His ankles," Carson said as he walked into the room.

Eric squinted into the light while the thugs wrapped tape around his ankles and the chair legs, then wrenched his arms to be secured over the back of the chair. Carson approached curiously, almost like he was viewing a zoo exhibit.

It was the first really good look at the man Eric had gotten since he was twenty-two, newly tapped to be a member of the Janus society and initiated through Inquisition-style bullshit like this. Back then, he hadn't known what it meant. Had thought it was just another Ivy League society, like Skull and Bones. Another circle jerk for rich assholes, a place to make sure you had your fingers on the right pulses, so later when you were really someone, you'd have the connections to make the world turn. He had done it out of loyalty, a way of following in his father's footsteps. It had been a last chance at gaining his family's approval, since he couldn't seem to do it with his career or his would-be-bride.

And then Penny died, and Eric had said "fuck it" to them all. To the company. To the family. And to Janus. Because really, what did he need of a secret society that protects the powerful when he had no intention of keeping power at all?

He hadn't realized it until now, of course, but Janus never saw itself as a mere society. Its members considered themselves gatekeepers—hence the name after the Roman god of beginnings and endings. Of passageways. And while membership meant support from all those gatekeepers and easier passage through the ranks of society, it also meant loyalty. Tithing. Permission from all.

Permission that Eric, unknowingly, had not been granted when he had decided to marry the illegitimate daughter of its powerful head—its *Caesar*. It didn't matter that neither he—nor Jane, for that matter—knew she was the product of a secret, one-night tryst before Yu Na, Jane's mother, had even left Korea. How could they have known she was related to John Carson, the man who called himself Titan within the ranks of Janus? Who had become *Caesar* long before Eric joined.

All that mattered was that those lines had been crossed when Eric had flouted Carson's orders. And now he was paying the price.

John Carson hadn't changed in the last ten years. Still a tall man, taller even than Eric's six feet and almost two inches. Still with a full head of wavy salt-and-pepper hair that gleamed with some kind of oil. Still clean-shaven but for the goatee that ringed his mouth with the precision of a stamp.

His dark greenish eyes—nearly black in this light—sparked

as he removed his suit jacket and handed it to the guard, who returned it to the outer room before rejoining them.

Carson nodded.

Jude stripped the duct tape from Eric's mouth with a burning tear. Carson crossed the room and squatted so he was eye to eye with his captive.

"I must say," he remarked. "You haven't aged well, Triton. You look at least ten years older than, what is it now? Thirty-two?" He looked to the other men. "Or is it thirty-three?"

"Not until January." Jude flipped through his phone, looking bored from his place against the wall. "He's a Capricorn."

Carson rolled his eyes at the astrology reference. Jude always had his quirks. "Close enough."

Eric glared at Jude, a man who had joined the society a year or two before him. "What the fuck are you doing here, Jude?"

Jude grinned and continued paging through his phone. "You didn't think I'd miss out on the fun, did you? Or have you forgotten how much I enjoy hunting big game?"

"Is that what I am? A fucking elephant to slaughter?"

A finger slid under his chin, forcing him to look straight and into the face he'd been dreading.

"More like a whale," Carson said as he turned Eric's face from side to side, like he was checking goods. "One that is in quite a bit of peril, I would say." He dropped Eric's chin and stood up straight. "You have been beached, Triton. It is your own fault, really. You swam too close to shore."

"Does that make you Captain Ahab?" Eric asked.

Eric didn't even bother to mask his contempt as Carson circled the chair. Jane would have had some fun with him right about now. Probably called him "Daddy Dearest." Teased him about his turtleneck. Asked him if he knew how to use contractions or if he spoke like a Bond villain on purpose.

In spite of himself, Eric chuckled.

Carson's dark eyes flashed dangerously. "This is Anton," he said, gesturing to the unfamiliar guard. "Do you know where Anton is from, Triton?"

Eric glanced at the man, who had a striking resemblance to King Kong. "Let me guess...Skull Island?"

There was a thick grunt, and then a blow to Eric's temple that made him see stars. Eric shook, and when he regained his vision, found Anton massaging his knuckles meditatively.

"Good God, Triton." Jude chuckled from the corner. "Some things never change. Almost thirty-three, and you still can't resist poking the bear, can you?"

"I wouldn't anger Anton if I were you," Carson said as he examined his fingernails, one by one. "He has a bit of a temper with people who aren't his friends. And comparing someone to a giant ape is not very friendly."

Anton grunted in agreement.

"Apologize," Carson prodded.

Eric just glared. "Why am I here, Carson?"

"Anton," Carson spoke as if the question hadn't been asked, "is from St. Petersburg. He trained with the KGB before he defected, oh, five years ago. He works for me now. Under my protection. So, you see, he's very loyal, since he knows that without my help, he'd have intelligence agencies from two world powers hunting him down like a dog." Carson bared his teeth like he was a wolf himself.

This time, Eric didn't respond.

"Anton learned a lot with the KGB, though," Carson continued. "Skills that have been very useful in my...line of work."

It wasn't hard to imagine why. All the members of Janus brought certain things to the table; "contributions" provided through their unique resources. The politicians brought power, of course, in the ability to control and effect policy in the favor of the society. There weren't many of them, considering how easily they were bought anyway. Those who owned large corporations usually had myriad different goods to provide for members' enjoyment—Jude, for example, earned his keep by trading in women, while another member whose family owned half of California wine country provided booze.

Eric didn't know what kinds of contributions his father and grandfather had made, though Jude had suggested to him a few months ago that some stock tips would be welcome. Nor did he know if his cousin Calvin, Nina's husband, was a member either —those kinds of discussions were forbidden if he wasn't. De Vries Shipping operated a solid half of the major ports on the East Coast, plus another fifty worldwide on top of its ventures in railway, trucking, and other forms of freight. You couldn't get anything in or out of this country, or many others, without DVS. And many of the members of Janus had a lot of things they wanted passing through those watery gates.

Eric wondered if Carson was one of those. John Carson was the CEO of Chariot, one of the largest engineering and research firms around, but more importantly, the biggest arms dealer on the planet. Carson's society moniker was Titan for a reason: he really did see himself as a god of destruction. And if he went around the world selling his wares to the highest bidders, such salesmanship undoubtedly required a strong-armed escort like Anton.

"Did he go with you to Korea?" Eric spat. "Let me guess, you were selling across the border. But I guess Kong here was a fetus back then. Like the daughter you abandoned, right?"

Jane.

Carson's dark eyes glinted dangerously, and Eric fought the urge to look away. It was strange, but when the man was angry, he really did look like his daughter. Both had those hazels that flashed almost green in bouts of rage. Jane's features otherwise took after her mother, Yu Na. But her height. That lanky yet lithe stride. Those moody expressions that changed with each new emotion. All of that was obviously inherited from the man in front of him.

Eric wondered how she was doing. If she had registered what had really happened. She wouldn't know that the man who had claimed her husband was also one of the most dangerous people on the planet. She wouldn't know why Eric had followed him out of the church like a dog on a leash.

But before he could wonder any more, something found his cheek with a harsh crack—an open-palm slap from Anton, whose hand felt more like steel than skin.

"Christ!" Eric shouted, shaking the chair.

"Next time, you'll speak about me and mine with a bit more respect, I think," Carson said.

Again, Jude chuckled, but seemed to regret it when he caught Carson's attention.

"Hermes," Carson said. "Leave us."

Jude's face slackened. He opened his mouth like he wanted to argue, but instead, gave a curt nod. His eyes darted toward Eric. "Have fun, Triton."

The heavy door slammed shut behind Jude. Carson pushed up the sleeves of his sweater, like he was the one getting ready to do heavy labor. Instead, the Russian was the one to pull a waxy rope, knotted at its base, from a hook on the wall.

"Before he left the KGB, Anton had a very good reputation in...what did you call it, Anton? Опрóс?"

Eric blinked. Carson's Russian accent was surprisingly good.

Carson turned back to Eric. "That means 'interrogation,'" he informed him. "There are some things I need to know. For example, the information you provided about the DVS merger was faulty. Why?"

Eric's eyes narrowed. "Maybe because I knew you were full of shit too."

Carson nodded at Anton. A second later, something whistled through the air behind Eric's head, and almost immediately, pain shot through his body, starting with the spot between his testicles and cock that had just been punched by the end of the knotted rope.

"FUCK!" The word erupted from Eric's chest like a siren. "Okay, *okay*! What, what, what do you want?" Sweat began pouring down his forehead.

"They call this maneuver 'Dutch Scratching.'" Carson circled around the other side of the chair, moving steadily, like a shark. "Fitting, I thought. Given the illustrious New Amsterdam roots of the great de Vries family." He reappeared in Eric's line of sight, then nodded to Anton behind him.

Zzzzip! The rope whirred past Eric's ear again. Another explosion of pain through his groin. His entire body jerked, and nausea pooled in his stomach. It was like getting kicked in the junk by a horse. Scratch that. Four horses. The fucking apocalypse was happening right on his balls.

Eric emitted a string of highly creative profanity at the ceiling.

"This is what is going to happen, Triton." Carson took another lap around the chair. "First, you're going to give me the correct information about another deal DVS is making. One that's not going to make me lose ten million this time."

Another nod.

Another zip.

Another thunderstorm of pain, nausea, and throat-cutting cries.

Eric could hardly swallow. But he could still stare at Carson with utter loathing. "Fuck. You," he bit out, barely able to keep his teeth from chattering.

Carson's hazel eyes narrowed. This time he didn't have to

nod before the knotted rope whipped through the air and under the seat yet again.

"FUCKING *FUCK!*" Eric keened to the ceiling. "Fine! Fucking *fine*, I'll tell you what you want."

Carson folded his hands over his belt buckle and smiled. It was a sinister face, tanned to an almost orange shade, the face of a man who enjoyed this kind of work. The work of torture.

"Yes," he said. "I think you will, Triton. But first, a lesson in loyalty. And respect."

He nodded again, then walked to the light switch. The room blackened once more just as a projector hummed on.

Pictures began to flicker on the wall in front of Eric. Pictures he knew. Pictures he recognized.

Of Jane.

Of him.

Together.

"What is this?" he muttered. "You fucking psycho, what *is* this?"

"Just the act of a protective father, I assure you," Carson replied.

"You're kidding. Father? You never cared about her before."

"On the contrary, I care about my daughter a great deal. Enough to allow her to be raised by a man much more...capable...of what she needed at a young age than I was. But I watched. From afar, I always watched. How do you think they were able to afford that big house? On a VA salary?" Carson chuckled. "That's quaint."

For a moment, Eric was enthralled. The face of the woman he loved more than anyone on the fucking planet was like an antidote to the poison of this place. Of these people.

But only for a moment.

The knot snapped around his seat and slammed into his perineum, tossing Eric so violently that the tape around his wrists and ankles felt like knives. It was a nastier pain than the scrotum, one that launched every feeling sloshing around his body, into his throat, down to his stomach, and back up again.

On the screen, Jane laughed.

Eric retched.

"Until it's done," Carson said to Anton as he walked to the door. He gave Eric one last look that verged on disgust. "I think it won't take long. It never does with his kind."

The heavy door closed again with a puff of dust, leaving Eric alone with Anton and his rope.

On the screen, Jane grinned. And the rope continued to work. Eric's last thought before he passed out was to wonder whether the face of the woman he'd once believed was his savior was really his downfall.

PART ONE

PROLEPSIS

Drip. Drop. Drip.
The mouse, he did a flip.
The clock struck one.
And all was done.
Drip. Drop. Drip.

"Drip"
—from the journal of Eric de Vries.

ONE

D*ing. Ding. Ding.*

The blunt edge of the butter knife touched crystal with gentle clinks that still managed to disseminate through the crowded ballroom. Within a few seconds, all five hundred members of New York's elite quieted while tuxedoed waitstaff darted silently between tables, delivering platters of duck *à l'orange,* Wagyu filets, or blackened branzino. It was the third course, which meant most of the room was tipsy, but not drunk. Full, but not yet tired. And the big band on the ballroom stage hadn't even touched the second set of swing classics, having supplied, until this point, Glenn Miller covers more fitting to a dinner soundtrack.

This wasn't the first speech of the night, but it was the one people anticipated the most.

My husband stood, his blond hair glimmering like a halo beneath the chandeliers above and twinkling lights wrapped around the statuesque white flower arrangements at every table. I smiled into my glass. I was the only one here who knew how devilish the man really was.

Husband. Holy shit, Eric de Vries was my *husband*. The staid, normal word sounded surreal in my head, particularly since six months ago, I was pretty sure I'd never get married. And certainly not to him. Eric was the golden boy of New York, the closest thing to royalty America had had since JFK, Jr. Tall and blond, with sturdy Scandinavian features and the bearing of a prince, he was the kind of person who existed in romance novels, not in real life.

And now he was mine.

Six months ago, we'd shocked this world by announcing our engagement. I'd walked out of a salon broke and fabulous in leather pants, combat boots, and freshly rainbow-colored hair. And then I'd slammed right into Eric, who had proposed the craziest idea I'd ever heard.

Twenty million dollars. Five years. Marry the only man who'd ever broken my heart and walk away never wanting again.

Except now, I wasn't going anywhere.

I was a character from a Kevin Kwan novel, my hair back to my natural brownish-black, but just as glossy as the celebration in front of me. My chunky glasses had been traded for contacts, and instead of my customary handmade duds, I was decked out in the *second* couture wedding dress of the night that cost more than my rent all of last year. The stunning Giambattista Valli was designed specifically for the reception with a sleeveless lace bodice, barely-there straps, and a tea-length skirt covered completely with ostrich feathers.

It was a hell of a long way from combat boots. Did I feel a bit like a stranger? Sure. Acclimating to this crazy world hadn't been easy. These people backstabbed with X-ACTO knives. But when Eric looked at me like that, honest to God, I couldn't have been happier.

That sly grin appeared, the one that he reserved just for me.

It was evenly mixed with boyish charm and a stern clue of what was to come after the guests left and we were alone. In front of others, Eric was reserved, content to let me be the bigger personality. I had the jokes, the splashy style, the attention-seeking hair while Eric observed passively. But behind closed doors, he was in command. Of my mind. Of my body. Of everything, every single sensation.

So, while his full lips smiled, his stormy gray eyes gleamed with a promise. *Mine*, they said. It was probably seventy-five degrees in this ballroom, but I shivered and clenched my thighs together. Hell yes, I was his. No receipts. No returns. One hundred percent property of *Mr. de Vries*.

Eric straightened his bow tie and turned to the quieted crowd. "I don't have nearly the grace of my mother," he said, nodding to Heather, who had spoken earlier in lieu of her deceased first husband—Eric's father, Jacob. "And I don't have the jokes of my ridiculous best man."

There was a friendly chuckle as the room turned its attention briefly to the man in question, Brandon Sterling.

"Don't even reach for my swagger, kid," he called out in a Boston accent thickened by alcohol. Skylar, his wife and my best friend, elbowed him in the side. Brandon just shuttered her concerns with a kiss. Once I would have been jealous, or at the very least pessimistic about the love those two shared. But now I understood it. I *had* a soul mate. The perfect man. And he was standing in front of me, toasting our wedding.

Eric just rolled his eyes and turned back to the crowd. "A lot of people were surprised when I announced I was getting married. And they were even more surprised when I introduced this one to the family. They said don't do it. They said it was all wrong."

I tried to remain passive as he listed all the reasons why we

were such a terrible fit. Different families. Different tempera-
ments. Different incomes.

Despite the joy of the day...I did find myself wondering now
if he considered us a mistake. After all, it was only hours ago that
I was screaming at him in the chapel.

*Steady now, Jane Brain. Don't let that head of yours run away
with itself.*

I swallowed my doubts as my dad's voice echoed from my
memories. More than anything, I wished he could have been
here. But since he was in a better place, the best I could do
would be to honor his death by listening to him now the way I
never had when he was alive. Eric was going somewhere with
this barrage. I'd come out the other end feeling fine. I knew it.

"Jane." Eric's eyes swam with love. "I didn't get to read this
at the church, so I'm going to do it now."

He pulled a familiar piece of paper from his pocket. I stared
at it. It was the crumpled poem he had given me just before the
ceremony, slipped around the edge of my door—the wedding
vows he wouldn't be able to say in the traditional manner but
wanted me to see anyway.

"Where did you get that?" I'd kept the poem with me during
the wedding, tucked in my tiny beaded clutch. I hadn't even told
him it was there.

Eric winked. "I have my ways, pretty girl."

Warmth glowed in my belly. That term was his way of
calling on the side of me that only wanted to do his bidding,
usually in ways that had me bent over a table, ready to receive
whatever "punishment" my insubordination required. Except it
wasn't really a punishment at all to be Eric's pretty girl. Not
one bit.

He unfolded the paper and held it up while he spoke into
the microphone:

Pretty girl. Woman. Siren. Fiend.
She with her
Lipseyescheekshairlegspussyskin
shouldersarmsbreaststhighsback
But more than that her
Mindgazehumorsmartstongue
wordstalentkindnesscandor
Makes me
Crazydevotedfrustratedsated
Inloveinlustinheatintrustin
All you are, Jane, all yours.
This is my
Hate vow
Love vow
Sex vow
My vow is that
Forever
Always
I belong to you.

The guests clapped, maybe too loudly considering they had just listened to this man describe our sex life, among many other things, in front of a bunch of strangers. But I didn't care. His words made me hum.

"I read that because I wanted to be clear," Eric said. "I wanted the nature of my relationship with this woman to be obvious." He held out his hand, gesturing for me to get up. "Jane."

I stood, and he pulled me flush to his solid body. His five-o'clock shadow gilt his square jaw, and his full lips smirked. Desire must have been written all over my face.

"I just want to say one thing." His low voice was amplified by the mic, but I felt like I was the only one in the room. "All of this," he said, waving the vows tenderly through the air toward the festivities. "These words I wrote for you?"

"Y-yes?" I asked, unable to look away from his deep gray eyes, the ones flecked with brown in the right light.

Eric held the mic closer to his mouth so everyone could hear him. "It's complete and total crap."

I blinked, about to kiss him until the words registered. Then fear crackled over my skin like an eggshell knocked by a spoon. "What—what?"

He dropped his arm from my waist, and I fell back into the chair, staring as Eric smiled widely at our audience.

His grandmother, Celeste, nodded knowingly from her table. "I knew it," she mouthed to Eric's aunts and cousins, who all nodded back, a row of pristine puppets.

"We knew it," they said like a fucked-up Greek chorus of perfect blonde hens.

"We knew it," said the crowd.

I stood again, my limbs trembling. "What—why? Why are you doing this?" I backed away from the banquet table that was suddenly empty except for my single plate of unfinished food. The room behind me never seemed to end.

"Because," Eric said with that nonchalant shrug that always equally infuriated me and turned me on. "You know the truth, pretty girl. You never belonged here in the first place. And you never will."

I whirled around, looking for Skylar. I didn't know what was going on. I wasn't sure I cared. I just needed to get out of here.

But instead of a hug, my best friend appeared with a can of bright red paint.

"How about a splash?" she asked with a wicked grin before tipping the bloody crimson all over my feathers. A row of children dressed in white snickered behind her.

My glasses fell off—which was strange, since I was wearing

contacts before, wasn't I? Then, before the screams could erupt from my throat, the floor of the ornate hall fell out from under me. I caught myself on the edge with just a few fingers, my feet flailing under me. One shoe fell. Then the other.

"Goodbye, Jane," Eric said with a haughty wave. Then he pushed the toe of his shiny black Oxford against my fingertips, dislodging one at a time. For the last one, he kicked. Hard.

And I fell into the hole. Into utter darkness.

———

DING. Ding. Ding.

I blinked my eyes open, squinting into the early morning light bouncing through my bedroom, twinkling off the condensation gathered on the windowpanes.

That dream. That fucking dream. I'd had different variations of it every night for the past ten days, since the world really had dropped out from under me. Sometimes we were at a court-house. Once it was in the middle of Central Park. But it always amounted to the same thing. Eric smiling. Eric leaving. Eric kicking me away. And I fell, always fell, out of control.

Like my entire life now.

Ding.

My cell phone alerted me with another message—I thought. Was that what had woken me up this time? It sure as shit didn't sound like silver on crystal in the harsh light of day.

I rolled over onto the goose-down pillow in Skylar's guest-house, where I'd been holed up since being left at the altar of the biggest wedding New York had seen in years. Thank God for wealthy friends, was all I could say. Thank God for Skylar and Brandon's giant estate in Boston, with its private granny flat and stone-walled security that kept out the prying eyes of Page Six. Thank God for the space they offered for me to relive my anguish, frustration, and rage time and time again without people watching.

Because, just like it did every morning, the whole nightmare flooded back.

Getting ready at the Waldorf, eager as a new bride should be.

Overhearing that once upon a time, Eric had slept with my nemesis and neglected to tell me.

Having a massive fight in the echoing chapel of St. John the Divine.

And then, just as we were about to finish the ceremony through gritted teeth, being interrupted by the tall, impossibly arrogant John Carson, who had announced himself as my long-lost father, objected to the wedding, and then beckoned Eric with a single Latin phrase: "*Deorum vocas.*"

Whatever the hell that meant. Not, I supposed, that it really mattered. Because with two more words to me—"I'm sorry"— Eric followed the man out of the church before the minister fully pronounced us married. His grandmother Celeste had collapsed in the front row...but Eric had kept walking. And no one had seen him since.

This wasn't real life. It was a plot lifted straight from *Dynasty* or *Days of Our Lives.* We were Jerry Springer guests with big bank accounts.

I pushed a hand through my hair—still black, but with that new streak of red I'd kept on Eric's request. I'd dyed my earlier color—a full head of pink-hued rainbow—back to my natural black-brown to present a version of myself I hoped would fit more with the glitzy, polished world of the de Vries family. But Eric demanded I put at least some color back in. He wanted the girl he fell in love with, he said. And like a fool, I believed him.

I flipped through the messages on my phone. There were four new voicemails from my mother, which I immediately deleted. I still hadn't forgiven her for keeping such a massive secret like my biological father from me. Not. Ready.

The rest were from Skylar. Some sent from the main house this morning while she and Brandon got ready for work. A few others probably from her office in downtown Boston. It was now eleven in the morning. Those two workaholics had probably been at it for at least three to four hours, even with two small children.

The phone buzzed in my hand, flashing with the wry, arch-browed face of my best friend. Wow, she was really not going to let this go today.

With a long, tortured sigh, I answered it.

"Sky, you are obnoxious, you know that? Some of us really don't have anything better to do than lounge around until noon. And we like it that way."

"You need to get up." Skylar's husky voice was sharper than usual, leaving no room for jokes.

I pushed off the big goose-down comforter and padded into the bathroom, where I set the phone on the sink. "What's so urgent that I have to be up by the crack of noon?"

I yawned as I put on my glasses—my favorite gold Guccis today—then scowled at my reflection and immediately took them off. My dark circles looked like checkable suitcases, and another night of tossing and turning had not been so good for the old mane, which would have looked right at home in an eighties hair band video. I could have doubled for Slash with the right top hat.

"Eric's back."

I stood up mid-wash of my face, water dripping down my chin. "He's back?"

"He called the firm this morning. And so did the de Vrieses' lawyer. Everything is set for the funeral this weekend."

I collapsed onto the toilet seat. Immediately following Eric's impromptu exit, his grandmother—the same grandmother who had concocted this whole marriage scheme to begin with—had collapsed right there in the church, dead before the paramedics arrived. She was in poor health, having fought cancer for several years, and Eric running out was just too much for her frail body. Her heart gave out. In seconds, the matriarch of the de Vries clan, one of the oldest and most powerful families of the Upper East Side, was gone.

Without Eric, however, I hadn't been allowed anywhere near the funeral plans or anything else to do with the woman with whom I'd become surprisingly close over the past six months. Celeste de Vries might have been the most Machiavellian schemer on the planet, but she and I had cultivated a sort of adversarial fondness for each other.

I was the exact opposite of what she'd intended by insisting her grandson get married to keep his fortune. The de Vrieses were demure where I was loud. Rich where I was poor. Eric's family was well-bred, blond, and perfectly polished; I was a half-Asian mutt who practically cosplayed Rainbow Brite.

But after so many lunches to plan the wedding turned into trips to the museum or Bergdorf's, I'd spent more time with the crotchety old matriarch in her final months than anyone in her family. And now that she was gone, I actually missed her.

Enough that when Eric's family refused to let me help with any of the funeral obligations, I had fled to Boston to nurse my wounds. But in a way, it made sense. If Eric himself had walked out on their wedding, what right did I have to anything else in the family?

Still, it hurt. It hurt a lot.

Of course it does, peanut. That's grief.

I shook my head. My own father's voice—well, the voice of the man I'd *thought* was my father—tended to pop up in lieu of a conscience since his death last year. Yeah. I wasn't in any place to be dealing with that.

The stab deepened as I realized that after coming back from...wherever he went...it wasn't my phone Eric finally called.

"So that's that, then," I said, unable to kill the forlorn tone. "We're officially communicating through lawyers now?"

I should have been happy. I should have been relieved. Our marriage was in a limbo state—a quick consultation with Skylar and the minister had confirmed it. While the minister had said he was happy to declare us husband and wife (as Eric and I had both spoken the key vows), the fact that neither of us had signed the marriage certificate (since the groom had basically sprinted away before his autograph was required) meant that the union wasn't legal. Not in the eyes of the state.

I was dodging a bullet, right?

Then why did this phone call feel like I'd just taken one in the chest?

"He didn't say," Skylar said. "He asked if you were all right, though."

"He couldn't have asked me that himself?" I demanded, growling more than I wanted.

"I really don't know, Janey."

Skylar sounded defeated. This was an awkward situation for her—being in the middle of us always had been. Eric was her friend and business partner, but I was her ride-or-die bestie. I knew her loyalties were first and foremost with me, but she obviously had sympathies for both me and my errant...whatever he was.

"So is that it?" I stood up and rubbed my still-damp face more violently than necessary, turning my pale skin pink. "You've been texting me all morning to tell me the Great Disappointment didn't actually fall off the face of the earth? He's just been ghosting me like every other dude bro this side of the Mississippi?"

Skylar exhaled. "No," she said. "The lawyer told me that

Celeste made some changes to her will. Jane, he's going to read it next weekend after the wake. And apparently, you're in it."

I sat down all over again, my bare feet slipping on the stone tiles. "You mean as Eric's spouse, right?" I shook my head. "I thought that was part of the prenup. Twenty million, but only if we were married for five years."

"No, no," Skylar said. "This is different. Tom—that's the lawyer's name—told me this is specifically for you alone. And he also said that Celeste requested the will be read to everyone in the same room. At the same time."

I stilled. That could mean only one thing. Eric would be at the funeral. The De Vries Shipping heir whose inheritance was dependent on his legal marriage to *me* was probably going to want to know whether or not his claims would be honored without his grandmother alive to verify them.

Honestly, I wanted to know that too.

"When?" I asked as I examined my single red bedraggled lock. Vaguely, I wondered if I would have time for a quick dye job, although almost immediately I realized I'd have to wait a while unless I wanted my hair to fall out completely. Suddenly I wanted this shit—this fucking reminder of Eric and his pretty girl bullshit—out of my hair, my life, my everything.

"The funeral is this Saturday."

That was in tomorrow. I knew this. I'd known it for over a week at this point. But until now, I wasn't actually sure I was supposed to be there.

"All right," I said. "I'll go. Of course I'll go. But first I need to visit my beloved's apartment here in town."

I could practically see Skylar rolling her eyes in front of me. "Jesus, Jane, *why?* You didn't even live in his Boston apartment with him."

But it wasn't what she thought. I wasn't interested in shoving my face into Eric's rows of designer suits, lolling around in his old icebox condo just to collect trinkets and remember better times. Fuck that.

"Because I'm done with his secrets," I said. "And if I have to face the entitled little twerp, I'm doing it with my eyes wide open. I have a key. It's not trespassing. Sky, it's time to do some digging."

TWO

I wasn't the only one interested in playing Inspector Gadget that day. Tweedledee and Tweedledum—otherwise known as Skylar and Brandon—were hot on my tail. The doorman looked up as the three of us entered Eric's building in the North End. I stormed into the lobby, shoving away the uncomfortable feeling of déjà vu.

The last time I was here, Eric and I had taken exactly two seconds to tear each other's clothes off. He had reawakened a part of me I had forgotten, like a tree blooming after a long winter, though perhaps not as elegantly. I did kick him in the ass, after all. And right after that, I'd agreed to marry him. It wasn't the most romantic night of my life per se, but it was certainly one of the hottest. And the memory of it made my chest squeeze.

Now the cherry trees in the churchyard across the street were bare-branched and trembling in the frigid November wind. And in jeans, my favorite Clash hoodie, and a leopard-print trench coat, I was wrapped up tighter than a pork sausage. These legs were closed for business, at least to this man.

"Paul," I greeted the doorman. "Do you remember me? I'm

Jane Lefferts. Eric's..." I drifted off. I really didn't even want to think the word "wife," much less say it.

"Of course," said the doorman with a slight tip of his head. "Congratulations on the nuptials, ma'am."

Skylar and Brandon made faces at each other. Fantastic. Someone had bothered to tell the doorman Eric and I were getting married, but not that it had been spectacularly torpedoed.

"Eric just asked me to get something for him from the apartment," I said as I pressed the elevator call button.

Behind me, Brandon snorted.

But Paul didn't act like anything was out of order—after all, why should he?

I stared at the black diamond that flashed on my finger alongside the matching band I hadn't bothered to take off. I couldn't have told you why. I wasn't ready to think about it.

We rode to the top floor in silence. Brandon and Skylar looked like they were waiting for me to pop as we rode to the top floor.

"Can you stop?" I said, if only to break the silence.

"Stop what?" Skylar asked.

"Stop looking at me like I'm a cardboard volcano about to blow over. This apartment isn't a cup of baking soda, and I'm not made of vinegar."

Brandon's face twitched. He had been helping Jenny, his daughter, with said science experiment just last night.

"You've really never been here?" I asked them. "I thought you two were his best friends."

Skylar shook her head. "He moved a few years ago, but he's not really one to hold a housewarming party or anything. You know Eric."

Brandon cleared his throat loudly. His meaning was clear. Did I know Eric? Did any of us?

"I know Eric doesn't tell people shit," I replied as the elevator doors opened. "If there is any information about my 'father,' this Janus society, or where Eric went, it would be here, not our place in New York. I decorated every square inch of that apartment. Eric left his personal crap in Boston. Clearly, I can't trust the man. Considering there's a good chance we'll end up in court sooner rather than later, I need to know what I've gotten myself into."

They followed me down the hall to Eric's corner apartment, where I stared at the shiny silver number on the door for a good thirty seconds.

————

"ONCE UPON A TIME," I said as I slowly drifted my mouth around the edges of his lips, "you used to know how to quiet this crazy mind of mine. You knew how to own it. Did you forget?"

Eric was a statue, but his eyes were stars. "Absolutely not."

My eyes closed, almost like I was meditating. But when they opened, Eric's lips grazed mine.

"Then do it," I murmured against his mouth. "Make me your pretty girl again...Mr. de Vries."

————

I TOOK a deep breath and shook the memory away. Then I stuck the key in the lock, and turned.

Inside, it was just as sterile and crystalline as I remembered, all white and silver and glass. Skylar and Brandon looked around with curious distaste while I immediately scanned for...something. What was I looking for, anyway?

Brandon ran a finger over the stainless steel island. "This reminds me of—"

"Your place when we split up?" Skylar finished. "I know. It's like a refrigerator." She wrinkled her freckled nose. "Good thing you didn't actually have to live here, Janey."

I shrugged. I didn't hate the apartment, exactly. The white, silver, and chrome decor was aesthetically pleasing and well put together, likely with the help of a decorator. It would have never been home, but there was more to a home than furniture.

Home.

Suddenly, I had a sharp, urgent hankering for the spacious apartment on the Upper West Side. I missed our big feather bed, the creamy prewar walls splashed with art, the eclectic mid-century furniture I had painstakingly collected for us. How many nights had we lain together in that bed, staring at the ceiling after giving with our bodies what had always been so much harder to give with our hearts? I had thought that in the end, we both finally let go of all those barriers. I had believed we were all out in the open. Bared. In love for the first time—it was always the first time with Eric—in my weird black sheep of a life.

How stupid was I?

After being left like that at the altar, I couldn't bear to spend one more night in that false haven. I had stopped there only to pack my biggest suitcase before escaping to Boston with Skylar and Brandon. For a while, I thought that when Eric found me missing, he'd come looking. But one, two, ten days later, nothing. Until the lawyer called.

Stupid, stupid me.

"So, what are we looking for, exactly?" Brandon asked as he wandered through the sparse living room. "What is there to find?"

"Everyone keeps secrets somewhere," I said, aimlessly pawing through the small bowl of keys and change by the door. "People are record keepers in the most random ways. Philanderers leave love notes. Serial killers have calling cards. Sam Berkowitz literally wrote letters to the police."

"Eric's not a serial killer." Skylar opened the fridge, which currently only held a few bottles of unopened Perrier. "He's been keeping his entire life buttoned up since we've known him, what, eight years now? You didn't even know who his family was until six months ago."

"I also never looked."

Skylar looked at me like she didn't believe me. I turned back to the key bowl.

"Two years ago we were working a case against this shark in Chicago," I said. "An underground gambling ring downtown. I came in at the tail end because it took ten years to rack up enough evidence against him to prosecute. He was *that good* at keeping it hidden. But what really got him were the emails he sent to his ex-wife bragging about how much money he had made without her. The guy cared more that his wife remembered him than he did about his own freedom."

Skylar scowled. "Idiot."

I just shrugged. "Human, I think. I wouldn't want my life's work to be forgotten, even if it was a brilliant crime. Or a brilliant revenge on your ex-girlfriend."

I really, *really* didn't want that to be true. But I couldn't help but wonder if this was supposed to happen the whole time. Eric never cared about his family before. What if he wasn't the genuine, if guarded person I thought I knew? What if he saw a chance to punish me for what I did to him nearly six years ago... and took it?

———

"AFTER THE EXAM, I was thinking I should make some

changes. I haven't seen my family in a while. It's time to check in."

"Oh?" I asked as I popped a cherry in my mouth and examined a study question.

Eric watched its progress with an intense, distracted look.

"That sounds nice," I said.

He blinked, like he'd just remembered the conversation we were having while studying for the bar exam. "I think you should come with me. Jane, I want to take you home. I want to do this for real."

His hand clapped over mine on the table, covering my scraped black nails with his smooth, pale palm.

I took a deep breath and set down my pencil. I could say this. I had to. "I think we should stop this."

Eric's head snapped up. "What?"

I twisted and turned in my chair like a toddler who needed to pee. "I...I can't, Eric, and you don't want to bring me home, you know you don't. Look at me..."

I gestured at my cropped hair with its four different colors, the ripped jeans, the chipped nail polish. Eric was a J. Crew catalog. I was a one-woman homage to Hot Topic.

"I am looking at you, pretty girl."

I blushed. "Stop. Stop that. See, that's what I mean. You call me that, but I'm not pretty. Not in the way everyone else will expect of someone with you. You said you're from the Upper East Side, right? Well, I don't know anything about your family, but I've been to that part of New York with Skylar, and... Well, let's just say you don't see a lot of women who look like me walking around."

"The Village is only a few miles from there. And New Yorkers love black."

"But do Upper Easter Siders love it with blue stripes through their hair or men's boots?" I asked, pointing at two things that I was currently sporting.

Eric leaned forward over the table and took my hands. "I. Don't. Care. When are you going to get it through that head of yours—I only want you."

For a moment, I almost said yes. I almost believed his face would actually beam the way I imagined. I almost bought into the idea that in some weird way, I would belong in his perfect, pristine world.

But reality has a way of keeping those things from happening. It ruins everything.

"I'm sorry," I said again. "It's over."

———

I MEANDERED into the kitchen and started pulling open drawers. Perfectly sharpened knives, way too much coffee paraphernalia. Nothing of interest.

"Well, I did a little more digging last night," Brandon said by the shelves in the living room. "Made a few calls. But I couldn't get straight answers from anyone about the Janus society. No one would confirm anything beyond what I already knew. Most people had no idea what it even was."

The way Skylar pressed her lips into a thin line told me she wasn't very happy her husband was asking around about this issue.

"John Carson, on the other hand, is pretty well-known," Brandon said. "The guy's a phantom, but he's the CEO of a major engineering firm. They make communication systems. Some combat equipment, but mostly munitions. Ray said they are a big recruiter at MIT, but John Carson is the kind of guy you can only reach if *he* wants to talk to *you*."

"You'd think he'd at least resurface after he stole his daughter's new husband," I said dryly. "After all, it's been thirty years, right? Don't I, as the presumed heiress, deserve an audience?"

Skylar patted me on the arm sympathetically. I didn't even want to think about the fact that I was turning thirty in a few weeks. I wanted to pretend this birthday wasn't evening happening.

"I think it's just leverage over Eric," I continued, ignoring her pity. "If what you described is the truth, then it seems pretty clear that all this society is interested in is power, or at least the potential for it. I have neither. I was just a means to get to Eric."

"Then maybe *that*'s why Eric went with him," Skylar offered. "Maybe he was trying to shield you."

"By jilting me at the altar? That was just mean." I shook my head. "John Carson is welcome to keep me in the closet with the rest of his skeletons, especially if he's responsible for Eric's bullshit. They can marry each other for all I care."

I yanked open another kitchen drawer with more force than was necessary. Ooh...even neat freak Eric de Vries had a kitchen junk drawer, eh? I rummaged through the half-used Post-its and a smattering of thumbtacks, loose twine, and other random items until I pulled out a worn Moleskine book lodged in the back. It was full of his jagged handwriting.

"What's that?" Skylar asked.

I flipped through the book. "Looks like an old journal."

It was a mix of prose and verse, with the latter dominating the pages. If the poems were dated at all, they were from about ten or eleven years ago, when Eric was at Dartmouth. That would have been around the end of his relationship with Penelope Kostas, his former fiancée, who had committed suicide just before they were supposed to get married.

"'Oh, bloody night,'" I murmured, looking at a particularly intense one. It had no date, but the imagery, love soaked in blood, gave me the shivers.

I didn't know much about poetry beyond my required college courses—I was more of a *Vogue* reader, to tell the truth—but I liked Eric's style. It was kind of all over the place, but he had a blunt, honest way with words that I appreciated. It was almost like he could say with poetry what his careful decorum wouldn't allow him otherwise. He had a tendency to use a lot of Greek and Latin allusions, which I guessed had to do with Penelope. She was Greek, he had told me.

"Nothing of use," I said, handing it to Skylar. "I don't know if he'd really want you to read that, but to be honest, I don't give a shit what that horse's ass thinks right now. Fuck him."

Skylar shook her head, but Brandon plucked the book from her with relish.

"I could use some pleasure reading." He flipped it to a page in the middle and read the first poem he saw:

> *Daedalus made his wings,*
> *Sewn of white and wax.*
> *And I, his son, first took them on,*
> *Before I gave them back.*
>
> *Still Icarus flew alone,*
> *While I had her beside me,*
> *She rained love, and her dewy body*
> *Threatened no one but Titans.*
>
> *Now I may be Icarus*
> *Without the father to warn,*
> *The folly of living*
> *Against others' sworn.*
>
> *Fly too close to the sun*
> *And you might drown.*

But I'm not too high, Dad.
She's just too far down.

Brandon grimaced. "Pretty corny, if you ask me."

I reached out for the book. "You don't have to read it."

"Oh, no, no. I'm not passing up the chance to post Eric's cheesy poems all over the office. That's called karma. If he's leaving me and Skylar to clean up his mess, the little fucker can deal with the consequences."

I ignored the insinuation that *I* was the mess being cleaned up. Instead, I went back to the key bowl and plucked an unobtrusive coin from the bottom. I turned it back and forth in my hand. It was Greek, or maybe Roman, with a face carved into each side. It looked a little like that coin Eric had been wearing around his neck, but this was tarnished pretty badly.

"Hey, I found something else," Brandon said. I turned to where he was paging through another thick book. He held it up. "Latin dictionary."

Again, Skylar rolled her eyes. "Babe, that's just for law stuff. Eric's not going to hide his family secrets in a dictionary. He probably took a case home."

Brandon just gave his wife a very long look. "How many times have you used a Latin dictionary in the past five years, Red?"

She shrugged. "That's different. I'm not in con law. There isn't much to use in family."

"Eric's not in con law either. I should know, since I'm helping with his caseload. And I don't know a whole lot of lawyers who highlight the parts of speech for *deus*." Brandon pointed a big finger to a section of the dictionary under the word *deus*—Latin for "god."

Skylar and I both crowded next to him to examine it. Sure

enough, the entire paragraph had been highlighted, with the word "deorum" underlined twice.

"That's what—the guy, Carson—that's what he said at the wedding. '*Deorum vocas*,' right?"

I shook my head. "What does that even mean?"

"It's bad grammar by itself, but roughly, it means, 'the gods calling.'" When Skylar and I looked up in surprise, Brandon raised a brow. "What? I googled it on the way back up to Boston."

"And you never thought to tell us this?" Skylar asked.

Brandon snapped the dictionary shut. "You didn't ask, Red. And Jane was upset. I figured when she wanted to talk about it, she would."

I perched on the corner of the couch. "I want to talk about it."

Skylar sat down next to me. "Brandon, does this mean something to you?"

Brandon pushed a big hand through his hair, looking very much like he did not want to answer that question. Which, of course, would only make Skylar press that much harder. He seemed to know this, because just as she was opening her mouth again, he sank to the armchair next to the bookshelf and started talking.

"I don't know much. Red, I already told you that. But Janus uses a lot of Latin and Greek code crap. Other than that...I know John Carson's face, but the guy does not exist on the internet beyond a line on Chariot's website."

"Just *think*," Skylar insisted. "You met John Carson before. What was he like? You didn't join Janus for a reason. Was it him?"

Brandon looked very uncomfortable. "Look..."

"I don't have time to beat around the bush here, Brandon," I snapped. "And I can't have daddy issues about a man I've barely met, so if *Pater Noster* is a bad egg, I need to know. Why didn't you join?"

"Because John Carson is a terrible fuckin' human being, all right?" The stress of Brandon's statement brought out his Boston accent to the point where the name "Carson" sounded more like "Cah-son." "I knew that the second I met him."

THREE

Brandon was all of sixteen when he started at MIT. It was a long story, the way the foster care system had taken him from a terrible upbringing in South Boston to the home of an MIT professor and his wife. But the basics were that the man turned out to be a whiz with numbers, graduating from the MIT economics department at nineteen before becoming a lawyer. Brandon was basically a cat with nine lives—currently, he was futzing around with electronics and being a doting father and husband.

"I think you need to start from the beginning," I said. "When did you meet my 'father'"—I literally could not say the word without wanting to vomit—"and what the hell happened?"

"And," Skylar put in, in a voice that was eerily quiet, "why did you call him 'Titan' at the wedding?"

If I had my guess, Brandon was going to catch hell later for not telling her this stuff before now.

Easy there, pumpkin. He's just trying to help.

I mentally batted away the voice of the man who had actually raised me. I didn't need to add more emotionally confusing fuel to this fire.

Brandon sighed and tugged at his hair harder, looking as if he would like to jump right out the window. "I studied econ at MIT, but I was also taking classes with the electrical engineering department, where Ray, then my foster father, worked. And I was good at it."

I nodded. This wasn't a surprise. Since leaving finance, Brandon had gone back to his engineering roots and spent most of his time making shit with a bunch of wires in his lab. That was the extent of my knowledge.

"Some of my work got people's attention. I was even on a couple of patents."

"At sixteen?" I asked, disbelieving.

Brandon nodded sheepishly. "Well, Ray was the principal author. But yeah, I got a bit of a reputation. Then, right after graduation, this asshole in a Harvard jacket gives me an address and tells me if I want my future made for me, I need to show up at this yacht." Brandon wrinkled his long nose distastefully. "I was nineteen, almost twenty. Unemployed because I was so young, dying to get out of Ray and Susan's house, but not wanting to go back to Dorchester either." Brandon shrugged, the movement monumental with his big shoulders. "So I went, thinking I was going to get some weird job offer. But instead, I was tapped."

"Tapped?" I repeated. It sounded like a game of duck, duck, goose, not a procedure for entering some weird society.

"It's a euphemism," Brandon replied dryly. "For 'kidnap you, make you sick as a dog on the open fuckin' ocean, and threaten to throw you to the sharks unless you tell them every secret you have.' John Carson wasn't on the boat when I arrived. Instead I met three younger members of some weird fuckin' society who addressed each other like Greek and Roman gods or demigods.

One was named Mercury, another was Achilles, but I don't remember the other one's name. They were all dressed in shirts and ties and looked very, very rich—which I was very much *not* back then, you know. Me at nineteen meant ripped jeans and a Sox hat."

"Just at nineteen?" Skylar scoffed with a pointed look at the Red Sox shirt her husband was currently wearing.

"So, what?" I asked, now totally absorbed by the story. "They just took you out to the ocean to invite you to their clubhouse?"

"In a way," Brandon said. "After three days of interrogating me they finally gave me a bit to eat and let me sleep."

"What did Ray and Susan say when you just disappeared for three days?" Skylar interrupted, looking genuinely horrified.

Again, Brandon shrugged. "I wasn't the best-behaved adolescent, Red. It wouldn't have been the first time I took off."

Skylar shook her head, looking very much like she wanted to give Brandon a piece of her mind on Ray and Susan's behalf.

"The funny thing is, it wasn't as scary as they wanted it to be," Brandon continued. "I knew tougher hoods in Dorchester. I told them whatever they wanted to know, gave them a few punches to the gut when they tried to get rough, and waited the rest out. On the third day, they brought me back. They said I'd passed the first test, and then they gave me a slip of paper with another address. Princeton, where I could meet the Titan, they said."

Brandon went, more out of curiosity than anything else. But again, he was kidnapped for the rest of the weekend to a house on the Jersey shore, interrogated again by another set of Brooks Brothers-wearing goons before being released with yet another invite.

"It continued like that for weeks," he said. "Secret meeting after secret meeting. Always with the promise of meeting Titan, but he never showed."

"Why in the hell did you keep going?" Skylar demanded. "Did you like being kidnapped?"

Brandon reached out for his wife's hand. "Hey. They didn't keep me, Red. Baby, I'm right here. And...I don't know. Didn't you ever want to fit in so badly, you'd do almost anything for it?"

I shrank. Yeah, I knew the feeling. I was pretty sure everyone in this room knew the feeling of not fitting in.

Skylar softened. "So what happened next?"

"Well, finally I did say fuck it. I had better things to do than serve myself on a platter for a bunch of entitled pricks to sucker punch. I figured by that point I was being initiated into something, but I didn't give a shit what it was. Two months later, I arrived at the Ritz ready to tell them all to fuck off. And that's where I found John Carson."

Carson, waiting for him in the penthouse, full of effusive praise and charm while he invited Brandon to sit down for an actual lunch.

"He liked the fact that I'd stayed discreet and never gone to the police," Brandon said. "And he liked a lot of other things about me. He said I had been chosen for my potential. Usually Janus was filled with inherited positions kept in the family." *Like the de Vrieses*, I thought. "But there was always one spot open for new blood each year. Someone with extraordinary promise. A true prodigy about to shine.

"Or," Brandon added, "be manipulated. But I didn't say that. I just picked at a cheese plate while he explained to me that I'd been chosen to be part of a very rich and secret society. They were 'kingmakers,' he said. Sometimes even actual kings. As a society, they protected the interests of the rich and powerful, so being a part of them assured I would become rich and powerful too. That I could rewrite the rules of the world I lived in. That I would never ever have to answer to anyone but myself."

The room was still—Skylar and I sat forward, elbows balanced on our knees.

"Then what?" Skylar asked.

Brandon sat back. "Then he had a couple of porters bring in the nicest fuckin' meal I ever saw, opened the door to a bedroom where three naked girls were waiting for me to join them, and left me a number on the table. He said to call within twelve hours if I accepted the offer. If I didn't, the number wouldn't work anymore. I'd be expected to forget any of this had ever happened. And if I ever spoke to anyone about any of it, I could also expect to suffer the consequences."

"So...did you...what did you do?"

I looked at Skylar, who was obviously trying not to fixate on the fact that her husband may have had a very wild evening at some point with three strange women.

"Well, think about it, Red," Brandon said gently to her. "Here's me, barely grown. I'd been living with Ray and Susan for seven years. Still had a knack for trouble. But more than anything else on the fuckin' planet, I just wanted to make some money. Because to me, after growing up the way I did, money meant freedom. It meant respect. Then John Carson invites me, a shit kid from Dorchester, to be in the most powerful association on the planet? Someone was finally offering me a key to the kingdom, you know?"

I brushed my thumb over the coin in my palm, toying with the hard edge. "But you didn't join?"

"I did not." Brandon bent over his knees, folding and refolding his hands like he was getting ready for a fight of his own. When he looked up, his blue eyes shone like the edge of a knife reflecting the sky. "Are you religious, Jane?"

I shook my head. "My mother went to church, but no, can't say I am now."

"I was raised Catholic," Brandon said. "And my mother—when she was actually sober—used to say you could see the Devil in people's eyes. I don't believe in any of that, but I swear to God, when I met John Carson for the first time, I thought the Devil himself was looking at me."

I swallowed, and my throat felt thick. It wasn't exactly easy being told that the person responsible for half your DNA might be, oh, Satan. Talk about an awkward introduction.

"Janus isn't a special society, Jane. It's just a gang, pure and simple, dressed up in tails and gold. I had already escaped that kind of life once. I wasn't about to jump into another version. No matter how good the prime rib."

For the first time since he'd started talking, Skylar actually looked at her husband with something like pride. Like she couldn't stop herself, she jumped up from her spot next to me and launched herself at him. Brandon, surprised, immediately pulled her into his lap and wrapped his arms around his wife's slight body while he stroked her hair.

My heart squeezed just looking at them. Not even two weeks ago, I had someone who looked at me the way Brandon was looking at Skylar. Maybe even more so. For a moment, I was taken back to the ocean, when Eric finally said those words I hadn't even known I'd wanted to hear.

———

"I'M DONE RESPECTING *your fucking boundaries when it comes to this. You want to walk away from me after tonight, Jane, fine. I won't come after you. But I'm not letting you go without telling you in no uncertain terms that I'm in love with you. I'm crazy about you. I knew the second you walked in that fucking bar, all the way back when we were practically just kids, that you were the only one for me."*

I shook my head. "N-no. It's not true."

"It is true. You stunned me then. You stun me now. You'll stun me every day for the rest of my life, because it's not what's on the outside that does it, Jane. It's what's in here. You're not just my pretty girl. You're the most beautiful fucking person I know, inside and out. And I love you."

My mouth dropped. I hadn't dared hope for those words for years, and now here he was, saying them out loud. And I couldn't believe it. "No, you c-can't."

Eric's face was fire. "Don't tell me what I can't do."

And then he kissed me again. Despite the cold water washing over us both, the kiss burned, through the waves, through my clothes, down to my toes that were starting to numb, to my fingers that began to wrinkle. It was a kiss that seared straight to my soul, branding me the way that only Eric de Vries could ever do.

———

MY FINGER DRIFTED LISTLESSLY over my lips. So much for that. Now I was snooping through his apartment, looking for evidence of his secrets. Trying desperately to figure out who this stranger was I had married. Or hadn't.

That wasn't love. I didn't know what it was, but love? No way.

A sudden ray of sunlight shot through the buildings on Hanover Street and caught on my ring, making the black diamond gleam on my finger. Suddenly, I felt ashamed for being her at all. If things were over between me and Eric—which I very much suspected they were—the only thing left to do was to go back to New York, pay my respects to his grandmother, and then move on with my life. Brandon was able to walk away from a man who offered everything in the world he'd ever wanted. If John Carson—whoever he was—was as bad as Brandon said, I needed to walk away too. And that meant from Eric as well.

I opened my mouth to say so, but before I could, the handle on the front door turned. And Eric walked in.

FOUR

"What the fuck are you doing here?"

The three of us froze. Skylar slid off Brandon's lap and stood up. Brandon brushed off his pants and also rose, looking rather like a cat licking itself after it had just been caught falling off a counter or something equally ungraceful.

I cleared my throat, but stubbornly remained seated. "I—we're looking for you."

Eric strode in. I only had a few seconds to take in the fact that he looked delicious in gray joggers, a black hoodie, and Yankees cap covering his cloudy eyes. It was a far cry from his normally tailored appearance, more like one of thousands of college students in Boston and less like the tycoon-in-training he was. His hair had even grown out a bit in the past ten days and was sticking out slightly from under his hat. If I hadn't been so stunned to see him, I might have jumped him.

Lucky for me, he got rid of that sentiment immediately.

"Looking for me in Boston? What in the actual fuck, Jane? This is *my* apartment."

"Well, technically, it's both of yours. Common law property and all that," Skylar put in.

Eric whirled around to her and Brandon, who both took uncomfortable steps toward each other. Brandon set the Latin dictionary back on the bookshelf and looked at anything but Eric.

"My own fucking partner and my best man," Eric sneered. "Dabbling in a little breaking and entering, huh?"

"Oh, get off your squad car, Officer Krupke," I snapped back. "This isn't *West Side Story*. I'm your *wife*, not a finger-snapping gang member. Skylar's right. Legally, this is my apartment too."

Eric's eyes flamed. "No, it's not. I never signed the license."

I opened my mouth, but no comeback emerged. The statement was like an arrow through the chest. It was true, of course, but I didn't think he would go there. And more than that, I was surprised by how much it hurt.

"We, um...look, Eric, we're just glad you're all right," Skylar mumbled as she reached for Brandon.

He wrapped a big arm around her shoulder, looking now like he wanted to punch Eric in the face. Hell, I wouldn't have argued. I kind of wanted to punch him myself.

"Hey, man, *you* disappeared for ten days," Brandon said. "And Jane's been worried fuckin' sick about you, not to mention Skylar and I haven't been too happy either. So now that you've decided to reappear, let's just take a deep breath, because I don't think you have the right to be mad at either of them. Not after what you've put Jane through."

Huh. Most of the time Brandon just seemed amused and mildly annoyed with me, like he was putting up with me for Skylar's sake. Turned out the big lug actually cared.

"Jane, do you need us to stay?" His face practically begged me not to say yes.

I shook my head. "No. Eric and I have some things to discuss on our own."

"We don't," Eric said.

"We do," I corrected him sweetly.

"Are you going to be all right?" Skylar asked me, though Brandon was already tugging her toward the door.

I swallowed and nodded. "Sure. Thanks, you guys."

Skylar gazed lovingly at her husband—I was pretty sure he was going to get lucky while they waited in the car. Eric and I just watched them awkwardly until the door closed.

Then I turned to find another devil staring at me.

"What's that?"

I followed Eric's gaze to the coin in my hand. "I found it in the key bowl."

"And you thought it was fine to take it?" His voice was sharp, almost fearful.

I frowned. "Well, I definitely want to now. Where the hell have you been?"

"That's none of your business."

Before I could stop him, Eric swooped down and plucked the coin out of my hand, then started down the hallway toward the bedroom.

"None of my business?" I sprang up. "We're *married*."

"No, we're not!" he called from the bedroom.

I found him in the closet, pushing aside rows of suits. If I had even made it this far before being arrested with guilt, I would have found the large black safe gleaming behind folds of wool and gabardine.

"Yes, we are," I said as Eric crouched down. "I asked the minister. *He* said we are. He pronounced it!"

"Well, the state of New York says we're not," Eric replied as he spun the combination lock. "And that's the entity I'm interested in." He opened the safe and retrieved several documents, which included a bunch of old books, several of which looked identical to the journal I'd found.

"Why do you keep a copy of *The Aeneid* in a safe?" I wondered as he stuffed the books into a duffel bag. One of the black journals toppled to the ground, and I snatched it before Eric could.

"Give that back."

"No." I scampered into the bedroom, paging through the book. More poetry. Lots and lots of poetry.

"That's private," he said as he charged after me. "Give it back."

"No!" I scampered onto the bed, not caring if I rumpled the perfect white sheets. Oh, this one was interesting...something about bloodred lips love bound. I paused, struck by the words.

"Stop going through my stuff, Jane," Eric snapped beside the bed.

I danced from foot to foot as I scanned a few more poems. "I'm sorry. Except not really, because when your husband disappears for ten fucking days, you kind of don't give a shit about rifling through his things. Not if it's going to give you some clues."

"You knew where I was, and so did Skylar. I called her office this morning."

The office. The fucking office. There was a small part of me that hoped the information had been off. That Eric had still planned to find me himself to tell me he was all right. To talk and fight and argue and...maybe even make up?

After ten days of alternately raging and moping, one small truth had emerged: I was still angry at him...but I also still loved him. And the fact that he didn't even seem to want to be married anymore really, really hurt.

"I didn't know you wrote so much poetry," I said, pushing

the thoughts away and deciding on another tactic. "It's beautiful."

"It's just immature crap."

"It doesn't read like that."

"Well, it is."

I turned another page, but then decided against my instincts and closed the book. Tentatively, I held it out to him.

"I am sorry," I said. "For snooping. You're right. If you want to share things with me, you can. And if you don't, I should respect that."

The hardness on Eric's face lessened a little, and once again, I contemplated wrestling him to the bed and forcing him to look me in the eye until that facade dropped completely. I could break him. It was something of a specialty of mine.

Eric stared at the small black book for a few seconds, then took it and dropped it into the trash can next to the bureau. I cringed, like the sound of the book smacking the bottom of the chrome container physically hurt.

"It's just childish fucking ramblings," he said and returned to the closet to pack.

I sank to the bed, unsure of what to do. But before I could come up with anything, Eric spoke first.

"You want to tell me what the hell you were looking for, aside from my shitty poetry?"

His tone was sharper than ever as he reemerged from the closet with five suits and a garment bag over his shoulder. I didn't blame him. It was the fourth time he'd asked me that since catching the three of us elbows-deep in his things. I still didn't have a good answer.

I got up from the bed and stared out the window to the tourists bustling around Hanover Street. It wasn't exactly high season in Boston—the first snow would happen any day now. But the North End, with its myriad Italian restaurants and proximity to the Freedom Trail, was always an attraction.

"Do you know your neighborhood stinks?" I asked. "We're seven stories up, but it's still like living in the middle of a garlic bulb. How did you do this for five years?"

I was baiting him. Goading him. I wanted him to charge across the room and cage me with those wiry arms. I wanted him to grip my chin and force me to look into those bottomless gray eyes. I wanted him to call me "pretty girl" and sweep away the mess of the last week along with everything atop his bureau so he could show me *exactly* how much I belonged to him, fight it though I might.

But Eric didn't reply. And the mess stayed where it was. Caitlyn Calvert, John Carson—it was like they were in the room with us.

"Jane."

I turned. Eric was zipping his suits into a garment bag.

"Stop," he said. "It's not going to work."

Yeah, he knew exactly what I was thinking.

"Can you really blame me?" I asked. "I had to find out something. I had to know where you were. Who my...who my father is. That is, if you're not going to tell me anything."

Eric looked up, but instead of answering the obvious question, he just asked another. "And did you find anything out?"

The gold coin—a much shinier version of the one I found in the bowl—glinted over his t-shirt. Hmm, so he hadn't taken it off. I stared at it for a moment, then turned away. "I guess there's a silver lining. I can fuck who I want now, can't I?"

Was that a growl I heard behind me?

I decided to go with it. "He's cute." I pointed at a middle-aged man taking out the garbage. His beer belly was about the size of a basketball, but Eric couldn't know that from across the room. "Oh, he's hot too." This time I was eyeing the garbage can.

I looked back at Eric, up and down like I was comparing two specimens. "Probably bigger than you too, if you know what I mean."

A muscle in Eric's neck twitched, but he didn't move. "Stop."

I bit my lip. He closed his eyes.

"I suppose it's a good thing we're not legally married then, huh, Petri dish? Maybe if I go to Marleigh's, Viv can hook me up with one of the guys there. Maybe the one I was flirting with the night I accepted your proposal."

"Stop."

"I bet his dick is huge. Like horse-huge. It's always the shy ones who are packing, you know."

"Goddammit!"

With sudden fury, Eric yanked off his baseball cap and hurled it against the wall with enough force that his hair flopped over his reddened, heaving face. He pushed it away, revealing the remnants of a big bruise over one eye.

"Jesus, what is that?" I stepped closer to examine.

Eric retrieved his hat and clapped it on his head. "Nothing."

"That's not nothing. That looks you were smacked with a two-by-four. Seriously, Eric, what happened?"

But instead of answering any of my questions, Eric just grabbed his bags and walked toward the door. "I have to go."

"Go?" I balked. "You just got here!"

"I came to get a few things and go back to New York for the funeral," he said, then walked down the hallway without waiting for me to answer. "It's tomorrow," he called over his shoulder.

I scampered after him. "Yes, I know it's tomorrow. Your *lawyer* called Skylar, remember? Goddammit, Eric, just *stop!*"

"*Look.*"

He swung around. I stopped short, and had to brace myself against his chest so I wouldn't plow into it.

Eric stared at my hands, flat over his broad pectorals. Even through the sweatshirt, I could feel the energy vibrating through his muscles. It was all too easy to imagine myself ripping the fabric apart just to run my fingernails up and down those washboard abs.

My fingers curled into the cotton, pulling slightly. Eric sucked in a tight breath. I bit my lip hard enough to sting.

"It's over," he stated in carefully enunciated words. "I think we both know that. I'm angry. And you're angry too, Jane. Let's just leave it."

Muddled images of red underwear and Caitlyn Calvert's snooty, surgically enhanced face flashed through my mind. Fuck, yes, I was mad. I was also worried. And confused. And attracted. And, and, and...

"Yes...no...well, yes, of course I'm mad, but—"

"You screamed at me in front of five hundred people, Jane," Eric interrupted again. "Is it really that surprising I walked out?"

"I did *not* scream at you!" I shouted. "Let's be totally clear here. I yelled at you and you yelled at me in a nicely barricaded chapel, all right? Just before we *both* said our vows in front of half of fucking New York City!"

"Vows?" he said nastily. "You mean the ones you fucking ground through your teeth right after flipping out about a one-night stand I had five years ago?"

"With *Caitlyn Calvert!*" I sucked in a deep breath. "You know, that two-faced bitch who kept trying to sink her French-manicured claws into you every chance she got for the last six months? You didn't think to say, oh, hey, remember that tacky thong you found in my bed five years back? Yeah, it belonged to that thirsty bitch."

"Exactly!" Eric exploded all over again. "Five fucking years ago! Right after *you* broke *my* heart anyway, Jane! Jesus fucking Christ, sometimes I think all you care about is your right to be angry at me. So, please tell me some more about how much those vows meant to you. It'll be a good story."

"You said my name," I said. "You made the promises, just like I did. That *did* mean something, even if I did want to slap your stupid face. So we fought. We always fight. That's what we do!"

"Well, I don't want to do it anymore. Not as your husband. Not as anything." He started walking away again.

"Eric, you have to deal with this!" I cried.

"I don't care!" He whirled around with a face like thunder. "I. Don't. Care. I'm done being *embarrassed* by you, Jane."

I stepped back like I'd been slapped. And really, it felt that way. He knew. He knew how hard I'd worked to fit in with his stupid, upper crust family. How much I'd changed myself for them just to avoid exactly that—his social embarrassment.

I prepared another sharp retort, ready to tell him he was an utter jackass. But something in his eyes flickered. Something was wrong.

"You don't really think that," I said. "You're lying."

Eric's eyes flashed, and he looked away too quickly. "I'm not."

"You are," I said. "You're a terrible liar, Eric. You always have been. You keep things close to your chest, have plenty of secrets, but you've never point-blank lied to me because you really can't. What is it? What are you keeping? I can help, I *know* I can."

His wide, full mouth opened slightly like he was going to answer the question. The mask dropped, and an equally muddled combination of emotions passed across his face. Anger, fear, passion, irritation, fondness, sorrow. Love. I saw them all and knew they were reflected on mine.

But then the mask resumed, more opaque than ever. Eric

swallowed, adjusted his cap, then looked straight at me. His expression didn't falter.

"Let me make this crystal clear. My grandmother, the one responsible for this sham of a relationship, is dead. It's done. Tomorrow we have to go to her funeral. The wake. The reading of the will. And after that, you and I are finished. I don't want to see you again. I don't want to know you, Jane. At all."

I shook my head, reeling. What was happening? Who *was* this guy, this genuinely heartless bastard? Eric had always been reticent, a bit stoic. Even cold sometimes. But heartless? I'd never really seen that. Even if I'd said it.

"But, but...the contract," I mumbled, losing my ability to articulate properly. "Your inheritance...I thought we...you'll lose everything."

Eric heaved his garment bag over his shoulder. His gaze met mine like a sledgehammer. "To be perfectly honest," he said, "I'd rather be single and poor than have a whore for a wife."

My hand met his cheek with a crack. I didn't even know I had done it until my palm burned, fire sprinting up my arm with the power. Eric took a few steps back, clutching his face with one hand. But to my surprise, he didn't shout. He didn't protest at all.

"Good for you," he said quietly instead as he touched the reddened skin.

And I could have sworn that in that second, the mask cracked once more. Just a little. The harsh determination on his stolid Nordic features wavered, like a tiny bit of remorse was squeezing through his pores.

But before I could prod it, suss it out completely, he swept around me and left.

FIVE

"It doesn't make sense," Skylar said for the fourteenth time over nightcaps.

Desperately in need of some comfort food after our altercations with Eric, the Crosby-Sterlings and I enjoyed some of their housekeeper's famous lasagna before Skylar and Brandon put their kids to bed. Now my friends were both sipping on whiskey while I made do with a glass of port. It was either that or vodka, and I suspected that Beluga was only in the house because of a certain Upper East Sider's tastes in liquor. I'd have a sugar-crashing headache in the morning, but I wasn't touching that crap.

"He's never acted that way before," Skylar continued. "In school, he was at worst indifferent, even though it was completely obvious he was in love with you."

"Was it now?" I asked. "Was the fact that he slept with Caitlyn Calvert an indication of his 'love' for me too? Or the part where he hid that shit while I had tea parties with the woman for months? When are women going to stop taking men's abuse as signs of affection? I think you're brainwashed, Sky."

"Please. Indifference toward *your* sexual exploits or forgetting to tell you something is not abuse, and you know it," Skylar retorted. "I've known the guy for almost ten years now, through all of your ups and downs, and I've never heard him say a bad word about you. And he's certainly never cared about your dating history, not that he even should, considering his own."

I shook my head. I was tired of thinking about this. Tired of replaying the entire argument in my mind again and again. Tired of hearing those final painful words ringing in my ears like fucked-up bells. That slap was still vibrating across my palm.

Whore. It wasn't the first time someone had called me that. Most people don't like women who are frank about their sexuality. They don't like women like me.

But Eric was always different. We'd shared more than one laugh together in the nest of our bedroom as we recalled past partners without an iota of jealousy. It had been a comfort, knowing I could be open about everything in my past with him, and him with me.

———

"DO YOU REMEMBER THE PHYSICS GUY?" I asked as we watched the first of the autumn leaves falling from the oak outside our window.

Eric's hand walked up and down my bare back, and he chuckled at the memory. "Was that the one who wore ridiculously tight jeans?"

I shook my head. "No, that was Greg, the music major."

"Right, right. I remember wondering if that guy was providing his own birth control with those things."

I snorted. "Maybe. He wasn't particularly well equipped, though. Like a tube of lipstick, that one."

His chest shook with mirth under my cheek. I smiled into the smooth, warm expanse and inhaled deeply.

"What about you?" I asked. "Were they all good, or did you have some horror stories too?"

"Well, there was an assistant at Sterling I nailed during my second year."

"Nailed? What are you, a carpenter from 1987? Were you 'banging the chicks' too?"

I received a quick pinch at my waist, causing me to squeal.

I smacked his chest. "Tell me! I swear to God, I don't care!"

Eric examined me for a moment, like he didn't quite believe me. "All right," he said finally. "She...she had a nice ass. So when we...got to that point where things were...going to happen, I turned her around to—"

"Can you stop pussyfooting around this story, Petri dish?" I interrupted. "You were about to fuck. I can handle it. Get to the punchline."

For that I received another round of merciless pinches to my own backside, causing me to laugh and wriggle uncontrollably.

"Listen, Lefferts," he said with a faux-stern expression once he stopped. "There is an art to storytelling, you know."

I broke down all over again while Eric just waited impatiently for me to collect myself.

"I asked what was wrong," I said. "Not who had the nicest ass in your roster."

"She had a tattoo," he replied. "I pulled down her underwear, and there it was. Right on the part that, well, you like smacked here and there."

I didn't even blush. He wasn't wrong, and I wasn't ashamed of it.

"What was the tattoo?"

Eric shook his head sheepishly, even though he wasn't the one with the embarrassing body art. "Tweety Bird."

I bit my lip. "As in Looney Tunes?"

"As in lemon-yellow, boner-killing, 'I tawt I taw a puddy tat' Tweety Bird," he confirmed. "And every time I, ah, gave it to her, the damn thing jumped like it was trying to fly." He shook his head as I erupted into laughter all over again. "It's not funny. Totally ruined those cartoons for me, I'll have you know."

"I'm not laughing at that!" I crowed as I wiped tears from my face. "I'm laughing at the fact that you do such a good Tweety impression. Can you do any others? How about Elmer Fudd? Or Daffy Duck?"

"That's enough!" A second later, I was flipped onto my front so Eric could cage me against the mattress from behind.

"She's got jokes," he said as he ran his hands up and down my back, lingering on my ass for a second longer than necessary. With a swift smack there, he quieted the last of my giggles. "Let's see who's laughing now, huh?" His hands slipped under my hips and jerked them up so quickly I lost my breath. "All right, pretty girl. On. Your. Knees."

A SMILE still lingered as I recalled those sweet moments. I didn't care where he had been. Just that we were together. And I'd thought he'd felt the same.

"I think you're just bitter, Jane."

Skylar and I both turned to Brandon, who had been listening to us go back and forth for the last ten minutes while he made a fire in the living room's enormous brick fireplace.

"About what?" I asked.

"You're holding a grudge. What *really* bothered you about Caitlyn Calvert?"

"Brandon!" Skylar warned him, but he waved away her protests.

I tipped my glass from side to side, watching the reddish liquid. "She...she's just terrible. And how many times have we heard Eric hate on women exactly like her. And then he invites her to his bed? The message couldn't have been clearer."

It wasn't that he had slept with someone else all those years ago, I realized. It was that he had slept with *her*. Someone so different than me, who fit into the posh world of the Upper East Side as seamlessly as I stumbled over it. There was a part of me that always worried Eric would rather have someone like that in the end. And by not disclosing the affair, he had confirmed it. Right before he called me a whore to my face. Everything Caitlyn was not.

"But he didn't invite her back," Brandon said. "And I bet he was hurting as much as you were back then. Guys do stupid fuckin' things when their pride is wounded."

"That sounds like loyalty talking," I replied as calmly as I could. Which was to say, not very.

Brandon picked up his whiskey and sat down on the wide hearth. "Loyalty for what? Eric and I only really know each other through Skylar and the fact that he used to work for me."

"You were his best man."

"For a wedding that wasn't even real." Brandon shrugged and poked at the fire, sending sparks up the chimney. "Here's what I know: the two of you are basically cut from the same cloth. You both got around, you both have pasts, and you both have more trust issues than the Vatican. Don't argue with me; it's the truth."

I opened my mouth, but closed it immediately. Because, of course, he was right.

"But I also know this," Brandon continued. "Two weeks ago, the guy couldn't stand to be away from you for more than a night. He ruined a perfectly good bachelor party to fly halfway across the world to get to you, Jane."

"Maybe that's just because Caitlyn was there," I said bitterly. "Maybe he was worried she would say something."

"I don't think his response has anything to do with some chick he banged back when the two of you were both playing musical chairs in nightclubs."

I blinked as a sudden rush from that night came back to me. Eric chasing me into his bedroom, yanking off my clothes. The hungry, focused look in his eyes that pinned me against the wall before he could even get there.

———

"TELL ME," he said again and again every time he removed another piece of clothing. My skirt. My bra. Everything fell to the floor alongside each pronouncement I made.

"You," I whispered each and every time. "I belong to you."

"That's right," Eric said once he finally stripped me naked. He placed both hands on my shoulders and pushed me gently back onto the bed. His fiery gaze drifting over my body like a pirate surveying his booty. But it wasn't greed that lit his expression. It was lust. Longing. Love.

———

"SO YOU THINK something happened while he was gone?"

Skylar's voice yanked me out of my daydream this time, but the gnawing in my stomach remained. That was the real bitch of the matter. As furious as I was at the man, I still missed him. Something deep and primal inside me yearned for him. Cared about him. I couldn't turn it off.

"I don't know," I said. "Someone gave him that black eye."

"I think you need to talk to your dad," Brandon said.

I blinked, taking an extra second to comprehend what he meant. Then I scowled. "John Carson is *not* my dad."

But Brandon and Skylar just blinked, like twin owls who felt sorry for their prey.

"Dammit," I muttered. "Okay. As soon as the funeral is over, I'll go see him. Or try to track him down or something else."

I'd returned to Brookline with new resolve: pack my things for the weekend, go to New York for the funeral, then get the hell out in time to start a new bar exam class in Boston. I wasn't going back to Chicago. Skylar had already said she could find me clerical work at the firm, and I had enough in my savings from the last few months to tide me over until I passed the bar and could find a real job in Massachusetts. Away from Eric. Away from this mess.

If only my heart could make as clean a break.

Instead, I tipped back the last of my port and stood up to clear our glasses. I had a long day tomorrow, starting with a several-hours drive back to New York. I didn't have any intention of showing up to Celeste's funeral looking like a tired old woman. And I suspected I would need some energy to face what was coming.

———

WE GOT up at the crack of dawn to drive down to New York together, but I had summoned the courage to go to Eric's and my apartment on the Upper West Side instead of getting ready at Skylar and Brandon's hotel room. All of my clothes were there, and I needed something more appropriate than the jeans and concert tees I'd been living in for the past ten days. I might have been bullied out of my marriage, but no one was getting between me and my fashion.

Thankfully, Eric didn't appear. It didn't even look like he'd come here at all. His clothes were hanging in the closet just as he'd left them before our wedding. Even the book of Romantic poetry he'd been reading still lay by the bedside, crooked atop a stack of other novels.

My heart ached as I recalled our conversation about the exact poem bookmarked.

———

"KEATS?" I asked, picking up the book. "Aren't the Romantic poets kind of maudlin?"

"All poets are a little bit maudlin, pretty girl," Eric murmured as he traced his hand meditatively over my stomach. "The Romantics just didn't bother to hide it."

"Which is kind of why I'm surprised you like it."

"Why? You think I don't have a heart?"

I shrugged. I was pushing for something, but I didn't know what. We were getting married in less than a week, but I still felt sometimes like I didn't know the real Eric de Vries.

"Keats's parents died when he was young. Did you know that?" Eric asked. When I shook my head, he nodded. "His father died when Keats was just eight. His mother when he was fourteen." His hand paused as he considered it. "You know, he had an inheritance, but he never claimed it. No one knows why."

He was quiet for a long moment.

"What's your favorite?" I asked, hoping to steer him away from that train of thought.

Eric blinked, then smiled. "Oh, that's easy. 'La Belle Dame Sans Merci.'"

"French?"

Eric shook his head and resumed the circles with his fingers. "Just the title. About a femme fatale, of course."

I made a face. "I really hate that trope. Why do women always have to be cast as a man's downfall?"

"I don't think it's a bad thing, necessarily," he replied. He leaned down and pressed a kiss to my breast. "Giving your life for the love of a good woman. Seems like a good way to go."

I watched as he progressed across my chest, pressing kisses over my sternum.

"What...what are your favorite lines?" I asked as he feathered his lips down.

He paused just over my nipple, and I felt the shadow of a smile press on the puckered skin. "You actually want me to quote poetry to you?"

But this time, I didn't have any retort. I remained still until finally, Eric sat up and combed his fingers through my hair as he spoke:

> I met a Lady in the Meads,
> Full beautiful, a faery's child,
> Her hair was long, her foot was light
> And her eyes were wild.

He pulled out the strand of red buried in black at the base of my neck and tugged.

"More," I murmured, pulling him down. I wasn't usually one for this kind of gooey display, but with Eric, I couldn't seem to get enough. "Tell me more."

Eric grinned. "Now who's maudlin, huh?"

I mimed like I was going to smack him, but instead I just enjoyed the feel of his steely arms under my touch. "Just shut up and keep talking poetry at me."

"'She found me roots of relish sweet'"—he sucked on my earlobe like it was candy—"'And honey wild, and manna dew'"— his mouth traced down my chest, pulling one nipple between his *lips and releasing it with a pop—"'And sure in language strange she said'..."*

I waited for him to finish, but with a sudden movement, Eric pulled my legs around his waist, his hardening length teasing my entrance just slightly. Morning light danced behind his blond hair like a halo.

And as he slid inside, his lips too slid past my ear, whispering the last lines of the verse that would sing through my entire being for days after: "'I love thee true.'"

———

I SHOOK THE MEMORY AWAY. Getting wrapped up in those moments was exactly what got me into this mess to begin with. It was too easy to forget what kind of duplicity Eric de Vries was really capable of.

I walked into the other bedroom that had become my studio/craft room when Eric and I had fused our worlds together instead of maintaining the platonic relationship he'd first proposed. A black wool midi dress I had just finished hung from a rack near the window. It was funny...I had no original plans for this dress, but I wondered now if I had made it with this day in mind. After all, Celeste had been so sick, living the past six months with the keen awareness that they were her last.

Celeste had loved to lecture me on my wardrobe (or the fashion choices she deemed unacceptable to my new "station"). With Chanel-clad superiority, she had said time and time again that my self-designed garments were too garish or rough, urging me to use Eric's money to buy more designer duds simply to fit in at society luncheons or just her home. For her, clothes were like armor.

Just like Skylar had warned me they would be in this world.

I fingered the dress, admiring its simple shape that I'd

modeled somewhat on Dior's New Look that Celeste loved so much. Black wool draped neatly across the bust, while sleeves trimmed with leather tapered around the elbow. Another panel of black leather wrapped tightly around the waist like a military-style corset, complete with a buckle I'd salvaged off another vintage dress. The pencil-style skirt reached a demure calf-length and was also trimmed with a solid inch of leather. It was my favorite thing I'd ever made—a mix of the brash edge I never wanted to shake completely and the classic, demure styles expected around stodgy Upper East Siders.

When I put it on, I felt like a warrior. Just like Celeste, in her own way, wanted me to be. After looking at myself for a few minutes, I removed the rings that I'd worn on my left hand for the last few weeks. It was only then that the transformation was complete.

SIX

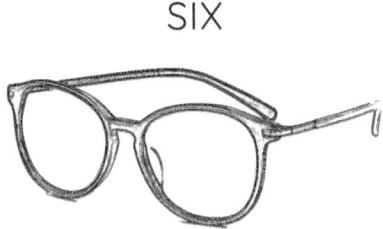

Unfortunately, my carefully chosen clothes weren't enough to fight the army of stares that confronted me upon my return to St. John the Divine. If Eric's and my wedding was the spectacle of the season, then the funeral of Celeste de Vries was its closing ceremony.

All—and I mean *all*—of the most socially significant families and faces of the tristate area had arrived for the event. It made sense now why the de Vrieses had waited almost two weeks after their matriarch's death to hold her funeral. Not only were they awaiting the return of the missing heir himself, but the glitterati that someone like Celeste would attract cast a planet-wide glow. Politicians, designers, celebrities, philanthropists. It was like walking through the pages of *Time* magazine's most influential people issue. Things like this took time to organize.

The hum inside the church intensified as I walked through the massive arched doorway behind Skylar and Brandon. Several people knew them—after all, Brandon wasn't exactly a slouch in this crowd. But most of the eyes immediately trained on me. I was the most recent disgrace of this family. Its stain, its utter shame. A car wreck everyone else couldn't look away from.

"Jane?"

I turned to find Nina, Eric's cousin, stepping away from a cluster of people. She wore a black Chanel suit and string of pearls in tasteful tribute to her deceased grandmother. Behind her, Violet, her mother, and Heather, Eric's mom, both peered at me. Violet's sleek blonde brows crinkled with disdain while Heather just looked as bemused as her Botoxed face would allow.

I gestured that Brandon and Skylar should find us seats. "Hi, Nina."

"I...we didn't expect to see you." Nina leaned in to touch her cheek to mine in that strange, non-kissing kiss only the rich practiced.

"What is *she* doing here?" Calvin, Nina's husband, appeared at her side.

I had met him a few times over the last six months, of course. He was a fixture at most of the family events and had floated on the periphery of Celeste's world, generally treating women like accessories while he smoked cigars and traded stories with men over brandy. This was the first time the man had ever actually approached me.

I wondered briefly if he was part of the same Janus society. Maybe he knew where Eric had gone But I saw no sign of that strange, two-faced coin anywhere on his person. And besides, wouldn't he have told them if he knew?

Maybe not, a small voice said. *Maybe not*. What did I know?

Not for the first time, I wondered how Calvin and Nina ended up together. Much like her cousin and the rest of her family, Nina was tall and lithe with quiet, Scandinavian good looks—blonde hair, a razor-straight nose, and deep gray eyes that pierced before you knew it. Calvin Gardner, on the other hand, was the kind of man who might have been good-looking in his youth, but who had slowly spread outward like a round of cheese left in the sun. His skin was slightly yellowish, like he'd rubbed it all over with too much tanning oil, and I was ninety-nine percent sure that his too-shiny chestnut hair was the product of a well-disguised transplant. He had a mustache reminiscent of the Monopoly Man, and his muddy brown eyes only seemed to spark when he sensed an opportunity to make money.

Nina eyed her husband like she had forgotten he existed. Her exhaustion with the man was palpable, and he hadn't even spoken directly to her.

"Hi, Calvin," I said. "I'm good, how are you?"

He just glared at me. "You're not part of this family anymore —you never really were. Why are you here?"

I surveyed the hundreds of people surrounding us, many of them watching our conversation. "Oh my God, I had no idea this was a small family affair."

"Calvin, of course Jane should be here." Nina gave her husband a sharp look. "Please sit down."

"Come on, doll, I was just joking."

Nina pressed her lips together irritably. "Please?"

With a rabbit-like wiggle of his snubbed nose, Calvin rejoined Heather and Violet in their corner.

Nina turned back to me. "Jane, I'm sorry. I was just surprised to see you after..."

"After my wedding crashed and burned, and then your mother sent me packing?"

Nina had the grace to look ashamed. Violet sent me a glare as Calvin whispered something in her ear. I was literally in my wedding dress, pacing the halls of the hospital along with the rest of Eric's family, when Violet informed me I should leave the family in peace. No one had argued. And so I had.

"We just..." Nina smiled politely at a few of the guests, but when her gaze met mine again, her eyes shone. "It's been a difficult few weeks. And with Eric gone..."

My bravado faded. Of course. I had no right to get up on my high horse with this family, as awful as they could be. Not today. Not when they were genuinely mourning.

"You didn't know where he was either?" I asked. I had tried to inquire multiple times, but none of my calls had been answered.

Nina shook her head, causing her perfect blonde waves to shimmer back and forth.

"Nina, I'm so sorry," I said. "Really, I am. If there is anything I can do to help, with anything, just let me know. Your grandma...she was special."

"She was difficult," Nina replied, but not without some fondness. She blinked back a few more tears. "But I loved her. Even when she adored Eric best of all, I still loved her."

I nodded sympathetically. I had spent enough time around her and Celeste to see all the small ways in which Nina had tried to please her grandmother. But there was a part of Celeste that respected some rebellion, that quality so obvious in her grandson, but which her other, much more obedient grandchild sorely lacked.

"So, Eric," Nina said, changing the subject. "Have you seen him then?" The subdued, yet frantic look in Nina's eyes told me she had not. "The lawyer said he was back, but..."

"Just briefly in Boston. He was—well, we didn't have a chance to talk much." I glanced at Calvin, who was still staring daggers at me from where he now stood with a collection of portly men in expensive suits. I wrinkled my nose. Their lapels were as big as my head. Money definitely didn't buy taste.

"The executor will read the will today, after the reception," Nina was saying. "In Grandmother's parlor. You should...he said you should come, didn't he?"

I nodded, and then, just on a whim, I reached out to squeeze her hand. Nina started slightly, but didn't pull away.

"She liked you," Nina remarked as she looked down at my bare hand, studying the fact that I now wore no ring. Then she released it with a thin smile. "She would be glad you're here."

And before I could respond, she made her escape to greet a few other mourners. I turned to where Skylar and Brandon stood waiting for me and ignored the other curious faces while we found our seats. I filed to the end row, sitting at the penultimate chair since there was already a jacket draped around the last.

"So the burial is at the family's plot at St. Mark's, followed by the reception at the penthouse," Skylar said next to me as she paged through the program. "Seems a bit weird, since she was Presbyterian."

I shrugged, unsurprised. "It's one of the oldest burial grounds in the city. The Stuyvesants were all buried there too. It was what she wanted."

Skylar gave me a queer look. "You talked about that?"

I shrugged again. Strangely, I had had a number of conversations with Celeste about her funerary wishes. She was very proud of the fact that her family was as old as some of the grandest in New York. Knowing the end was nigh, she had not been quiet about her wishes.

"She knew what was coming," I said, fighting the quaver in my voice. The more I thought of those conversations, the more I found I missed the old girl. She might have been a controlling autocrat, but she cared deeply about her family, and after some time, her sharp tongue was almost entertaining.

A blast of organs interrupted the chatter of the church, and there was a rumble of hundreds of people rising to their feet as the choir behind the crossing began the opening hymn.

"Are we supposed to sing too?" I asked Skylar.

She looked at me like I was crazy. "I'm barely even Jewish," she whispered back. "How would I know?"

Brandon elbowed her and nodded at the program, pointing to the lyrics, then to the liturgy printed below it.

"Ah," I said. "There's a script."

Brandon just rolled his eyes, and all humor evaporated as the minister passed, followed by the casket carried by eight men I recognized as cousins and friends of Eric's family. Eric, however, was nowhere to be found.

We watched as the casket was brought to the crossing and set on a stand between two towering displays of white gladiolas and uncountable candles. Everything was exactly as Celeste would have wanted: lush, but tasteful.

The pallbearers returned to their seats as the hymn ended. The minister approached the microphone and began the service.

"In the name of the Father and the Son and the Holy Spirit. Amen."

A few people around the church crossed themselves, including Brandon. The majority stood still and listened to the minister speak.

"The Lord is near to the brokenhearted, and saves the crushed in spirit. *Psalms* 34:18. May grace and peace be yours in abundance in the knowledge of God and of Jesus our Lord. *Peter*." The minister took a deep breath before continuing: "We are gathered here to praise God, to witness to our faith, and to give thanks for the life of our sister, Celeste Annika de Vries. We come together in grief, acknowledging our loss. May God grant us grace that in pain—we may find comfort, in sorrow—hope, and in death—resurrection. Dying, Christ destroyed our death. Rising, Christ restores our life. In baptism, Celeste was sealed by the Holy Spirit and marked as Christ's own forever. Let us pray."

The entire congregation bowed their heads as the minister

continued with a traditional prayer. It wasn't completely unfamiliar. Unlike the bombastic affair of my wedding, this was a service I knew, having been towed to Bethany Korean Presbyterian from time to time while growing up. Dad wasn't much of a constituent, but that never prevented Yu Na, when she was feeling penitent, from trying to save her only daughter.

There was a shuffle from the back of the church as one of the heavy doors opened and closed, but everyone kept their heads dutifully bowed even as footsteps hurried up a side aisle. I peeked over and found Eric sliding next to me at the end of our row, his black suit rumpled and eyes swollen as he bowed his head in prayer.

"Please be seated," said the minister.

The congregation obeyed.

"Eric?" I said in a low voice as we sank into our chairs.

He glanced at me. "Shhh."

I shimmied closer. "Eric."

Tentatively, I reached out to touch his shoulder, but, like a skittish cat, he jerked away.

"Don't—don't touch me," he said, and when his flickering eyes met mine, I jerked back. There was something different there this morning. The vitriol from that night in Boston was gone, and now, all I saw was fear.

"Eric." The name was now a whisper. "What happened? Where have you been?"

His eyelids dropped, and he inhaled a long, almost tortured breath. "Nowhere you need to know about."

We sat not six inches apart, listening to the same minister who had married us offer a different reading, followed by a variety of platitudes about absolution and grace. I couldn't have said what was in them—all I could think about was the man next to me. Eric sat still and straight the entire time, never looking once at me, just keeping his focus on the gladiolas. Thirty, forty minutes passed. His gaze didn't waver once.

"And now we welcome Celeste's grandson, Eric de Vries, to say a few words about his grandmother."

I gaped as Eric stood shakily, pressed his charcoal, paisley-printed tie over the plain white shirt, and limped to the front of the church. In the front row, Nina, Calvin, and the rest of the de Vries family's mouths dropped in surprise, then shut quickly when they realized everyone was watching them. The entire building was deathly silent as the prodigal son took his place in front of the casket, unfolded a piece of paper, and began.

"I'll make this short. Grandmother never liked a bunch of talk. Maybe that's why, just a few weeks ago, she pulled me aside and asked me to delivery her eulogy when the time came."

A smattering of light laughter rippled through the church. Eric rubbed the back of his neck and stared at the paper.

"My grandmother wasn't the easiest person to know. She was strong. She was stubborn. She really, really liked having her way. Kind of like me. Kind of like everyone in our family."

Again, a round of chuckles sounded.

"She also didn't always have a lot to say, but when she did, she made it count," Eric continued, buoyed by the sound. "And when she asked me to return to New York after a long time away, she wanted one thing. One dying wish. For me to be happy."

There was another rumble. No doubt that wasn't the story much of New York knew. I wasn't an idiot. Conspiracy theories had been flying around this city since Eric and I had announced our sudden engagement. Some thought I was pregnant. Others thought I had blackmailed him somehow. Very few knew the conditions forced upon us in order to bring Eric back into the family fold.

But it seemed Eric had settled on the conclusion I had determined as well. That perhaps Celeste had required this ridiculous plan because she knew her grandson better than he thought. She knew that when pressed to get married, he would still only choose a life that would make him happy. Someone he...loved.

The word landed in my chest with a thump. It felt like a mockery. We weren't anything close to love now—just wreckage of lust and lies. I wasn't even sure anymore if love was something Eric or I were capable of. Not with each other. Maybe not with anyone.

I swiped at a tear that escaped from under my glasses. Beside me, Skylar squeezed my hand.

"She wanted her family to live like she did—on their own terms," Eric continued. "But she was one of the lucky ones. Not everyone can live their life exactly the way they want, but Celeste de Vries did. She made no apologies, even up until the end."

Eric swallowed visibly, and I gripped the edge of my seat so hard my knuckles turned white.

"We may have fought. We may have sparred. But before she died, she gave me what I wanted more than anything in the world."

His eyes met mine, and suddenly I found it hard to breathe. Eric's voice was soft, barely audible, even with the amplified sound.

"And for that, I'll always love her."

My heart pounded in my chest, echoing his every footstep as he made his way back to his seat, his broad, strong back oblivious to the barrage of stares.

The final lines of the commendation sounded around us, but I could no longer make out the words. Eric shook as he stared at the floor. I sat still, unsure of what to say or do. Did he mean me? Was *I* what he wanted most in the world? Or was it his family? His fortune?

But before I could sum up the courage to ask, the edge of

Eric's hand flattened against the edge of mine where our seats met. And then, very slowly, two of his fingers slid over my skin and wrapped around my ring and pinky fingers.

I stared at them while the minister's sonorous voice echoed through the air.

"What—" I finally whispered.

"Don't."

I looked up. Eric was looking at me, his deep gray eyes bottomless pools of sorrow and pain. Was this just for his grandmother, or was it for us? We had hurt each other so many times before, but I had never seen him look at me like that. I had never seen him look so afraid.

He turned back toward the minister, who was now guiding the congregation through The Lord's Prayer.

"Eric," I tried again. "What happened—"

"I said don't."

His lips barely moved; it was a whisper that only I could hear. But still, I heard it, and even though he would not meet my eyes, another finger joined the first two and squeezed. I looked down and was surprised to find the platinum of his wedding band still glinting against the dark wood.

Then his hand opened, and mine slipped into it. He held it long after the final rites were finished. Long after the casket was carried out of the church. It was only when we had to leave for the burial service that he finally let go. I turned to put on my coat, but when I looked up, ready to walk him out the doors, he was gone.

SEVEN

The burial was short and relatively simple compared to the church service. Skylar, Brandon, and I hovered on the outside of the group, unsure of where exactly to stand. Only a few people really cried, but I thought it was more out of respect than because they were sad. Celeste wouldn't have shed more than a tear or two at her own mother's funeral. Any more would have been utterly distasteful.

Celeste only wanted certain people present at her interring, and even fewer at the gathering afterward, which was limited to family and close friends only in the salon of her apartment. Skylar and Brandon were not allowed to attend, which was how I found myself walking into the elevator of her building alone.

"Hi, Gracie." I waved hello to the affable doorman who had actually cried when Eric gave me my engagement ring. "I'm here for the reception."

"Afternoon, Ms. Leff—Mrs. de Vrie—Ms. Jane." He seemed just as confused about my marital status as I was. *Yeah, join the club, buddy.*

I made for the elevator, but just as it was about to close, a large, familiar hand blocked it. Eric entered, his face freezing when he saw me.

"Oh," he said. "Hi."

"Hi yourself," I said as the other doorman closed the old-fashioned grate and began escorting us to the top floor.

We rode in silence with twin stiff postures, our hands clasped at our waists like dolls.

"You look nice," Eric remarked.

I looked down. "It's just a black dress."

When he looked me over, I swore I could feel his heated gaze through the layers of leather and wool.

"I remember you modeling it when you were making it," he said. "It looked nice on you then too."

I wanted to ask him what he was playing at. Shouting at me one second, praising me the next. I was the one in this relation-ship who imparted the emotional whiplash—he was always the steady hand. Maybe Brandon was right. Maybe something really *had* happened to him while he was gone. The question was, what, exactly?

"You're not wearing your rings."

I held out my hand, as if just realizing that I had removed the jewelry. "It's...they're just here."

I pulled out the long chain I was wearing around my neck. The simple platinum band and my engagement ring, set with its enormous black diamond, dangled from the end like a hypno-tist's tool. Eric followed its progress, back and forth, then fixed his deep gaze on me for a second before he looked away.

I looked down. His ring finger was now bare. I hated—*hated*—how much it hurt.

"You took yours off?" I asked.

His hand clenched. "Right, well. I suppose we're not married, are we?"

His harsh words in Boston thundered in the back of my mind.

"Nope," I said in a voice that was sharper than I intended. "I suppose we're not."

Before he could reply, the elevator doors opened, and Garrett, Celeste's butler, was waiting for us. We filed into the familiar penthouse foyer, which now seemed like a terrible parody in the absence of its owner.

"Welcome, sir," Garrett greeted Eric with an oddly formal bow and hung there a moment too long. "Miss Jane."

"Hello, Garrett," Eric greeted him. "How are you holding up?"

"As best as we can, sir."

Garrett offered a curt nod, but the creases around the old butler's eyes seemed darker and deeper than usual. It struck me then that the de Vrieses weren't the only ones mourning. Garrett had been Celeste's butler for close to sixty years, since she was a young bride herself. The ancient man must have been wondering what in the hell he was going to do with himself without his mistress.

"The rest of the family has arrived, sir," Garrett said as he turned and began to lead us slowly through the maze of hallways that tunneled around the penthouse.

"Eric," I whispered as we walked.

"Not now," he said over his shoulder.

"We need to talk."

"No, we don't."

"Yes, we *do*."

At that, I received a sharp, silvery glare. Eric glanced at Garrett, who kept walking like we weren't squabbling like children in front of Celeste's prized Gustav Klimt.

"Jane," Eric said. "It's done. We're done. You need to get it through your head."

"You're so full of shit, you're basically a compost factory," I retorted. "Were we done when you held my hand through the service like a child? I know you're in pain, but you're also jerking me around. You disappeared for almost two weeks, and I have a feeling you're going to do it again as soon as the lawyer tells us whatever he has to say. So, we need to talk. Now."

Eric just shook his head and turned away like *he* was dealing with an errant toddler, not me. "Later," he said. "When you've calmed down."

"I am not doing this again with you!" I hissed, grabbing at his shirt sleeve.

Eric whirled around with a face like thunder. The bruise over his right cheekbone was yellowish now, but still evident.

"Who did that?" I asked as I stepped forward, floating my hand over the spot. "Was it him? Was it my..." I couldn't bring myself to say "father."

He jerked away, like my fingers were a knife. "It's none of your fucking business."

"None of my business? I'm your *wife*, Eric."

"No, you're not!" he snapped. "We've been over this. Neither of us signed the license. I left before we could, and I'm sure as fuck not doing it now. *We're not married, Jane.*"

"You keep saying that," I said. "But we said the vows. We exchanged the rings. The m-minister pronounced us man and w-wife. I asked—according to h-him, we're married."

I hated—absolutely *hated*—the way my voice warbled, how I couldn't stop the tears rising, and that my face was heating up. I hated that I cared, that I had opened my heart to this man at all. Sure, I had been furious before we said our vows, but I still said them. I still—God help me—wanted the bastard.

Because I thought I had belonged to him, and him to me. We were a mess together, but he was *my* mess.

Wasn't he?

Eric took a deep breath, and slowly, the anger flowed out of his body just as quickly as it had arrived.

"Jane," he said more gently. "You're off the hook, all right? My family, everything. You'll be compensated for this madness, and you don't have to deal with this insanity anymore. It's better this way. Really, it is."

"I don't believe that," I said, reaching for him again. "Eric, please, I know I was angry at the wedding, but we're—we're not finished. Right?"

"Eric?"

We both turned at the voice calling down the hall, a voice that was liable to make me snap in fucking half.

Eric and I spoke in unison: "What the hell are you doing here?"

Caitlyn Calvert emerged from the parlor entrance, immaculately dressed in a demure sheath dress with a Peter Pan collar. Her tawny, light brown hair was pulled back in a neat French twist. Blue eyes blinked innocently at the two of us. She was Bambi reincarnated as an Upper East Side socialite.

"Eric," she cried as if we hadn't both just cursed at her. "Oh, Des, we've been *so* worried about you! Where have you been?"

"I'm sorry, *what?*" I stepped in front of Eric before she could get to him. "You practically ruined my wedding, you psycho! What in the *fuck* are you doing here?"

"Jane, is that coarse language really appropriate at this time?" she asked irritably. "I'm Nina's best friend. Of course I was going to support her and the family. Why are *you* here? I thought you wouldn't be particularly eager to show your face after you embarrassed Celeste the way you did."

"That's enough." Eric's voice was machete-sharp, and I was relieved when his cutting gaze aimed right at Caitlyn. "Cait, you need to leave."

"What? Des, let's just calm down." She extended a slim

hand, like she wanted to cup his face. "You don't want me to leave—"

"I do," Eric said. "You think I don't know what you did? You knew exactly where Jane was before the ceremony."

"Desi—"

"Nina told me everything on our way to the gravesite. You made sure Jane knew we slept together because you wanted to break us up. Isn't that right? Or maybe you just wanted to embarrass her."

Caitlyn's doll eyes blinked like she was having a conniption. "Eric...it was just a...I really didn't—you can't say that night didn't mean anything to you! I was special!"

I snorted. "You and half of Boston."

The woman really had no clue whom she was dealing with. Sleeping with Eric, the king of the one-night stand was about as special as trying on a pair of jeans. Back then, if he didn't take you home, he wouldn't even remember your name.

Special? And as far as I knew, only a dead girl and I could lay claim to that particular title. I wasn't sure that was something to admire, but there it was.

"I'm not your Desi. I'm not your Eric. I'm sorry that night meant more to you than it did to me, but you have to let it go," Eric said. "The question isn't whether it meant anything to me. The question is why I never wanted more. Because really, Caitlyn, why would I want a hamburger when I had steak at home?"

For a second, I saw Eric's grandmother in his eyes. It was the first evidence I'd ever seen that Eric actually shared her DNA, but it was obvious—the family-born ability to cut a person down with a single glance.

Caitlyn actually sank like she'd been chopped at the knees.

"I—"

"Get out of here, Caitlyn," Eric said. "I don't care what Nina or Calvin say. Until the lawyer says otherwise, this apartment belongs to me, and you're trespassing. So get the hell out before I have my security drop you down the garbage chute."

Caitlyn's mouth opened and closed like a fish before she slowly backed away.

"You'll regret this," she said as her face twisted in anger. And then she turned and flounced toward the elevators.

"Well, that was a waste of Botox," I remarked as she disappeared down the hall. "I think she ruined the whole procedure with that scowl of hers."

Eric was flexing his fingers like he'd just won a fight with a knock-out punch. He didn't, however, look particularly victorious. "Yeah. I guess."

"Aside from the part where you plagiarized Paul Newman, that was pretty impressive."

Eric looked up. "What?"

"The thing about the hamburger. He, um, said that about his wife, Joanne Woodward." Suddenly, I couldn't stop fidgeting. Playing with my chain, examining my manicure, toying with my hair. Was this how you broke up? By pronouncing your love for a person to someone else?

When I looked up, Eric's eyes were wide, all traces of anger vanished.

"I know," he said quietly. "I read it in a magazine a few months ago. I remember thinking that it made a lot of sense."

A few months ago was when he had finally confessed that he loved me. When he chased me into the ocean to shout it over the surf crashing on a sandbar. Then he dropped to his knees on the walk back to his family's house, clasped his waterlogged watch around my wrist, and asked me to marry him for real, not just for a check.

A few months ago was when we stopped being an act and became something else.

"I'm not a piece of meat," I said, though the argument was

weak. Who was I kidding? I'd be anything he wanted if he would just come back.

Eric's eyes closed, and when they opened again, the longing I saw there was so forceful I almost had to step backward.

"I know," he said. "You're so, so much more, Jane."

But instead of pulling me close and kissing me, like I wanted to do with every fiber of my body, angry or not, he took a step away and rubbed the back of his neck violently.

"Look," he said. "I won't go, all right? But I just need to get through today. Can you do that with me, Jane? Afterward, we'll talk. We'll make a proper end of it. I promise." He blinked. "I don't want to leave again without saying goodbye."

For a moment, I felt frozen there under the paintings and the gilt crown moldings.

"Come on," Eric said, holding out his hand. "We'll get through it together."

I looked at his hand for a moment, unsure of what I should do. But in the end, I took it, not caring how pathetic it made me. I took it because I wasn't sure if this time would be the last.

EIGHT

fter a few hours of eating shrimp cocktail and making polite, awkward conversation in the parlor, Eric, his family, and I piled into the late Jonathan de Vries's office to listen to Celeste's lawyer read her will. It was an unnecessary gesture, of course, but this was what Celeste wanted: a formal family gathering orchestrated at her whim. A pronouncement. A bit of theater.

Heather and Violet took seats on a big leather couch against the built-in bookshelves. Nina and Calvin assumed the chairs in front of the desk while Eric and I, still holding hands, stood under the Ansel Adams landscapes in the back of the room. Some other extended family members loitered in between, but those invited were a select few.

The lawyer briskly entered the room holding his briefcase and looked very self-important as he took a seat behind the giant carved desk. The room quieted as everyone watched the man remove the will, a deceptively small document, from a leather-bound folder and spread it carefully across the desktop.

He cleared his throat. "Good evening, everyone. First and

foremost, please accept my deepest condolences regarding the loss of Mrs. de Vries. She was a great lady and will be dearly missed."

Not a face in the room moved. Not even a sniffle. The lawyer cleared his throat again.

"For those of you I have not had the privilege of meeting, my name is Thomas J. Clark from the estate firm of Clark and Levine. You may call me Tom. I have been appointed executor of the last surviving will of Celeste Annika Van Dusen de Vries."

He looked around meaningfully, as if speaking the name of the deceased would chase out some fake attendees from the room. No one moved.

"It was the wish of Mrs. de Vries to have her will read to those specifically named in it before submitting the document for probate, which is why your presence has been requested here today. I personally drafted the will for Mrs. de Vries several times over the past few months, the last iterations dated August eighth and November second of this year."

There was a low murmur—clearly some substantial changes had been made that the family was not aware of. Beside me, Eric stiffened. The dates meant something to me too. The first was, after all, the day after our engagement party in the Hamptons. The date we had become something...more. The second, of course, was the day of our wedding.

Absently, my hand moved to toy with the rings dangling down my dress front. Eric watched their progress with a veiled expression, then fixed his gaze to the front of the room. A few seconds later, however, I felt a large hand slip around my waist, and he pulled me against his tall, strong body.

"I will now read aloud the last will and testament of Celeste de Vries, per the wishes of the deceased," said Tom. "As the document is relatively short, please wait until the end of the reading with any questions, which I will answer to the best of my abilities."

He looked around for a brief moment. Still, no one in the de Vries family moved.

"Just read it, Tom," snapped Calvin. "It's been a long day."

"Yes," said Tom. "Well.

"'I, Celeste Annika Van Dusen de Vries, resident in the City of New York, County of New York, State of New York, being of sound mind, not acting under duress or undue influence—'"

"Just get to the parts where she says who gets what, please," Calvin cut in. "We know all of this. She was sick, but she wasn't incapable."

"Calvin!" Nina hissed at her husband.

"What?" he asked.

Eric shook his head and mumbled something under his breath that sounded suspiciously like "dick," but I couldn't tell for sure.

Tom blinked around the room. "Would everyone prefer that I do that? She truly did request that we read the document in its entirety, but it's not strictly necessary, I suppose..."

His uncertain gaze landed on Eric, who stiffened.

"I think it's best if you skip to the sections that pertain directly to everyone here, Tom, and summarize the rest, if you don't mind," Eric said, much to the visible relief of everyone else. "Calvin's right. It has been a long day. We're all fairly beat."

"Especially those of us who've actually been here for the last two weeks," muttered Calvin. But no one else in the room backed him.

Tom, however, just looked relieved. "Very well," he said as he reexamined the document. "It directs that the funeral expenses be paid out of a fund she set aside for the purpose, which has been done. She also appoints me as her executor, which I am. And then she splits up her assets to beneficiaries—"

Everyone in the room immediately straightened.

"—which I'll read without addresses, as follows:

"To my daughter, Violet Arabella de Vries Astor, in addition to her current trust and holdings within the de Vries corporation, I leave my jewelry collection in its entirety, my car and driver, and the property and holdings at 1184 Southampton Road, Southampton, Long Island, along with the following sum for its maintenance—"

Violet preened, clearly happy with her lot. She had received the massive estate in Long Island, which, by my Zillow explorations, was valued at somewhere around one hundred and forty million dollars. And that wasn't even counting the cars, art, furnishings, and any other priceless commodities on the property.

"To my daughter-in-law, Heather Denise Keeler née de Vries née Stallsmith, I bequeath her current residence, the townhouse at 170 East Sixty-seventh Street, New York, New York, along with the contents of the following accounts to maintain said property—" Tom looked up. "Er, would you like me to read the account numbers too?"

Huh. I hadn't realized Heather, despite being remarried, still lived on de Vries property. Celeste must have cared for her more than I assumed.

"Good lord," Calvin muttered to Nina, who did her best to shush him again. "Of course not. Just read on, man. Honestly!"

Tom readjusted his glasses before he continued:

"To my dedicated butler, Garrett Donaldson, I leave my property at 8614 Park Avenue and everything in it, excluding the jewelry listed below, as well as the contents of the following accounts for the property's maintenance, HOA fees, and taxes until his end of life—"

An audible gasp interrupted the man once again—this time it was from Violet.

"She *can't* be serious!" she cried. "Mother left the penthouse to a *servant*? It's one of the most valuable properties in her estate! It's been in the family for nearly a hundred years!"

"I assure you, ma'am, it's correct," Tom replied even as he checked the will again. "She was quite adamant about it. Mr. Donaldson has served the family faithfully for most of his life, or so she said. She wanted him to live out the remainder of his in what she said was his home as much as it was hers. The remainder of the building, however, stays within the general estate, I assure you, but she wished for the penthouse to be subdivided and gifted to Mr. Donaldson."

I smiled to myself. This also, I hadn't expected—Celeste de Vries becoming a tool for the redistribution of wealth, at least a little bit, upon her death.

"*Vive la révolution*," I murmured.

Eric looked down with a muffled grin that revealed one dimple. "Your French is still horrible," he said below the chatter of the room.

I hid a smile of my own. It seemed in poor taste to make fun of the grieving, but it did feel a little like Celeste was probably cackling over this exact moment from beyond the grave.

"All right, all right," Tom said. "You can fight it if you like, Mr. Gardner, but I'll tell you right now, Mrs. de Vries took every precaution to guard her wishes. You'll be hard pressed to find a judge who will overturn this in any state, much less New York."

There was another rumble of dismay—clearly the penthouse was a hot commodity with this group, although I wouldn't have wanted to touch the winding old labyrinth, myself. I'd be too afraid David Bowie or a bunch of puppeteered goblins would burst into song behind every corner.

"Dance, magic, dance," I sang to myself quietly.

Eric just frowned at me blankly.

The group quieted when Calvin rapped his knuckles on the edge of the desk.

"What else?" he barked. "What else did dear Grandmother decide to 'surprise' us with? Can you give us the Cliff's Notes?"

Tom cast a sharp look in Calvin's direction, but seemed to think better of his retort as he went back to scanning the document.

"Well, there's another sum and property for Nina Gardner— seventy-five million plus an apartment on Lexington. Another few small amounts designated for great-grandchildren—small for her, that is. Ten million each in a trust, to be released at age thirty or when they get married. Another few odds and ends to the gardeners at Southampton who took care of her roses, and another small amount for her brother, Rufus. Ah, and to Ms. Jane Lee Lefferts, the sum of fifty million dollars, to be dispensed immediately into the following account, provided she meets a certain condition of Eric's inheritance."

Tom proceeded to rattle off the USBC number, but it was masked by the second round of uproar that traveled around the room.

"*What?*"

"She must be *joking!*"

"She gave fifty million dollars to *her?*"

I, however, was just finding it hard to breathe at all. Fifty million dollars. *Fifty million dollars.* More than double what I'd originally been promised for marrying her grandson.

I couldn't even begin to fathom that kind of money, couldn't even understand what it looked like. I only knew this was a life changer. Not just for me or my mother. But for anyone in my family who came after me. This was an income source for literally generations.

Celeste hadn't just given me money. She'd given me and my family absolute freedom.

"There is absolutely no way my mother would have put that in her will," Violet was arguing.

"She's a nobody!" Calvin practically screamed with her. "The bastard of John Carson and his yellow whore! She's already made this family a laughingstock once, and Grand-mother wants to *reward her* for it? I won't have it. None of us will!"

"Calvin, *shut up!*" Eric's voice echoed through the room, a thunderclap in a storm.

I hadn't noticed until then just how hard I was gripping his arm, finding it difficult to stand upright on my own. I was light in the head, and certainly in no condition to give Calvin a taste of his own sharp medicine.

Calvin turned in his chair toward us, and I fought the urge to hide behind Eric's solid body, which stood taller than ever as he faced the roomful of hatred on my behalf.

"Eric," Calvin said. "After what she did—"

"What did she do, Cal?" he asked. "Got reasonably angry because I kept a secret from her? And then married me anyway to save my face? *I* was the one who walked out on her, Calvin. If anyone embarrassed the family, it was me, not Jane."

"Even so," Violet chimed in. "She's not a de Vries. Mother wouldn't even let Nina take over the chairmanship at DVS because of her last name. There is absolutely no way she would give this much of her personal fortune to...to...someone like *her*." She thrust her French-nailed finger at me so viciously I thought the gel tip might fly across the room and ping me in the head.

"Aunt Violet," started Eric, the hand around my waist tightening even more.

"It doesn't matter," I finally croaked. Everyone stopped talking and looked at me. "I won't take it. I don't want any of it anyway. Not if...not if it's going to cause this kind of discord."

"Well, at least she has *some* sense," Calvin grumbled.

But Eric just frowned and shook his head vehemently. "She's taking it," he said. "Jane, don't argue with me. These people have put you through enough. You're taking the money, and then you'll be rid of us, all right?" He looked around at his family. "We're not married. The license was never signed, and it won't be. Ever. So we're going to give Jane this gift that Grandmother intended and let her go. Got it?"

There was a final grumble, but oddly at the finality in Eric's voice, everyone turned back to the lawyer, ready to receive the final bombshells in the will.

"Get on with it," Calvin snapped again. His face was turning red. "There's really only one thing anyone here wants to know now. Did she leave the company to Eric, Nina, or decide to ruin us all out of spite?"

Was it my imagination, or did Nina smart at his words? I blinked, and the next moment, Eric's cousin was sitting next to her husband as placidly as ever, her smooth face without a ripple of disturbance.

Everyone turned forward again. Clearly this was the question of the evening.

The fingers at my waist pulled tensely on the fabric of my dress. Did Eric still want the company? Was he eager to be free? I honestly didn't know.

It wasn't really the company, of course. DVS was a publicly traded corporation, but the de Vries family still held exactly forty-nine percent of its shares—not enough to maintain veto power at board meetings when they wanted, but certainly enough to tank it—and the family's trust funds—if Celeste had decided to sell it off, as she threatened, instead of bequeathing it to everyone else.

Tom took a deep breath, looking very much like he wanted to escape out the window behind him. "I'm afraid, Mr. de Vries, the final item may deter your plans for Ms. Lefferts." He looked down at the will.

"To my prodigal grandson"—there was a groan from Calvin —"Eric de Vries, I bequeath my shares of De Vries Shipping Corporation under the following stipulations:

1. He will assume the chairmanship of the board (with the votes from the board) within two months of this notice and by their vote;
2. He will ensure a place on the board of directors for his cousin, Nina Gardner née Astor, and an executive position within the company;
3. He will live in congress with one Jane Lefferts Lee, in or out of wedlock by his and her choice, for a period no less than sixty days from November second of this year."

Immediately, the room burst into uproar all over again as everyone shouted and yelled about it.

"So he *doesn't* have to be married now?"

"Sixty days? That's it?"

"What in the hell is happening?"

But Eric was as silent as stone. Instead, he was staring at me, his face pale as the moon and his eyes as wide as craters.

That fear I had seen before had returned. Panic.

"She knew," he whispered. "Fucking hell."

"She knew what?" I asked.

But Eric had no more answers for me. Instead, his gaze shot to Calvin, whose skin had also blanched considerably. "What have you done?" Eric demanded.

Calvin's piggish face only turned a few shades whiter, but for once, he remained quiet.

"No," Eric said, standing up. He turned to Nina and the rest of them. "We can't. You...you don't understand."

"I'm sorry, sir," Tom said as he held up the will. "It's what the document says. And I'm sorry to say it, but if you do not comply, I am to arrange for the partitioning and sale of the company shares to the highest bidders and donate the proceeds of the sales to a list of approved charities. If the family wanted to purchase them on their own, I'm afraid even the combined liquid wealth of everyone in this room would not be anywhere near enough to purchase forty-nine percent of DVS."

Behind them, Calvin's face screwed up even more, and in front of him, Nina's smooth brow crinkled in confusion, mirroring the twin faces of her mother and her aunt.

"What is going on?" Nina asked as she looked between Eric and Calvin. "Eric, what did Calvin do?"

"It was you, wasn't it?" Eric said. "You did this. She was free, Calvin. She was *free*. Did you tell Grandmother? You did, didn't you?"

"I didn't say a word," Calvin whispered, though guilt was scribbled all over his face.

Eric just shook his head, the arm around my waist fell away, and he shuffled toward the door.

"No, but if you hadn't told John about her in the first place —" he started.

"I didn't tell him anything!"

"Well, someone did."

"Eric, just wait a second—" I tried.

But before anyone could say anything else—or before I could ask one of the million questions running through my mind—Eric received a text message.

"We'll talk about this later," he said. "I have to go."

And then, despite the general uproar in the room, he left.

Two seconds later, my phone also buzzed in my coat pocket.

The message was from an unfamiliar number and was short and terse:

The old dairy in Central Park.
Ten minutes.
The both of you.
–C

I stared at it for a long time. It didn't take a genius to know who had sent it. John Carson. Dear old Dad. Apparently, he had a few things to say to the two of us. Well, I had a few things to say too. And there was no time like the present to get them out.

NINE

I burst onto the street still buttoning my cashmere coat, my breath spilling into the chilly November air in bright white plumes. Eric, of course, was nowhere to be seen among the rush of cars and pedestrians on Park Avenue.

"You have *got* to be kidding me," I muttered as I looked frantically up and down the street. This was the second time I had chased Eric out of this building just to have missed him. Living in this ridiculous, diamond-lit world was starting to feel like déjà vu.

"Ms. Jane?"

I whirled around to find Gracie, the doorman, watching me timidly.

"He went straight toward the park, miss," he said, pointing a white glove westward.

I swore. Profusely. He must have received the same basic text that I had. Well, fine. I had a few choice words for Daddy Dearest myself. I was about done with him yanking me and Eric all over the fucking city like puppets on a string.

"Gracie," I said, turning back around. "Can you tell me the quickest way to get to the old dairy?"

———

TWENTY MINUTES LATER, I'd ruined a perfectly good pair of vintage Givenchy pumps tromping through Central Park. I'd walked around the Met after leaving Celeste's building with the intent of making my way to the old dairy and waiting there for Eric and John Carson in the shelter of the Dutch-style building. My hair was a frizzy mess from the light drizzle, my gold cat-eye glasses were fogging up, and my toes were soaked from stepping in more than one deceptively deep puddle on the park paths.

But just as I passed the back end of the Met, the sky really opened up, and rain began to dump.

"You have got to be kidding me," I said to the clouds. "Really? *Now*?"

The clouds, of course only responded by raining harder. I decided my best bet was to walk south to the transverse road crossing the park and grab a cab or bus to the West Side, where I could dry off in the safety of my own apartment.

But no sooner had I trotted down one of the south-running trails than I stumbled upon the statue of the Polish King Jagiello. And there, sitting on a bench, completely oblivious to the rain-drops hanging off the end of his long, straight nose, was Eric. They were a funny pair—the bronze monarch on the horse, swords crossed above his head as he rode into battle; Eric, the despondent heir, head bowed while he twisted a wet brown leaf back and forth between his fingers like a forlorn schoolboy.

He hadn't even bothered to put on an overcoat, instead soaking up the cold mid-November rain like a sponge in his Tom Ford. A shame, really. That suit was one of his favorites.

I paused, no longer caring that my clothes were also getting ruined. Across the path, raindrops bounced off Turtle Pond like bullets breaking skin. Eric, however, just stared moodily at his sad little leaf, completely unaware of my presence or the pounding rain.

For a moment, all of my anger returned. How could he just sit here like today hadn't happened? Like the *world* wasn't happening? It was the epitome of childish. Was this what he was going to do every time things got hard? Run away and sulk? Maybe it was better that we didn't stay married. Maybe it was better if I just said hang the money and walked away from him and his completely.

I started to say just that, but something stopped me. His hand twisted around with the leaf, and in his palm, I caught the telltale glint of gold: the two-faced coin that had hung around his neck for the past several months.

All of this had something to do with Janus. This secret society. Eric wasn't a coward by nature. Hell, he was the one who came to me asking for my participation in this charade. Hadn't he stuck up for me, had my back through all of it?

Who had his now?

His hand stopped moving, and the leaf fell to the ground. He continued to stare at the coin, clenching and unclenching his fingers around the quarter-sized metal piece.

"Well," I said, shooting for levity but hitting something closer to cynicism as I approached. "If it isn't the errant heir himself."

Eric looked up, seemingly unsurprised to see me. "Hey."

I bowed. "How goeth it, my liege?"

He rolled his eyes. "Don't call me that. You of all people…"

I sighed and sat down beside him. My dress and coat were already ruined, so who cared if I had a wet ass? "You've been running away from me for weeks, and now you're going to give me a hard time for jokes?"

He just sighed and went back to playing with his coin, tipping it between one palm and the other.

I looked at the sky, which wasn't letting up. Pieces of my hair were pasted to my cheeks like papier-mâché. Around us, the park was desolate. It felt like the whole city was mourning Celeste's passing, not just us.

Absently, Eric pulled on his tie, first on the bottom, then up at the top, loosening its choke around his collar before he went back to playing with the coin and chain.

"Eric," I said as kindly as I could, though I was fighting to snatch the thing out of his palm. "I think it's time you tell me what's going on. Before we see...*him*."

At that, he finally looked up with a start. "What do you mean 'we'?"

"I got a message just after you left. Pops requesting my presence at the dairy. I take it you got the same one, and that's why you darted out of there?"

Eric swallowed. "You are not going anywhere near him, Jane." His voice was quiet, but vehement—the first sign of anything besides despondence.

"Oh, really?" I said. "I get the feeling our reunion is unavoidable. The scion has been called home, so to speak."

Eric shuddered. "You don't want to know how close that is to the truth."

I set a hand on his knee. He shook it off. I frowned.

"Then maybe you'd better tell me," I said. "Because I have the sneaking suspicion that if I'd known about all this crap before, we might be in a better spot."

"Jane," Eric said quickly. "You have to know, I never knew who he was to you. I never—Jane, I swear to God, I *never* knew."

Whatever I was expecting, that wasn't it.

"I know," I said. "I believe that, at least. You've kept a lot from me, but I can't believe you'd keep a secret like my paternity. But now that the cat's out of the bag, you might as well tell me the rest. Who is John Carson to *you*? Why does the thought of him make you look like you're planning to dig a tunnel under this weird Polish statue and live there like a Ninja Turtle?"

Eric just shook his head vehemently. "The less you know, the better."

"That is one hundred percent untrue."

His eyes turned just a shade darker than the rain clouds above us. "Look. I have some money. My own, not my family's. Your loans are paid off already, and it should be enough to—to get you started on something else. Whatever that's going to be. Away from here, Jane. Do you understand? You have to leave."

I shook my head stubbornly. "I'm not going anywhere. What is it about my...*father*"—I practically spit out the word—"that has you acting like a scared fucking rabbit?"

But instead of replying, or saying anything at all, Eric stood up suddenly and took off into the trees.

"Goddammit," I muttered. "Not again."

I jogged after him, trying my best to make him out clearly through my rain-smeared lenses as he dodged across the traverse, earning the ire of more than one cabbie in the rain. He walked briskly into the "Ramble," the horde of trails crisscrossing several acres of the park with no apparent rhyme or reason. The asshole had the privilege of being in much better shape than I was, *and* he wasn't wearing heels.

But apparently I was running on adrenaline.

"Eric!" I shouted as he turned another bend. I stumbled as one heel broke. "Fuck!" I cried.

He paused, having clearly heard me, but when he saw that all I suffered from was a broken shoe, he took off once more.

"You asshole!" I shouted as I kicked off the ruined footwear, picked them up, and started sprinting after him. Once he came into sight, I hurled one shoe at him, which glanced off his shoulder. I wasn't much of a runner, but at least I could throw.

"Stop following me, Jane!" he shouted, even though he stumbled a bit.

"No!" I hurled the other shoe. This one hit the tree in front of him.

He whirled around. "Yes!"

"No!"

I leaped forward, and we both went hurtling into a pile of leaves at the base of a naked birch. We tumbled a good few feet together until both of us were covered with cold, wet leaves and mud. My shoes disappeared somewhere in the soggy refuse along with my glasses. The world around me grew blurry, but Eric, now close and personal, remained perfectly clear.

"Goddammit!" he shouted as he pushed me off him. "You never know when to leave well enough alone, do you?"

"That's because if I didn't, you'd just toss me to the wolves, you bastard!" I threw a handful of wet leaves, which hit his shoulder with a splat.

We were both a disaster now—Eric's suit was soaked and smeared with dirt; my dress was basically just a mud flap. Why did it always have to come to this? Practically drowning before we could actually talk?

Eric sat up, his chest heaving.

"You need to get out of here," he said in between tortured breaths. "Jane, you need to trust me. Don't wait around to meet him. Don't stay. I'll deposit some money into your account or you can call Skylar and Brandon."

"What about your family? What about your company?"

"I don't care about any of that, Jane! You just need to *go!*"

Before I could protest more, Eric got up and started jogging back into the park, seemingly immune to the torrents of rain. Thunder clapped.

"What in the hell," I muttered as I scrambled up and after him. My toes were starting to turn blue. "Eric, wait up!"

"Stay away from me!"

I took off, catching him just as he ducked under an arch. "Eric! Shit! Will you just *wait*?"

I caught his sleeve just before he could run out of reach. It wasn't enough to hold me, though, and I fell to the pavement, only to be caught just before I slammed into the sidewalk.

Eric pulled me upright, and we stared at each other for three long seconds, hands cuffed around each other's arms, caught in a warped circle of our own making. Streams of water flowed down his beautiful face, drops hanging off his nose, lips, chin, even his eyelashes.

He scanned my face in the same hungry way.

Then we both lunged.

His lips crashed into mine. Or maybe mine crashed into his. Either way, I was swept up in something that was simultaneously like fleeing and coming home. *Mine*, my subconscious screamed with every angry, hardened bite of his lips and thrash of my body.

Eric coiled around me, then shoved me against the arch's stone wall so that his entire hard, wet body was flush against mine. My hips thrust against his, seeking contact, comfort, revenge. I wanted to punish him for his absence and welcome him back all at once. Never had I felt so confused.

"Why?" he breathed, sucking in air like he was drowning. "Why do you have to be so fucking stubborn?"

"Because it's *you*, that's why!"

I yanked him back, eager to feel his tongue twisting and turning with mine. The world was cold, but his mouth heated my core. He seemed to be fighting the connection, as frustrated as I was that neither of us could quite get close enough.

"I told you to go," he gasped in between harsh kisses. "It's for your own good. Why don't you ever fucking listen?"

"You ran away." I kissed him again, this time with more bite than lip. "You left me at the altar. How was *that* for my own good?"

"I was saving you, not leaving you," he growled and shoved his erection violently into my hip. Both of us moaned into each other's mouths.

I yanked at the back of his hair, forcing him to look at me. "Saving me from what?"

Eric's stare focused on my swollen lips, and his pupils dilated like an animal's. A slip of tongue emerged, and he licked at a reddened spot at the corner of his mouth—apparently, I had drawn blood. It was clear that he wanted to do a lot more to me than just kiss; hell, I was ready to lift my skirt for the man right there, no matter who might be walking down the path.

But then, his head fell to my shoulder, and he inhaled like he hadn't breathed in minutes. "You're not going to let it go, are you?"

"No," I replied immediately. "No, I'm not."

"Why?"

I pulled at his hair again, this time more gently, and when he lifted his head, I framed his sharp, chiseled face between my palms. His deep gray eyes were wells of sorrow and shame. He shuddered, but I didn't think it was because of the cold.

"Because," I said. "Because I love you, that's why."

The final admission was a punch to the gut—both of our guts, if his face was any indication. Because it was the truth: there was something about Eric, about *us*, that was special. It didn't matter that I was still furious with him about Caitlyn. It didn't matter that he had disappeared for almost two weeks. I couldn't just walk away. Not now. Maybe not ever.

"You shouldn't."

"But I do."

His forehead touched mine. "I know," he said. "I love you too. Goddammit, I do."

We stared at each other for what seemed like hours, gray eyes meeting hazel in a clash as intense as the storm around us. There was another smash of thunder, and the downpour intensified even more. Suddenly the fact that I was wrapped around Eric's body like a vine didn't mitigate the fact that it was forty-five degrees outside and pouring. A violent shiver traveled through me.

Eric stepped back and took my hand. "Come on," he said in a voice that was more dejected than I was comfortable with.

"Where are we going?" I asked, though I followed him, barefoot, up the way we came.

He looked down at himself, then me. "Back."

"To Celeste's penthouse?" I cringed. The idea of leaving muddy footprints anywhere near the judgmental crowd we'd left behind made me want to live under this arch forever. I honestly thought Celeste might rise from the grave to snap about stains on her Oriental carpets.

Eric shook his head. "We'll go home. And try to figure out how in the hell we're going to survive Carson when he finds us."

TEN

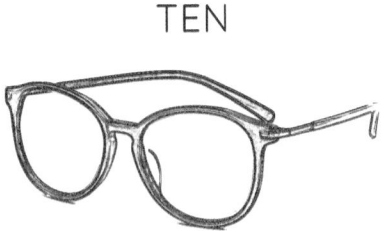

We caught the most expensive cab in the world across the park (it took several soaked hundred dollar bills out of Eric's wallet to convince any driver to take us in our muddy condition) and to our apartment on West Seventy-Sixth Street. Eric hadn't touched me during the entire ten-minute ride, though I caught him staring at my lips every time I looked at him. A muscle ticked at the bottom of his jaw, like the man was literally a time bomb held at bay only by the cab's muted Russian music and the fact that the irate driver kept checking on us through the rearview mirror like we were wild animals about to rip up his stained vinyl.

Well...he wasn't completely wrong.

I followed Eric up the steps of our brownstone and then the stairwell, staring at his perfectly formed ass with a mix of loathing and desire. Like two scoops of ice cream, that. It was irritating, really, the way his pants were stuck to it. The way the muscles moved back and forth, back and forth, right in front of my face. Taunting me.

And so, by the time the door locked behind us, I was a giant knot of desire and anger, ready to tear the man apart in more ways than one as I shoved on a spare pair of glasses sitting by the key bowl. Everything that had happened in the past few months —hell, the past five *years*—was roaring through my head at supersonic speed.

Caitlyn Calvert.

John Carson.

Red panties.

"Rock the Casbah."

The bridal march.

Every single mind-bending orgasm the man had ever given me.

Eric peeled off his jacket, giving me a prime view of the way his shirt was pasted to the etched lines of his back and chest. The soaked white was closer to gray in this light and matched the stormy hue of his eyes.

When he caught sight of me standing there, he scanned my body, then immediately closed his eyes like he was in pain. "Christ, Jane," he muttered. "For the love of God, go change your clothes."

I looked down. My dress was black, so I wasn't giving the wet-t-shirt show that Eric was. But the thin, gauzy fabric had been stretched in the mud and rain, and right now the neckline was pulled indecently low so that my cleavage—what little I had —was fully on display. My nipples puckered from the cold. Well, *mostly* from the cold.

"Crap," I said, yanking up the collar, but unable to get it to stay. It was just too misshapen. Finally I let it drop. "You know what, fuck it. It's not like you haven't seen it before."

"Jane, come on—"

"Grow up, Eric," I snapped, though I folded my arms over my chest. "Stop acting like you haven't seen about a million women exactly like this or worse."

Eric sucked in a long, tortured breath. "A million women," he said through his teeth, "aren't *you*."

We stared at each other for what seemed like hours. His torso rose and fell with each exceedingly difficult breath. Eric's own chest, abs, biceps were on display too—every sinewy muscle on the man was taunting me through the translucent white fabric. Not to mention the way his pants weren't leaving much to the imagination as his desire became obvious, pressing against his zipper. And he wanted *me* to cover up? Please. The man looked like a *Playgirl* shoot.

"You have to go," Eric said like my X-rated thoughts weren't playing through my mind.

I snapped my head up. "Are you kidding me? I have to *go*? You said we were coming back here to figure things out." Call me crazy, but I was sort of looking forward to continuing what we started. We had some catharsis to get to, followed by a hot shower.

"I did figure them out. Jane, get changed, and then you need to leave New York. Brandon and Skylar are still here, right? You can go back to Boston with them. Brandon and I can hire extra security for you, and—"

"I'm not going anywhere," I interrupted. "And you are more of an idiot than ever if you thought I was. I literally just chased you down through the mud, Petri dish, donating two very expensive shoes and my favorite glasses to Central Park while I was at it. I look like a wet rat that just got flushed through the entire New York City sewer system. So if you think I'm going to just walk away without getting some goddamn answers, you must be more out of your mind than I thought."

His eyes narrowed at the nickname I knew he loathed. "Jane—"

"No!" I shouted. "We tackle each other in the park, and then you kiss me like you can't possibly do anything else. And now we're here, and you're right back to acting like a scared rabbit. I demand the truth, Eric. Where in the *fuck* have you been?"

"I can't tell you that!" he burst out.

"Can't tell me what? That you were kidnapped by my long-lost 'father'? That he's the head of some uber secret society that can't decide whether it wants to use Greek or Roman code names? That they 'tap' the unsuspecting shoulders of New England's elite college grads and proceed to scare the shit out of them until they are nice and compliant?"

Eric jerked his head up with alarm. "What in the fuck. You are *not* supposed to know any of that."

I shrugged and tossed up my hands. "Well, too late now. The medieval cat is out of the bag, my love, so you might as well just spill the rest."

"Who told you?" he demanded, starting to pace, the water in his shoes squelching comically as he did. "Calvin was never officially inducted—all he knows is that Jude and I are part of something he wasn't in college. He's been trying to get in ever since."

"I don't know who Jude is," I said. "But Brandon wasn't fully inducted either, so he says. Sounds like *he* came to his senses before it got to that, but he knew a bit to share. And I didn't have to chase him like a lunatic for the information either."

"Idiot," Eric muttered.

"What was that?"

"I said he's an idiot," Eric enunciated clearly. "If he thinks he's going to get away with talking about Janus, he's really, *really* fucking stupid."

"How would anyone find out?" I asked. "Are you high? Your paranoia is off the charts."

"He'll find out," Eric said darkly. "Carson *always* finds out."

I sat back onto a barstool while Eric continued to pace the living room, completely oblivious to the muddy tracks his shoes were leaving all over the expensive alpaca rug. *Joke's on him*, I thought as I watched. It was his dumb black Amex that paid for it anyway.

He stopped in front of the big fireplace and turned to me with sudden determination.

"Look," he said. "I'm asking you to leave for your own good. I don't want you anywhere near Janus or Carson. You have no idea what they are capable of." His face turned visibly whiter on the last few words, and he grabbed the mantle, needing to steady himself.

"Why?" I demanded. "What is it, exactly, that you think they're going to do? What happened to you?"

"He..." Eric shuddered. "No. I'm not going there. Not now."

I scowled. "You know, the more I hear about it, 'Janus' sounds less like some illustrious secret and more like MS-13 dressed up in coats and tails. We shouldn't be running, Eric—we should be calling the police."

Eric laughed, a sad, slow cackle that lodged a pang of dread in my belly. "If you think the police would do anything other than exactly what Carson wants, you're more of a fool than he thinks."

"Please," I said. "John Carson doesn't know me from Adam. Where has he been for the last thirty years, huh?"

"Your father," Eric spat, "has absolutely forbidden me to be with you. He's made it *very* clear."

I screwed my face up in confusion. "What? Who the hell is he to say—"

"John Carson is the most powerful man in a brotherhood of the most powerful men in this country, Jane. He's someone every world leader listens to. He's someone who is absolutely fucking not to be trifled with." He glanced toward the window in the general direction of the park. "Which, unfortunately, is what we're doing by not showing up at the park, as it happens. Jane, you need to *go*."

I snorted. "You make him sound like Zeus on the mountain-top. Tell me, does he have a lightning bolt too?"

Eric didn't even crack a smile. "In a manner of speaking. Only his looks like a nuclear warhead."

"What?!"

"Chariot Industries just overtook Lockheed last year in arms development. They supply weapons to most major buyers on the planet."

I rubbed at my forehead, now recalling that Brandon had said something similar. But still. This was ridiculous. Just because the man made weapons didn't mean he was going to use them on us. "So...what, he's going to shoot you with a missile if we stay together? Why does he care so much anyway?"

Eric shook his head. "I don't know, Jane. I wish I did."

He sank to the hearth and stared hopelessly at his hands. I slipped off my stool, then padded around the furniture and joined him. We sat there for some time, shivering as the cold set in. No one bothered to light a fire. I wasn't sure there was a point.

"You put your ring back on," I remarked when the platinum on his fourth digit caught in the twilight sun peeking through the storm clouds. "In the park. You put it on."

Eric flexed his hand. There were other remnants of bruising on his knuckles. For the millionth time, I wanted to know what had happened to him while he was gone.

"I—it was always in my pocket." He started to pull the ring off, but when it didn't move easily, he left it on, stroking it gently with his thumb. "I never wanted to take it off, Jane. But when I saw you'd removed yours, it seemed like the right thing again. But now the will..." His head fell again, and that same forlorn posture overcame him once more. "God, this is such a clus-terfuck."

I couldn't help myself. I still didn't completely understand what was going on, but I had to do something. I tapped him on the shoulder. His eyes met mine, wide and scared.

"Hey," I said. "You're not alone in this. That's what these things mean, right?" I pulled out the chain under my dress and dangled my rings in front of him. "Say the word. And I'll put them back on."

Eric watched the rings for a long time. "I wish I could," he said. "I wish—fucking hell, Jane, I wish we could just leave all of this shit behind us and run away."

"Why can't we?" I wondered. It was an honest question. That didn't sound too terrible right about now.

But Eric just expelled a long, low breath. "Because we can't."

"That's not an answer."

"It's the only answer you'll get."

"Why?" I pushed. "Because I'm too simple to understand it?"

"No, because you're too fucking *special*!" Eric fell forward, caging his head between his hands. "Don't you get it? I left because I love you, you stupid, stubborn girl. How many times do I have to tell you that I left to keep you safe!"

For a few minutes, I watched him wrestle with his torment.

"I don't need you to protect me," I said finally.

His voice was a croak. "You have no idea what you're saying."

I raised a brow. "That's not your choice to make."

Eric stared at me.

I stared at him.

I stared at the way his muscles taunted me through his wet shirt.

I stared at the drop of rain dangling off an errant lock of blond hair.

"Jane." Eric's deep voice seemed very far away. "You need to stop looking at me like that."

I blinked. "Why?"

"Because," Eric said. "This isn't supposed to happen anymore." Like a magnet, however, he just leaned closer.

I stared at the plump lines of his mouth. "I think it already did."

"You know what I mean."

I raised a brow. "Do I?"

His mouth inched forward. His entire body shook with want.

"Eric," I whispered.

He closed the gap.

His kiss was now soft, tentative, closed-mouthed. It feathered over the bottom, then the top of each of my lips. So unlike his usual style, where he took what he wanted without apology. Eric was nonchalant to the point of immovable so much of the time, but when he kissed me before, I always knew he meant it.

Something in him was broken. And it broke my heart too.

I slipped a hand around his neck and pulled him closer, urging him on.

"I can't," he whispered, though he opened to me more. "But goddammit, Jane, I can't stop either."

"Can't stop what?" I murmured, enjoying the way his tongue dove around mine.

His lips drifted down my throat, leaving goose bumps in its wake. "Wanting you. Needing you. Fuck."

I cupped his face between my hands so he had to look at me again. "Then don't."

He groaned, a guttural, animal sound that vibrated through his lips and into my soul. Slowly, we stood up together, practically traveling as one, pawing at each other's wet clothes. I didn't care that we still had so many secrets lying between us. I only ached to be close. Ten days. Two weeks. Whatever it was, it felt like a lifetime.

Eric kissed me again. And this time, he fucking meant it.

His hands were everywhere. They traveled around my waist, my arms, around my neck, and over my sternum. Then he pulled away, and his hands dropped to the neckline of the dress that lay loosely over my décolletage. He took a firm hold of the fabric and ripped the dress in half.

"Hey!" I yelped, though I was being nearly as rough with his jacket and shirt.

Eric smirked as he yanked the cloth from my shoulders, tearing the zipper along its seam the rest of the way down my back. "I'll buy you a new one." The dress fell to the floor with a splat.

I eyed the heap of wet wool and leather somewhat ruefully, even as I pulled at his pants. "But I made it."

"You'll make another." My chin was yanked around, and he kissed me again, hard and fierce. "Tell me the truth, pretty girl. What matters now?"

We toppled into the bedroom, cold limbs warming as we sought each other through the last bits of clothes. My underwear was tossed to the wall; his boxers landed on a lamp.

"Us," I murmured as his mouth found my nipple and sucked. Hard. "Oh, *fuck*, Eric! Just us."

"I'm sorry," he whispered in between kiss after kiss across my chest. "So fucking sorry. For Caitlyn—"

"I don't care about that anymore," I said, though I knew it wasn't completely true. The whole matter just seemed very, very far away now.

He sucked briefly on my other nipple. "Goddammit, Jane, you have no idea...no idea how hard that was—"

"Shut up," I said as I grabbed his hair and forced him to look up. "I don't care about that stupid wench anymore. Stop apologizing and just fuck me, will you?"

His eyes flashed with that familiar glint—the one that loved and hated when I challenged him this way. His hands slipped up the backs of my legs, then grabbed me behind my thighs. Less than a second later, I was tossed onto the mattress, landing on my back with a thump.

"You want me to fuck you?" Eric growled as he crawled over me. "Like what? An animal?" His teeth closed over my nipple once more, this time with some bite.

"Ah!" I arched into the pain. "If the sh-shoe fits."

He buried his face between my breasts. "You have no fucking clue, gorgeous."

"Ah!" I shrieked. "Eric!"

But my cries were swallowed again by his kisses, now just as torrid and bruising as the ones in the park. We were both starving for each other. Desperately, I reached between us, eager to guide him home.

Eric broke the kiss and pushed up on his forearms. He peered down at me, though the movement just allowed me to take his thick erection more firmly in my grip. His eyes closed briefly, and when they opened, glinted like steel. Slowly, he reached down and removed my hand. His long length lay on my thigh as he moved one of my hands over my head, then the other, and trapped them both under his forearms.

"Impatient, are we?" His cock slipped between my thighs, teasing the slippery warmth awaiting him.

I rocked my hips up, hoping to draw him closer. "You seemed like you needed some help."

"I seemed..." He trailed off, somewhat amazed. "I think you forgot who's really in charge here, pretty girl."

The name seared my heart like a brand. And I only wanted more.

Eric sucked on my lower lip harder. I moaned into his mouth.

"Say it," he growled as just the tip of him found my entrance.

I twisted and turned, trying to flee and get closer to his broad, strong body. "Say—say what?"

"You know what." He pushed in further, but only just.

"Oh, God," I moaned, squirming even more. I wanted him deeper, but at the same time, I didn't think I could take it. "Oh, God, *Eric...*"

"Say it," he commanded as he charged forward. "Tell me what I want to hear."

He pushed inside completely, and his sudden presence there, along with the friction of his hips right over my clit, pushed me directly over the edge of a cliff I hadn't even known I'd been standing on. A sudden orgasm swept through me; one I hadn't even been expecting.

"OhGodEricIloveyouuuuuu!" I cried as I shook from head to toe, limb to limb.

And it was only then that he started to move. Solid, consistent. Filling me again and again, reuniting our bodies and our minds in that way only he knew how to do. Just as my initial euphoria faded, Eric's consistent, even rhythm inspired the bloom of a new sensation, one that went so much farther than the surface.

He pulled one of my legs over his shoulder and sat up on his knees so he could look down at me, drifting his other hand around my face, over my breasts, stomach, hips. My hands threaded together over my head—even without his hand there, I still felt pinned to the pillows.

"You're so fucking beautiful, Jane," he whispered as he continued to move, deep enough now to make me arch with every blow. He dropped a kiss on my ankle, and his other hand found my clit, drifting a thumb lightly over the sensitive spot. "A goddamn work of art."

I had heard them before. Those words. In that voice. But it didn't make them less erotic or any less meaningful. I was still so frustrated with the man, but I couldn't deny that I loved him. Needed him. When he did this to me, nothing else in the world seemed to matter.

I spun out in that beautiful dream of pleasure and desire. His name filtered from my lips again and again until another wave of pleasure rose in front of me like a shooting star.

"Eric," I whispered, this time too overcome to shout.

His gray eyes widened. "Jane." His voice was hoarse as he lurched over me. "I'm...goddammit, I'm going to come."

"Do it," I urged. "Just let go! I'll be right with you."

Eric's gaze was a hammer, and I was the nail. The force of his expression alone bound me to the mattress as he pounded away. But just as he tensed every one of his cinderblock muscles, clearly ready to relieve *all* the pressure in each of those merciless blows, there was a loud knock at the front door.

"Triton!"

Eric froze. I opened my eyes.

Who. The fuck. Was that?

"Triton!" The deep male voice was familiar. Resonant, even through the thick prewar walls.

"What are you doing?" I hissed. I pushed at Eric's chest. "Whoever that is, fuck him. Don't stop!"

I was so close—*so* close—and just needed a few more thrusts, a bit more friction to reach my own zenith for the second time.

But Eric just stared at me in utter horror as the voice sounded a third time:

"Triton! Open the door!"

Like the voice was a shot through his chest, Eric exploded off me, stumbling backward naked and still erect, looking as disoriented as I felt. I pushed up onto my elbows, suddenly angrier now more than ever.

"Hey!" I snapped. "You cannot be serious right now, buddy. We talked about this. Orgasm-withholding is a hard limit!"

But Eric didn't respond. His eyes were flying around the room, searching for clothes. He grabbed the first things he could find from the closet—a pair of ratty joggers and a clean white dress shirt, shoving them on without underwear as he hopped from one leg to another.

"Eric!" I yelled as I sat up completely, holding the bedsheet to my chest. Outside, a few car horns blared in concert with me.

His eyes widened, like he hadn't completely realized I was still there, naked on our bed, still throbbing from the orgasm that had never happened.

"Jane," he croaked, glancing between me and the window, where a fire escape hung outside the double-paned glass. "Get dressed. And *run*."

And then, before I could respond, he left the room, slamming the door shut behind him.

ELEVEN

Since all of my clothes were still in my workroom next door (we hadn't yet rebuilt the master closet to accommodate both of our wardrobes), it took me a few minutes to find some of Eric's that would actually stay on. Eventually I located a pair of pajama pants and one of his expensive white Oxford shirts, which I knotted around my waist, looking like I'd walked out of a TLC video circa 1992. That was me, apparently. Ain't too proud to beg.

I made sure my makeup wasn't melting down my face *Crow*-style, then exited the bedroom still tying my hair into a bun on top of my head. Fuck a good impression. Whoever the hell had interrupted this reunion with my "beloved" was going to be on the receiving end of my wrath, not hospitality.

"All right," I said as I entered the living room. "Who in the *hell* at the door was more important than what we were doing? Last I heard, Triton was The Little Mermaid's dad, not anyone who lives in this apartment."

Eric turned from the door. His shirt was still buttoned only halfway up, offering a distracting view of his abs and chest. The coin dangled around his neck again. If he hadn't looked so terrified, I would have towed him back to our room, even if the Queen of England herself had joined us.

A sudden stream of evening sunlight through the bay windows cut through the storm, making the coin gleam. Eric's face crumpled.

"Jane? I told you to—"

I waved his words away. "You didn't really think I was going to do that, did you, Petri? Now, who's our guest? I'm guessing Papa stopped by. Are they *deorum vocas*-ing again? Do we need to have a talk about appropriate fucking moments for reunions?"

Eric folded his mouth into a thin line and shook his head. I couldn't tell if he was more irritated with me or himself at that moment.

I turned to the person whose tall, imposing figure filled the doorway. It was, of course, the same man who had burst through the doors of St. John the Divine two weeks ago.

John Carson looked down his long, slightly hooked nose at me with an imperious gaze that matched the oiled salt-and-pepper curls so assiduously groomed to his scalp. His eyes gleamed with intent. Slim and tall, he was immaculately dressed in a navy three-piece suit, over which an open raincoat floated around his person like a cape. He looked like a very wealthy, Burberry-clad Dracula, a fact I didn't like to admit since I could also see the resemblance to me.

The same hazel eyes.

The same long limbs.

The same smug mouth twisted in a knowing grin.

Fuck, fuck, *fuck*.

My insides suddenly scrambled as I came face-to-face with a man who could only be my father. I blinked, swallowed heavily. And then called on my plentiful supply of bravado.

"You have a bit of a habit of breaking up awkward moments,

did you know that?" I said as I approached. "First my wedding, and now my husband's homecoming. Perhaps you should wait until you're properly invited to these things. If you are at all."

"Jane," Eric murmured.

I just rolled my eyes. From my vantage point, the fact that my maybe-husband had left me at the altar, that he was currently staring at me like a terrified gerbil, that he had literally pulled out of me *mid-orgasm*—all of this was because wannabe Mr. Burns kept busting in on everything. And yeah, I'll be real. I was most angry with the last one. I didn't care if this guy was the Pope—he wasn't getting away with fucking up my sex life.

"How did you get up here?" I asked as I folded my arms. "Carson, is it? Because I'm sure as hell not calling you 'Daddy.'"

The man blinked. Slowly, his smirk widened, and he bowed. He actually bowed, like some archaic character from an Edgar Allen Poe story.

"You have got to be kidding me," I muttered.

"Jane," he said as he extended a long hand. "It's a pleasure to meet my daughter properly at last. I wouldn't have chosen these circumstances, of course, but we'll make do."

I examined the hand for a minute, took it, and immediately wished I hadn't. Carson's hand—I couldn't for the life of me think of him as John, and definitely not Dad—was cold and overly smooth, like bone. It was like greeting a cadaver.

"You would have preferred a creepy meeting place in the rain?" I said. "Eric and I politely decline your offer. *We* decided to come home. The two of us. Alone."

As I emphasized the word "we," Carson's pleasant expression disappeared.

"You know," he said. "Some might say it's rude to ignore an invitation. Or an order. Isn't that so, Triton?" he asked Eric.

"We had more important things to do," I cut in. "Like

consummating our fucking marriage, asshole. Or did you show up to watch? Pretty kinky, but incest isn't my thing, just FYI."

Eric buried his face in one hand. Carson's tightened even more as he cast a look over the room behind us. His gaze caught the abandoned wet clothes, and his jaw clenched visibly.

"I believe you are mistaken," he said as he walked inside, carefully avoiding the debris and muddy tracks. "From what I understand, the marriage is not legal." He turned by the kitchen island. 'Isn't that correct, Triton?"

Eric mumbled something under his breath that sounded strangely like "Yes."

I shot him a dirty look, which he avoided.

I turned back to Carson. "We're figuring it out. It's a family matter."

His laugh was like listening to a rock bounce down a stepladder—jarring, rhythmic, and clipped. "I suppose that entitles me to negotiations, doesn't it, my dear? After all, no one ever asked your father's permission. And Eric, of course, dearly paid for it."

Carson's eyes floated over Eric's body, which shuddered visibly. I stepped closer to Eric. He only stepped away.

"What did he do to you?" I whispered.

But Eric wouldn't answer, just shook his head and turned back to Carson "Things are more...complicated now."

Carson looked Eric over. "Cute, Triton. Very cute. But try as you might, you'll never have your grandmother's negotiating skills. A viper, that one."

His tone was overtly admiring, like Celeste had been a force to be reckoned with, but not without some spite. Well, she had been a force. I could testify to that personally.

"What do you want?" I asked, unwilling to beat around the bush. I was tired of being jerked around in this little charade.

"Simple," Carson said. "To protect my legacy."

I frowned. "Your what?"

"Young de Vries here had his orders. Several times, I might add. To stay away from you."

I frowned. "*Me?*" I shook my head. "Why me?"

Carson tipped his head. "Call it a protective father's instinct. It's not your fault, my dear, that Eric has such a hard time taking orders."

I turned to Eric, who just held out his hands.

"I couldn't," he said weakly. "I couldn't walk away from you."

My heart twisted in my chest. Yeah, I knew how that felt. Still, something wasn't adding up.

"I don't buy it," I said. "So what, your little two-faced clubhouse decided the boss's daughter was off-limits?"

Carson's head snapped up. "She knows about Janus?"

"She's smart, Carson. She figured it out." Eric shrugged, but didn't mention Brandon. For once, I was grateful for his impervious exterior.

Carson scowled. "Inexcusable. We'll attend to that later."

Was it me, or did Eric shrink at the implied threat? From a man at least thirty years his senior?

I, on the other hand, was puffing up like a blowfish. "This is ridiculous. What does it matter what the evil Boy Scouts say? Why did you have to get involved with them anyway? Just walk away like you did last time."

"Oh, Eric didn't walk away," Carson corrected me. "He thought he did, but in reality, he was released."

My forehead screwed up in confusion. "What? Why?"

"Five years ago, Eric wasn't an active member of our little group," Carson said. "A black sheep running off to play attorney?" He scoffed. "Please. We had no use for him then."

"But you do now?"

Eric took a deep breath. "Jane, DVS operates nearly a third

of the major ports in the world right now. Our contracts basically control what goes in and out of almost every country on the planet. I'm the controlling shareholder now. That makes me...valuable."

"That's enough," snapped Carson. "It's bad enough she knows about the society. The rest is none of her concern."

"None of my concern?" I parroted. "How's that, Dr. No? You are literally twisting my life around because of all this nonsense. That definitely sounds like my concern. Do you usually interfere with the lives of your members with this kind of manipulative horseshit?"

"Of course not," Carson replied easily. "But the other members haven't tried to marry my daughter."

And there it was. The key difference. The reason for his interference. Me.

"You've—I—we—" I stumbled over the words until I could think of just one thing—the thing I'd been avoiding for the last two weeks. "I need to call my mother."

"I wouldn't advise that." Carson took a few steps closer to me. "Yu Na was told to stay far away from my activities long ago. She accepted my settlement and married that..." His hand waved, as if recognizing Carol Lefferts as an actual person wasn't even worth his time. One of his thin eyebrows arched. "What, you don't think she and the psychologist came up with that house payment on their own, did you? There is also the fact that her VISA was processed within days, not years."

Carson leaned down so he could look me straight in the eye. It wasn't far—he was tall, but so was I.

"Yu Na has good reason to be afraid of me," he said. "As does Eric. I'd hate to give my own daughter a taste of that medicine, but it's not out of the question if she doesn't behave."

I opened my mouth to tell him to go fuck himself, but something in Eric's eye stopped me. He shook his head minutely. So I remained quiet and took a step back. *Proceed, asshole*, I thought. And like he heard me, Carson did.

"You see, my darling, I have a bit of a problem. There is an unfortunate price, it seems, of working with the elements I do. A cost of being at the forefront of modern technology."

"You mean weapons of mass destruction?"

Carson cast another long look at Eric. "Someone *has* been talking."

He shook his head.

"You're the CEO of Chariot Industries," I shot back. "And I have access to Wikipedia."

Carson frowned, but continued to pace. "I see. Well...let me be frank, then. A man reaches a certain age, and he wants a legacy to leave behind. He wishes to know he will not be forgotten."

"So you found out your swimmers are sterile, and I'm all that's left. Your little half-Korean mistake?" I had to laugh. "Well, that's rich."

"It is what it is," Carson replied between his teeth. "The facts as they are."

"Well, the facts are also that I want fucking nothing to do with you," I said. "I don't know you, regardless of whatever money you gave my parents. I don't want your 'legacy.' I don't want anything at all from you."

Carson shrugged. "I harbor no illusions about the possibility of our relationship," he informed me. "Nor, quite frankly, do I want one. You are much too old and much too..." He waved his hand up and down, as if to indicate something unworthy about my general being. "No, you would never be an appropriate heir. I shall make do with closer confidants. But I have one requirement. That *my* superior bloodline does not under any circumstances mix with this...swill."

"The de Vrieses?" I frowned at Eric. "What do you have

against one of the oldest families in America?" It was ironic, I knew, that I was actually defending a family who had treated me like a kitchen scamp for the last six months, but here we were. I'd take their snooty Dutch noses over this asshole any day of the week.

"That's none of your concern!" Carson barked. "One way or another you *will* learn some respect. I advise you learn it quickly before you receive the consequences of your disregard. Since he loves to talk so much, perhaps *Eric* can give you a preview."

I looked to Eric. His head gave an infinitesimal shake—the universal sign for *shut up, Jane.*

"What is the deal with rich people and their legacies?" I blurted out "Look, Goldfinger, I hate to break it to you, but your DNA is not that special. And neither is mine."

"Ah, but I must disagree with you, my dear," Carson put in. "You see, history proves different. Some genetic legacies are more powerful than others. It's the strong who inherit the earth, not the weak."

I looked at Eric. "Is he serious? This is over some kind of freaking eugenicist garbage? Are we in the middle of the nineteenth century?"

"If this were the nineteenth century, my dear, you wouldn't exist."

I snorted. "Someone needs to go back to history class, Johnny boy. You think you're the only rich white man to take advantage of a poor Asian woman? It's a timeworn stereotype, so really, *you*'re the one out of date. Not to mention ordinary as fuck."

"*Jane,*" Eric hissed.

"Don't bother, Triton," Carson said, his eyes blazing at me. "Her concerns do not matter anyway." He paused. "However it emerged, I would hate to know that my legacy will go to waste. You're rough, but there is enough of me in you that it is worth my effort to take an interest in where it...goes."

I scowled. "You talk about me like I'm a broodmare."

Carson just shrugged, which told me the comparison wasn't totally off base. But before I could argue, something else occurred to me:

"But Eric's part of your little club," I said. "If you want to talk bloodlines, his family has deeper roots here than just about anyone besides the actual indigenous people. The de Vrieses didn't come on the Mayflower, but that's only because they bought Manhattan ten years later for twenty bucks."

"Technically, that was Peter Minuit," Eric put in. "My ancestors were among the merchants that helped him settle."

Carson smiled, like the detail strengthened his argument that the de Vries line was corrupt.

I just rolled my eyes. "Are we done with the pedantry, boys?" I turned back to Carson. "You want a pedigree? He's got one. I should think you'd be happy—if I wanted a relationship with you at all, *which I don't*—that I ended up with the colonial crown prince of Manhattan should tickle those shaved whiskers of yours bloody pink."

"Be that as it may," Carson said, barely able to contain his irritation. "That's how I feel. And it's how it shall be. Anyone —*anyone*—but a member of the de Vries family."

"Except there's one problem, Carson."

Finally, Eric managed to find his voice as he stepped in front of me. He picked his jacket off the floor, pulled out the wet, wadded remains of our copy of Celeste's will—given to each family member in the office—and handed it to Carson.

"Page five," Eric said softly as Carson laid the document on the counter and started peeling it apart.

"Stupid woman," Carson muttered to himself as he scanned the ways in which Celeste had divided her estate. "Two hundred million dollars in real estate to a butler?"

He continued to murmur to himself, chuckling every so

often until he came to the section concerning Eric and me. Then his face turned an ungodly shade of red as he read the short paragraph. And read it again. And again. Until finally, when he was just about to spout like a tea kettle, he looked up, fairly shaking with fury.

"What. Is. This?"

Eric shrugged. And for once, it was the best thing I'd ever seen. "It's my birthright," he said softly. "Tied to the woman I love."

Carson spluttered. "You had to get married to keep your inheritance. You told me yourself, it didn't matter to whom."

Eric just cocked his head. "Grandmother changed the terms. Jane and I are both granted our own trusts, but the conditions were altered. We don't have to stay married. We don't even have to get married again at all. We just have to live together for sixty days. Jane receives fifty million, and I keep my family's forty-nine percent and remaining assets. If I do nothing, the executor has instructions to sell it all. Which means, of course, DVS loses all its contracts around world ports." He quirked a brow. "Something tells me you might be interested in that, considering the way Chariot has been investing in DVS stock for the last ten years. What's your stake now? A full one percent?"

Carson's jaw dropped and stayed there for several seconds.

"I might be new to this job," Eric said. "But I'm not stupid. You want me in Janus? You summoned me, after all, Carson. Was that to keep your enemy close or because I served some interest? I remember. You never do anything unless it benefits you in some way. Or, of course, anarchy. So which is it? I can't be a someone without her, Carson. I'm no one without Jane."

My brain wasn't sure how to take that. But my heart definitely thrilled.

Eric winked at me. "Maybe Grandmother wasn't such a viper after all, huh, Jane?"

I grinned. I had *never* been so thrilled that Eric's grandmother was a Machiavellian genius. Carson looked back and forth between us frantically, and I bristled, feeling triumphant. More, however, than I should have.

"Yes, well..." Carson tapped a long finger on the counter, then suddenly swept the entire will into the garbage container on one side of the island. "She wasn't smart enough to include a procreation clause or anything else like it."

Carson's shocked expression morphed into a smile. The kind that, like the Cheshire cat's, seemed to be present before the rest of his face appeared around it.

"Sixty days," Carson said. "And you will. Not. Touch. Her."

I snorted. "Yeah, that's going to happen."

"Oh, it will. It will. Won't it, Triton?" He reached across the island to Eric and pulled his coin out of his shirt.

"This," he said, "was your father's, not yours. I recognized it when I last saw you."

With a sudden wrench, he ripped the chain from Eric's neck.

"Hey!" Eric yelped.

Carson examined the coin for a few moments. "I should take it," he said. "Until you've earned back the right."

But instead, he dropped the necklace on the counter, where it collapsed into a pile.

I stared at Eric, who was staring at the coin. I started to grab for it, to hurl it out the window or back at this horrible, snide man who was somehow related to me. But before I could, Eric's broad hand covered it and pulled it away. I watched in shock as he tucked it into his pants pocket with great care.

"You're kidding," I said. "You're not really going to agree to this, are you?"

"Jane," he said weakly. "I—I have to."

"Well, I don't!"

I stomped my foot on the ground like a child. Carson seemed to enjoy it. I whirled around at him.

"Listen, you pompous prick. There is no fucking way in hell you're going to dictate *any* parts of my life or his! I don't know who you think you are, but—"

Suddenly, my wrist was snatched, and I was swiftly walked backward into the wall in four long steps.

"Hey!" Eric shouted just as I was slammed against the exposed brick, its jagged, uneven texture cutting into my back. "Easy!"

"*This* is a family matter," Carson bit out as he glared down at me. "I've forgiven your ill manners because of the unfortunate circumstances of our meeting. Haven't you considered *why* your prince over there is so terrified of me, Jane?"

I quivered, from fear yes, but mostly anger. "No."

That same smile appeared, revealing white teeth that had to be capped, but several stained ones near the back. Carson's breath smelled lightly of cigars. I hoped cancer was eating him alive as we stood there.

"People who cross me usually regret it. Painfully so."

"Is that a threat?" I asked.

"It's a fact."

A low, almost inaudible laugh hummed from the back of Carson's throat. He released my hand, and I crumpled against the wall and down to the floor, holding my sore wrist to my chest.

"It's fine," Eric said as Carson turned around. "We'll do it."

"*We'll* do it?" I cried. "*We* will do it? Don't I have a say in this at *all*?"

"Jane, please," he said, as nonchalant as ever, but with a pleading note that almost broke me. "It's two months. Just...just two months."

But that wasn't it. It wasn't the asking me to live platonically that made me so upset. It was that he was choosing this farce—this fucked-up parody of a marriage—over the truth and passion and grit that had always been between us.

Eric had broken my heart so many times before, but this time, he smashed it to pieces. Because it was clear to me, for the first time since he'd walked back into my life six months ago, that the only thing that really mattered to him was his own fucking skin.

Well. I could look out for mine too.

I pushed up from the floor, still cradling my hand, fighting not to swing out at both of the smug, entitled fuckers in front of me.

But before I could say anything, Carson seemed to accept Eric's consent for us both. He tapped his finger to his nose and walked to the door.

"Sixty days, Triton," he said before leaving. "And I'll know. You know I will."

The door closed behind him and the click of the lock echoed through the apartment.

I turned to Eric. "You're insane if you think I'm going along with this. If this is how it's going to be, I'll just leave now."

"Jane—" Eric's voice cracked as he pulled the coin out of his pocket and stared at it. That stupid, flashing piece of metal that seemed to mock us with its brightness.

He looked up, and I could see every argument he had flashing across his otherwise immovable face. That he had to do this, not for himself, but for his family. For Nina and her kids. For his mother and aunt. For the people, bad and good, who were grieving a woman who had done everything she could to maintain a legacy for them through her sole heir.

I deflated like a sad, tired balloon. Every emotion I had seeped from me like the air out of my lungs. All except for anger. At him.

"Fine," I said through gritted teeth. "I'll do it. Not for you. For Nina. For my mother's future. I'll stay for sixty days, and not one fucking day longer. But if you think I'm going to make it easy on you, think again."

Eric stared at me like a monster was rising in front of him. And who knows? Maybe one was.

I pushed up on my toes to look him right in the eye. His gaze, however, drifted to my lips like it always did. I shuddered. Dammit.

Anger, I thought to myself. *Hold on to your anger*. It was the only way I would be able to do it.

Somehow, we'd have to live together for sixty days. Sixty days without touching. Without kissing. Without fucking.

I moved in with Eric six months ago absolutely hating his guts, and I lasted two weeks. Two months would be impossible without holding on to that hate. Doing everything I could to keep it alive.

"If I have to live this miserable, stupid charade with you, I'm going to make you regret it more than you've ever regretted anything in your life."

I moved closer so that my lips hovered inches from his, and Eric's steely gaze drifted down, fixed on them.

"Is that a threat?" he asked, his voice barely above a whisper. Dangerous and scared all at once.

"No," I said as I stood as straight as I could. "That's a promise."

INTERLUDE I

"Good lord. Would you look at this?"

Eric turned to find his cousin Nina, with a moth-eaten caftan that was half gold sequins, half magenta silk. She held it against her slim body, and the sequins glimmered, the same color as her hair.

"Just call me Madame Esmeralda," she said, swaying the fabric back and forth. The movement caused miniature plumes of dust to fly into the air. Nina sneezed and tossed the item into a box designated for donation.

They had taken it upon themselves to go through the remainder of Celeste's things so that Garrett could use the storage space beneath Celeste's Park Avenue building. A castle on top of a landfill, Eric thought. Yes, they could have hired an estate manager to do the majority of the work for them—and they would, after this bit was finished. A good half was just clutter—papers and decayed clothes from decades gone, things Celeste hadn't even considered for thirty, forty, even fifty years or more. A sizeable portion of whatever the family declined to keep would end up at Sotheby's on auction. The rest would go to donation. Violet and their great-uncle Rufus, had already retrieved the few belongings they wanted. Now it was Nina and Eric's turn.

"I think Grandmother had a bit more fun back in the day than she let on," Eric said from his place amid several boxes of books.

He held up an album of pictures, one in which their grand-mother was actually wearing the garment Nina had just tossed aside. Celeste was perhaps thirty in the photo, the mother of two small children—Violet, Nina's mother, and Jacob, Eric's father—and a full-time New York socialite during the swinging sixties. In the photo, she was as poised as ever, but held her Manhattan high alongside her husband, Jonathan de Vries, and a roomful of New York's highest society toasting the 1965 New Year.

Nina sidled around the debris to take a look.

"They look so glamorous," she admired. "And look at Grand-father. He's positively besotted with her."

The note of envy in her voice made Eric glance at her, but before he could respond, Nina had already gone back to her sort-ing. Eric examined the photo more closely. Jonathan de Vries had died long before any of his grandchildren were born, but it was clear that he was the life of the party. Celeste stood as impe-rious as ever despite her small size and the bedazzled dress, but looked a bit like the cat who had gotten the cream. Meanwhile, Jonathan's arms were spread magnanimously around his wife and son, five-year-old Jacob, with a cigar perched between his bright white teeth and a twinkle in his eye as bright as the North Star. A marriage of opposites, sheltering their heir, Eric's father.

Eric put the photo album in a box marked to take home with him.

Even the wealthy hoard, Eric thought as he closed one card-board box and opened another. Maybe more than others. Maybe that was why he had always erred toward a more ascetic exis-

THE KISS PLOT   141

tence during the ten years he'd been estranged from these people.

"Calvin still can't believe we are even doing this," Nina remarked as she approached a rack full of clothes hanging in plastic bags. "He wanted to fight the will in court and take the penthouse from Garrett. He's still mad you told him it would be impossible."

"Well, it would, even if I thought it was the right thing to do. Grandmother knew what she was doing. And her lawyer, despite his bumbling, is the best estate attorney in the city." Eric's eyes widened as he discovered a trove of old poetry books. "We still own the rest of the building. And besides, would you really want to live in that mausoleum?"

Nina's silence told him she would. Eric felt guilty. He forgot sometimes that Nina had grown up in this apartment much more than he had. And that Celeste's decision to turn the company over to him, the black sheep, instead of her dutiful granddaughter likely still stung.

"I think he deserves it," Eric reverted back to Garrett as he paged through a first edition of Shelley. He tucked the book in the take-home box and picked up another. "He's been around since our parents were kids."

Nina raised a brow under a broad-billed sun hat that made her look like a duck. "Do you think...no, never mind."

Eric looked up. "What?"

She shrugged—a family tendency—as she turned around and opened a spare box of antique silver. "I was just wondering if they had ever...you know... After all, they did live there alone together for such a long time."

Eric screwed up his face. "Garrett and Grandmother? I doubt it. First of all, he was, what, at least fifteen years her senior?"

Nina's expression made it clear what an impediment she

thought *that* was. After all, their grandfather had been forty-seven when he married his twenty-two-year-old bride in the early fifties. And Calvin was sixteen years older than Nina.

Eric smirked. "Okay, okay. It's possible, I guess. It has been almost thirty-five years since Grandfather passed."

"And she never wanted to remarry," Nina added as she fingered a fork. "Do you want these?

Eric shook his head. "No, Mom gave Jane and me a set as a wedding gift." He didn't mention that he would likely have to give it back. "Grandmother wouldn't be the first to enter into a marriage of convenience anyway," he added wryly.

Nina put the silverware aside and removed her hat. "Is it really that bad? After all, they ended up happy. And you and Jane always seemed so...well, I always thought there was a spark." The envy in her soft voice reappeared—masked, but only just. It was a family talent.

Eric picked a few more books and tucked a first edition of Joyce's *Dubliners* in the "keep" pile. "It's complicated. First that bullshit with Caitlyn—"

"Who is *so* sorry, by the way, Eric. Really, she is."

"Yeah, I bet." The acid in Eric's voice fairly dripped. "Don't bother defending her to me. What she did was unforgivable."

"Eric, she was just confiding in me—"

"With Jane in the room. You told me yourself you thought she was in there."

Nina was quiet. There was no way for her to defend Caitlyn's actions, and they both knew it.

Eric softened. He understood Nina's life better than most. Caitlyn had grown up with them and was probably one of the few people who understood Nina and the unique stressors that came with being a de Vries. She would have seen how Nina was groomed from birth to occupy her social stations, and like her, she went along with a marriage that wasn't arranged *per se*, but might as well have been. Eric had never understood why Nina had married Calvin, that sniveling horse's ass. But then again, he hadn't really been around to voice his concerns either, had he? Caitlyn was Nina's compatriot, even after her own marriage ended.

"Oh, before I forget, Garrett sent this down when I gave him the last of our keys." Nina maneuvered around several other boxes, careful not to get dust on her pressed gray pants, and picked up a large, rectangular package near the door to the storage unit.

"It's Grandmother's Klimt," she said, this time not even bothering to hide her envy as she handed it to Eric.

Eric didn't have to open the package to imagine what was inside. The painting was one of the most valuable pieces in the entire penthouse, and that was saying something. It was similar to Klimt's more famous *The Kiss*, a portrait of a couple embracing done with a collage-like gold leaf technique. The story was that it was a portrait of his great-grandmother and her first husband, done before he died in the first World War. After, Annika Arendt had fled Austria and married George van Dusen —Celeste's father. But not without taking her prized painting of the love of her life.

"We should just donate it," he said. "I'm sure the Met would take it off our hands."

Nina didn't answer. They both knew he wouldn't do it. She had seen Jane admire the painting more times than Eric.

"Garrett said she intended to give it to you and Jane as a wedding gift," Nina said, turning back to the clothes. "Lucky you. All Calvin and I got was her spare set of Heisey glassware. And I'll remind you that midcentury settings were *not* back in style yet."

Eric snorted. "She never did like Calvin."

"She liked his pedigree, that's all. No one liked Calvin. No one likes him now." Nina said it casually as she examined a few more Puccis on the rack.

Eric put the painting against the wall with the other box of things he was planning to bring back with him and returned to his boxes of books. "You know, you don't have to stay with him. Not if you don't want. Fuck the rules."

"And sully our family's sterling record? How could I?"

"That's my job, is what you're saying?"

All he received was a very unladylike snort. They were both aware of the double standard between the two of them, the last of the direct de Vries line. Despite the fact that Nina had always been perfectly behaved while Eric had literally deserted the family for ten years, it was Eric who had received the lion's share of the family's fortune and power.

"It's all right," Nina said as she heaved an armful of clothes off the rack and set them in the donation box. "There is Olivia to think about too. Calvin and I get along all right as long as we don't have to spend too much time together. Not all of us are lucky in love, Eric. Which, by the way, means the ones who are should take advantage of it."

Nina's gray-blue eyes were large and open, without judgment. It was a welcome, unexpected sight from one of his family members. But Eric couldn't meet them. He didn't know what Calvin had told her about the ordeal with Janus—he was still relatively sure at this point that his cousin-in-law, desperate for entry to the illustrious society, was the one who had been keeping an eye on him and Jane for Carson. Much good it would do him. Carson hated a rat, even if he had use for one.

"Do you think Jane would want any of these?" Nina asked, interrupting his brooding. She held out a colorful, psychedelic print. "They are so beautiful, but there are really only so many costume parties one can get away with after the age of thirty." She sighed, as if the number represented some kind of death knell. "Jane might like to do something with them, don't you think? She's so talented."

Eric glanced at the rack. "You know, she probably would. I'll bring whatever you don't want to the apartment. Jane can go through them there."

Nina nodded. "If anyone knows what to do with these gems, it would be her."

Eric mumbled his agreement. He was trying *not* to think about Jane, though it was a fairly impossible task. It had been one week since Carson laid down his rules. One week of living with a stomping, irritable, annoyingly beautiful half-Korean who seemed intent on wearing the smallest clothes possible and reapplying her goddamn lipstick every ten minutes. She knew what she was doing. Jane *always* knew how to press his buttons.

But. The society. The coin that hung around his neck like an anvil. Eric had no doubt the apartment was surveilled despite the fact that Tony, his head of security, screened it nightly. This was Carson. The man wasn't just demanding—he was obsessive. The only way out was to live the next forty-three days was exactly the way he had so far: according to the rules. Work late. Stay in his room. Above all, keep Jane safe.

He wasn't an idiot. He knew why Grandmother had chosen the sixty days. Jane was right. In the eyes of the church, they were in fact married. The minister had confirmed it and signed the license, which was now locked in Eric's desk at home, signed by neither the bride nor the groom. Therefore, no marriage had been filed with the state either. And in forty-three days, the entire thing would be nulled, as New York State law decreed a marriage license was valid for only two months after the date of a marriage. If the signed document wasn't filed by then, the whole thing would be nulled.

Celeste had gotten the wedding she wanted—one last hurrah for the de Vries dynasty on her watch. The addendum to the will was her gift to Jane and Eric, allowing them to make their marriage a choice rather than a requirement. The wily old fox. She knew them both better than they realized.

Too bad they couldn't accept the gift even if he could make it that long.

The idea scarred, though Eric knew it was for the best. He still didn't understand why, exactly, Carson was so determined to keep him and Jane apart, but he assumed it was some kind of fucked-up penance for staying away for so long. Janus didn't take it well when members defected. When Eric had only just joined, one member who wanted to leave was penniless a month later after his entire company was purchased out from under him. The man drank himself to death within a year.

In retrospect, Eric had gotten off easy.

"Eric?"

Eric snapped out of his thoughts. "Hmm? What's up, Nina?"

"I said, you might want these. They look like Uncle Jacob's."

Abandoning the books, Eric wove his way around an Art Deco dining set and a very stiff-looking French country chaise to Nina. She pointed to the collection of tatty books and papers stacked inside another box: several yearbooks from Yale, a few framed photos, and a shoebox full of letters and postcards. The top most book was beaten black leather, inlaid with the name *Jacob Arendt van Dusen de Vries* in gilt letters across the front. Eric fished it out and flipped through the pages.

"A diary?" Nina asked, looking over his shoulder.

Eric nodded. "Looks that way. Huh. I didn't realize Dad kept anything like this. I don't even remember him reading anything besides the *Times*."

Nina went back to picking through a box of handbags. "It's not exactly Shakespeare," she said.

"That it's definitely not," Eric replied.

The writing was short, terse, and utilitarian. Eric knew that in families like the de Vrieses, there were often long-standing traditions of keeping records. Dynasties knew they were dynasties. There was a strange meta-awareness in how they lived, knowing that they were more likely than not to make it into history books or catch the eye of biographers down the line. Often, they obsessively recorded their lives, wanting to control the narratives that would be potentially be made about them. The victors really did write history before they won anything at all.

His grandfather's and great-grandfather's journals and letters were both housed at the New York Public Library archives with other parts of the illustrious de Vries family papers. When nothing had been donated after Jacob's death, Eric had just assumed that his father hadn't written anything.

Eric flipped through a few more of the pages. They were fairly bland accounts of business trips, a line or two dedicated to lunches or dinners with people. His mother cropped up in several of them around the time they married, but not much was said beyond the color of her dress or the time Jacob picked her up for dinner. Like so many journals of its kind, it required the reader to investigate between the terse lines for the emotion beneath.

December 25, 1987
Christmas at Mother's. Violet brought the new baby. Eric
broke several ornaments. Tried out a new gin martini
recipe.
Five course meal with the Jameses on Lex. Home for three
days until the next trip to Beijing. Heather pleased with
her bracelet.

They were such short phrases, but Eric had no difficulties imagining the Christmas at his grandmother's parlor. His great uncle Rufus would have been tippling too much gin, Violet would have been wrangling three-month-old Nina, and Eric, at two, would have been pulling and yanking on every shiny, priceless antique imaginable, much to Celeste's dismay. Was it just him, or was there some humor embedded in this account? That his father had thought it important to log his toddler's intransigence among all of the other festivities brought a hint of a smile to Eric's face.

He read a few more pages—droll accounts of a business trip to China and Japan. Port negotiations as his father learned the family business.

Just before he closed the book, another entry caught Eric's eye:

> *February 10, 1988*
> *Home finally. Detoured to Seoul on my way back from*
> *Beijing. J was angry over some girl he met there. Had to*
> *rescue him from a hotel in Hwaseong. On the upside,*
> *hoping we can put this mess behind us at last. After all,*
> *isn't he the one who would constantly tell us, "Ne quid*
> *expectes amicos, quod tute agere possis?"*
> *Heather liked the jade earrings. Next time I'll get the*
> *necklace too. They match her eyes.*
> *Eric now speaking in full sentences. We are trying for*
> *another, but no luck yet.*

Eric drifted his fingers over the final words. Short, but loaded. A brief paragraph dedicated to some anonymous friend, but he could feel his father's frustration, clear as day. Just as he could hear the echoes of adoration in each account of his mother's small reactions.

"What does that mean?" Nina asked, back to snooping over his shoulder, this time with an oversized cashmere sweater draped around her shoulders. She pointed at the Latin phrase Jacob had quoted.

Eric turned. "My Latin's rusty, but roughly, I think it means something like, 'Expect nothing from friends, do it for yourself.'"

Nina made a face. "That's depressing."

"Yeah, whoever 'J' is, he sounds like kind of a dick." Eric rubbed a finger over the passage.

Nina cast a sly grin at her cousin. "It's probably code for Grandfather."

"In 1988? Years after he died?"

Nina shrugged. "Someone else, then. I still can't believe you took Latin for four years. Grandmother was *so* angry at you for refusing German or French."

"We had good tutors," Eric replied as he went back to sorting. "There was no need."

It was a little strange, though. Because it wasn't *that* unusual for Ivy League assholes from a certain generation to quote Latin at each other. Like Rolex watches or priceless heirlooms, it was another signifier of their wealth and status—old, useless shit that no one but the rich cared about. He had thought at the time that Celeste would be thrilled he was carrying on the tradition, but Nina was right. Back then, Grandmother had put up quite the damn fuss.

For Eric, taking Latin in college was more of an homage to his father than anything else. Like the anonymous "J," Jacob de Vries also had a penchant for quoting Latin. Virgil was his favorite. Eric probably knew half the TH*Aeneid* before he was ten. Now, of course, he realized that Jacob probably read it more out of duty to Janus. But as a child, Eric had just thought it was an interesting story about the birth of Rome.

He picked up the box of his father's things and carried it over to the wall, next to the wrapped Klimt painting. He would take that, the first editions, and the rest with him in his car. There were some things too precious to trust to an assistant.

"Don't forget the clothes," Nina called from the other side. "Unless you want Bridget to send them."

She winked, fully aware of the effect a box of vintage couture would have on Jane, the biggest fashion addict in New York.

Eric sighed. He knew the effect they would have too, but he wasn't sure it was a good idea. Sixty days in an apartment with the woman and being unable to touch her was already the seventh circle. But what made it worse was how much it clearly hurt Jane too. His own pain, Eric could take that all day. But hers...fucking hell. That made him want to slit his wrists just to save her the trouble. Better she hated him. Better she considered him a thoughtless ass.

Still...it was like he couldn't help himself.

"I hope you and Jane figure out a way to make it work," Nina was saying. "If Grandmother's sixties collection helps patch things up, I'm taking full credit."

"I don't think it's going to happen." Eric's voice was flat. Cold.

"Calvin said something like that. I was hoping he was exaggerating, like usual."

Eric looked up from his things sharply. "What did Calvin say?"

Nina shrugged as she examined a pair of red shoes. "Not much. Something about her father disapproving of the match. I suppose it's understandable. Mr. Carson always scared me half to death. And he never did like Grandmother, did he?"

"Didn't he?" Eric wondered.

Nina gave him another look. "If you'd been around for the last ten years, you would have known that. I don't know how it started, but you should have seen them at events. Like sniping cats, always."

Eric frowned. "Over what?"

Nina shrugged. "How should I know? Shipping contracts? Port access? Any number of things could have angered the man. Chariot Industries makes boats too, don't they?"

Eric twisted his mouth around. "I don't actually know."

Nina put on a pair of green Chanel sunglasses and looked over the rims. "You should probably learn the business you're going to head, Eric."

Eric just ignored Nina and sidled around the mess to retrieve the box of clothes anyway.

"I really am a fucking masochist," he muttered as he carried it to the others. Because he would take it home. He'd offer it to the woman at whose feet he'd lay the fucking world. Give her whatever he could because he couldn't offer what he—and she— truly wanted: himself.

But as much as Jane's luscious lips and sharp tongue made his chest ache with want, Carson's threats were always there.

Ten days in that dungeon.

Alone.

Hurting.

By the end of it, Eric had barely remembered his own name, much less what he had done to deserve it. At this point, it didn't matter anymore. He would do almost anything to avoid that. And he would do *everything* to avoid Jane receiving the same fate.

———

"NEXT TIME it will be her turn," sneered Jude, his well-groomed face assuming a gargoylish form as the swinging light cast deep shadows across it. He tapped Eric's face with the knotted rope that

now made Eric flinch at just the sight of it. His whole body was on fire and had been for hours.

Please, no, he thought. Not her.

Jude's face broadened into a wide, nasty grin, and Eric realized he had spoken aloud. Then Jude nodded, Anton drew back his hand, and Eric didn't think at all for a very long time.

————

ERIC SHOOK HIS HEAD. In the week and a half since he'd been dropped off on the Staten Island Ferry, the memories seemed to have gotten worse, rather than better. Just the night before, he'd startled himself awake from a dream. In the room next to his, he could have sworn he'd heard Jane get up.

But no one knocked on his door. And as he began moving his boxes onto a cart to roll up to the street, he had to admit a truth. It hurt that she didn't care enough to come in. But it was better that way too.

PART TWO

APOSIOPESIS

Oh, kiss me, sweet nymph,
With thy poisoned lips,
With ruby's red shade that cuts to the quick.

Oh, Dido, cry out,
Hysteria's spout
Trapped not by deed, but words that you shout.

Oh, save me, sweet sprite
With thy hair like the night,
Like Diana, so fierce, so eager to fight.

I'd fly to the mark,
Without liquor or spark,
It's thy light that saves me from oppressive dark.

"Memory"
—from the journal of Eric de Vries

TWELVE

I sat up on my bed and blew at the bright purple polish on my toes. What had that lecture said again? Divorce law wasn't my strong suit. Never had been.

The question on my computer's screen flickered like a strobe light, waiting for my response. I really needed to stop staring at my computer.

I closed my eyes to focus. Profiting from matrimonial disgrace was really Skylar's area, not mine. I hadn't thought about this stuff since law school, and going through these questions for hours a day was making my brain bleed from boredom. I blew again, inhaled the fumes from the polish, then opened my eyes with triumph before I clicked on the correct answer.

"Ha!" I crowed when the screen blinked the green confirmation. I'd take my victories where I could get them these days.

In the last week, I'd thrown myself into studying for the December test date for the NYLE—the New York State Law Exam—followed by the February general bar in the event I wasn't able to get the second part waived. I might have had money coming my way, but I wasn't interested in being a layabout. And really, I had to do *something* to pass the time while I lived with the equivalent of a knife stabbing me in the chest every damn day.

Maybe it wouldn't have been so bad either if the knife in question wasn't such an impassive prick. Eric bowing to John Carson cut to the bone—but not nearly as much as his feigned indifference.

Eric made good on his original promise. We lived together, but just barely. He was gone almost every morning before I woke up, usually arrived at the apartment after ten or eleven, and headed straight for the shower, then bed. Gone were the easy nights where we bickered over someone's latest culinary experiment and recounted our days. Even his books of poetry had disappeared from the two shelves in the living room. He'd done his best to erase himself from my life.

It only made me angrier. And more likely to act out during the scant hours when he was there.

The last seven days had turned me into a jealous teenager. I had reapplied my red lipstick so often I'd already replaced the tube. I had paraded around the apartment in my tightest jeans and called him Petri dish every chance I got. I even left porn running with my bedroom door open for a solid hour before bed one night—not that I got anything out of it other than a headache. There are only so many times you can listen to silicon-trussed women whining fake orgasms in ear-splitting falsettos before you lose your sex drive completely. At the end, Eric just walked out and didn't return until two a.m. One guess where he went.

I was being petty and I knew it, but it quickly started to feel pathetic too. Like it hurt me more than him.

And did I get anything for my sacrifices? Not even a groin adjustment, my friends. Nothing. Nada. Zip.

The crazy thing was, I wasn't even sure I wanted to be a lawyer anymore. But every time I considered the alternative—potentially fulfilling my secret childhood dream of designing clothes—all I could see was Eric's stupid smile whenever he suggested the idea.

Well, fuck that. I was a damn good prosecutor before I got canned for my boss's change in politics. I could be one again.

Just as I was getting into the next section of the online lecture, the opening bars of "Rock the Casbah" tinkled at me from my nightstand. Yeah, I'd have to change that ASAP. I grabbed it, but the name on the screen made me grimace.

Yu Na, still making one of a million efforts to call me since *that day.*

Okay, yes. This conversation was overdue. We'd been playing phone tag since Carson's ultimatums—now it was she who had been playing hard-to-get.

Leave it alone, Jane, begged all her voicemails. *Please, just leave it be.*

Yeah. No.

I swiped right. "*Eomma,* I don't want to talk unless you're going to answer my questions."

"You picked up the phone, Jane. Maybe you do want to talk."

I ground my teeth. Our conversations always had to be arguments, didn't they? Apparently, she wasn't going to let a little thing like lifelong deception get in the way of that.

"*Eomma,* what do you want?"

"What do I want? I want to talk to my daughter, that's what I want. I want to know she's okay. You stayed in New York. Why, Jane?"

"Because...I..." I didn't know how to tell her. I didn't want to admit that yet again, I'd agreed to a bribe—a really, really *big* bribe—to live in this stupid fucking apartment for two months to save Eric's skin, his family's, and if Carson's threats were real, mine.

"Because this is where I live," was all I could come up with. "For now, anyway."

"What does that mean?"

"Nothing."

"Jane!"

"You know what?" I sprang off my bed and started pacing around the room like an awkward penguin, toes arched uncomfortably to keep from spoiling. "How about we hold the third degree from now on? It's really inappropriate considering you're a complete liar."

"I am your mother, Jane! I have a right to know if my daughter is okay. I have a right to know what she is doing!"

"I am *living my life!*" I shouted louder than I wanted, letting out weeks—no, months—of frustration and buttoned-up rage at the one person who was basically offering herself as my scapegoat. "I am trying to recover from the fact that my mother lied to me my entire life and that my biological father is basically Darth Vader with a nice suit. I am *reeling,* and I needed some fucking space to do it!"

There was a long silence, so deep that it seemed to consume the constant hum of noise that surrounded me in this city.

Then:

"Your father would not like the way you are talking to me," Yu Na said in a quiet, though bitter voice.

"Which one?" I replied nastily.

"The only one you have!" she practically shrieked.

I cowered, even though I couldn't see her. On some level, I could feel her laser stare all the way from Chicago.

"Carol was your father," she continued. "I never wanted you to think any different. He raised you, he loved you, he cared for you. He was your daddy, Jane. You know that!"

THE KISS PLOT   159

Hastily, I swiped a tear that escaped down one cheek. Goddammit. I hadn't really taken a second to internalize all of this, but now the pain was really sinking in. I had loved Carol Lefferts with my whole heart. He had been a wonderful father. Kind. Supportive. So much that even more than a year after his death, his voice still spoke from memories past, an avatar for my conscience.

Family's more than blood and bones, kiddo. Takes sweat too.

I shook my head. I had shoved that voice aside for weeks now because I couldn't bear to think of it as a lie.

But it was. *He* was.

"Except he wasn't my dad, was he?" I said stubbornly, though my voice quaked. "He was just playacting, right? Pretending for the sake of the poor fatherless baby and her wench of a mother."

"Jane!"

"I just want to know one thing," I continued. "Did he at least want to tell me?"

"Who?"

I shook my head. "*Daddy.*" The word cracked on my tongue.

There was a long pause, and for a second, I thought she might have hung up. But at last, she spoke again.

"He wanted to tell you every day, Jane." She took a deep breath. "He always said you deserve to know. He was right."

There was a long pause as both of us digested that fact. I nurtured both sadness and relief—at least he had loved me enough to want to tell the truth. Even if it was just another lie to protect me, I wasn't sure I cared anymore. I still needed the father I knew to exist, even if only as a memory.

"And I...the man who...John. It *is* John Carson, right?"

She paused for several beats. "That is what he told me."

I frowned. "*Eomma*, let's not play games. Was it that asshole at the wedding or not? Because he is kind of screwing up my life, so if there's a chance the paternity test might come out negative, I'd really like to know."

I could practically hear her shrug. Shit.

"What did he say to you back then?" I found myself asking. "You said he threatened you. What did he say he would do?"

Another long pause. But again, she answered. "He say...he just said I would regret if I ever told anyone about him."

I sank to the corner of my bed. My anger still simmered, but the obvious fear in her voice dampened it some. "*Eomma.* Come on."

It took a minute of wheedling and guilt-tripping—a skill I had learned from her, as it were—but eventually she told me why she had been so terrified to tell me or anyone else about the true paternity of her daughter.

She had a friend, she said. Another flight attendant. The one who had actually invited her to participate in the low-key prostitution ring that had brought her face-to-face with John Carson and instigated my birth. Seo-hyeon, who called herself Adele to westerners, had started the ring when another rich American propositioned her. She was entrepreneurial and had quickly roped several of the other girls into her scheme, including Yu Na.

It all went well. Until it didn't. Until the Seoul police started sniffing around, and one night, Seo-hyeon disappeared.

"They found her two weeks later in a storage ditch by a melon field. Strangled with her clothes—that red dress she always loved—and wrapped in a plastic bag. Maybe it was him. Maybe not. No one knew."

My mother spoke like she was reading off a police report. I, however, had no problem imagining the scene. Although I worked mostly on petty crimes in Chicago, I'd seen my fair share of real violence in the police reports that filtered around the Cook County SA's office. I shuddered, considering what it must have been like to learn a friend had been killed that way.

"When I tell him I was pregnant," Yu Na continued, "he tell me not to say anything. He give me money if I stay quiet. Or else, he said, I would end up like her. Me and my baby. Like Seo-hyeon." The combination of mourning and fear in her voice was palpable.

"You never thought to speak to the police?" I asked. "In Seoul or in Chicago?"

"What would I say?" my mother replied. "A man named John told me I have to pretend he is not the father of my child? I didn't even know his last name until his friend told me, Jane. Years later."

"Then how did he send you money?"

I didn't actually need her to answer. Cash, money order, wire transfer. There were all sorts of ways to send funds anonymously if you really wanted to do it.

I swallowed. The longer she spoke, the more the fear in her voice assuaged the anger in my heart. I was still mad, of course, but I could—kind of—understand why she had kept her secret. Maybe I would have too if I thought some terrifying American businessman was going to send me to the fishes.

But then I had to wonder: just how many people had my kingpin of a sperm donor (I refused to think the word "father" about the man) threatened over the years? And, if he was actually responsible for murders...just how many?

"Promise you will stay away from him, Jane," my mother kept saying again and again.

I couldn't do it. Because the more she told me, the more I wanted to chase the bad guy. I had these skills once. Contacts. Investigative methods. It seemed a shame to let them go to waste.

"Jane!"

"Hmm? What? Oh, sure. I don't want anything to do with him. I promise."

She exhaled, like the words actually meant something. Well, for now they did. "You will come home soon to visit?"

"I..." I pulled at my sweater. I honestly wasn't sure I could handle being around her right now. "I'll think about it, *Eomma*, okay?"

There was a long pause. Then: "Okay."

I blinked. It was so unlike my mother to take my first response as a final offer. But then again, we had never been in this predicament before.

"You will come home for Thanksgiving?" she asked.

I cringed. "I...I have to study for the bar, *Eomma*. I have to stay here." I had no idea if this was true, but I wasn't going back to Chicago.

She emitted a long sigh, but before she could respond, there was a knock on my door.

Eric, actually being useful for once. And early.

He gave a shy wave and carried in a large cardboard box.

"*Eomma*, I have to go. Talk soon."

Eric loitered awkwardly around the door until I hung up.

"Got a minute?" he asked.

I set my phone on my nightstand. "Oh. Hi."

"Um, hi. How are you doing?" Eric leaned against the door-frame and looked me over like he was searching for scratches.

I frowned. We'd barely spoken for a week, and now he wanted to check in? He set the box down by the door, then aimlessly toyed with the gold coin hanging over the open collar of his shirt.

I glared at it. "I'm fine. What is it?"

Eric blinked, apparently completely adapted to my terse syntax. Then he scanned the study materials scattered across the bed and frowned. "What are you doing?"

I closed my laptop. "Preparing for an acrobatics career. What does it look like I'm doing, Petri dish?"

He walked in to get a better look at the materials, ignoring the daggers I was shooting him. Aside from the double bed on one side, this room was otherwise cluttered with my sewing machine, bolts of fabric, boxes and bins of trim, buttons, zippers, and anything else I needed to make my clothes. It was my creative space, my sanctuary. Prince Spineless Manwhore had not been invited, nor was he welcome.

Not that he cared. The vintage mannequin wobbled on its stand as he nudged it upon approach.

"You're really studying for the bar again?" he asked. "Why?"

I rolled my eyes. "God, you're really getting brainwashed. Did you think I want to spend my days at pastel-colored luncheons and serving on the boards of a million charities? Just because I planned a wedding with your family doesn't mean I want to be like them."

My throat hurt, like the word "wedding" was actually a weapon that could cut on the way out. A muscle in Eric's jaw ticked.

"I didn't say that." He fingered one of the pamphlets bearing the exam deadlines. "I just thought—"

"You thought what?"

He dropped the pamphlet. "I thought you were more interested in this"—he waved a hand toward my mess of a studio —"than going back to law. I thought the plan was that you were going to take some classes at FIT or something like that."

I picked up the NYLE pamphlets protectively and held them in my lap. I hated that he was fairly correct in that assumption. I hated that every time in the last week I'd even considered sketching, his approving face had come to mind. But most of all, I hated that he thought he knew me well enough to say these things. Like he had the right.

"I'll have you know I was an excellent assistant prosecutor," I said as I reopened my computer.

"I never said you weren't—"

I just held up a hand. "Don't bother, Petri dish." The thin silver bracelets on my wrist jangled. "Don't you have some chlamydia to spread? Just because I'm your roommate doesn't mean I have to play ball and chain. Go do what you do best and leave me alone."

Eric opened his mouth—the full mouth that a part of me still wanted to suck on like a freaking Jolly Rancher, dammit—and watched as I purposefully grabbed the lipstick from my night-stand and proceeded to draw it over my lips for the fifth time that day. With every passing second, his gaze grew darker, until at last he turned abruptly. I watched his irritatingly perfect ass as he strode away, fighting the urge to call him back and apologize. But what for? He was the one who was basically extorting me to live here. He had no right to be angry.

Did he?

It wasn't until Eric had swiped his coat off the couch and left, apparently to do exactly what I had suggested, that I finally tiptoed over to the box and peered inside.

YSL. Pucci. Mary Quant. It was a box full of psychedelic originals from the 1960s, stuff that would fetch thousands in a vintage shop, but which Eric had brought here—apparently for me.

I pulled out one particularly gorgeous mini-dress with a swirling blue and green pattern so specific to that time. In a second, I could easily imagine how to style it with a highlight aesthetic. Tease my hair into a beehive. Find a killer pair of black thigh-high boots. Lean into the cat-eyed makeup that basically rendered me feline.

I could do it and then wait at the counter with a martini, ready to pounce on my prey as soon as he walked back through the door. This box said he wanted it, right? He was practically begging for me to meow the apathy right out of him.

Instead, I shoved the box under my work table and returned to my study materials. That was the smart thing to do. The practical thing to do. The path of action that wouldn't continue breaking my stupid heart.

THIRTEEN

T he next day, I still couldn't stop thinking about that conversation with my mother. Yu Na might have been scared shitless about the man, but I wasn't. Something about him didn't quite sit right. If her friend had been murdered in such a terrible fashion, hadn't anyone gone to the police? Was the man actually capable of murder, or did he just use the event to scare Yu Na? What was he doing in Korea in 1987 to begin with?

Round and round I went, but every internet search was a dud. John Carson really did keep his web presence to an absolute minimum, despite the growth of the company he helmed. Chariot had taken larger and larger government contracts over the last thirty years, but the only press I could find on John Carson was in praise of his business acumen in taking a thirty-million-dollar family trade in windshields and turning it into some real money. Beyond that, the man appeared spotless. He was a ghost.

I needed help. I tapped on my phone, considering whether or not to call some friends in Chicago. But then I remembered someone else. Someone local. Skylar had given me the number of Matthew Zola, the assistant DA who had prosecuted the Brooklyn gangster for terrorizing her family at one time.

The DA who currently worked in the organized crime and racketeering bureau.

The DA who might be able to help me land a job along with some leads of how to find John Carson.

Hmm. Not a bad idea.

He also seemed to be a DA who had nothing better to do on a Sunday night than work late—he picked up his office phone on the first ring.

"Matthew Zola."

"Ah...hi there. We, um, we've met before, and..." I made a face at myself in the mirror over my work table. What in the hell was wrong with me? Where was my game?

"Who is this?"

"This is Jane Lefferts," I said bluntly. "I'm a friend of Skylar Crosby's. We, um, we've met before, a few years ago."

"Oh!" The instant familiar tone calmed my heartbeat immediately. "Hey, Jane. How are you?"

"I'm good," I lied. "Just great. Hey, random thought. I don't know a lot of people in New York, and I'm here for the next few months, so...I was wondering if you wanted to grab a drink, or..." I winced again. I sounded like an awkward teenager feeling out a movie date, not an almost-thirty-year-old woman who could buy an entire theater if she wanted.

But to my surprise, Zola replied, "Sure, that sounds great. How does tonight sound?"

"Tonight?"

"If you're free. I need to get out of the office anyway."

He suggested a lounge on the Lower East Side, to which I readily agreed, since that part of town was pretty much the polar opposite of its uptown cousin.

"Perfect," I said a little too eagerly. "It's a date."

———

TWO HOURS LATER, I was putting the finishing touches on my hair just before I exited the bathroom wearing one of the YSL dresses from Celeste. Don't judge. You'd put on an original Mondrian dress too if it was dropped on your doorstep in mint condition. After practicing my cat-eye makeup for a solid hour, I had just popped in my contacts and finished teasing my hair into a bouffant half-updo that was one hundred percent shagalicious and went perfectly with the window-paned print and primary colors. I was a one-woman Mod Squad.

"Jesus!" I cried as I walked smack into Eric, in unexpectedly early. "Where the hell did you come from?"

His hands clasped my shoulders to steady me, and a cloud of cologne, soap, and a light scent of dust floated between us. God, he smelled good. And...suspiciously female.

I sniffed. "Chanel No. 5? Really, Petri dish? You could be a little more discreet."

Eric glowered as he took in my dress, hair, and makeup. "I was with Nina, finishing going through Grandmother's storage. I see you went through the clothes."

I looked down and back up at him. "Yeah. Well. A classic is a classic. No one in their right mind turns down YSL, even if it comes from you."

He folded his lips together. "Nina actually thought you would like it."

I really didn't like the way that idea hurt. I mean, Nina was nice and all. And shouldn't I have preferred that Eric wasn't trying to win me back with vintage fashion?

I should have. I should have, but I didn't.

The realization robbed me of any quips. "So that's it? It's all Garrett's now?"

Eric shrugged off his jacket and hung it on the back of one of the chairs at the breakfast bar. I took in the navy pants covered in dust, the way his blond hair was uncharacteristically ruffled, and the smudges of grime on his white shirt.

"The estate planner will finish the job, but yeah. We're done going through the rest. Garrett is changing the locks this week."

I watched silently as he moved around the kitchen, locating a glass and taking out his favorite vodka from the freezer.

Then my eye caught the corner of a couple of new boxes stacked next to the door, as well as a large, paper-covered package. "What are those?"

Eric turned from where he was pouring himself a stiff vodka. "What? Oh. Just some other things I wanted. Books mostly. Didn't you see the other box I brought yesterday?" He nodded toward a cardboard box next to a bookshelf.

I shook my head. "I must have missed that." I wandered over to the new boxes and snorted when I picked out the first book. "Rilke? Do you even read German?"

"First editions aren't meant to read. They're to collect."

"The only person who would say anything like that would have to be as rich as Midas, and just as bored. Which, I guess you are. Or will be in another six-ish weeks."

Eric just gave me a long look over his glass, but didn't reply.

I set the book back in the box. "What about that?" I asked, pointing at the larger package.

Eric tossed back the vodka and poured himself another. Dang. Collecting books must really be taxing.

"Open it and see," he said.

So I did, because I really wasn't interested in the way just his posture, leaning rakishly over the counter, made me want to unwrap him instead. What the hell was it about the man and dress clothes? I'd worked for years alongside all manner of stodgy men in suits and ties—not once had they done anything for me. But all Eric had to do was lean over with his shirtsleeves rolled up and top collar unbuttoned, and I was ready to jump a man whom I hated more than just about anyone right now.

Elbow porn. If it's not a thing, it should be.

"Be careful," he said behind me. "It's really fragile."

I didn't turn around. "Thanks, Dad."

But as soon as I had opened the package, it was obvious why he wanted me to be cautious.

"Is this...is it..."

"It's real."

Inside was the painting. *My* painting. The one I'd admired every time I'd been to Celeste's penthouse. The gorgeous original Gustav Klimt that hung in one of her many hallways. Two beautiful figures locked in a scattered embrace. Broken and splintered when you looked at them closely, but such a lovely whole together.

It was my favorite item in that apartment. I looked forward to seeing it every time I visited.

Eric pushed off the counter and came to stand next to me to look at the painting, now perched on top of the boxes and leaning against the wall. It wasn't a large piece—maybe sixteen by twenty-four inches. Just a mid-sized portrait. But so, so beautiful.

"It's for you," he said. "Apparently she told Garrett that she wanted you to have it and forgot to put it in the will. The old guy always hated it anyway and decided to make good on the promise."

"That's very generous of him," I murmured as I floated my hand over the gold leaf. "He could have gotten a fortune from Sotheby's."

Eric shrugged. "Maybe he thought he had enough."

"It should probably be in a museum."

"If that's what you want."

I turned. "Do you want that?"

"I think you should have it," Eric said. "I always liked the look on your face when you saw it. Like you were sharing a secret with these two." He looked up. "Consider it an early birthday gift."

We watched each other, and for a second, I thought maybe we were leaning into each other.

"That dress," he said, his words a little more drawn out than usual. "I like it."

I looked down at the seminal black and white print, with its primary colors blocked in strategic corners. It was structural and overt—Yves Saint Laurent was known for his use of "masculine" aesthetics during the sixties, even in women's fashion. The red matched the violent streak in the back of my hair. In it, I felt strong, but still classic. Like I could say "fuck you" to the dauphin here without feeling like a coarse peasant.

"Well, I didn't wear it for you," I said, pushing past him to retrieve my clutch from an end table.

Eric blinked, finished the remainder of his drink, and walked back to the kitchen to mouse around for some food and a third finger of vodka.

"Still," he said. "You're awfully dressed up for a night at home, even for you. What are the big plans?"

"I'm going downtown for dinner. Orchard Street, I think."

"Oh, nice. There's a great bar down there called the Green Goose. Order a Manhattan. I was just there the other night, and Corinne makes the best in the city."

And there it was—the reminder that Eric was already back to his old ways. Boozing and whoring himself out like a dilettante prince while I sat at home getting carpal tunnel. Not from that, you fiends. From online legal practice tests.

"Are you taking a cab?" he said, following me into my room, where I was filling up my clutch. "Why don't you take my driver? You look too good to be walking around downtown alone."

Eric watched as I brushed my skirt down and checked my painstakingly curled hair. I pulled out my makeup for the final touch-up. He didn't move.

"What are you doing?" I demanded with a mouth still held in an o-position.

Eric shifted uncomfortably. "Do you really have to do that right there? All the goddamn time? This is hard enough as it is, living together."

"You don't want to see it?" I asked. "There are three other bedrooms in this apartment open to you. Move to one of them."

He remained where he was, however, hypnotized as I reapplied my liner and lipstick. His pupils dilated, and he made no attempt to hide the fact that the front of his pants was getting pretty tight.

Ha. About damn time.

"So who are you meeting?" he asked after he sipped his drink a little too quickly.

"A friend." I examined my eyes, making sure my liner hadn't smeared. I wasn't sure if this new magnetic stuff was for me, but it was working so far.

"Which friend?"

"I have a date." I turned around triumphantly and looked around for my phone. Ah, there it was, on the bed. I tried not to think about the time Eric had stripped me down. Right there. On that exact corner.

Eric's gray eyes narrowed. "You have a date?"

I lifted my chin. "I—yeah. A dinner thing. With Matthew Zola, Skylar's prosecutor friend." It was only a half-truth, of course. Yes, Zola and I were having drinks and probably food, but that was about it. And yeah, I was overdressed. Maybe for this exact moment.

"A dinner thing?"

"Why do you keep repeating everything I'm saying? Did you turn into one of Celeste's myna birds while you were going through her stuff?"

"Because I can't believe you're saying it!" He tossed back the vodka like it was water, not 100-proof liquor.

"Please." Suddenly he was much too close. "Like you give a shit. Don't worry, I'll come back here tonight. We won't break any rules, I promise. You'll still get your bazillions."

I pushed him in the chest, but he didn't move. The gold chain swung between the folds of his open collar.

"Maybe you should be a little more worried about yours too, pretty girl."

"What is *that* supposed to mean?"

"It means," Eric said, "that I've had a lifetime of practice dealing with assholes who only wanted to line their pockets with the de Vries name. Get ready, gorgeous. They're going to come after you, too. And last I heard, assistant prosecutors don't make shit. What do you think, should I come with you? Ask Zola to marry me too?"

My hand flew out before I could help myself, but Eric was too quick. He ducked out of reach, and I ended up going flying, right onto my mattress.

"You're an asshole!" I yelped as I struggled to get up.

"Never said otherwise," he agreed nonchalantly, though his face was reddened, as if he'd just run up several flights of stairs.

"How many times over the past few weeks did you tell me, again and again, that we weren't married?" I asked as I chased him back into the kitchen.

Eric's back tensed as he opened and shut the cupboards, presumably looking for food. "I don't know, but—"

"And did you not just insinuate that all I care about was your money anyway?"

"Yeah, but that was just—"

"And did I or did I not just tell you that I would stay here *platonically* for the next two months, despite the fact that it is clearly killing both of us to do it?"

Eric turned with a deep scowl. "You also said you'd go out of your way to make my life a living hell. Is this what you meant? Dressing up like a hot go-go dancer, off to fuck random men while I give myself cirrhosis wondering where you are?" He gulped the rest of his vodka, as if to prove the point.

"Oh, that's rich, coming from the man guzzling martinis all week with God knows how many crabs-infested barflies. I hope you're double-bagging it, Petri. You're going to need an extra-long lab visit next time."

Eric's face darkened even more. "You have no clue where I've been, Jane."

"And I don't need to. I can hear your crooked steps. And I know you, Eric. You only wear the Tom Ford cologne when you're looking to get laid." I leaned across and sniffed again, ignoring the way the familiar scent caused tingles to run up and down my legs.

When I stood up, he was practically vibrating with anger. *Good.*

I grabbed my coat off a barstool and threw it over my dress in a decidedly dramatic fashion. Lauren Bacall had nothing on me tonight.

"I guess I'm keeping both my promises," I told him. "Don't wait up."

FOURTEEN

I took an Uber with a complete stranger just to piss Eric off. It worked—his tall shadow was shaking in his bedroom window as we drove away. Point Jane.

Zola was waiting for me at a lounge in the Lower East Side. It wasn't until the driver pulled up to the address I'd provided that I realized it was in fact the Green Goose, the exact place Eric had recommended. Dammit. Point him.

"Who the fuck names a bar after an off-color water fowl?" I muttered to myself as the car pulled away from the curb. "Goose is the least sexy name on the planet."

But when I entered the bar, I immediately felt at home. The Lower East Side was a long way from the tall, posh buildings that surrounded Central Park. The lounge itself was nestled in the basement of a sagging brick walk-up that had the beaten charm of a building that used to be "bad," but was now repurposed to New York's young bohemian contingent who either hid their Wall Street wealth under ripped jeans and concert tees or lived five to a bedroom just to afford Manhattan rent. As I looked around the lounge, I was just as likely to see biker jackets as crinoline, combat boots as ballet flats. Vintage labels mixed with full-sleeve tattoos, and there were mohawks and bobs alike.

I smiled. These were my people, eclectic and weird. And not for the first time, I wondered what life would be like once I could trade the radius of Central Park for a bit more...diversity.

I approached the bar and flagged down the server, a cute, femme guy with a nose ring.

He gave me a look that should have set my dress on fire. "What'll you have, gorgeous?"

I wrinkled my nose—not just because Eric sometimes called me that, but because this guy looked young enough to be my offspring. Okay, maybe not that young. But close enough.

"Just a PBR." I set a five on the stained bar top.

Nose ring nodded lasciviously. "Vintage. I like it."

I scowled, unsure if he was referring to me, my dress, or my beer choice. My thirtieth birthday was in three days, just before Thanksgiving. I wasn't particularly happy to be entering the more "mature" stage of my life. Weren't people supposed to have their shit together by thirty? My life was messier than ever.

"I had to stop drinking that stuff a few years ago. Gives me heartburn."

I turned to find my "date" for the night taking a seat at the bar next to me, looking a hell of a lot better than any public servant had any right to look.

I'd met Matthew Zola a few times. After the trial that involved Skylar's family, he remained friends with the Crosby-Sterlings, attending their random extravaganzas with the rest of the ragtag group of family and friends they had assembled over the years. He looked the same as ever—about six feet, but with the bearing of a taller man, lean and wiry with shiny dark hair combed neatly back, penetrating eyes fringed with long black lashes, and a full mouth that was always curled in a slight smirk. Zola was a good guy, as clean-cut as it got. But sitting there in a plain leather jacket, white t-shirt, and jeans, he still had an edge that, like his five-o'clock shadow, couldn't quite be erased.

I grinned. "Hey there, stranger. Nice to see you again."

He offered a distinctly European kiss on each cheek—I knew his family was Italian or something, so I wondered if he'd picked it up from them. Then he ordered a beer for himself. The bartender gave him the same firestarter look he'd given me, served the drink, and dashed off to flirt with the other clientele. Zola smiled at me with certified bedroom eyes. And I almost scowled.

Because despite the fact that I was enjoying a drink with a man whom I had flirted with off and on for years, I felt nothing. *Nothing.*

My mojo, that finicky, conniving little bitch, had decided to go missing. Again.

"You're a bit underdressed for the office," I remarked, pushing all negative thoughts to the side.

Zola looked down at his casualwear and smirked. "Sunday. No court. You look...wow. Really great."

"Do you live far from here?"

"Oh, a bit, yeah," Zola replied. "But it's all right. You gave me an excuse to come into the city. I don't get out of Brooklyn much. Traffic, you know."

I nodded, though I really didn't know. Despite having spent the last six months in New York, I wasn't very familiar with much beyond the basic Manhattan neighborhoods below 125th Street. And, of course, one neighborhood in Queens with a rock-climbing gym.

"Where, ah, where in Brooklyn are you from?" I asked, though I wouldn't really know the difference.

Zola finished his sip of beer. "Well, I'm from the Bronx originally, Belmont. My parents still live there, but the rest of us left."

I smiled. Bronx neighborhoods were basically Latin. "The rest of you?"

The lawyer smiled, his mouth twisting sheepishly. "I have a few brothers and sisters."

"How many is a few?"

The smile widened. "Ah, five."

I blinked. "Bit of a stereotype, aren't you? Big Italian family?"

"Italian and Puerto Rican, for your information," he said. But his grin informed me he wasn't irritated by the question. "They're like roaches—I can't get rid of them. My sister lives with me in Brooklyn. Sheepshead Bay. We couldn't afford to be any closer to the city. She's a teacher; I'm an assistant prosecutor. Public servants, you know?"

I did know. Man, oh, *man*, did I know. Chicago was almost as expensive as New York, and I did not relish the idea of going back to a studio. Nope. Wasn't happening. Not if the next almost-six weeks killed me.

But even so, it was nice sitting here with Zola, listening to him talk about completely normal things like his family's crowded townhouse and the price of rent in Brooklyn. It was the first time in months I'd had a conversation with anyone who didn't consider forty-five-dollar steak a cheap meal. I liked it. I missed it.

I drained my PBR and signaled to the bartender for another.

"Someone's looking to get sloshed," Zola remarked.

I shook my head. "Just letting off some steam. So...Skylar mentioned you work in the racketeering bureau here still."

"Oh, yeah. She said you might be interested in a job. The new DA wants to beef up my bureau, actually."

"Oh?" I had no experience with organized crime, but I wouldn't say no to an option.

Zola waggled his dark brows. "Wanna go after some big baddies?"

"Like who?" I asked. "The last big case that made the news were those rich people who paid their kids' way into Harvard and USC."

"Well, we did help the feds a bit on that one. None of them were de Vries, by the way, but we did hear whisperings..."

I remained silent. It wouldn't surprise me in the slightest to find out that anyone in Eric's family had bribed their kids into college.

"Most of the crime we have is on a smaller scale, sure," Zola rattled on. "But you'd be surprised. Every now and then, someone big turns out to be involved. There was this heroin ring in East New York that was ninety percent small-time dealers, plus a basketball star for the Nets. It's crazy, you know? Like these fat cats would rather risk their lives to stuff a few extra thousand in their pockets that they wouldn't even notice." He shook his head. "They do it because they can."

I nodded. I'd heard of similar kinds of thrill seekers in Chicago too.

"So, are you taking the bar in February or have you applied for reciprocity?" Zola asked, referring to the potential to waive the UBE because I already had admission in Illinois.

I nodded. "I applied, but in the meantime, I'm studying for February. I have to take the NYLE in December anyway."

Zola waved away that concern. "My dog could pass the NYLE."

"You have a dog? What kind?"

He scoffed. "I'm a lawyer. I don't have time for a dog. I meant that figuratively."

I grinned back. Zola was cute when he was awkward. Cute, and yet, still doing absolutely nothing for me. Which was weird, because the man was fucking gorgeous.

He arched an eyebrow at me. "So, here's my real question, though. Why in the hell do you want to practice law when you just married into one of the most powerful families in New York?"

I sighed. "You heard about that, did you?"

"Jane, it was on the cover of every paper in the city. The whole world heard about it. But I, uh..." He pointed his beer bottle at my hand. "I can't help notice there's something missing there."

I examined my naked finger, then tucked it into my lap. "You want to hear the real joke?"

He cocked his head, waiting.

I shrugged. "It's fake. All of it. Eric had to get married for money...and now that Celeste died, we found out that she adjusted her will. We only have to cohabitate through the end of the year, and then we're done. No marriage. Nothing."

"Ah," he replied. "Which explains why you want to work. You want out of their shadow."

I held a finger in the air like a lightbulb had just appeared. "Bingo."

Zola examined me for a moment, tapping his lips. "Don't hate me for saying this, but that doesn't look like the face of someone who's only marrying for money."

"Oh?" I asked. "And what kind of face does it look like, then? Inexplicably fabulous, I hope."

"It looks sort of like someone with a broken heart," he said, then turned his attention back to his beer. "So why did you really call me? You could have just sent me your resume if you wanted a job."

"I need..." I looked up with sudden awareness. "Hold on." I pulled a dollar from my purse and handed it to him. "Can I trust you?"

Zola looked at the dollar. "Ah, shit, Jane. You know I can't take that."

"It's not against the law."

His slim black brow rose. "Actually, it is. Prosecutors can't have a private practice here. I guess you're not that far through the course yet, are you?"

I sighed and withdrew the bill. When I set my hand back on the bar, Zola covered it with his own. I looked up.

"I can't be your lawyer," he said. "But I am a friend. And you can trust that. Are you into something?"

I shook my head, causing my hair to move around my face. "No, not...not me."

"Eric, then?"

"Maybe. I don't know."

Zola's dark eyes were earnest, but kind. "Tell me."

For a moment, I was struck with indecision. This was exactly what Eric was scared of. That I would share his secrets, my biological father's secrets, and imperil both of us. He was convinced that Carson had some way of listening or tracking or seeing whether or not we were telling the truth.

Gingerly, I removed my phone from my purse and stared at it for a long time. I felt paranoid just wondering about it. Not like I-had-one-too-many-hits-on-a-bong paranoid. Like Edward Snowden paranoid.

But Zola didn't seem surprised when I dropped the phone camera-first into my glass of water.

"You know, you could have just asked the bartender to put it in the microwave over there," he remarked as we watched it sink to the bottom of the pint glass.

I sighed. "Some say I have a flair for drama. They might be right."

His black brow rose again. "I think you better tell me exactly what's going on, Jane."

I took a deep breath, then checked around the bar. Yeah. Even with my phone deep-sea diving, I still didn't feel safe. "What do you say we go for a walk?"

Zola chuckled. "You've watched too many gangster movies."

"No, I'm just antsy. Come on, Matlock, let's get some air."

———

WE MEANDERED DOWN ORCHARD STREET, and Zola shoved his hands into the pockets of his jacket while he waited patiently for me to speak. I recognized the trick. Sometimes when you question a witness, the best thing to do is wait them out.

We turned right onto Houston, and it wasn't until we passed Katz's, the famous diner where Meg Ryan faked an orgasm in *When Harry Met Sally*, that I finally started talking, soothed by the hum of traffic.

"Have you ever seen anything to do with secret societies?" I asked.

Zola peered at me. "What, like the Illuminati? I didn't take you for a conspiracy theorist, Jane."

I shook my head. "No, not like that. More like Skull and Bones."

"Those Yale assholes?"

I chuckled. "It's a real thing."

"Yeah, I know it is," Zola said. "Half the criminal defense attorneys in the city went to Ivies like that. Meanwhile, I made do with CUNY."

I nodded, but didn't mention my alma mater. Since Zola knew Skylar and Brandon, he also knew that Thanksgiving at her house was basically a Harvard alumni party.

"So, what?" he asked. "Eric's in a society, and you don't like it? Don't those guys just dabble in some mild vandalism and wear hoods and shit?"

I giggled. Then sighed. And then opened my mouth, and before I realized it, the entire story flooded out. The wedding. The coin around Eric's neck and the other strange men who wore ones just like it. My biological father, John Carson. And my mother, who was scared shitless of him.

The way Eric seemed to be too.

"So, wait, you're telling me Eric was abducted for ten fucking days by a bunch of Latin-loving assholes who wear matching jewelry?"

I chuckled. I quite liked that characterization.

"And no one reported it?" Zola prodded further. "Why didn't you call the police?"

I rolled my eyes. "I was a little mad, you know."

He shook his head. "That's cold, Jane."

"Skylar called for us." I stared at the sidewalk, ashamed. Why hadn't I looked harder?

"And what did they say?"

"Later that evening, they received a call from Eric saying he was fine," I said. "Only that he wanted us to leave him alone, and he'd be back for the funeral. They dropped it."

The family had bought it, mostly because he had done it once before. So I bought it too. It had stung like hell, but somehow I'd swallowed that pill right alongside being left at the altar.

"And now this...society...headed by your long-lost dad...is forcing you to live together without sex for sixty days?" Zola frowned.

I did too. It did sound weird. "I just...something is off. Why would Eric agree to it if they hadn't done something to him? Something really, really awful? His face was all messed up when he came back. And then Carson threatened me too, you know. Plus that stuff he told my mom."

"Jane, that's speculative at best, and you know it. What if Eric was just pissed and wanted some space? What if—and I really hate to say this—what if he realized he just didn't want to get married?"

"Because he said he loved me!" I shouted, loud enough for a couple of passersby to startle. But as soon as I was done, I immediately felt exactly like someone I had never wanted to be—that girl. The one who says her asshole boyfriend is an angel when everyone's not looking. I might as well have yelled "you don't know him like I do!"

Zola, to his credit, just continued walking, unruffled. But I knew what he was thinking. And I was right.

"Jane," he said after another block had passed. "I'm going to suggest something you're probably not going to want to hear. I don't know you. And I don't know Eric. But I do know that people do weird things when they are grieving—"

I shook my head. "No."

"And a lot of guys will say a lot of things to get laid—"

"No, no, no—"

"And from what you've been telling me, it sounds like you two have a history of maybe being a little vindictive with each other. So maybe—"

"Listen," I snapped. "Eric left me one way and returned ten days later with a black eye and some pretty insane paranoia. I guarantee if you saw us together, you'd understand what I'm talking about."

Zola gave a long, low exhale. "What makes you think that I—"

"Because half of what you do is read people, Zola," I interrupted for the last time. "I know that because I used to do it too. You're telling me that after, what, seven, ten years cross-examining people who are determined not to snitch, you don't know if someone is lying? If they are feigning indifference? If they care about something when they say they don't?"

We stopped, finding ourselves at last at the end of the island. Across the FDR highway and the East River twinkled the lights of Brooklyn. To the south lay the Williamsburg bridge, under which I could see the tail end of a small container vessel. It wasn't one of the de Vries boats—they were all much bigger and operated out of South Street and New Jersey. But it still made me think of the man who owned them all.

"Fine," Zola relented at last. "Fine, I'll take a look. But, Jane?"

I turned. "What?"

"When I tell you there's nothing there, you have to believe me, all right?"

I smiled. "When you tell me that, I'll believe you. But you won't."

FIFTEEN

Zola and I meandered back down Houston and split a pastrami sandwich at Katz's—I couldn't resist—before he took the train back to Brooklyn. I got a cab back uptown and considered the best way to sneak back into my room, sight unseen. My rage had faded, and now I just felt full and tired. I wanted nothing more than to take a hot shower, curl up in my bed, and try to forget the other, much more comfortable bed where I had spent most of the last six months happier than I'd ever been.

That was the real loss. It wasn't a ring on my finger or millions of dollars. It was that in the darkness with him, when I had watched the moon cast its blue light over his smooth skin, I had felt for the first time in my life that I wasn't just a black sheep, rebel daughter, quirky friend. With him, I had found my niche, like a crooked jigsaw piece snapping into its place. I had belonged. Until he cast me out.

I entered the dark apartment with heavy feet. Eric was out, I realized with an even heavier heart. I shouldn't have been surprised. I had thrown my date-that-wasn't-a-date in his face, and he had already been half drunk when I left. It would have been completely in character for him to finish the bottle and find someone else to temper his frustration. Probably on her knees.

I hated that I knew that's what he would do.

Maybe Zola was right after all. Maybe I was just a pathetic, jealous ex.

"Did you have a nice time?"

"Ahhh!"

I jumped at the sudden sound of Eric's deep voice reverberating through the darkness. I dropped my purse and whirled around. As my eyes adjusted, I spotted him in one of the Danish chairs by the big bay window. The moonlight cast his face with that bluish glow I'd just been remembering, making the tips of his blond hair appear almost metallic and the rest of him—half-clothed in nothing but his slacks from earlier—look like a carved statue.

A work of art.

I pressed my hand to my racing heart. "What are you doing here?"

Eric slouched further and toyed with something in his hand. His necklace dangled from his fingers, the streetlight reflecting off the gold coin as it twisted and turned on its chain.

"I live here," he said acerbically.

I rolled my eyes, then hung my coat in the closet and set my clutch on the foyer table. "I know that. I just mean, what are you doing here, sitting in the dark? You look like you're ten seconds from shoving your head in the oven."

Eric snorted. "Don't tempt me."

I didn't reply. I didn't like the serious undercurrent in that suggestion, and suddenly I felt guilty for even joking about suicide.

"I was just sitting here thinking about our little situation," he said, his tone almost dangerous. "Torturing myself. Coming to terms with the fact that I just might be a bit of a masochist." He blinked, his eyes two bright, angry stars. "I always choose women I can't have. First Penny. Now you. It's like a sick fetish."

I stared at him, unsure of what to make of this. Eric wasn't usually the type for drama—that was my card.

"But," he continued, "if I'm going to be a glutton for punishment, I might as well finish the job."

I blinked. "What does that mean?"

Eric rose slowly from the chair and padded across the dark room. He looked a mess—rumpled hair, shadowed eyes—but an absolutely gorgeous, shirtless mess as he stalked toward me.

"I've been trying to make this easy on you," he said with every careful, if slightly wobbly step. "But you are fucking determined to make it as hard as you can, aren't you?"

"You asked for this," I replied, taking a step back. "I would have just walked away."

Eric tipped his head back, causing a few rumpled blond locks to fall back, and emitted a harsh laugh at the ceiling. "I suppose that's what you're good at, right? Just walking away?"

My rage returned. "I'm sorry, but *I* was the one who was jilted at the altar, asshole. Not you."

Eric's head jerked upright like it was attached to a rubber band. "You will *never* understand what that cost me, Jane. What *you* cost me."

"You're right. Not if you don't tell me."

He stared at me for a long time, quivering a bit, whether from anger or drink, I couldn't tell.

"Do you have any idea what I went through when I was... gone?" he growled. "For you? Do you?"

I stilled. This was the first time he'd said more than a few words about what had happened to him during those ten days. Apparently, he'd had enough vodka that it turned into truth serum, but only with vague, ambivalent bullshit.

"How much?" I dared him. *Tell me. Don't tell me. Tell me* something.

"They wanted me to forget about you," he said before taking another long swig from the bottle. "And they were willing to hurt me to make sure I would. And they did. A lot."

I remained quiet, waiting for him to tell me more. As an ADA, I had seen more evidence of physical crimes than most ever would, but the idea of someone hurting Eric made me feel sick. And violent. And furious. So much more than I felt toward him.

"It hurt so much. But not as much as knowing you were fucking some other man tonight." His voice was like gravel, coarse and cruel. He took another step forward, caging me against the counter. "Knowing some other asshole was right where only *I* am supposed to be. Fucking. Killed."

I scrambled onto a stool. Eric moved between my legs, but still didn't touch me. He just...hovered.

Desire sliced through me. I wanted to shove him away and yank him close at the same time. Kiss him and slap him all at once. And Eric, ever the statue, didn't move a single tensed muscle.

"Pain," he whispered. "Pain is all I feel. Except when I'm with you. But now, that hurts too."

One by one, my defenses fell.

"What if...what if I told you we did nothing?" I asked

Eric's hot gaze carved a path up and down my body. "Is that the truth? Don't lie to me."

I nodded. "It's the truth."

"Did you want to?"

I wanted to say no, but my voice was frozen by the harsh hold of his eyes. Eric sucked in a breath, then brought the vodka bottle to his mouth and slowly licked around the edge before tipping it up and emptying it completely. His full lips wrapped around the thick glass, and I stared enviously at the sight of his tongue, small and pink, slipping inside the bottle. Twirling. Teasing.

Fuck.

Eric floated his other hand over my body, then reached over my shoulder and plucked a pussy willow branch from the bouquet on the counter. The soft nubs drifted over my neck, pressing just hard enough not to tickle, but light enough to elicit a trail of goose bumps. I remained silent as Eric brushed the branch over my shoulder and down my arm. Completely benign, perfectly unremarkable places. And yet, as the fronds pulled at my neckline and tickled the hollows under my jaw, I had never been more turned on.

"Eric," I whispered, unable to move.

He just watched the progress of the soft buds as they floated down to my collarbone and back up my neck again.

"What about now?" he murmured, hypnotized by the path of the bud. "Do you want to now?"

I gulped. Then I nodded. I couldn't lie.

His expression flashed with satisfaction.

"I can't touch you," he said. His eyes met mine, big and pleading, as if to say, *but I wish I could.*

I squirmed, both out of frustration and commiseration. I understood he was scared, even if I didn't fully comprehend why. Just as I also understood the currents of desire flowing back and forth between us were unavoidable. Wanting this man was as natural as breathing.

Before I could stop myself, I unzipped my dress, then pulled my arms out of it, one at a time. I let the structured fabric drop, leaving me bare from the waist up.

Eric grunted and sucked on his lower lip as he looked me over. I moaned softly. I wanted to do that.

The pussy willow branch painted a path over my breasts, between their taut peaks, over their swollen nipples, through the shadow of their curves. I twisted slightly back and forth, begging wordlessly for a stronger touch, a pinch, a slap. When I closed my eyes, I could almost imagine it was his fingers, not a flower bud teasing my skin into a pebbled frenzy. I could almost pretend he was tracing kisses around the tip of one nipple, then the other.

I sucked in a breath. When I opened my eyes, Eric was biting his lip so hard the skin around his teeth had turned white. Like a magnet, his gaze met mine, and a low, guttural groan emerged from deep in his chest.

Slowly, almost like I was trying to touch a wild animal, I brought my hands up to clasp his cheeks, but he shook his head against the motion.

"We can't," he said. The growl was low. "You know that, Jane."

We were inches from each other. It wouldn't take much. All I had to do was lean forward, tap my lips to his, and he wouldn't have been able to do a thing to stop me.

But I also knew I wouldn't do anything without his consent, just like he'd never do anything without mine. No matter what, that was the one promise neither of us had ever broken. As mad as I was, I wouldn't start now.

"Why?" I whispered, unable to keep the quake from my voice.

Eric's entire body shook. "Please believe me," he said, so quietly he almost mouthed it.

"But I can, right?"

His eyes opened again, newly sharpened. "You can…"

"Do it?"

I took the pussy willow and tossed it over my shoulder, onto the counter. Eric watched, transfixed, as I brought my hands to my breasts.

"Yesssss," he hissed as I took each nipple between a forefinger and thumb, then pulled slightly, plucking on them like strings on a violin.

He set the empty vodka bottle on the counter. While I continued to torture myself in the way I wished to *God* he would, Eric unbuckled his belt and unzipped his pants. He reached into his boxers and pulled out his erection, which, in my expert opinion, looked painfully hard. He shuddered as he wrapped his hand around it, and his gaze quickly dropped between my legs. It was immediately evident what he wanted.

"Do it," he whispered. "Show me, pretty girl."

The name. *That fucking name.* It was so benign, so innocuous, I should have been even angrier that he used it whenever he wanted. He knew its Pavlovian effect. He knew I couldn't say no when I heard its siren call.

Nor would I now. Because in truth, I wanted the release too. I wanted to feel someone's touch—if not his, then mine—push my skirts up to my waist. I wanted to feel the tickle of hands on my inner thighs, the slight intrusion of a pair of fingers pulling aside my underwear.

So I did it. I peeled off my tights and underwear and let the dress fall to the floor. Then I sat back on the stool, feeling every bit the rebel and the work of art this man had always proclaimed me. I yearned for his touch, so I supplied it for myself, slipping one finger, then two over my clit while my other hand continued to pinch and pull at my breasts. I leaned back against the counter, deliciously on display as I worked on my own pleasure, entranced as much by the sight of Eric fisting his own sex in rhythm with my fingers.

"Oh!" I cried out.

But Eric paused his own ministrations—a pause that looked as painful as my own—held a finger to his mouth, and shook his head. And I knew without arguing that that was my choice. Do this silently, or not at all.

Wildly, I nodded. *Yes, I understand.*

His hand started to move again, this time faster. A few times, the tip of his cock just barely touched my thigh in a wet, dewy kiss of skin on skin that made Eric jerk and bite back a moan himself.

My fingers moved faster as well. I wanted this so badly, and that familiar precipice was approaching more rapidly than it ever had. My head was thrown back, eyes clenched shut as I braced myself for the fall into ecstasy. But just as I was about to topple over, another intrusion tugged me back into the present.

Something cold. Something hard. Rounded, but still blunt-edged.

I looked down to find Eric still massaging his cock, but with his other hand slipping the tapered end of the empty vodka bottle between my thighs. He held it at the end and stood between my legs.

"Holy shit," I whispered, but made no move to stop him. Real talk: if I had been alone in my room, I would have already taken care of the job with my rabbit. Three times over. My legs were already splayed open through no movement I could recall —I was dying for something down there. No, I was dying for *him* down there. And he knew it.

But he wouldn't break his word. Even now.

"Is this—is it okay?" he asked, his voice barely above a hum.

I stared harder. The bottle didn't move, poised just at the juncture of my legs, but not actually invading that private space.

But yes, he was really doing this. I looked at him. And then I nodded again.

"Do-do it," I told him.

A hint of a smile lifted on one side of his face.

The bottle slid in maybe an inch. Maybe less. I rocked my hips into it. Eric pushed it in a little further. It was the hottest thing I'd ever seen.

Eric's gray eyes met mine. "Don't stop, pretty girl."

Maybe it was the fact that I'd barely heard that name in weeks, and he'd already used it twice in the last few minutes. Maybe it was the fact that as hard as I tried *not* to think about Eric whenever I did pleasure myself, his face, his entire body, always appeared. As if attached to an electric current guided by those two words like light switches, my fingers started moving again, with the same rhythm as the cool glass sliding in and out of me, as the steady movement of Eric's fist around his cock. The three of us moved together, almost as one—fingers, bottle, fingers, a crazy finger trap of a situation, until I was practically lying on the counter, open to whatever penetration he was willing to give.

Eric pushed the bottle in again. My fingers pressed harder. I exploded. And so did he.

Ahhhhhhhhh! I opened my mouth in a soundless scream, my entire body seized with pleasure, but also pain of this man's absence. Eric shook over me, every beautiful muscle in his sculpted body on display as he emptied himself over my thighs, my stomach, even my breasts.

His mouth shivered too, hovering maybe a millimeter from mine as he braced himself on the counter's edge, trying to catch his breath. His lips, soft and inviting, brushed mine so lightly, I wasn't completely sure they actually did, or if it was just the heat of his breath. Eric shuddered, a full-body movement that seemed to move through mine like a wave. Then he closed his eyes and stood up. The bottle slipped out, and I collapsed against the counter.

"Bed," he said hoarsely while he moved around to toss the bottle in the garbage.

Unable to move while he padded into his room to clean up, I sat there. I swallowed heavily, then reached around to grab a napkin off the counter—one of an expensive monogrammed set we'd received as wedding gifts from an Astor or a van Dusen cousin. I swiped the linen over my legs, almost rueful to clean off the evidence of Eric's loss of control.

Pathetic. I was so pathetic.

Was this all we were anymore? Would we dance around each other in a tense tango for the next fortyish or so day until we couldn't fucking take it? Give up to silent, tortured orgasms in vodka-infused darkness?

Whatever happened to real, functional relationships?

Have you ever had one of those, Jane Brain?

I shook my head. I did not want to think about my dad—either of them—at a moment like this.

The sound of Eric's knuckles rapping on his doorframe pulled me out of my thoughts. I turned to find his tall, elegant body silhouetted in his bedroom door. He tipped his head, remaining silent, though his meaning was clear.

I finished cleaning myself off, then abandoned the wreckage of my dress and the napkin to follow the man wordlessly into his room—what was our room. I followed him onto the plush king bed, allowed him to wrap me in the duvet before sliding under it himself, lying on his side to face me.

He smiled, and the bittersweetness of it broke my heart and made it sing all at the same time.

"Thank you," he mouthed without sound.

I just nodded. And together we lay, watching each other as sleep crept nearer.

But for some minutes more, after Eric had drifted off, I considered: how could I still love someone I hated this much? How could I hate someone I loved so intensely?

Both questions swam around my mind in circles for a long time as I watched him sleep. And by the time my eyelids drooped shut, I didn't have any more answers than when I started thinking. I wasn't sure I would ever know.

SIXTEEN

B y the time I meandered into the kitchen the next morning, Eric had left for work. Again. And when I waited up that night for him to return—all I wanted to do was talk about that strange interlude—I ended up falling asleep on the couch at some time past midnight. But I woke again in his room the next morning, this time fully clothed. Apparently, someone broke his "no touching" rule to carry me to bed.

The next day I went to sleep in my own room, but when I woke up the following morning, there was a head-shaped imprint on the pillow next to mine. The night after that, I tossed and turned on the night of a very uneventful thirtieth birthday after dodging my mother's calls and accepting a few messages from friends. But I did nothing else to celebrate, alone until Eric appeared in my doorway in nothing but his briefs, tipped his head silently toward his room, and padded back into it. Of course, I followed.

On the pillow, there was a book wrapped in coarse brown paper. He nodded, and I unwrapped it carefully, not needing to be told I should keep quiet. Inside was a large book of Mario Testino—one of my favorite fashion photographers. The images were lush and rich and beautiful. Just like the man in front of me.

"Happy birthday, Jane," he whispered as his fingertips floated over mine.

Then he lay down, and I followed suit. We blinked at each other for a long time in the darkness, and eventually fell asleep, watching, but not touching, resting, but not speaking.

On Thursday morning, I walked into the kitchen to find Eric making coffee.

"You're actually here," I said as I took a seat at the counter.

He looked up from his plunger contraption. I wasn't allowed to mess with Eric's designated coffee-making area of the kitchen —it looked like a laboratory, not a cooking station.

"Oh," he said. "Well, yeah. We have to leave in about an hour."

I frowned at his tone. Was there something I was missing? "Where are we going?"

"Boston, right? You're going to Skylar and Brandon's too, aren't you?"

Still sleepy, I looked around the apartment, and things suddenly clicked. It was Thursday. Of course. Thanksgiving. I was expected in Boston this afternoon.

I swung back around. "Um, no. You are not going to Boston."

Eric pressed the button on his milk frother. "What? Of course I am."

I shook my head vehemently. "No, you're *not*. I need time with Skylar. I don't know what the hell we've been doing for the last four days—"

"*Nothing*," Eric interrupted. "We've been doing absolutely nothing."

His utter denial of all the intimacy that was still between us just made me that much angrier.

"*Exactly!*" I snapped. "No touching, right? I'm basically living in a strip club parody."

"Jane!"

"Well, just because I have to share this fucking apartment with you like the ghost of gentlemen's clubs past doesn't mean I have to share my holidays too. I'm going to see my best friend. I don't need you tagging along like Casper."

Eric worried his jaw for a moment until the frother beeped behind him. He gave me a view of his t-shirt-clad back while he finished making his drink. "Brandon invited me last weekend, Jane."

"So, what? Skylar invited me weeks ago."

He carried two mugs of perfectly foamed cafe au laits to the counter and set one in front of me. "Brandon was my best man," he said calmly.

"Skylar was *my* maid of honor," I countered.

"I'm their kids' godparent."

"So am I!" I exploded. I shoved a hand into my hair, then angrily tied it up into a bun. "I'm sorry, but this is bullshit. I have claims on the Crosby-Sterlings in the event of a split. They are *my* home base, not yours. Go share a turkey with Nina and Calvin. You'll have plenty of relatives eager to kiss your feet now that you've officially been named in the will. It will be fun."

Eric sighed and rubbed his jaw, which was covered with an irritatingly sexy layer of stubble this morning. "Did it ever occur to you that I might need a break from this situation as much as you?" He blinked, and the shadow of his lashes hung heavily over his cheekbones. "It hasn't been easy on me either."

The look on his face from Sunday flashed through my mind. *Pain*, he'd said. *Pain is all I feel. Except when I'm with you.*

My shoulders slumped. I really didn't want him there, but

not because I truly hated him. And he had a point—it was this situation that was eating us up, not each other. When he was around, I felt so confused. It was impossible to compartmentalize my life the way Carson insisted, and even harder to compart-mentalize my emotions. Being around Skylar and Brandon, who had such an obviously loving marriage, would only cast Eric's and my situation into higher relief against theirs.

But Eric, who could usually read me enough to understand my body language, still didn't offer to stay. Which told me that, yes, he probably needed the companionship of his real friends as much as I did. Or maybe he was worried about meeting the requirements of the will. Did cohabitation also leave no room for holidays or vacations?

Fuck.

I'd never know.

"Fine." I pushed off the stool and stomped back into my room to pack, then immediately turned back and swiped my coffee off the counter.

Eric just watched with an irritating smirk.

"I'm only accepting this because you don't want to ride all the way to Boston with me uncaffeinated." I avoided his eyes as I took a long sip. Lord, the boy really did know his way around a French press or whatever that thing was. Much better than the instant crap I was drinking in Chicago.

"Whatever you say, Lefferts." Eric turned to clean up.

I paused by my bedroom. "And to be perfectly clear, we're staying in separate bedrooms."

Behind me, there was a distinct snort. I slammed the door.

"The helicopter leaves at noon," Eric called through the walls. "Tony will drive our bags up later."

I opened the door and peeked back out. "Helicopter? Try the Chinatown bus, buddy. We may be rich, but we're not assholes."

Eric rolled his eyes, but didn't stop drinking his coffee. He also didn't even bother giving an answer. Because, of course, the smug bastard knew I wouldn't hesitate to trade a four-hour bus ride for private helicopter. Even if it meant I was harnessed next to his arrogant ass.

———

SHORTER RIDE OR NOT, Eric's presence on the way to Skylar and Brandon's house seemed to exist solely to piss me off. For the entire flight to Boston, he was determined to play Annoying Tour Guide, constantly smacking his arm across my chest to point out various boring lighthouses and townships on the coast. On the way to Brookline from the helipad, he kept trying to fix my clothes. My hair was messed up from the headphones, he said. And by his metric, my tag was showing at least five separate times. I wasn't sure what tag that was, since I had made the fucking shirt myself. Discovering the cherry-printed silk at a fabric shop in Albany Park was a coup last year.

By the time we had picked up the wine and challah bread on our way to the house, I was about ready to smack him. He had traded items with me four times before we even got into the car.

"Here, let me hold that," he said, sticking the wine bottle between his legs so he could grab my seatbelt and latch me in.

"OhmyGodyouhavetostop!" I blurted out, batting his hands away. "Why are you so damn fussy today? I can buckle myself, for fuck's sake!"

Eric shrank back into his seat, then clutched the wine and looked out the window.

"No reason," he mumbled.

"Obviously it's not no reason," I retorted. "I think the last time someone fastened my seatbelt for me, I was five. What's up?"

His eyes darted toward the Town Car driver, then back to me before he folded his arms across his chest.

"Nothing," he said as the car turned down Skylar and Brandon's street. "I was just trying to be nice."

"Well, next time you want to be nice, treat me like an adult, not a toddler."

He shot a sly look my way. "Pretty sure I'm not allowed to do that anymore."

My mouth dropped. His thumb drifted over the top of the wine bottle, and Eric smiled—the kind of smile that would have had me falling out of my seat if I had anywhere to go. My heart gave a loud thump. I squirmed uncomfortably.

Bastard.

Eric was still smirking when our Town Car pulled into Brandon and Skylar's circular driveway.

"Aunt Janey!"

I opened the door to find Jenny, Brandon and Skylar's daughter, pelting out of the house and into my arms. Luis, her chubby brother who actually *was* a toddler, made a beeline for Eric, who picked him up.

"Hey, kiddo!" I swept the little girl into a bear hug. "How's kindergarten, eh? Are you murdering the ABCs?"

"Murder?" Jenny asked, her little red brows screwing up in confusion. She turned to where Skylar was following the kids out the front door. "Mommy, what's murder?"

Skylar gave me an exasperated look. "Jane."

Beside me, Eric chuckled. "Don't listen to your inappropriate Aunt Jane," he said to Luis, taking the little boy's hand and waving it back at him. "She's a bad influence."

Luis squealed, the kind of full-throated giggle that only children under three can pull off. Then he kicked his legs furiously until Eric set him down, freeing him to sprint toward the orchard around the side of the house.

"Well, you better go get him," Skylar said as we all watched Luis's crooked run for the trees. "He'll just keep going until someone tracks him down."

"Yes, ma'am." Eric grinned, gave her a mini-salute, and jogged after Luis.

Skylar turned to me and her daughter. "Jen, go tell Daddy that *his* guest is here, okay?"

Jenny nodded and headed back into the house after I set her down. Skylar rubbed my arm while we watched Eric chase Luis around in the trees. What was it about watching a full-grown man get down on the level of a small child? Every butterfly in my stomach was flapping around in there.

"I didn't know Brandon invited him," Skylar said apologetically. "He did it last week when I was at work."

I shrugged, guilty that my friend felt she had to choose sides at all.

"Don't worry about it," I said. "I should have invited him myself."

"That's magnanimous of you."

"Sometimes I can be the bigger person. It doesn't happen often, but I think I can manage it as long as we keep ten feet between us."

Skylar pressed her lips together—it was obvious she still thought this whole thing was ridiculous. She wasn't wrong.

I turned toward the front door. "Let's go inside. It's freezing, and I'm ready to eat my weight in mashed potatoes. If I can't have sex, a carb coma is the next best thing."

———

"SO, what's with the construction site on the other side of the orchard?" Eric asked after we had said our hellos to the rest of Skylar and Brandon's family. He was referring to one of the two outer cottages, which had looked from the outside like it was being completely gutted.

Skylar and Brandon's parents—Ray, Susan, and Danny—were camped out in the living room watching football with the kids while Sarah, Skylar's bubbe, shooed everyone out of the kitchen. The four of us lounged in the solarium, munching on carrot sticks and trying not to get too drunk on empty stomachs. I accepted a glass of wine from Skylar while Brandon fixed Eric a vodka on the rocks.

Eric smirked at me over his drink and took a sip.

"It's my new lab," Brandon said proudly.

"Sterling Labs just won a big government contract," Skylar said. "Which, of course, Brandon took to mean he needed to construct an entire facility on our property."

"Hey, I didn't want to leave you and the kids all day long," Brandon said. "If I had to commute to MIT, I'd never be home. You wouldn't like that, would you?"

"I just told him it couldn't actually be in the house. Some of us have issues with work-life boundaries."

"I'm sorry, who was it who brought home three boxes of depositions last weekend?" Brandon retorted as he flopped next to Skylar on the loveseat. He slung his arm good-naturedly around his wife and kissed her fondly. "I'm just kidding, Red. She's a killer, this one. *Boston Magazine* is doing a profile on my girl, did you hear?"

"No, I didn't," I murmured, unable to stop watching the way my friend glowed under her husband's affections.

Eric's shoulder brushed mine. It wasn't an arm around my waist, but when I started at the sudden contact, then looked at him, he was also watching our friends with naked envy. He also did not move away.

"Would you like a tour?" Brandon asked.

I didn't, but it was obvious by the look on Brandon's face that he was dying to give us one.

"Oh, go ahead," Skylar said, getting up. "You guys can be his fresh audience while Bubbe and I finish up. I still have to make the cranberry sauce."

"And that's all you're allowed to do!" Sarah piped up from the kitchen, where she was currently whipping a giant batch of potatoes.

Eric and I followed Brandon out of the main house and across the orchard that was still hanging with a few lingering leaves. The construction site around the cottage had been abandoned during the holiday, but it was clear that some major work was going on.

"Cottage" was a misnomer. When Skylar and Brandon originally bought the property, it had come with two granny flats—one-story, two-bedroom guesthouses that they had originally imagined for Skylar's dad and grandmother to use. But Sarah had been adamant about staying in her own house, and where she went, her son did too. So they had simply been a guest lodging for people like me.

Until now, apparently. Eric and I followed Brandon into the gutted house, which bore absolutely no resemblance to the quaint place where I had stayed several times. The walls had been completely demolished, the carpeted floors torn up, and the kitchen was all but eradicated.

"This is remodeled?" Eric asked doubtfully.

Brandon shook his head as he stepped around some of the debris. "Oh, ha. No. The top floor is the last step. The house had to be elevated first so we could dig the downstairs."

"Dig?" I said. I remembered some construction going on here a few weeks ago, but hadn't asked about it, as upset as I was. Now I felt kind of dumb for not noticing more.

Brandon stopped in front of a thick steel door. Eric and I

watched as he pressed his thumb to a fingerprint scanner, unlocking a set of stairs into the ground. "I hope you're not scared of enclosed spaces."

"Suddenly I feel like I'm in the middle of a video game," I said. "Do people still play the Legend of Zelda?"

"Only the best ones," Brandon replied.

We followed him down the stairs, past another code-guarded door, and into a room that was at least twice the size of the entire structure above us. It was clean, a far cry from the lab I remembered in the attic of the main house. Two of the walls were lined with stainless steel worktables, a bank of dark-screened computers stood against the far wall, and a small conference table occupied the middle of the room.

"This is the lab," Brandon said with supreme satisfaction. "Sterling Labs is getting serious."

"It seems more like a bunker," I remarked. "Are we expecting a nuclear attack anytime soon?"

Beside me, Eric chuckled.

Brandon just tipped his head from side to side good-naturedly, like it was an actual possibility. "I don't know about that," he said. "But part of the requirement of the contract was that we had certain security measures in place. I did my part. I consider it an investment in my company."

I looked around doubtfully. "You don't think this is a little overkill, Ian Fleming? I feel like I'm in Q's lab from MI-6."

Again, I was rewarded with a snort beside me.

"Spies are real," Brandon argued. "And everywhere, according to the State Department." He turned to Eric. "Speaking of which. Are you still trying to find..."

He trailed off with a glance at me—obviously indicating that he would wait until I was gone to continue the conversation.

I snapped a finger in front of him. "Right here, gentlemen."

"It's fine," Eric said. "And yeah, I am."

"You're trying to find what?" I asked, irritated at being left out of the loop.

"The bug," Eric said. "The way that...you know...the way he knows if..."

I blinked, and then his ambiguity made sense. Carson. The bug. Eric was trying to figure out how we were being tracked. *If*, I thought, *we were being tracked at all*. I honestly wasn't convinced it was more than a stupid threat.

"I don't think it's visual," Eric was saying to Brandon. "If it was...we would have heard from him. About certain things." He glanced at me, and his ears turned slightly pink.

Because you fucked me with a vodka bottle? I didn't say it out loud, but the haughty look on Eric's face told me he knew exactly what I was thinking.

"I'm guessing it's some kind of audio signal," he continued. "But I can't for the fucking life of me figure out what it is. Tony scans the apartment every day before I go in. My office too. We can't find a damn thing."

"Why do you think it's audio?" I asked. "Why do you even think there's a signal at all?"

Eric turned to me, a bit dejected. "Because of this." He pulled out his phone and swiped to a message before handing it to me.

Titan: Be careful. You are getting attached.

I scrolled up and down, but that was all there was. No exchange. Nothing. I looked up. "That's it?"

"Look at the time stamp."

12:32 *A.M.*

I handed the phone back to him.

"That was about an hour after you returned from your... date," Eric said, just barely unable to hide the acerbity in his voice.

I opened my mouth, then closed it. Suddenly my forearms were covered in goose pimples. We'd fought. He hadn't said much out loud that night, but it certainly would have revealed his jealousy.

"That's all?" I couldn't help but wonder. "Just 'be careful.'"

Eric's eyebrow rose. "Why would there be anything more?" he asked, though his expression dared me to say it out loud for the same reason I knew he would not—that we were somehow quiet enough that no one had understood what we were doing.

I frowned. Certain things made sense now. Why he was so quiet—deathly so—in the apartment. Why he never seemed to respond to anything in meaningful ways. Why he never asked me verbally to sleep with him, but found ways to make it happen anyway.

He knew I wouldn't be able to stay quiet if we did what both of us were dying to do. But he couldn't stop himself completely either.

I wasn't sure if I should be mad or satisfied by the realization. *Maybe some of both*, I thought.

"Well, at least you don't have to worry about it in here," Brandon said as he gestured around the room with pride. "One of the benefits of a secure location, I guess. This conversation stays between us for now."

"Secure?" I asked. "Like a safe?"

Brandon nodded. "Basically. We outfitted it like a Faraday shield to block any electromagnetic radiation, but also made sure radio waves can't interfere either. It's like being locked in a microwave." He patted the wall beside him. "In other words, if there's a signal coming off one of you—your phone or something like that—it's not getting out of this room, and nothing gets in.

Those computers over there are one hundred percent local. All we have is a land line to communicate with the outside."

Eric stood stock-still. I frowned at the telephone in the corner.

Brandon turned, looking between us both. "Did I say something wrong?"

But Eric and I just turned to each other as the meaning of what Brandon was telling us sank in. Was it possible that in this moment we weren't actually being watched? Recorded? Overheard in any way?

Before anyone could respond, there was a sudden blare of the telephone in the corner. All three of us jumped.

"Shit," Brandon muttered as he crossed the room. He picked up the handset. "Hey, Red."

I sighed. Of course it was Skylar. No one else would have known we were here, much less the phone number. ·

"Jenny did what? And now Luis is—actually, never mind. I'll be right there." He hung up the phone. "Sounds like the kids unleashed holy hell on Sarah while she was making the gravy. Jenny just tipped two pies on the floor, and apparently Luis dumped a bowl of cranberry sauce on his head." He made for the door, but paused when he realized we hadn't moved. "You guys coming?"

I didn't answer. I was glued into place.

Eric cleared his throat. "Do you, um, think we could look around a bit more? DVS wants to build a space like this at, uh, one of the offices. It would be good to have a model."

Brandon's brow rose. "Have a 'look around'? Sure, sure. Just, ah, clean up when you're done." He caught my eye and winked. "Who's the rabbit now, Jane?"

Then he turned, leaving Eric and me alone together. And this time, without any kind of audience.

SEVENTEEN

The door closed behind Brandon, swallowing his footsteps and leaving Eric and me blanketed with tension. The room was silent, and Brandon's last words about the "security" of the building echoed.

Nothing could get through.

No signals.

Nothing.

Eric turned to me with a gaze so fierce that I stumbled backward into a pod of rolling office chairs, sending them into a traffic jam behind me.

"Jane." Eric's tone was almost dangerous as he stalked toward me.

"Eric."

I pulled one of the chairs in front me, oddly wanting to put something between us. Not because I didn't want him to touch me. Because the intensity with which I wanted it was...terrifying.

Eric picked up the chair and hurled it behind him.

"Whoa," I whispered. "That was...violent."

"It was in the way."

I glanced at the chair. "I think you just broke the wheel."

"I'll buy Brandon another."

"I don't think he'll be impressed."

"Jane." Eric's big hands wrapped around my waist and yanked me to him. "Shut up."

He kissed me, and for a moment, I couldn't think. His lips, soft, pliant, but also demanding, quieted my mind in that way they always could.

Well, almost.

Shut up.

"No." I pushed at his arms, shoving him off me. "Fuck you, *no*."

"Jane—"

"Don't tell me to be quiet! Don't silence me, you asshole."

"I'm not—"

But it was too late, everything was bubbling up, like I really was that volcano ready to explode.

"You and that vampire dick who calls himself my father are manipulating me like a fucking puppet, and I've *had it*! Even if it's just down here, I DON'T WANT TO BE QUIET!"

Eric pushed a hand through his normally combed blond hair. The action made a few strands stick up, charmingly boyish over his intense expression.

"Okay," he said finally. "Okay, I get it. That asshole has been pulling my strings for months too. Between him and my dead grandmother, I feel like a damn marionette." He exhaled a long, low sigh. "But it's been torture. Don't you get that? Fucking *torture*. Worse than the actual torture that fucker put me through."

"Yeah, it's not exactly fun being a fucking chess piece, is it?" I snarked.

Eric glowered. "I don't mean that. I mean having to coexist

with a woman who drives me crazy but makes me want to live. Having to share our fucking home with you and not be able to touch you. Kiss you. Not be able to love you, Jane! FUCK!"

He rubbed a hand roughly over his face, which he hadn't shaved before coming here. The leftover stubble, combined with his aristocratic brow and the locks of hair flopped over his forehead, made Eric look like he had walked right out of a Jane Austen novel—the chilly, dark-eyed Darcy of any woman's fantasy.

He caught me looking, and his hand dropped. A smirk spread across his face. "You misunderstand." His voice was soft, but foreboding. "I don't want you to be quiet, pretty girl. I want you to stop talking so you can start screaming."

We stared at each other, chests heaving, for more than a minute.

Then we lunged at each other again, and this time, I didn't fight him off.

His kiss was loud, hungry, full of grunts as he devoured my mouth and sucked hard on my neck and chest. Good God, I was going to have more bites than a malaria patient by the end of this —but I didn't care. I wanted him to mark me everywhere he could.

We made quick work of each other's shirts, resisting the desire to send buttons flying. After all, we did each have to walk out of here in one piece. As I ran my hands up and down his rigid muscles, he had the cups of my bra yanked under my breasts, palming them both almost violently.

"Ah!" I cried out as he pinched both nipples.

"You have a safe word, gorgeous." His deep voice rumbled against my throat just before his teeth found it. "If it gets too rough, use it. But I want to hear you sing like that for the next twenty minutes."

We toppled onto the conference table together, clawing like animals in heat.

"We don't have much time," Eric heaved as his hands went exploring, pulling up my skirt so quickly I worried it might rip.

"We—don't—ah!" I couldn't even get a full sentence out before I was turned over facing the table, underwear pulled down and thighs forced apart.

My protests didn't matter. I was ready for him anyway. I'd been *ready* for the man for weeks, damn him.

"FUCK!" Eric roared as he shoved into me, both of us on our knees atop the lacquered wood, rutting like a damn National Geographic special. His voice, louder than I'd heard it in over a month, bounced off the soundproofed walls and back through my body.

He was big. Bigger, somehow, than I remembered him, as if time had either shrunken my parts or grown his. One hand kneaded ferociously at my backside, the other reaching around for a harsh handful of breast. He pounded away, moaning like an animal against my back while I flattened across the table, unable to do anything but take it. I was trapped beneath him. But it was the only place I wanted to be.

"Touch yourself," he ordered, his breath hoarse against my neck.

"I—oh!" I cried out as he thrust again, much deeper than before. Lord, the man was really taking no prisoners.

Then Eric stopped, wound my hair around his fist, and yanked me up so my back was flush to his chest. My scalp screamed, but the rest of me throbbed right along with his cock inside me.

"*Don't* make me repeat myself, pretty girl," he said through gritted teeth, his voice harsh and unforgiving in my ear.

He seized the lobe between his teeth and bit. I squealed.

"Are you going to make me wait?" he asked before biting again.

"Noooooo," I moaned, unable to speak clearly through my desire.

I set my fingers on the spot he wanted. Over my shoulder, Eric watched, the growl against my clavicle indicating he was pleased.

"Your nipple," he said. "Pinch it."

"But—"

There was another yank of my hair. "I've got my hands full, gorgeous. And we've got about ten minutes left. Pinch your nipple and your clit, because I'm not going to last much longer, and I need to feel you squeeze my dick while I come."

I obeyed, because there was no way I couldn't. My other hand found my nipple and twisted it just as he had before, creating that deliciously sharp pain to match the growing ache between my legs.

"Eric!" I shouted as once again, he pummeled forward. All the sensations in my body were starting to run together. His cock. My fingers. Every erogenous zone I had was porous as pleasure and pain seeped together into a nameless sensation that would be my undoing.

"Are you close?" Eric demanded. "Fucking tell me you're close, pretty girl."

I wasn't close. I was done.

"ERIC!" I screamed as I fell forward. My hands dropped as I shook, overcome completely by the feel of him inside me, taking over everything.

Eric's strong arms caught me, holding me tight as he chased my orgasm with his own. Behind me, his body clenched. Everything about him seemed to expand.

"Fucking hell, Jane," he gritted out before taking my earlobe in his teeth and biting not-so-softly as he emptied himself completely. One, two, three more thrusts before we both sagged against each other, then fell to the table.

"Holy shit," I mumbled into the lacquered wood.

"No kidding." A sweet kiss landed on my shoulder, and for a second, Eric pressed his cheek on the spot.

We lay like that for a few more minutes, but before anyone could say another word, the sound of footsteps descending the stairs had us rolling off the table like secret agents, landing in a pile of limbs and laugher on the carpet.

"Ow!" I giggled. "Where did my glasses fall?"

"Forget your glasses, Lefferts. Where the fuck are my pants?"

The door opened.

"Sorry, I just left my cell phone—"

Brandon walked in and immediately stopped two feet inside. His sharp eyes scanned over the room, landing on the toppled furniture, the scattered clothes, and eventually finding us peeking over the other side of the table, hidden only by the chairs lined up in front of us.

"Jesus Christ, you gotta be kidding me." He shielded his eyes like he was blocking the sun. "Don't waste time, do you?"

"Nope!" I crowed, earning a pinch at the waist from Eric, though he didn't look particularly mad at me.

Still blocking his vision, Brandon grabbed his cell phone off one of the work tables and felt around for the door. "There's disinfectant under the other table," he barked. "Use it." Then he marched up the stairs, muttering "fuckin' animals" under his breath.

The door closed behind him. Eric and I looked at each other and immediately burst into laughter.

"He's just jealous," Eric said with a grin. "Two kids under five? I bet he's getting laid about once a month these days."

I snorted. "I don't know. The two of them still can't keep their hands off each other."

"Don't remind me," Eric replied. "Until May, I worked with Skylar every day for years."

I tittered again, earning another kiss that quickly turned into something more intense. I sighed into Eric, relishing the taste of him. The feel of his body pressed to mine. I missed this. I missed *him*.

Eric's features softened slightly as he traced my cheek with the back of his hand. The gold coin dangled between his perfectly sculpted pectoral muscles. I fingered it gently, wishing I could rip it off. It was heavy—probably because it was made with solid gold. Antique metals had a different kind of heft.

"I hate this," I said, pulling lightly on the chain. "I hate *them*."

Eric looked down at my hand, then slowly pushed it away, forcing me to release the coin.

"I'm working on it," he murmured and got up to search for his clothes.

"Working on it how?" I stood too and started putting my bra and skirt back into place. "You promised that fucker that you wouldn't touch me. We're going to walk out of this room, and you're going to treat me like a stranger again because you're scared of the boogie man. I don't know why you don't just tell him to go to hell."

Eric pulled his belt through the buckle with a little more vehemence than was strictly necessary. "People don't say no to Carson."

"People, sure. But you're not people. You're Eric fucking de Vries." My cherry print shirt taunted me from under the tossed chair. I grabbed it and shoved an arm violently through one sleeve. "You know, sometimes I think I'm more aware of that than you are."

Eric gave me an irritated look as he put on his own button-down. "Trust me, you're not."

"Then why put up with it? What's the difference between the two of you anyway? You both basically own half the planet, right?"

"The difference is that he almost killed me, Jane."

I stopped fussing with my clothes as all blood drained from my head. "What?"

Eric looked up. "Just...pretend I didn't say that."

"Are you kidding?" I yanked out my ponytail holder and starter finger-combing my waves. "You don't just admit someone tried to commit murder and then pretend nothing was said. This was when you were gone, wasn't it?"

The sudden lack of color in Eric's face told me everything I needed to know. "Jane," he said through his teeth. "Just drop it, all right?"

He started putting way too much attention into rolling up his shirtsleeves.

I strode up and smacked his hand away. "Hey, J. Crew!"

The scowl was back. "You don't know what you're asking. And even if you did, I can't tell you about it. For your own safety."

He made for the door without waiting for an answer.

"Uggh!" I cried. "You are *so* frustrating sometimes, you know that?"

Eric let the door close again and turned. "You're mad? I'm just trying to keep you safe!"

"Yes, I'm mad at you!" I shouted. "I'm mad because you don't have the guts to stand up to him with me. I'm mad because I feel like I'm the only one fighting for *us*!"

"I *am* fighting for us, Jane!" he roared back. "I'm fighting for *you*! I'm fighting to protect *you*!"

"I DON'T NEED YOUR PROTECTION!" I shrieked. "I

need your love. I need your *trust*, Eric. Was I the only one who felt like this was some kind of homecoming? Right here on Brandon's ugly conference table?"

Eric swallowed. "You know you're not. I needed that just as badly as you did."

"Well, then what is the fucking point of this life if I can't spend it with the one person who has ever made me feel...well... anything at all worth keeping?"

He stilled, like an animal caught in headlights. "Do you...do you really feel that way?"

I swallowed. Had I never said it? Had I never completely told him how I felt? He had shouted it to me over the waves of the Atlantic Ocean, and I had definitely said "I love you." But maybe it was true—maybe I'd never really told him. Not like this.

Well. No time like the present.

"I'm not a poet like you," I said, hovering a hand over his face. "I've always been better at speaking with actions." I gestured to my clothes and thought of the apartment I'd so carefully curated for our life. I tried hard my own ways to let him know how I felt. "All my life, the world felt like a cage for someone like me. People and places telling me what I could be, how I should act. They wanted me to settle down. Speak softer. Dress better. Be nicer. Easier. Calmer. But you...when I'm with you, I just feel free." I pulled at his collar. "*You* free me."

Eric's thick gaze didn't waver. "That's pretty fucking poetic, Jane," he whispered.

I closed my eyes as emotion vibrated through me. When I opened them, the world seemed off-kilter. He was the only part of it that felt straight and solid.

"Please," I begged. "Please don't put me back in that cage."

He shook his head. I understood the conundrum. Common sense said that relationships, monogamy, marriage—every metaphor in the world spoke to how suffocating they were supposed to be. For years, I had assumed it was the case. And yet, here I was, admitting the oxymoronic truth—that it was only when I was tied to a person—*this* person, to be exact—that I was truly free to soar.

"You don't think this entire life is a cage?" he wondered. "Sometimes I regret inviting you into it at all. It was selfish."

I shook my head. "No. No, I don't."

"But, Jane—"

"Don't you understand?" I asked. "My only cage is the one without you."

Eric watched me for a long time, his eyes traveling up and down my person, almost like he was trying to memorize every fold of clothing, every strand of hair. I pushed my hair aside angrily, but didn't otherwise move.

"If you only knew," he said at last, so low his voice was almost swallowed there, between the thick, impenetrable walls.

But instead of reaching out to me, instead of assuring me that things would change—instead of telling me as I so needed to hear that we *would* face Carson and figure out how to be together—he just turned back to the door and opened it, standing aside like the gentleman he had been groomed to be.

"Ladies first," he said, unwilling to meet my eye. "Come on, Jane. We'll be late for dinner."

EIGHTEEN

We trudged back to the main house in silence, no longer touching, not even looking at each other. If those crazed minutes in Brandon's lab had let out something important, Eric had shoved it back in and locked it up with ten more padlocks.

His head hung as he walked, like a despondent Charlie Brown.

My hands clenched and unclenched, more like a caged animal than ever.

When we entered the kitchen, Skylar took one look at my disheveled appearance, made excuses to her grandmother, and dragged me upstairs to change. All Eric had to do was pat his hair in a few places to look like a catalog model again, but apparently, I resembled Courtney Love after a serious bender.

"I'm not even going to ask," she said as we entered the giant walk-in closet she and Brandon shared.

I shrugged. I was pissed at Eric all over again, and all sorts of confused, but I felt absolutely no shame about getting my rocks off. I did need to fix myself up, though.

"Your hem is torn," Skylar remarked wryly, pointing to the wide rent in my skirt. "And your shirt is missing some buttons."

"That asshole," I said as I fingered the frayed edge of the limp fabric. Apparently, he really had ripped the clothes from my body. The bias cut on this shirt had taken me weeks to get right. I scowled. I wanted to march downstairs and ram the ruined silk down Eric's stupid, stubborn throat.

Skylar shook her head. She clearly thought Eric and I were no better than a couple of bonobo chimps.

"Just grab a dress," she said, gesturing at her side of the closet. "You're too tall for any of my pants anyway. Or else there are leggings in the bureau on the right if you want to borrow some."

"This is basically the wardrobe department of *The Good Wife*," I remarked as I leafed through the single rack of clothes that didn't include suits. She had a taste for pencil skirts—the woman must have had at least twenty—but they were definitely not my cup of tea. "Do you own anything without shoulder pads, Mrs. Florrick?"

"Very funny," Skylar called out from the bed, where she was taking a much-needed load off. "It's just work clothes. You know how dress code works in court."

I popped my head out. "Seriously, though. You're a zillionaire. Where are all the good duds?"

Skylar shrugged. "I like my sweaters and jeans when I'm at home. Brandon and I aren't like you and Eric. All the furniture in this house doubles as a jungle gym, we prefer upholstery that can hide stains, and no one dresses up unless we absolutely have to."

I smiled at the idea that there was actually some similarity between Eric and me. I had always considered us such opposites, but we both did like clothes. And our apartment filled with art

THE KISS PLOT   227

and fine furnishings. We both liked beauty for beauty's sake. Always had.

As quickly as it had buoyed me, the idea immediately brought me back down. Because, as Eric had so emphatically said through his actions, there was no future there. No matter how slyly compatible we were.

Fuck him.

"Hey, can you decide already? I feel bad abandoning Bubbe in the kitchen, and I don't want to be MIA when Zola gets here too. He should arrive any minute."

I popped back out of a row of blouses. "Zola's coming?"

"He sometimes does," Skylar said absently. "You know that."

I knew that Zola was a good guy and had remained a friend of the family. I also knew that sometimes, yes, he *had* shown up at random holiday events. We'd even flirted a few times—hey, you would too if a handsome Italian was sitting across the sweet potatoes from you. But nothing ever happened. What's the saying? Don't shit where you eat turkey?

And more importantly, why hadn't he mentioned it when we met this week?

"It was a last-minute thing," Skylar answered my unspoken question. "Actually, he was wondering if you would be here." She gave me a pointed look. "I almost thought he still had a thing for you. Remember when you met back in the day?"

I wrinkled my nose, choosing not to mention that Zola was probably taking the opportunity to call my bluff about Eric's and my behavior.

Or maybe, I considered as I remembered Eric's reaction to the man, that was exactly what I needed.

I turned back to the dresses and chose a slinky red knit number—one I happened to know Skylar almost never wore because she thought it was too revealing for a mother of two. I, however, had no such qualms. It would look hot with the boots I was wearing and just might drive a certain blond shipping heir crazy.

"Red," I said as I pulled the dress out. "Red is the order of the day."

———

WE RETURNED DOWNSTAIRS TO A FAMILIAR, warm scene: Sarah and Susan bustling dishes out of the kitchen to the spacious dining room; Luis and Jenny running around underfoot with telltale bits of sweet potato and cranberry sauce peeking from the sides of their mouths; and Ray, Eric, Brandon, and Matthew Zola making their way to the table from where they had been watching football. Almost everyone had a drink in hand and was eagerly eyeing the big table full of food. It was idyllic and warm, exactly the way Thanksgiving should be. Full of family, friends, and loved ones.

A pang lodged in my gut as my mother's face flashed through my mind. Multiple expressions, actually.

That's because you know she should be here, Jane Brain.

There was my dad—my *real* dad—twisting my insides even more. I could be mad at her. But, I realized, keeping us apart was exactly what a man like Carson wanted.

"I just need to make a call," I said to Skylar, ignoring Eric's concerned look as I ducked out.

I found my coat and purse in the kitchen and pulled out my new phone, dialing as I went outside. She answered on the second ring.

"Jane?"

I took a deep breath, but before I could even get out "Hi, *Eomma*," I burst into tears—loud, noisy tears that truly ached with every breath.

"Jane?" she asked again, her voice rising. "Jane, is that you? What is the matter?"

"*E-e-omma*," I stuttered. "I j-just wanted to say Happy Thanksg-giving."

I could barely manage the words. Less than two years ago, I had been sitting at the table with her, my dad, some of his buddies from the VA, plus a bunch of other cousins and aunties in Chicago. The table was covered with a diverse mix. There was the more traditional American Thanksgiving foods—Dad loved a roasted turkey and usually made the fixings to go with it. His coworkers (and sometimes patients) could be counted on to bring a grocery store pumpkin pie or cranberry sauce in a can. Meanwhile, my mother and her family would fill in the gaps with a bunch of Korean food: *japchae* noodles, maybe a potato dish or dumplings. Three types of homemade *kimchi*, and probably at least two different desserts. It was eclectic and weird, but it was ours.

"I miss you," I blurted out, only just understanding how true the words were. "*Eomma*, everything is a mess. Eric, the wedding, we—"

"Hush."

The word was spoken kindly, quietly, but was still effective. My mother wasn't the type to use nicknames. Unlike my dad, who had a backpack full of monikers for me, my mom was like a lot of Koreans who didn't readily call their children by anything less formal than their given name.

Ironically, the only other person I really knew whose family treated him that way was Eric. Yet another random thing we had in common.

"You should be here," I said. "Or I...I should be there. Holidays are for family, *Eomma*. I'm sorry about how I've treated mine."

Suddenly, there was nowhere else I'd rather be than my

parents' house in Evanston, wrapped in one of the old seventies afghans my dad insisted on keeping. My mother would jabber away in Korean with her cousins, and Dad and I would make small talk with his coworkers and try to decipher whatever sporting event was on the TV. I felt harsh, nasty pangs of regret for every holiday I'd spent without them, for every time I'd avoided my mother's calls, for the three years I'd spent in Boston instead of around my dad while I could. The house in Evanston might be gone along with him, but that didn't mean the soul of our family wasn't alive and well.

It didn't matter that I'd found a new family of two over the last six months only to lose it again. It only mattered that I'd squandered the one I'd always had.

"Christmas," I started to promise before I realized it wasn't possible.

I had to stay with Eric until after the New Year to meet that sixty-day requirement. I wanted to promise the lunar new year, but realized again I had to stay here to take the bar a week after that. No, as much as I wanted to run home to squeeze my mother right this minute, I wouldn't be able to do it until the spring.

My heart ached that much more.

"Jane?"

I cleared my throat. "Yes, *Eomma*?"

"I love you," she said.

I blinked my tears away in surprise. She rarely said that sort of thing. Our closeness was more bound up in bickering, shopping, harping on daily life. She showed she cared by *caring*. Open displays of affection usually made her very uncomfortable.

"We don't say it enough," she said quietly. "And today, we are thankful, right? I am thankful for you."

I opened and closed my mouth, unsure of how to reply to this uncharacteristic compliment. I was overflowing with regret and the desire to fix something, *anything*, in this mess of my life.

Maybe my next move wasn't to hold on to a relationship that was clearly doomed from the start. Eric might have felt like home more than anywhere else I'd known. But in six weeks, we'd be completely free of each other, and I'd be worth fifty million dollars. I could buy my mother back her house in Evanston. Give up men for good. Maybe we could live there together, two bickering old maids. She could teach me how to make her dumplings and *kimchi*. All the things I'd resolutely refused my whole life. I'd finally learn Korean, sew blankets, spend my spare time playing *godori* and be the good daughter she always wanted me to be…

"I am thankful," she continued, "I have a strong daughter that can make her own life. Much better than I ever could."

And just like that, the house, the life of two old crones squabbling at each other on the porch—it all disappeared. I blinked, and I was back on this porch, back in this life. But lifted, somehow, by my mother's faith and my own determination to make it right.

Whatever that meant.

"Thanks, *Eomma*," I said. "I love you too."

There was a shout behind her, and before she could reply to me, my mother rattled off something indecipherable in Korean, something I couldn't understand. Would never really understand.

I had never felt so clearly that we lived different lives. Or understood better that it was the way it was meant to be.

"Call me soon," she ordered.

"Okay," I said, still swiping at tears. "I will."

"Okay," she said, and in that strange, yet familiarly abrupt way of hers, she hung up the phone, leaving no room for sweet goodbyes or kind words made of nothing but reassurance. The conversation was over. The important things had already been said.

"Everything all right?"

I put my phone in my coat pocket, then turned around to find Zola stepping onto the porch. He was a bit more dressed up than I'd seen him last weekend, in a gray button-down shirt and black pants. With his dark hair and olive skin, he looked a bit roguish. But his eyes were open and friendly. There was no mask at all.

He gestured with his half-full wine glass. "They sent me to find you. Ray's carving the turkey, and they're dishing up."

I offered a small smile and ran my finger under my glasses. "Yeah. Yeah, everything is okay. I'll be right in."

But instead of leaving me to gather myself, Zola took one look at me, set his glass on the railing, and crossed the deck to gather me into his arms. He left no space for refusal, and while I stiffened at first, once it was clear there was no ulterior motive, I allowed myself to enjoy the comfort.

Because in my mind, it wasn't him who was hugging me. It was another solid, lean body. Another pair of arms that were wiry, but strong. It was the subtle hint of Tom Ford I was smelling, and it was a gold-stubbled cheek pressed against my forehead.

When I closed my eyes, I could pretend it was Eric offering me solace, not this kind man who barely knew me at all.

I allowed myself exactly three long breaths before I stepped out of Zola's embrace. My eyes were dry again, and I felt like I could eat pie with everyone.

"Thanks," I said. "I—I needed that."

Zola smiled kindly. "You looked like it. The holidays are hard when you're not getting along with family. I've been there."

"Yeah?" I pulled off my glasses to check my eyes in my window reflection. "Why aren't you with yours now, by the way? I thought you had a big Italian family."

"Well, my ma would kill me if she knew I was here instead of in Belmont. I'd never get away with it at Christmas, but sometimes I feel like a little white lie doesn't hurt for the sake of my sanity."

He reached out and squeezed my hand, and I squeezed back, grateful in this moment to have a friend.

But before I could reply, I spotted a shape lurking behind the sliding glass door. Because of the way the afternoon light bounced off the window, it was hard to spot him at first, but as soon as I did, his gray eyes cut through every distracting flash. Eric, watching me with an expression full of hurt, but also anger. And I realized that he had seen the entire thing.

NINETEEN

When Zola and I found our seats across from each other at the big farmhouse table, Eric was nowhere to be seen. All of the dinner attendees were seated. Parents, friends, kids, even Annabelle and Christoph, Skylar's French half-siblings, had emerged from their bedrooms for the meal.

"Where do people keep going?" Brandon demanded as he helped Sarah bring out the platter of carved turkey. "The food is getting cold. No one wants a lukewarm bird."

"Relax, babe," Skylar chided him like she was speaking to a child.

"Don't worry, Brandon," I said. "You'll still get dessert if you finish your green beans."

For that, I received a blue-eyed glare.

"Oh, Aunt Janey," Jenny said, "Daddy *always* eats his veggies, 'cause he knows if he doesn't, I won't either."

"Yeah," Luis agreed beside her.

I smirked at Brandon, who just took a long drink of beer. I

didn't think the man particularly cared that he was wrapped around his daughter's little pinky.

"Eric had to take a phone call too." Skylar appeared with a couple of bottles and proceeded to pour everyone a drink, ignoring thirteen-year-old Annabelle's pleas for a taste of the wine. "Sorry, Anna. The kids get sparkling cider."

"But Brandon said I could have some special for tonight!" Annabelle argued. Her French accent, I noticed, was almost completely erased after several years of boarding school in Andover and weekends here in Brookline.

"Why?" asked Christoph, whose accent was completely gone. "You're just a kid."

"I am not!"

"Brandon!" Skylar turned to admonish her husband, but the big man pretended to hide behind Sarah, whose five-feet-and-change form wasn't exactly up to the task. At the sight, however, even Skylar couldn't help but crack a smile, and everyone relaxed as she went back to pouring the kids' beverages.

"Don't worry, kid. Wine's not that great."

Eric flopped into the empty seat between me and Annabelle, warmth practically radiating from his body. There was a slight sheen on his skin, like he'd just been running, and as he spoke, I caught a hint of vodka off his breath. He ignored me completely and grinned at Annabelle, with whom he was obviously familiar. *Of course*, I realized. Eric had probably spent nearly every holiday I didn't in this house for the last five years, considering he had been so deeply estranged from his own people. He knew the kids like they were his own nieces and nephews.

"How's Andover treating you, Belles? Are you on the head-mistress's good side yet?" Eric asked.

Annabelle gazed at him adoringly. "H-hi, Eric. We—I mean, Chris—was hoping you'd be here for Thanksgiving this year."

Eric's smile widened. The girl practically melted. I rolled my eyes. He really couldn't help himself, even with a gawky eighth grader, could he? Jackass.

"We, um, we heard about the wedding." Annabelle's eyes danced to my bare fingers, asking the questions that reporters *still* called me about.

Eric smiled again, but this one was much grimmer. "Ah. Well. Don't believe everything you hear, beautiful."

The girl flushed all over again, but before she could reply, Eric reached for his wine glass and took a nice long drink.

"I thought you didn't like wine that much anymore," I murmured.

He set the glass down. "It's a party. I'll adjust." His eyes were glassy, and I could still smell the vodka, even under the wine.

"Who were you talking to?" I asked in a low voice. "Or was it a private conversation between you and Brandon's stash of Beluga?"

Eric refused to look at me, turning his wine glass back and forth instead. "Nina called to say Happy Thanksgiving."

"Oh? That's really sweet of her."

The steely look erased any lingering goodwill. "Yeah. Everyone says hi. Including Caitlyn."

My skin prickled. "What?"

His slim blond brow rose. "You heard me. She said to tell Jane and Desi hello, apparently. So I said hello back."

That idiotic nickname of hers—the one that marked him as *hers* somehow—made it very difficult not to break my wine glass. "You didn't. Not after. After we—after you—"

"Let's not do this here," Eric said with that calm that absolutely infuriated me.

"Then when?"

"How about never?" he said between clenched teeth and the fakest smile I'd ever seen. "Since you're too busy prepping your next move, I don't really see the fucking point."

His eyes flashed at Zola, who was too immersed making Christoph laugh with some bad French to notice. On his other side, however, Annabelle's eyes widened at the sudden profanity.

"Stop it," I hissed.

"Stop what?" Eric suddenly drained his entire glass of wine in one go, then immediately refilled it. "Seems to me *you*'re the one who lacks self-control, Lefferts."

My eyes widened. "Ex*cuse* me? Who tackled who on the—"

"Ahem!" Eric coughed loud enough to interrupt me, and before I could recover, there was the sound of a chair screeching against the hardwood as Brandon lumbered up at the end of the table, and everyone quieted.

"I—well, *we*, Skylar and me—wanted to say thanks to everyone for coming today. We, ah, honestly didn't expect *everyone* to show."

There was a small titter of laughter. Brandon was always good with a crowd, even his own family.

"But we're damn glad—"

"Daddy!"

"Ah, *darn* glad you did," Brandon finished with a meaningful look at Jenny. He held up his glass, and we all mirrored him. "Cheers," he said. "To family and friends."

"To family and friends," we repeated dutifully.

"Whether or not they stay that way," Eric muttered.

"I'm sorry, what?" I asked.

"Shouldn't we say grace or something?" Brandon asked loudly just as everyone was reaching for the food set out up and down the table.

"Daddy!" Jenny moaned again. "I'm *hungry*!"

Skylar bit her lip. I snorted. Sometimes you really can't take the Catholic out of the boy, and according to Skylar, Brandon had gotten a bit more...pious...since taking in Annabelle and Christoph on the weekends. Having a teenage girl running around his house had recently inspired the epiphany that Jenny would also, at some point, have boys sniffing around. Apparently, he had started taking the kids to Mass with him every so often and had been talking a lot of abstinence crap at Jenny. Which, of course, only induced Skylar to make wry comments about how well those celibacy vows were working for the church, and to buy various sex education books for all the kids in the house.

"Grace?" Ray put in. "Brandon, I'm a scientist. I don't believe in God. And you don't either, for that matter."

"I never said I don't believe in God, Ray," Brandon replied, looking nervously at Christoph and Annabelle, as well as Jenny, who was observing with a keen eye. Luis, still too young to really follow the conversation, was already dipping his spoon in the sweet potatoes Skylar had put on his plate.

"Well, I do," Sarah said, whose love for Brandon couldn't be quashed by a mere difference in religion. "The Jewish one, at any rate." She looked kindly at Brandon, and he grinned back at her.

"Come on, you *shiksa* goddess," I jeered at Brandon, making Skylar, her dad, and Zola all snort. He was really too easy to tease. "Just clear your conscience so we can eat. My stomach is growling a prayer right now."

"Daddy, what's a *shiksa*?" Jenny asked.

"It's a pretty gentile girl, *matoki*," Sarah said automatically, petting her great-granddaughter on the head. "Brandon, maybe just a simple blessing? My Daniel is very good at that sort of thing."

"Ma." Danny just shook his head. Skylar patted him on the shoulder. She knew he didn't really like being the center of attention.

"What?" Sarah asked. "You love being on the stage playing the music, don't you?"

Jenny screwed her freckled face up in confusion. "Daddy's not a girl. How can he be a *shiksa?*"

"I'm not, pea. Auntie Jane thinks she's being funny."

I couldn't stop giggling, however, and soon, Christoph and Annabelle had joined me, while several other people hid smiles. Eric, however, remained stone-faced.

"Very nice, Jane," Brandon said.

But when he bowed his head and crossed himself, his daughter as well as his wife's siblings all automatically mimicked the movement. Apparently, Mass wasn't completely lost on them.

Across the table, Zola sighed and did the same, and slowly, the rest of the adults bowed their heads out of respect as Brandon gave a short, awkward blessing that was only slightly better than "Good bread, good meat, good God, let's

"Poetic," I remarked to Eric.

"It had a rhyme scheme," he said without any humor. He dished himself potatoes and turned to pass them without offering me any.

I handed him my plate. "Um, do you mind?"

"I do. But I'll do it anyway." Eric smacked a spoonful so hard they splattered across the plate.

"So, Matthew," Sarah asked from the other side of the table as she gestured for Zola's plate to serve some turkey.

"Zola," he corrected her with a good-natured grin. "The only person who calls me Matthew is my mother when I'm in trouble, Mrs. Crosby."

"And why aren't you with her?" Eric asked nastily as he accepted the stuffing from Annabelle.

This time I didn't ask for some—he just dumped a bunch

right on top of my potatoes. I used my fork to separate them, then passed my plate down for some green beans.

Zola looked up uncomfortably as he took his plate back. "Well, my parents' place is pretty small, and I have a lot of siblings. And now they have kids, so..."

"What's wrong with kids?" Eric asked. "There are kids here too. Do you not like them either?"

Zola looked around at the children currently present, all of whom seemed to be very interested in his response. "Ah, no, no, they're great. And I love my nieces and nephews. It's just...I see them a lot, especially at Christmas, so I usually take Thanksgiving to get away for a bit, you know? See other friends. Other towns."

"Other girls?"

Zola paused mid bite of turkey. "Ah, sure. Sometimes there are girls present." He smiled at me. "Like today."

Eric looked like he wanted to hurl the bowl of cranberry sauce he was holding at Zola's face.

"Why are you so interested, Petri dish?" I asked. "Did you need a wingman to help you refill your sample?"

Eric's eyes narrowed at the use of the nickname. "Maybe," he said, just because he knew it would hurt. "But apparently he doesn't need one. He was able to make his move all on his own, wasn't he, pretty girl?"

"Ah...I'm sorry?" Zola's gaze ping-ponged between Eric and me. "Hey, man, if I did something—"

"He's talking about the fact that you hugged me on the porch," I said, though I was still staring at Eric. His blond hair was now deliciously mussed, and his silvery gray eyes had gone completely black. If I hadn't been so furious with him, I would have wanted to drag him back to the lab.

But the entire table had gone quiet—they were all watching this little display. All I wanted was for Eric to make it end.

Sadly, he did not. "I'm talking about the fact that you molested some guy right here in front of me and the kids, Jane."

"Oh my *God*," I snapped. "It was a hug, not softcore porn."

"Guys," Brandon warned us.

"What are they talking about?" Susan asked Ray. He shrugged and kept eating potatoes like nothing was happening.

"It was inappropriate," Eric retorted. "And embarrassing."

"Kind of like this conversation?" I returned.

"Eric," Skylar tried. "Jane. You guys, come on—"

"Maybe she wouldn't have needed a hug if someone hadn't made her cry," Zola said.

I turned to him. "Oh, that's not why I was—"

"Maybe she was crying because some fucking creep wouldn't take his hands off her," Eric rejoined.

"Language!" Sarah snapped, clapping her hands over Luis's ears.

"Whoa," Christoph muttered. He looked at his sister. "He sounds like your friends at school, Anna."

"Which friends are these?" Brandon asked suspiciously.

"Eric!" I stood up and glared at him, ignoring the curious stares of the people all around the table. "Outside. Now."

He swallowed and shook his head. "No. We can't."

I expelled a quick, frustrated sigh. "Then the lab again," I said, ignoring our onlookers' surprised, confused faces. "It's quiet there. Brandon, would you mind letting us in?"

Eric stood and grabbed my arm. "Fine, let's go."

"Hey, can you not drag me?" I yanked my arm back, and when he didn't release it, Zola and Brandon were both standing.

"Eric," Brandon called. "Calm down, man. We're already going."

"Stop grabbing on me!" I batted his shoulder, but his hand didn't move, so instead I dug my heels in and pulled him back.

"Hey, man. She said stop!" Zola reached across the table toward Eric. And it was the absolute wrong move.

"Get your fucking hands off me!" The words flew out of Eric's mouth, and before I could stop him, his hand dropped my arm as the other went swinging across the table at Zola, who ducked away neatly.

Brandon hopped around the crowd and pinned Eric to the wall in exactly two seconds.

"Let me go!" Eric roared, hands pinwheeling outward. "Let me fucking go, Brandon!"

"Mommy," Jenny whispered as she clung to Skylar. "Mommy, what's wrong with Uncle Eric? He looks mad at Aunt Janey. And he said 'fuck.' A lot."

"Don't say that word, pea," Brandon said between gritted teeth while he struggled to hold Eric still.

"But Uncle Eric said—"

"Skylar, can you get the kids out of here?" Brandon snapped as he twisted an arm around Eric's shoulder, holding him captive in a tight half-nelson.

"What is wrong with you!" I hissed at Eric from where I had backed against the wall, holding Luis away from the nonsense. "You are acting *crazy*! It's like having Thanksgiving with Jekyll and fucking Hyde!"

"Now Aunt Janey said 'fuck' too!" Jenny squealed.

"It's just a word," Annabelle remarked in a droll voice that somehow only thirteen-year-old girls can manage. "Anyone can say fuck. Fuck, fuck, fuck."

"Everyone stop saying fuck!" Brandon shouted.

"Fuckin' A," Danny muttered in agreement.

"Dad!" Skylar snapped.

Sarah appeared next to me and swept Luis into her arms with more spryness than any octogenarian should have.

"*I* will take the kids upstairs," she said, her thick Brooklyn accent more apparent than ever. "All of them. And let the *big* babies get their acts together."

She gave her granddaughter a meaningful look, which she then directed at Annabelle and Christoph. Both children immediately rose, carrying their plates.

"Skylar. You get these boys under control, you hear? Or else they'll have me to deal with."

Every man in the kitchen—including her son, Danny—blanched at the idea of being on the receiving end of Sarah Crosby's sharp tongue. She exited the room with everyone thirteen and under, followed soon by Susan, then Ray and Danny as they made excuses to watch the rest of the football game.

Skylar waited until their parents and kids were gone, then turned to face who was left with the same imperious expression that had won her a reputation as a shark in court.

"Get it together," she ordered. "Otherwise, you can get the hell out of my house. All of you."

There was a tense minute where everyone left stared at each other with wide eyes, like they were waiting for someone to toss a grenade into the middle of all of it. But, as if by some telegraphed message that signaled the threat had passed, we all relaxed. Brandon released Eric in a slump against the wall, Zola heaved a big sigh, and I flopped back into my chair.

"I meant no harm," Zola said. "And I have no motives with Jane, all right? We're just friends. Anyone can see the two of you are—"

"Nothing," Eric cut him off with another sharp look. "We're nothing. It's an arrangement at this point, as I'm sure she informed you over dinner."

Zola blinked, his dark eyes sharp, but full of empathy. It occurred to me then that this was why Zola had come to the dinner. Like any good investigator, he couldn't resist a solid lead. And as mortifying as this little altercation had been, it had at the very least convinced Zola that I was right. Eric was acting extremely out of character. Someone was forcing his hand.

The prosecutor's gaze traveled over Eric's sullen form, like he was looking for something. *The bug*, I realized. Of course. Zola was curious about how in the hell Eric was being tracked.

Zola believed me.

"Yeah," he said finally as he picked up his glass of wine. "She did. Which, to be honest, is really why I'm here instead of breaking bread with my own family. I was wondering if I could help."

TWENTY

A few minutes later, we gathered around the kitchen island with full plates, refilled glasses of wine, and deep breaths.

"What do you mean, you can help?" Eric finally asked warily as he took a bite of turkey and cranberry.

He now looked a far sight from the normally poised, put together almost-chairman I knew. The buttons of his shirt had torn open, his hair was pitched to one side, and his face was flushed from exertion, a stark contrast to the circles underneath his dark gray eyes.

Some of that wasn't just from the near-fight, I realized. The last several weeks had really taken their toll on him. He looked awful. Tired. Stressed.

Zola didn't answer. Instead, he looked around the room for a second, and then, apparently not finding what he wanted, pulled out his phone, typed out a message, then turned it toward us.

Where's the bug?

The meaning was clear. Everyone in this room was aware, on some level, that the Janus society was listening to Eric, and thus was listening to this conversation. It had to be done carefully.

Eric shrugged, and that glazed expression I was truly starting to loathe resumed its position. An expression of helplessness. Numbness.

I wanted to slap it out of him.

Zola frowned, then typed another message before turning the phone back.

Your phones?

Eric shook his head, and I did too.

Zola pressed his lips together, and it was clear that he was wondering if the bug was real to begin with. I understood—I'd wondered the same thing. But there was no other way Carson would have sent the message he had. Maybe he'd sent others too —I doubted Eric would have shown me.

"Can I see that?" Brandon said, gesturing at the medallion gleaming around Eric's neck.

Almost protectively, Eric touched the coin I had come to loathe. "Why? Don't you have one?"

"I was cut in the third round," Brandon said, like he was talking about baseball tryouts, not initiation into a billionaire mafia. "Can I look at it?"

"Ah, sure," Eric replied, then somewhat reluctantly unclasped the necklace and handed it to Brandon.

Brandon set it carefully on the stone counter like he was going to take a close look. Then he reached a long arm behind Skylar like he was stretching, took a pewter mallet off the counter that Sarah had been using to crush walnuts, and brought it down on the gold coin with a smash that shook the house.

"Brandon!" Skylar shouted. "We just put in this granite!"

"Red, you had this counter done five years ago. And the kids have smashed it way harder than I just did."

"What in the fuck, man," Eric croaked—he had been too busy staring at the necklace to say anything at first. "That was my father's! What did you just do?"

"I thought this might be it," Brandon said, ignoring Eric completely. "Ray!" he called out for his father, who appeared so quickly from the living room that I wondered if he'd been lurking outside anyway, eager to return to the excitement.

With an irritated look at everyone in the room, Ray nudged between Brandon and Zola. He picked up the coin, and it was only when he held it up in the light that we all saw what Brandon found so interesting. It wasn't a coin at all.

To start, it was split completely in half. Not down the middle, but around the sides, like a tiny can of shoe polish with its crooked top now bent beyond repair. And from between its seams, something else green and metallic peeked from inside.

"Ah," Ray said with academic interest as he peeled off one side to examine what was hidden there. "A miniaturized acoustic recording device."

The rest of us stared at each other. Recording device, I got. But I didn't understand what the rest meant.

"State of the art," Ray remarked to his son. "John Rizzo was working on something like that in conjunction with the NSA, but I don't think they were able to achieve operational capability." He turned to Eric. "Where did you get this?"

But Eric couldn't speak. His mouth was open as he stared at the coin. "Is that...is that the way..."

"The way John Carson has been stalking you?" Brandon finished for him. "Yeah, looks that way." He took the coin back from his dad, and everyone in the room immediately clamored around the table as Brandon set it down on the counter to begin dissecting it.

"Red?" He beckoned to Skylar without looking up. "Baby, can you get me a glass of water, please?"

Skylar fetched the water quickly, but instead of drinking it, Brandon immediately dropped the coin into the liquid.

"Hey!" Eric snapped, as if being slapped across the face.

Brandon looked up impatiently. "I'm sorry. Did you want that sycophantic asshole to continue listening to this conversation? I might have broken the transmitter, but I won't really know until we take a closer look."

Eric swallowed. "He really was doing it that way?"

"Probably. But everyone should put their cell phones in the microwave just to be sure." Brandon glanced around at the five other faces (minus Ray's) that were staring at him in horror. "Don't worry, I won't actually cook them. The microwave blocks transmissions." In response, he received more blank stares. "We're just being safe."

Ray snorted. "Just leave them here. We should go to the lab anyway. We won't be able to see anything without a microscope."

Brandon perked up at the mention of his new lab. Skylar just rolled her eyes and slid off her barstool.

"I'll tell Bubbe we'll be a while," she said. "They can come back down and eat without us."

———

FIFTEEN MINUTES LATER, we had all left our phones at the house and filed back into the underground lab. Eric glanced at me as I stumbled past the broken chair.

"Animals," Brandon mumbled again—clearly he'd noticed, too.

"Send me the bill," Eric said as he took a seat and pulled one out for me.

I sat down, and he rolled close to me, moving to take my hand. But I rolled right back away. Bug free or not, he wasn't getting away with his bullshit at dinner. Not yet.

Ray had immediately taken the tiny chip over to a microscope on one of the steel worktables. "Good God," he erupted a few minutes later. "Bran, come look at this."

Brandon lumbered over and peered into the microscope. "Holy shit."

"Do you see that? It's an acoustic transducer nano-array circuit," Ray said. "Using a solid-state memory unit."

"And at that size," Brandon added in awe. "I didn't even think that was physically possible. How do you think they overcame the acoustic wavelength size discrepancy?"

"Ahem!"

Brandon turned to his wife, who had just cleared her throat.

"Translate, please," she said pointedly.

"Yeah," I added. "Not everyone here speaks Klingon."

Brandon returned to the conference table while his father continued examining the coin. "Okay, how's this? It's the smallest wireless recording device that Ray, a circuitry specialist at MIT, has ever seen or heard of." He jerked a thumb back at the microscope. "That's definitely your bug, my friend. And it explains why Tony never detects anything when you're waiting outside your place. You've been wearing it around your neck."

Eric just stared numbly at the table. "I've been...it's been..." He buried his face in his hands. "Oh, *fuck*. I've—goddammit, I've taken that thing everywhere with me. Every board meeting. Everywhere in the entire fucking company." He looked up in horror. "It was in my grandfather's study for...Jesus, since my dad died. Carson's been listening in on my family for twenty years?"

"Of course not," Ray said from the microscope before the shock of the idea actually gave Eric a heart attack. "That kind of technology is brand new. There's no way anyone has been capable of a transmitter this small for more than a year. Maybe two."

"Was there any time he could have changed it for the old one?" Brandon asked. "Maybe when you weren't, I don't know, conscious? Sleeping, or..."

By the look on Eric's face, it was obviously the "or."

"He must have done it when I was passed out," he said, staring ahead, but at nothing at all. "When I was...away."

I swallowed thickly. What *exactly* happened that had caused Eric to pass out?

But before I could ask, he turned to me sadly. "Jane, he heard—"

"We were quiet that night," I said, though I wasn't sure myself that the noises we had made were completely silent.

Be careful, he had said. We were...weren't we?

"Were you quiet down here?" Brandon asked pointedly.

I frowned. Eric flushed. Ray pretended not to hear us while Skylar rolled her eyes so hard they almost fell out of her head. Zola just looked amused.

"I thought you said the room was sealed," Eric said.

"It is," Brandon replied. "But this thing can record locally and then transmit once it's out in the open."

Eric and I exchanged twin expressions of horror. Yeah, the pervert could have heard every single scream. *Fuck.*

"You never thought to have Tony scan *you* for bugs?" Brandon wondered. "Not just your office or phones?"

"I never thought," Eric said dazedly. "Fuck. *Fuck*, the bastard collared me. Tagged me like an animal, and like a fucking idiot, I had no clue!"

"It might not have mattered anyway if they scanned for it," Ray pronounced as he prodded at the coin with some kind of long steel needles attached to a bunch of cords. "It has its a random noise, spread-spectrum countermeasure." He removed the necklace from the microscope and examined the warped head of Janus with renewed respect, then put it back under the lens. "Remarkable."

"More like disturbing," Eric replied.

"So, who made it?"

We swung toward Zola, who had been listening to everything and taking assiduous notes on a legal pad he'd brought with him.

Ray frowned. "Well, it doesn't have a manufacturer's label," he said. "Of course, it wouldn't for this kind of surveillance." He looked up. "We could probably check for the patent, but this is so new, I bet it's still being processed. Still, maybe three labs in the world could even approximate this kind of surveillance technology." He pointed at the crushed metal and tiny chip inside. "As far as we know, the Chinese don't have anything like it, and neither do the Russians."

"Ray consults for DARPA," Brandon clarified.

Ray shrugged. "Half of the MIT labs are military funded. But I've had clearance since 1978, you realize. All three labs that make this sort of thing that I know of are in the U.S. And they're all private contractors. Lockheed, Gruber, and Chariot."

Zola made a note. "Illegal surveillance," he said to everyone. "So he did it himself. Everything stacks up."

"Fuck," Eric muttered. "He's going to...when he finds out we know."

Unable to stop myself, I set a hand on his shoulder. Before I could take it away again, Eric covered it with his and squeezed tightly before letting it go.

"It's what I wanted to tell you when I came," Zola continued. "I looked into this guy Carson after we met, Jane. Or tried to. It's going to take some major investigative power to learn anything concrete, I'm afraid. The man is clean as a whistle, and he lives behind a wall of political and military protection."

I nodded. "I thought that might be the case. I couldn't find anything either."

"You were looking into him?" Eric asked me.

I turned with a scowl. "Well, of course I was looking, you idiot. What do you think, I was sitting around playing on my sewing machine? Pretending like some bastard didn't just march into my life, steal my childhood and my husband on the same day, and then proceed to blackmail the two of us? *Obviously* I've been trying to find out about him. But he's basically the hardest man to catch on the planet. If I hadn't met him in person, I'd assume he was a phantom."

"Well, of course it's the case," Brandon said. "I could have told you that. I believe I did."

Everyone turned to him.

"You were in the society too?" Zola asked, now scribbling furiously.

Brandon shook his head. "I was tapped, but I didn't join. Partly because I couldn't find out much about John Carson beyond his title. And I couldn't find out about anyone else because they all used the fake Hellenistic names."

"What do you mean?" Zola asked.

"Greeks," Eric said lamely. "And Roman, mostly. They use *The Aeneid* to come up with code phrases too."

Brandon rolled his eyes. "Can I just say that Titan is a stupid choice, by the way? It's not even a real name—just a type of god. Yours makes more sense—Triton, son of Poseidon, god of the sea. Shipping, ocean. It had a logic to it. Carson's is just lazy."

"This is why you didn't join?" Skylar asked with a raised brow. "Because their naming procedure was inconsistent?"

Brandon cast her an impatient look. "No. I didn't join because the guy who tapped me was shady as hell, like I told you. Some random asshole in a big suit invites me into his super-secret club by blindfolding me and forcing me to sit in a fuckin' dungeon for three days. What do you think I said?"

"You've been there?" Eric asked with a shudder. "His...place?"

Brandon gave his friend a queer, knowing look. "Might have. They took me to a few different spots. But I wondered where you might have ended up."

Eric didn't reply. I swallowed and fought the urge to take his hand when he flexed it, looking for mine.

"But you met him?" he asked Brandon incredulously. "You got to that point and he just let you...go?"

Brandon shook his head. "Well, it wasn't that easy. He did try to talk me out of it. But after three other abductions, I was done with that shit. So I finished my lunch, told John Carson to go fuck himself, and left after that last meeting. Except leaving still meant being blindfolded and dumped in a ditch somewhere in Western Connecticut. I got a couple of good punches in, though, even with the blindfold." He shook his head, looking like he wouldn't mind delivering those punches again. "Took me nine hours to get home from there. Bastards."

His south Boston accent was starting to emerge, demonstrating just how much he hated remembering this guy. Carson had long morphed into "Cah-son" again. By the way Skylar was grinding her teeth, she sensed the tension as well. I could sympathize.

"What about the other members?" Zola asked. "Jane, you mentioned someone Eric called Jude when we last spoke. Is that his real name? It's not Greek, right?"

"That's Jude LeTour," Brandon said. "His family negotiates a bunch of Asian imports. Glorified middle men."

"Hermes," I murmured, thinking of the Greek messenger from whom Jude took his name.

Eric shook his head. "None of them will talk. Trust me. Carson makes sure of it."

"I'd still like their names," Zola said. "You never know what will make people move. People who are a part of these kinds of organizations aren't quiet out of loyalty—it's because they are protecting themselves. There's always a pressure point."

"There is," Eric said bitterly. "And John Carson knows all of them for every single member. I really can't—"

"Yes, you can," I put in. "You have to at some point."

But Eric just remained tight-lipped.

"What?" Skylar asked. "What is it?"

"He's worried," Zola suggested. "Because two years ago, Chariot became the biggest military industrial lobbyist in Washington. They were responsible for increasing the military budget by about fifteen percent, and most of that went to them."

"So?" Skylar said. "That doesn't give John Carson an excuse to break the law and extort people."

"No," Brandon said gently. "But it does mean that a lot of very powerful people won't give a shit if he tries."

Eric sank his head into his hands again, looking very much like he couldn't breathe. Brandon reached behind him to take Skylar's hand—whether to comfort himself or her, I didn't know.

"So...what does this mean?" I asked. "He can't track you anymore now that we ruined his thingy. Can't we...Jesus, can't we just tell him it's over? I'm his daughter, after all, maybe he'd... maybe he'd listen to me."

"Jane." Eric's voice was flat. Lifeless. Even I didn't believe my own suggestion.

"I have some friends at the FBI," Zola said. "I'll contact them, see if there is an investigation already running into the Janus society or John Carson. In the meantime, you two have a choice: go back to your life and wait for him to send another whatever that thing is, or you can tell me the rest of what you know, and maybe I can help you get some protection while I start my own investigation..."

He trailed off. Again, it was clear that no one in the room thought we could just escape someone like my biological father.

"We could probably handle our own protection," Brandon said snidely, earning an elbow from Skylar. He wasn't wrong, though.

I turned to Eric, prepared to fight. "I don't want to go back," I said plainly. "I can't do this. It's...we're not going to last. He'll break us, and honestly, part of me thinks that's exactly what he wants."

Eric was quiet for a minute. Then he reached out and took my hands. This time I let him.

"I don't want to live in that apartment, pretend we're strangers," I said quietly. "I d-don't want to pretend to hate you anymore." My voice cracked on the last bit, basically blaring my truth.

But when he looked up, all I saw was that same truth reflected. He was scared, of course. Much more than me—he knew firsthand what kinds of personal terrors John Carson was capable of. But Eric's mask, the one he used to protect himself at all costs, was gone.

He squeezed my hands even tighter, his thumb brushing over the empty space where my rings should be.

"I don't want to hate you either," he whispered. "I can't, Jane. I just can't."

"So what do we do?" I asked, my voice uncharacteristically small. "Do we—do we face him?"

"No," Eric said, looking at me with wide eyes. "We run."

TWENTY-ONE

Zola's next suggestion was to research Carson's company rather than the man himself.

"That makes sense," Skylar remarked as we bent around her computer back at the house. "What do historians always say? Follow the money?"

So we did. And while John Carson appeared to have hardly any web presence, after he became CEO of Chariot approximately twenty years earlier, his mark was obvious on the company's life. After becoming one of the original purveyors of biological weapons during the fallout of the Vietnam War (and suffering the public blowback for it), Chariot quietly went back to electronics and parts manufacturing for a solid twenty-five years. They didn't seriously get back into warmongering until after 9/11, though it was clear they never completely abandoned the research.

"Look at the shareholders' reports," Zola muttered, pointing through a few charts. "Their profits tripled. Every year."

"Whoa," Brandon said from his place on the couch, where he appeared to be looking at the same documents. "Looks like that's also when they became a major supporter of a bunch of the war hawks in congress too. Did you see?"

When we looked closer at nearly every political contest, local and national over the last twenty years, Chariot's political donations were nearly on par with the Koch brothers or Tom Steyer. Simply put, John Carson appeared to have nearly every major politician in his pocket, and had for the last two decades.

"I'd bet a thousand dollars that John Carson helped co-write the Patriot Act," Ray said. "No more warrants on domestic surveillance? They would have been all over that kind of technology."

"So Chariot now just makes stuff that spies on people?" Skylar asked between her teeth. "Or other stuff too?"

"Ohhh, they make a lot more than that," Ray said gravely.

"Weaponry. Systems. Missiles," Brandon chimed in. "You name anything that blows shit up, they make it. And they sell to about half the countries on the planet, or have since John Carson took over from his father in the nineties. Think Tony Stark before he became Iron Man, and that's basically your dad, Jane. Well, maybe not Tony Stark. Obadiah Stane's a better fit. Iron Monger, you know?"

He bounced between Skylar's and my blank looks. Brandon always was a closet comic book fanatic, but it was actually one of the things I liked most about him. Underneath his sleek exterior, the guy really was a total dork.

"Since when did *you* become anti-gun?" Skylar asked.

Brandon glanced nervously at me. He didn't realize I knew about his past—the one where he used to run around with hood-lums in South Boston until he was about twenty-one or so. I happened to know he still kept a loaded gun in a safe next to their bed. It was cause for many an argument between him and Skylar.

"This has nothing to do with that," Brandon replied acerbically. "Over the last twenty years, Chariot Industries became the largest arms dealer in the world. John Carson has most of the federal government in his pocket, and probably most of the military too. NRA. GOP. DNC. Name your political acronym—he controls them all and sells bullets to everyone else on the planet that matters. He is the last person you'd ever want to piss off."

Eric sank further into the sofa, where he hadn't moved since we'd all migrated back to the house.

"Oh, fuck," he moaned softly to the ceiling. "What the fuck are we going to do?"

We spent another few hours combing the internet for anything else that could get Zola started on an investigation he now insisted on spearheading. Even if the Brooklyn DA didn't want to take it on, he had friends at the FBI who might. But Brandon was right: John Carson was a ghost. The fourth-generation head of a company that first made its millions profiteering during World War I, there were virtually no photographs of him past the age of fifteen or so.

"Here's...oh, no, I think this is his father again, Jane," Zola said when he found yet another picture of a heavily side-burned Gabriel Carson from the seventies. "Your grandpa sure liked a good leisure suit."

I scowled. "He was *not* my grandfather. None of these people are my family."

Zola shut his mouth—it wasn't the first time I'd snapped at someone for making that kind of remark.

"Here!" Brandon said triumphantly. "Found him!"

We crowded around his laptop to look at a grainy *People Magazine* spread from the late eighties.

"That's not him," I said. "That's Gabriel again."

"Not him," Brandon said. "*Him.*"

He pointed a big finger at a man lingering behind the principal three in the photo. It was unclear, but if I squinted, I could make out the features of a much younger man who had the same hooked nose and curly hair as the one who had so rudely disrupted my wedding. His eyes were dark, and he scowled in the photo.

"It says President Bush and the First Lady with Gabriel Carson *and son*, in Kennebunkport, 1988."

I shoved my face closer. "Holy shit. That *is* him, isn't it?"

I backed up so the others could see. He stood with the Bushes, one of the most important political dynasties in history. It was well documented that George W. had been a Skull and Bones member during his time at Yale. Maybe he had been a member of Janus too.

"Send me that link, will you?" Zola asked. "Right now, it's the only identification we have. But I'll need it to start the investigation."

"And you're sure your friends at the bureau won't tip him off?" Eric asked for the fifteenth time.

Zola nodded. "These guys are friends of mine from the Marines. We did two tours together. Patriots, all of them."

Eric nodded, and Brandon typed away while the rest of us adjourned to the living room. The photo felt like the hammer coming down on a nail. Our fate, somehow, was sealed with the realization that John Carson wasn't just a strange, vindictive man who seemed to appear out of thin air to ruin Eric's and my life. He was a real person. And real people had real weaknesses.

———

A FEW HOURS LATER, after Zola had left to get the last train back to New York, Eric and I finally lay down together in the dark.

We had not, after all, decided to sleep in separate bedrooms.

But oddly, neither of us had gotten undressed, just lain on the bed in our clothes and faced each other on the pillows.

Everyone had decided it would probably be best to leave in the morning. An evening storm had hit Boston with the first snow of the season—even if Carson knew the coin was out of commission, no one thought he would retaliate until at least the morning, and that was only if he really was monitoring it that closely (Eric seemed to think he was, but I had my doubts that a very busy CEO was *that* obsessed with our sex life). At best, he'd send a new one with a strict order to wear it immediately *or else*. At worst, his thugs would try to force Eric into a van again.

"If he tries to abduct you...well, it's not like we don't have security," Brandon added as we made our way upstairs to the bedrooms. He'd already called in two extra security men to guard the house that night, just as a precaution on top of Tony plus Skylar and Brandon's usual detail.

So we decided on England, and from there, Europe. A perverse version of the honeymoon we never took.

"The U.K. has a good relationship with the U.S., but they don't buy from Chariot," Ray had informed us before leaving. "Lockheed wrapped up those contracts years ago, and I happen to know the current Prime Minister really does not like Chariot or any of its champions. It's unlikely John Carson has MI-6 at his disposal."

It didn't make us feel completely better. But it was something.

So we packed our things that night, ready to make our move as soon as we could. Eric had only placed one phone call—a telegram to be delivered to Nina's apartment tomorrow evening, informing her that we were taking a sudden honeymoon for a few weeks and requesting her to step in at board meetings. It wouldn't go over very well, but it was a stopgap at least. Because we were together, we wouldn't be violating the terms of Celeste's will, and on top of that, it wouldn't tip Calvin off immediately as to where we were.

"I don't want to run," I finally admitted as I turned onto my back. "It feels...wrong."

Eric sighed. "We've been over this. It's temporary. Just until Zola, Brandon, and I figure out what to do next. Brandon and I aren't Jeff Bezos, but we've got resources between us. And Zola has at least a few people at the FBI on his side. We just need to figure out what Carson wants. His pressure point."

I shrugged. "Maybe it's just easier for you. This is what you do, right? Run away?"

Eric frowned. "Is that really what you think?"

"It's becoming a bit of a pattern."

He stared at me. "Takes one to know one."

"That's not fair. When was the last time I ran away from you?"

"I had to chase you into the ocean. You ran then."

I didn't say anything. It was true. But it wasn't the same thing. Over the last six months, for the first time in my life, I had become the more tenacious of a pair. I had changed. I had stuck around. I had wondered where this man had gone. And it had hurt. So. Much.

"I'd follow you anywhere, you know," Eric said quietly.

I remained silent. Would he, really? When he'd been so eager to leave?

Eric reached and turned my cheek so I was looking at him. I closed my eyes. He waited until I opened them again. And still, there was that open, almost plain face that sometimes flashed with such extreme, heart-wrenching charisma, I almost couldn't take it. There was that earnest sorrow. The mask had evaporated.

"I'm sorry," he said. "For the way I've been acting. For that comment at dinner about Caitlyn. For everything."

"Did you really talk to her?" I asked, surprised by how much the idea really hurt. In the grand scheme of things, Caitlyn Calvert's pettiness seemed so small now. But she fit into Eric's world in a way I didn't. There was a part of me that might always feel threatened by that.

He shrugged. "Over speaker with everyone else. To be honest, she's a big reason I didn't want to go to Violet's for Thanksgiving. They're...well, I missed Nina. But Jane, you're my family now. You have to know that."

He pulled my chin toward him and examined my lips a moment. His mouth trembled, and I could feel mine do the same. I wanted to kiss him, but at the same time, that never seemed to rid us of the past that hung around like a ghost.

Eric seemed to understand. Instead of a controlling, forceful movement, he simply stroked the side of my cheek. Then only after our breathing calmed, he placed a chaste kiss on one corner of my lips. I welcomed the touch, but the rankling from the past several weeks still lingered.

He broke away with a sad expression. "It's going to take more than that, isn't it?"

I quirked a brow. "You think?"

Eric sighed, but didn't argue. "We could go back. Be room-mates for the next month. Pretend the necklace was run over by a car and let him give me another until you can leave for good. I never—Jane, I swear to God, I never thought it would be this insane for you. You don't have to bear this shitty burden. I don't for one goddamn second think I'm worth it."

I toyed with his hands. His fingertips were calloused—from climbing, he told me once. So unlike what you would expect from a blueblood like him.

"The problem in the church wasn't that you screwed Caitlyn five years ago," I said, surprising myself when I changed the subject completely. "I just want to make that clear. It's that you never told me. Just like you never told me about your family, your dad, Penny, Janus..." I started to feel dizzy with all the secrets this man had kept. "It's that even now, I'm still kind of in the dark..."

"Jane..."

"What did he do to you?" I asked suddenly. "Really. I need to know."

Eric stilled. "Who?"

I turned so I could see his face clearly. He didn't have to look at me, but I wanted to look at him during this conversation.

"Carson," I said quietly. "Why—what are you so scared of? Really?"

There was a long silence—long enough that I thought he wasn't going to answer. Then Eric's hand stretched and took a harsh grip on the sheets.

"He...kept me in a room," he said. "In the dark. Only ten days, right? Long enough to make me feel like I was going crazy."

I sucked in a breath, though I had a feeling this was only the tip of it.

"And when he did come in...he was angry, Jane. He was angry I'd defied him. He was angry about you. So he punished me. And he did everything he could to make sure I would associate that punishment with you." He laughed, then, a sharp, blistering sound that hurt my ears. "He did a pretty good job of it at first."

I waited a bit longer for him to elaborate, but it soon became clear he wouldn't. Well, not without my prodding.

"How?" I pushed as gently as I could.

"Jane, you don't want to hear about this."

"Yes, I do. You went through this for me. At the hands of my fucking sperm donor. Tell me. Please."

There was another chest-moving sigh. But eventually, Eric told me what happened.

I stared at the wall with my cheek buried into my pillow, wishing I could touch him while he spoke, but also sensing it would not be welcome. Because his story was gruesome.

It had taken two days, maybe three. There was a hatchet-man, some former KGB goon who wielded torture tools like a musical conductor. Rib-cracking kicks to the side, or blows to the temple that made him see stars. Some casual waterboarding. Dutch scratching, which was a far too humorous name for beating the hell out a man's crown jewels with a knotted rope. They'd made Eric hate almost every part of his body—including the one I loved most. And when they weren't doing that, they'd forced him to watch a slideshow of photos...photos of me. Right before they would start it all over.

"That's insane," I whispered as he finished his terse, but effective descriptions.

"He is," Eric said. "Carson got mad, though, when he left a bruise. The point, he said, was always to remain discreet." He barked a sardonic laugh. "That black eye wasn't very discreet, was it?" He pointed at the skin around his eye that had all but healed at this point.

"Seriously, though." I pushed up from the bed, full of anger. "Who the fuck does this guy think he is, Vito Corleone? You can't just rip people off the streets and torture them, for Christ's sake!"

"Most people can't, no—"

"We need to call the police." I wiggled insistently, like the extra movement would make me feel like I was doing something. "You should have told Zola all of this. He could call the FBI. Someone needs to know."

"Jane," Eric said. "It doesn't matter."

"But he—

"It doesn't matter," he crooned, stroking my back like I was a frenzied animal. "It really doesn't matter."

"What? How can you say that?"

"Don't you see?" he asked. "It didn't work."

I blinked, sucking in breaths to tame the rage burning in my chest. "It...didn't?"

"John Carson wanted me to walk out of that room hating you, Jane," Eric said, pulling me up his body so I sprawled over him, but we were face-to-face. His hands slid up and down my arms. "But I couldn't. I knew it the second I saw you again in my apartment. That he hadn't even scratched the surface of what I felt. I could never hate you. Not even close."

His gray eyes suddenly looked so much older than they had even two weeks ago. And was it just me, or had a few new silver hairs made their dashing appearance near his temples?

"I've been waiting for you to come back," I whispered, suddenly terrified by the truth that had been haunting me: that maybe he never would. All the anger I'd felt over the past few weeks really just came down to protecting myself from the fact that this man could hurt me more than anyone else. And had.

"Maybe I thought if you knew...you wouldn't want the real me," he admitted when I thought he wouldn't respond at all.

I smacked a palm half-heartedly on his chest. "Haven't I shown you everything I am? Crazy dyed hair and all?"

"That's just cosmetic. My secrets run pretty deep."

"What did you say? You just wanted me? Well, I just want you."

Eric sighed. "I don't want to keep secrets from you anymore," he said quietly.

"Then don't."

"Even if that means we have to be a secret together?"

"You'd walk in, and it was like I wasn't there," I said as a tear escaped. "All those years we fought. We yelled. We sparred. But you were never like that. You never treated me like I was invisible." I sniffed and swiped at another tear. "I gave you everything, didn't I? But you held yourself back."

Eric didn't move, his tortured expression cast in stone as he listened. But then, suddenly, he pulled me to him, clasping my head against his broad chest so hard that his fingers dug into my scalp.

"I was protecting you," he said fiercely. "Do you understand now why? He's a monster, Jane. I didn't want you anywhere near him. And when he grabbed you—even the fucking *suggestion* that he would do anything to you like what he did to me..."

"I...I know." My voice was muffled against his chest.

"I couldn't talk because they were listening, but I wanted to tell you everything, Jane. *Everything*."

"What about before?" I pushed, though I didn't fight his embrace. "Even before the wedding, you kept things from me."

"I didn't mean to. I swear to God, I didn't mean to. I— fucking hell. Before the wedding, those months..."

He finally released me, and I pushed up on my forearms, still balanced across his chest. He cupped my face between his hands, cradling my cheeks like he was mining for gold.

"Every moment I've spent with you—from the beginning, Jane, not just the last six months—every fucking moment has been the happiest of my life. Fighting, fucking, laughing, talking. I'd take them all again. Every single sorry one of them, so long as they were with you."

I watched him for a long time, doing my best to read his face. That mask still didn't appear. Every fear he had was still written plainly over his features. He looked tired, sad, worried, and upset. But more than that, he looked very much in love. With me.

"I'm still mad at you," I said as I closed my hands around his wrists, holding them where they were.

"Then why?" he asked. "Why fight so hard? With me? For

me? Because you do, Lefferts. I know I'm not worth it, but I'm so goddamn glad you do."

"Because the fucked-up truth is, I'd rather be mad at you than pleased with anyone else."

A small smile peeked through the gloom. "No one loves to fight me like you do?"

I couldn't hide my own smile either. "Something like that."

And then, because I couldn't not, I kissed him again. It wasn't an angry kiss, or the kind of kiss so steeped in lust it choked. It was the kind that just belonged. Like we always had, against all odds, right here. With each other.

Eric's mouth opened to mine naturally, and he released my face so he could wrap his strong, lean arms around my body and roll me to my back, caging me against the bed. Caging me and freeing me all at once.

"Jane," he whispered as he nuzzled my neck, pulling away Skylar's black cardigan, and then tugged at the thin straps of the red dress. "Jane, please."

But I didn't want him to beg. Not now. More than anything, I wanted to make him feel strong.

My hands wove into his thick blond hair, pressing his face lower as he inhaled my skin. My fingers slid lower, under his collar, helping him from his shirt as well until finally he pushed up on his knees, giving me a fine view of his solid, muscular form as he removed the shirt completely.

"Come here," he urged, pulling on one of my hands until I was kneeling with him.

We quickly shed the rest of our clothes, eager to find skin to warm skin in the dark. The world was so cold beyond the secure walls of this house, surging toward us, closer every second. And yet, we couldn't do anything but this. Because if Eric and I were going to win this battle, we had to find each other here in the dark. We couldn't stand alone.

He pulled me back on top of him once we were both free of all our impediments. Even my hair was stripped of pins, cascading all over my shoulders, a shadowy waterfall to shelter us both.

"Give me your mouth," Eric said even as he took it, his kisses hungrier this time, lush and full.

"I missed your voice," I mumbled against his lips. Living in silence, him unable to speak. I hadn't realized until now how much I thrived on his thoughts, not just my own.

He hummed into the kiss, then slid his tongue to co-mingle with mine, twisting and dancing in that delicious way that prompted deep moans from both our chests. Another kind of language, but ours just the same.

"Say it," I whispered as his mouth floated over my neck again. "I want to hear it."

Eric flipped me onto my back. "Say what, gorgeous?" He landed a kiss on one breast, then worshipped the other before he continued his path downward.

"My name."

I felt a smile against my navel. "Jane."

But I shook my head and pulled at his hair. "No, the other one."

His chin balanced on my hip. Slowly, a sly grin twisted across Eric's otherwise stolid features, casting it alight with fire and charisma. A fire blazed in my belly. The grin widened.

He pressed his lips to the soft skin of one inner thigh, then the other before he tugged lightly on the hair down there. Then he touched his nose to the quiver of nerves that made me shudder. "Pretty girl."

I hummed and arched into his waiting mouth. "Again."

"Pretty girl." He said it again, but this time it was more of a vibration as his lips found my clit, and two of his dexterous fingers slipped inside me. They curled. He licked. And my entire body bloomed.

"Eric!" I cried as he took me closer and closer to that blissful cliff.

But just as I was about to topple over it completely, he pulled back and crawled right back up my body, maintaining that skin-to-skin connection both of us craved.

"Spread your legs." His voice was low, but stronger than I'd heard it since *before*.

I hissed as the long, solid length of him pulsed against my thigh. It was like our hurried, animal fuck in the lab hadn't even happened. This time every cell in my body wanted to unite with his.

He didn't wait for my answer, just took my lower lip between his teeth and bit lightly. I did as I was told.

Eric's eyes shuttered as he entered, one slow inch at a time, filling me, testing me, stretching my capacity. He waited a moment while I adjusted to his size. And then, as his poet's eyes held mine in their thrall, he finally began to move.

His body found its rhythm quickly, muscles corded as he held himself to measured beats. With every thrust and pull, he drove us both higher and higher, past the point where any of the outside world could threaten our pleasure anymore.

Then he stopped, like he had just realized where we were.

"What?" I asked "Why—why are you stopping?" I rotated my hips toward him, but he didn't move, just continued to watch.

"Are we really doing this?" he wondered. "You and me against the world?"

My body cried for him.

"Yes!" I whispered fiercely, clasping his face between my palms. "You and I were born to fight, Eric. Against each other, sure. But for each other...absolutely."

He stared at me for a long time, and then he lunged forward.

"Eric!" I shouted, unable to hold it back. "Oh, God, p-please!"

"Give me all your screams, Jane," he growled. "I'll swallow them, every one."

"ERIC!" I cried again, but he did as he promised, taking my cries with deep, forceful kisses, savoring the depths of my voice as an orgasm crested through us both.

Our bodies melted into each other, clinging to each other, slick and heated even as the cold from the outside pressed in on us more. Somewhere out there, a man who called himself my father wanted only to ruin a bond that now seemed critical to life itself.

I had never felt so sated. Or so scared.

"Eric?" My voice was smaller than it had ever been.

"I know." He pressed his forehead against mine. Mind to mind. Soul to soul. "I know."

"We have to go now, don't we?" I refused to open my eyes. I didn't want to see the answer I knew would be on his face. "We shouldn't wait until morning."

But I felt Eric's nod anyway. In the dark, his arms tightened further, like he thought the wind howling outside our window might rip me away.

"Yes," he agreed. "We have to go now."

INTERLUDE II

"Penny? Pen, are you home? I tried to call your cell, but it went straight to voicemail."

Eric closed the door of his mother-in-law apartment as he entered the familiar dim space. He dropped his messenger bag on the crowded rumple of shoes beneath the coat rack and hung up his raincoat. He shook out his hair, absolutely soaked from the sudden downpour that had hit just as he was exiting his last exam of his undergraduate career. One final late nor'easter was pushing through New Hampshire that day, right on the tail end of spring, almost like it was trying to chase the Dartmouth undergrads out of Hanover for the summer. By this point every year, the small town itself needed a summer vacation.

"I finally got that paper back from Professor Lockhart, Pen," Eric continued as he meandered around the kitchen. He pulled out a plate of the spanakopita Penny had made last night and pulled up the cellophane to sniff it.

Sweet, he thought. Still good.

They were down to the last groceries of the week, but Penny wouldn't get paid until Monday. Eric hadn't found summer work yet, and after they announced their engagement a few months ago, his allowance had been completely cut off. Penny, saint that she was, had insisted that he finish the semester strong instead of finding a job immediately.

"Forget about it," she said, over and over again. "There'll be time for that after you get your degree."

The first phrase, pronounced "fuhggedaboudit," had sounded so adorably Queens that Eric had teased that she sounded like Robert de Niro. She'd just smacked him on the arm, then dragged him into the bedroom to make him apologize the right way to her sweet curves.

Eric smiled to himself as he recalled the memory. Maybe he could tease her now so she could take her revenge again.

"So, I was thinking we should just do it, Pen," Eric said as he meandered into the bedroom, pulling off his t-shirt and unbuttoning his dampened jeans. He rifled through the second drawer of the beaten bureau looking for a pair of shorts. "I don't need to walk, you know? No one is going to be here to watch me anyway. The Grande Dame is still holding a grudge, after all, and Mother's too busy in St. Tropez with that fool she married to bother. I'll have the school send my diploma to your parents' place in Astoria, and then you and I can just hightail it to Atlantic City. Then, I don't know. We could still wait tables for a while. Maybe even save up for a little honeymoon before the move to Boston. Catskills, maybe, or what about Miami? Pen? What do you think?"

When she didn't answer, he finally looked up. That had been the plan, after all, to save up for a year before he started law school at Harvard. He had deferred specifically for that reason. Meanwhile, Penny had been asking him to set a date for weeks, but he'd evaded her, waiting for his family to come around before he made any other moves.

Today, though, when he'd called his grandmother's house and

been given the shake by the butler for the tenth time, it had finally sunk in. They were never going to approve of Penelope. It was them or her. But Eric had already made his choice.

"Did you fall asleep in the bath again?" he asked as he walked into the adjoining bathroom. "You really have to stop—"

And there, his heart stopped completely.

The water in the tub was the color of roses in full bloom, a deeper red than he'd ever seen. It was also cold. Chilled like the late afternoon air.

Penny's wrists, neatly sliced up to her elbows, sunk to her pale thighs, the rest of her emerging from the opaque liquid like a freshly carved statue, her still-wet brown hair pasted back from her face. But her blue eyes, normally so bright, were open, glazed, and horribly dulled. The skin around her mouth and eyes bore the stains of tear tracks and tiny new wrinkles of horror. Perhaps at what she had just done.

"No." The word, soft and hardly spoken, still ripped from his throat.

Eric fell to his knees before he'd even reached the big clawfoot tub, diving into the water to lift Penny out of the bloody mess. The red slashed across his shirt, his shorts, staining even the rain still pearled on his skin and hair. He fell to his knees, cradling the girl's cold body against his chest.

"No, no, no, baby, no!" Frantically, Eric searched for a pulse— at her chest, her neck, her wrist, anywhere.

None, of course, could be found. The wounds at her wrists weren't even bleeding anymore. The water had gone cold. She'd obviously been there for hours.

He dug his phone out of his pocket and had to dial the number four times before he could make it through.

"Nine-one-one?" He was shouting, but somehow couldn't even hear his own voice. "There's—oh, fuck, Penny—m-my fiancée. I—fucking, God, she...she's killed herself!"

He answered the woman's questions as best he could, stam-
mering through the address, Penny's state, what he'd found. As the
operator spoke, keeping him on the line, an item in the wire waste
bin caught Eric's eye.

"Fuck," he said.

"Sir?"

Keeping Penny clasped against his chest, he leaned over and
pulled the pregnancy test out of the garbage.

Two pink lines. One, then the other.

Eric's chest heaved, and he rocked the dead girl back and forth
in time with the pounding shakes of his body.

"Oh, God," he cried over and over again. A siren wailed in the
distance. "Please, God. No."

———

ERIC AWOKE GASPING, like he was underwater, drowning
in that sea of red all over again. He sucked in a deep breath, then
another, but nothing calmed the wrenching stab in his chest.
Fucking hell. Penny. He hadn't dreamed like that in years.

Sweat ran in rivulets down his brow. The air felt thick,
almost liquid. He was hot despite the cool mid-December
weather in Florence and the fact that the flat he and Jane were
renting near the San Lorenzo market seemed to have absolutely
no insulation. Winter was coming in Tuscany, but he felt like he
was trapped in a sauna.

Eric pushed down the comforter, careful not to disturb Jane.
Beside him, she slept, her face relaxed into porcelain perfection.
Eric watched her, willing his breath to fall in time with her own.
And slowly, it did. So strange, really, that a woman who drove
him as crazy as this one was also the key to maintaining his
sanity.

Two days. They had two more days before they had to leave

again. He didn't like to stay anywhere more than a few days, maybe a week at most, which, combined with the fact that he was reluctant to spend money in ways that would call attention, meant that he and Jane had basically been living like college-aged nomads for close to a month.

First had been London, where they had used an under-ground friend of Brandon's to get them fake passports. They'd escaped on the earliest flight out of Logan in the dead of night, arrived in the U.K. at close to one p.m., and moved on to the continent a few days later, sticking to ground transportation where possible. Paris, then Fountainebleau, where Eric had taken his frustrations out on the rock while Jane meandered the markets. After that, it had been down to Toulouse, followed by Nice and Monaco. From there, they took a flight to the south of Italy, moving their way up the boot and enjoying the sunshine until they rented a room in Florence from a landlady who liked cash better than real names.

For the first time in his life, Eric regretted not being closer to his family, if only to have a better idea of whom he could trust. And for the first time since her death, he truly missed his grand-mother. The old woman wasn't warm, but she had been shrewd enough that Eric liked to think she could have out-schemed John Carson. She would have understood what he *really* wanted out of this cat-and-mouse game he was playing. And then she would have known how to box the fucker into a corner, wrap him up, and send him on his damn way.

But Celeste was gone, and Eric still didn't even know all of the company's resources. He had been learning the ropes over the past six months, sure, but the tiny, unspoken rules were the hard part. Which cabinet members' loyalties lay where, which senator owed favors for which PAC donations, which comptroller could be bought, and which had to play it straight. And on and on and on. For a company like DVS, these kinds of alliances weren't just limited to New York City or even the United States. They spanned the damn globe. Sometimes Eric had a feeling he would never really learn these intricate parts of the job because he should have picked them up his entire life. The way a true heir would.

And so, also for the first time in his life, he wished he hadn't walked away from his family's legacy. Because it took more than a bank account to fight someone like John Carson. It took generations of knowledge, passed on between trusted advisors and a dynasty. Much more than a couple of former lawyers and a smattering of friends battling a network of spies they weren't even sure existed.

The other problem was that they would stick out nearly anywhere just by virtue of their own differences. They had no real shelter from the storm. Jane had suggested staying in Northern Europe for a while, where Eric would blend in with the tall, blond Vikings. Jane, unfortunately, would not. They could do the opposite and go somewhere in East Asia, but then it would be Eric who would stand out.

"Besides," Jane said as she knocked down that idea too, "most Koreans would know I'm mixed anyway, and definitely that I'm American."

For that reason, they had decided to stick to large metropolitan areas—more diversity meant more opportunities to fit in. London, a huge melting pot of culture, had been a good fit for the first two days until Eric had received a telegram from Boston informing them that Carson knew they were missing, and TSA informants had told him where they'd gone. So, London was short-lived, because there was no way in hell Eric was going to sit around waiting for Carson to truck him back to that hurt locker.

Jane's eyes opened, and before she turned, Eric took a moment to observe the multitude of color in their depths. Hazel

—green and brown and yellow and gray, flecked together in a perfect collage. Jane's eyes often reminded Eric of the Klimt paintings she loved so much. The gold freckles around her irises glimmered like the leaf technique.

Jane turned, sensing she was being watched. "Well, hello there," she murmured sleepily. There was still a slight smudge of makeup rimming her eyes, giving them a smokier allure than usual.

Paris. Carcassonne. Naples. Florence. It didn't seem to matter where they went. They always woke up like this. Wanting.

Eric remained silent for a few more seconds, enjoying the clear pleasure Jane took with his body as she trailed a hand up and down his torso. It was fair, after all—he enjoyed hers too. Amid the chaos of the last few weeks, this had become something of a morning ritual. Sometimes—okay, most of the time—those gentle touches turned into quite a bit more. But they were a constant, like they were making up for those few weeks they were forced to stay apart—maybe even the years they had lost by their own accord before that.

"Will you ever grow bored of me?" he wondered just as her hand started to drift downward, chasing the ridges of his abdominals. She took her time in between his chest muscles and over his abdomen. Jane could make fun of his climbing habit all she liked, but she seemed to like the end results.

She squinted to see him clearly. She was nearsighted, so he wouldn't be too blurry without her glasses. The expression was more out of confusion.

"I don't know. It's about as likely as you getting bored with me, I guess."

She looked back up at the ceiling. Eric tapped her cheek, and she turned back to him.

"Never," he said softly. "Not in the last eight years. Not in a hundred more."

A small, shy smile flickered on her face, then was replaced by one with more bravado. "Well, good," she said, popping over to smack a kiss on his lips. "That's settled then. No one is bored. And no one will be." She looked him over more critically. "I'll tell you what, though. I will get sick of that god-awful hair. I already am."

Eric picked at a strand of his dyed hair. He would admit—the black didn't suit him particularly well. But it had seemed a smart precaution to take in a part of the world where nearly everyone had dark hair.

"You don't like it?" he asked.

"You look like Edward Cullen," Jane said. When Eric tilted his head questioningly, she rolled her eyes. "A sparkle-skinned teen whose testicles didn't fall before he turned into the undead. It's not all bad. He reignited the sexual desires of an awful lot of middle-aged women."

He balked. "Just because of the hair, I'm a sparkly teenager?"

Jane shrugged. "Eh. Maybe. I'm not feeling particularly generous. It's too cold to be nice."

Before she could continue her ribbing, he rolled over her and stopped that line of thought in its tracks with a kiss. Suddenly he needed to feel her body, still naked from last night, wrapped around him like a vine.

He needed to feel safe.

The thought, ironically, made him feel even less so.

The sun turned a corner around one of the buildings, and suddenly the light slashed across Jane's face through the blinds.

Eric froze. "Fuck."

"What is it?"

He shook his head and pushed off her. "I—nothing. I'm just not in the mood."

This happened sometimes. In certain lights. Certain strobes or flashes, when they hit Jane's face in the right way, took him right back to that room.

Jane sat up, her long dark hair falling over her shoulder in ribbons. She had gone all the way back to black and had taken to straightening it. ("Anyone looking will think I'm a Japanese tourist.")

"No," she said gently. "I don't think so. You tried this crap last night too. What's going on?"

Eric picked up a strand and twirled it around his finger, enjoying her natural, more unruly wave after she fell asleep with it wet. He loved the way no part of Jane ever seemed to be able to conform completely.

"Bad dreams," he mumbled, avoiding her gaze.

She examined him for another long minute, like she was trying to decipher his thoughts. And then her mouth found his, and Eric was done thinking at all. His head fell back into the pillow, and now both of his hands found their way into her hair when she moved down his body. Fucking *hell*, the woman had a mouth that could turn the Pope from celibacy, and she was working magic with it under the sheets.

"That's better," she said once she'd brought him twice to the point of no return only to pull away.

With some effort, Eric managed to lift his head. "You minx. Finish the damn job, will you?"

"Well, that's not very gracious."

That cocky smile appeared. She wasn't wearing her lipstick, but her mouth was still reddened, slightly swollen from her efforts. Eric wanted to bite it.

"Come here," he ordered.

The smile widened. "In a minute."

She slid up the rest of him like a snake, taking the time to tease him with her parts—the brush of her hair over his hips, the tickle of hardened nipples across his chest, the drag of her snatch over his swollen tip. He bounced at that contact, and Jane smiled as she sat astride him. He usually preferred to be the one in charge, but for a moment, he liked seeing her like this, under the illusion that she could be in control.

Ah, fuck. Who was he kidding? Jane had been in control of him since he'd met her.

"Am I going to have to cuff you?" she asked when he jerked at the feel of her sheathing him, inch by inch.

His gaze was heavy lidded, but sparked at the dare. "I'd like to see you try, pretty girl."

She leaned down, enshrouding him with her hair, her sweet floral scent settling around him like a mantle. Her lips drifted around and inside, and she squeezed him. He jerked again.

"I think you and I both know that I could have you begging for them in about two minutes," she said, squeezing again. Her hips tilted forward, then back, allowing him to slip in and out, just by an inch or so. Teasing with delicious friction that wasn't quite enough.

And then, like she couldn't help it, she moved again to take him completely.

Eric might have smiled with satisfaction if he wasn't so over-taken. God, she was a thing of beauty—long and lean, riding him like an animal, reaching down between her legs to take what she wanted right along with him. No apology. No shame.

He tried to help out, sneak his fingers next to hers.

"No," she said, smacking his hand away. "This time you need to just watch. You need to just take it."

She began to move faster, and the light in the window seemed to expand. Eric's mouth opened, and his fingers dug into her thighs, seeking purchase somewhere while she drove them both mercilessly.

"Jane, I'm—fuck, I'm going to—"

She peered down at him, but didn't stop. Usually she'd let him pull out, let him cover her, mark her. She liked to see the evidence of his loss, her gain. It was another of her ways of assuming control in a situation where he tried to keep it for himself.

But this time she didn't. She just continued to rock, back and forth, driving him closer, closer, her fingers vigorously chasing the same goal.

And then, like a rocket, she exploded.

"ERIC!" Her voice, husky and full of sleep, reached the ceiling as she began to shake. And before he knew it, Eric was shaking too. He pulled her down, wrapping a hand around her neck, the other at her back. Keeping her flush to him, body to body, mind to mind.

He spilled into her.

And she took him. She took it all.

Jane took everything he'd ever have to give.

He could only hope it would be enough.

PART THREE

PROLEPSIS

Are you so blind, oh, woman of mine?
Can't you see the wretch that I am?
Flying this high, we soar, we die,
Cresting o'er sky and land.
The man in robes, the fools, the probes
Want questions we dare not ask.
So nights are spent with your jasmine scent,
Noses buried beyond our tasks.
Now hope alights before we take flight;
Will the hunter arrive with his killers?
Should his aim be true, should our faults accrue,
Would you stand fast as a pillar?
Be still unlike your heart of a sparrow
So that out of love, I might block the arrow.

"Fear Sonnet"
— from the journal of Eric de Vries

TWENTY-TWO

I stretched like a cat, long enough that my toes brushed against the rusted metal bed rail at the end of the mattress. Outside, the bustle of Florence was audible. Whoever said Italians were lazy was a damn liar. The San Lorenzo neighborhood had been waking me up at seven a.m. on the dot every morning with the sounds of trucks and market stalls opening first thing.

The central market, just a few blocks away was probably already bustling after the local restaurateurs had scavenged the prime pickings. The heavy scent of espresso bubbled up from the cafe at the bottom of our building, and every so often, a shout of conversation snuck past the arched single-paned windows flooded with gray December light.

I turned over groggily. Eric's side of the bed was empty. That in itself wasn't particularly unusual. He didn't sleep well—hadn't since we'd left the States nearly four weeks ago—and usually went for a run or did some kind of exercise in the early morning hours while I continued sleeping. He didn't like leaving me alone, but we both figured out quickly enough that he would start acting like a trapped rat if he didn't get *some* outlet every day. Me, I was good with walking around museums or the market. My cardio back home was window shopping—there was no reason to change that here.

I found him on the other side of the room, checking the burner phone we'd been using for the last few days and fiddling with his god-awful hair. Despite the chilly December air—our rooms depended on an archaic heater that only worked occasionally—he was shirtless in a pair of leggings and running shoes, the sinewy lines of his back still covered with a sheen of sweat. I licked my lips.

"It's no use. You still look ridiculous," I said, pushing up onto my elbow while holding the sheet to my chest. I'd tried to sleep with clothes on, but Eric wasn't having it. Even though we fell asleep apart, he tended to wrap around me in his sleep, like some part of his subconscious desperately needed skin-to-skin contact. I wasn't one to argue. I missed him too.

Eric pulled at his hair once more. It wasn't as bad as it had been at first, when the shock of black made him look like Edward Scissorhands. Now that the black had settled, he was more on the level of a low-level Cure groupie.

"I look like a local," he said to the mirror, then turned around, giving me an impressive view of his blocked abs. He'd lost some weight since we left—his anxiety kept him from eating enough, despite all of the amazing food we'd enjoyed. It wasn't too much. If anything, it made his already impressive physique that much more eye-searingly cut.

"You still look like a vampire," I corrected him. "Absolutely no one anywhere would ever confuse you for an Italian."

"What about now?" He popped on a pair of Ray Bans and struck a pose.

"Vampire Jack Nicholson."

The sunglasses were hurled at me. I dodged them, giggling until Eric tackled me onto the bed.

"Ah! Get off me, you sweat factory!" I batted him ineffectively.

But my protests were lies, and Eric knew it. Once again, his lean body against mine felt less like a cage and more like an open door. I closed my eyes, enjoying his lips drifting over my neck. His hands pushed away the sheets, seeking the curves of my rib cage and waist like he was memorizing every inch of my body.

"I hated it so much," he said for the tenth time, pausing to press his forehead to mine. "Not being able to touch you." He pushed up. "It's like breathing to me. You know?"

I nodded. I did know. I had felt the same way.

"Come here," I said, pulling him back down for another kiss. His lips, firm, yet soft, molded to mine, sinking me even deeper into the feather bed. With this kind of ecstasy, it was almost possible to forget we were on the lam.

But on the lam we were, and after close to four weeks of it, I had to be honest: I was getting a little tired of pretending we were poor students. Money wasn't an issue, of course, but the living in squalor was. Eric insisted we stay away from the places people would expect a de Vries to stay. Five, four, even three-star hotels were out. We rented cheap rooms in pensiones, but only because I drew the line at hostels. I wasn't the slightest bit interested in sharing a room with a bunch of pimply teenagers trying to find their next score of molly. Eric and I needed *space*.

Eric sat back on his heels and fingered my wrists, noting the still-reddened skin there from the scarf he used last night to bind them behind my back.

"Sorry about that," he murmured with a hint of a smirk.

I smacked him on the shoulder. "No, you're not."

"No," he admitted as his right dimple made an appearance. "I'm not. And I'll probably do it again."

But instead of making good on his promise right then, Eric got up and meandered back to his duffel bag, which had accumulated a few changes of clothes during our trip. He pulled out a shirt and plugged in the decrepit old iron. Five-star hotels were a no go, but Eric wasn't willing to forgo his tailored style.

"I booked us tickets on the next train to Genoa," he said. He removed his running shoes, waiting for the iron to heat. "From there we can see what's available and just go. We'll send another telegram to Brandon before leaving."

I flopped back into my pillows and sighed. This had become our new normal. New burner phones in every city to contact only each other. Brandon had set up an account at Western Union specifically to receive telegrams from Eric, who sent them only when we were about to leave places, to let them know we were okay. Meanwhile, he collected messages left for him over the course of each week. Brandon was the point of contact with the private investigators hired to dig into John Carson's history. The idea was to figure out what he really wanted, or at least some weaknesses to exploit. Because no one believed for one second that this strange vendetta had anything to do with the man's love for me.

Eric pulled out a pair of charcoal wool pants to press. "I know. I'm sick of it too."

"I just want to go home," I replied to the ceiling. "Not that our grand European caper hasn't been lovely."

And it had. It really had. Shitty accommodations aside, we'd seen all the stuff in Europe I'd never been able to see as an actual poor college student. Art and architecture I'd only seen in textbooks; more markets than I could shake a stick at. I would have been in heaven if it hadn't been for the potential threat lingering around every corner.

"We haven't even heard from Carson," I continued. "Don't you think there's a possibility he just gave up?"

The wry look on Eric's face told me he did not. "John Carson waited exactly ten years before contacting me again. I just ran off with his daughter, whom he forbade me to touch. I don't think he's just going to let it go."

"I still think we should talk more to your family. Not Calvin. Nina. Even Violet."

For that, I received no response at all. As far as the de Vries clan knew, we were just taking a delayed extended honeymoon over the holidays. The board of DVS hadn't been happy about it, but since Eric didn't hold an actual position in the company, and they wouldn't vote him in as chairman until after he had officially assumed ownership of the family's stockholdings, all there was to do was wait.

But Eric acted as though we had no allies within his family, and I wasn't ready to concede the point. Nina, for instance. Or:

"Your grandmother—"

"Who is dead." Eric's tone was hollow.

I swallowed. "Who is passed, yes. But she knew, Eric. She knew something like this would happen."

"Maybe." He turned his pants over and started ironing the other side.

We'd had this conversation a few times already, debating the extent to which Celeste had really anticipated John Carson's maneuvering, and why. At first, Eric had thought it had been part of some greater scheme, but now he wasn't so sure. He thought the sudden change was just a simple gift to us—a marriage by choice, if that's actually what we wanted.

"Why else would she have changed the terms of her will so last minute?" I argued.

"Maybe she just liked you, Jane. A lot, apparently."

A hint of a smile fluttered over Eric's face—he was so serious most of the time, especially since we'd left New York. I wanted more of that levity.

"I don't mean that," I said. "Celeste and I seemed to under-stand each other by the end. The gift to me was after the engage-ment, but the other one—the one requiring cohabitation—that one she made the morning of the ceremony. Why didn't she care if we were married anymore?"

Eric stared at his empty left hand—neither of us wore our rings—for a very long time. Long enough for the answer to dawn on him as it had on me.

"She really did know he was going to show up, didn't he?" he murmured. "She must have seen Jude and Faber when they showed up at the rehearsal dinner."

I nodded. "She did see them. She was shouting for you, don't you remember? And they had the same coins, you know. Eric, do you think there is any possibility she recognized them like my mom did?"

Eric swallowed thickly as he clearly followed my train of thought. "Fuck."

"She knew there was a chance the wedding would be stopped somehow. That someone would show up and—" My eyes practi-cally popped out of my head as another thought occurred to me. "Eric, you don't think they had anything to do with her..." I couldn't quite say it. Was that what all of this had come down to? Murder?

My mother's story whispered from the back of my mind again:

He tells me not to say anything. He gives me money if I stay quiet. Or else, he said, I would end up like her.

Dead. In a melon field.

I had scoffed at the idea that John Carson was an outright murderer at the time, but after learning at least some of what he had done to Eric, now I wasn't so sure. This new hypothesis about Celeste wasn't helping.

But Eric just shook his head. "I've known these guys a long

time. They don't take kindly when people don't keep their secrets, but I've never known anyone to stoop to murder. Just, you know, cruel and unusual torture. The dead aren't useful to them anymore."

I sat back in the pillows, unconvinced.

"She was sick, Jane. Really sick. I'm not surprised the drama of the day took it out of her."

I wasn't sure how to respond. People who were capable of kidnapping and torture didn't seem to have a particularly strong moral compass. But I had to default to his judgement on the matter.

"So the catch-22 wasn't to trap us," Eric murmured as he hung his pants over the back of a chair and started on a shirt. "It was for Carson."

"Sixty days," I said. "Just enough time for us to do it on our own." To do exactly what we'd done. Run away. Stand up to John Carson.

I looked down at my messenger bag, which, unbeknownst to Eric, held the unsigned marriage certificate. The sixty-day deadline was approaching. In another ten days, just after New Year's, we wouldn't be married at all. The license would expire, and everything we had done would be nulled.

I considered saying as much, but I didn't think Eric really cared about the marriage at this point. I had no idea what his plans were for after that deadline. We said this was a honeymoon, but a part of me wondered if he would think it wasn't worth the trouble after a while.

Maybe he was just biding his time until we could say goodbye for good.

With a deflated sigh, I rolled out of bed and rifled around the ground for the t-shirt I'd tried to wear to bed last night. One look in the mirror told me that I'd have to bear another cold shower in the tub in the corner of the room. I grimaced. It made me look and feel like a plucked chicken. Not hot.

Now finished with his ironing, Eric stripped off the rest of his sweaty clothes and jumped into said shower like the water wasn't icy cold. I watched appreciatively through the translucent curtain. Eric glanced over and caught me staring. He pushed back the curtain so I had an unadulterated view of his ridiculously cut body.

"Like what you see?" he asked coyly.

I tapped my lip. "You look like an ad for an at-home gym."

His face screwed up in mock confusion. "Is that a good thing?"

I didn't reply, just kept ogling.

"I'll take that as a yes," he said with a sly arch of one darkened brow. "You're welcome to join me, you know."

I sighed. The bad dye job didn't matter. After seeing the David in person just yesterday, I could definitively say that Eric was even better looking—and *much* better endowed—than Michelangelo's famous statue.

"Jane," he said. "Come on. The water is actually warm today. Get in here."

His tone brooked no argument, and before I could think twice, I practically skipped across the room to join him. If thinking about the future wasn't a viable possibility, then at least I could live in the moment.

TWENTY-THREE

"We have the rest of the day," Eric said a little over an hour later as we stood at the bar downstairs and enjoyed a couple of cappuccinos for breakfast. He had splurged with a brioche too, and I was picking off little pieces of it when he wasn't looking. "Signora Deflorio said she'll keep our bags until we meet our train at five."

"That was generous of her," I said. The miserly old landlady couldn't even be bribed to turn up the heat while we were here. "Or was it generous of you?"

Eric shrugged in a way that told me my second guess was the correct one. Then he took a sip of his coffee and made a face. A coffee snob to the nth degree, he barely tolerated the dark-roast styles of French and Italian espresso. I had already heard enough lectures on third-wave coffee and the merits of light roasting methods to last me a lifetime.

Before he could launch on yet another coffee tirade, I jumped in. "So, what's on the list? Another trip to the Uffizi?" We had spent the majority of Tuesday there after we'd arrived, and Eric couldn't get enough of the Caravaggio collection.

He set down his cup. "I thought maybe we could walk around town since it's actually nice today."

We peered out to the bluebird sky above Florence. It had been rainy most of the week, so our sightseeing had been confined primarily to museums and churches. There had been no idle walks by the river or winding around the Florentine streets, like all the travel websites promised.

"Exploring," I said. "Okay, I like it. Lead on, sir."

———

"DON'T you think that makes you stick out more than a phone would?" I asked for the tenth time as we stepped out of the central market with a backpack full of goodies for lunch later. Prosciutto, a couple of tomatoes, bread, and a half-bottle of wine to carry to wherever Eric was planning to take me today. It was cold and windy, but the sky was clear, and the off season meant minimal tourists. A good day for a picnic.

Eric turned the adorable paper map he insisted on using instead of a phone. Having been here before, he actually knew some parts of Florence reasonably well, but occasionally he needed some help, and that was usually where we got into trouble.

"It makes me look like a tourist," he replied. "Just like everyone else."

"Maybe if you were seventy. All right, Grandpa, where to?"

He turned to his map, studying it for the fifth time. Something I had learned about Eric on this trip was that he was only a good guide if he knew the place. But once he was disoriented, his sense of direction was terrible.

"Well, I was thinking maybe we could swing by Dante's house first—I just want to see the outside. Then we can back-track a little and cross via the Ponte Vecchio, since I know you wanted to see the shops. Which I think is...that way." He pointed in the opposite direction of the Arno river, which the Ponte Vecchio crossed. Which he should have known, considering we'd walked across it approximately a zillion times in the last six days.

I grabbed his finger and rotated it in the right direction. He watched the action, then a slow smile crept across his face. Before I could say anything, he leaned down and kissed me.

"Thanks, gorgeous," he said against my lips.

I readjusted my glasses—the kiss had knocked them off-kilter and fogged them up too. "Anytime. Shall we?"

"It's only a thirty-minute walk all the way to the piazza, I think. Can those shoes take it?"

I looked down at the gorgeous black booties I'd bought in Paris, which went perfectly with my daily outfit of jeans and sweaters. I'd tried to steal a couple of Eric's shirts just to change up my spare look, but he wasn't having it.

"These boots were literally made for walking," I said. "And that *is* what I'm going to do."

One side of Eric's mouth quirked again, and my insides hummed. How *did* he always manage to do that?

"Come on, Nancy," he said, slinging a long arm around my shoulder. "Let's go exploring."

———

"I CAN'T BELIEVE you skipped Italy when you came to Europe," he said for the twelfth time as we approached Ponte Vecchio, the famous medieval bridge crowded with jewelry shops over the Arno river. The stacked bridge also provided a helpful shield from the winter wind coming off the river.

"Well, I was twenty, and on a shoestring," I said. "I had a rail pass and approximately twenty-five dollars a day to live on. Italy was too much of a detour." I said it flippantly, but I had to admit he was right. I had missed something big by skipping Italy.

"It's my favorite country in Europe. Everything here is beautiful. Even the ugly stuff is beautiful."

Eric gesticulated toward the stolid, tile-roofed buildings that bordered the river up and down both sides. Florence wasn't a huge city, but its center was dense, with tight, stone-colored streets that wove behind the main avenues like snakes.

I looked up and down the river as we crossed the bridge. I hadn't really seen anything ugly in Florence, but the grime of age coated the bottoms of the stone and stucco buildings, and everything sat just a little crooked as the city had sunken unevenly into itself over centuries. It wasn't ugly, though—not at all. I would say more that it had seen some stuff. Florence, maybe even more than most cities in Europe, wore its history like a pair of perfect leather boots, the kind that just look better with every scuff.

"Penny and I came to Europe in college too," Eric said. He chuckled at some unspoken memory. "Man, I had to beg her parents to let her go. But I sponsored the trip from my trust, so they couldn't really argue much—this was before Grandmother cut me off. They were just upset they couldn't take her to Greece themselves."

I listened curiously as we took a tiny side street to get out of the wind whipping off the river. It was a nice day, but it was December, after all.

Eric, however, continued to chatter uncharacteristically. For most of this trip, Eric had been too busy looking over his shoulder to engage in carefree conversation. I'd gotten used to his paranoia over the last month, but that didn't make it enjoyable.

"It was for a month, and we did the rail pass thing too. Hostels and all of that. Penny was always kind of uncomfortable with luxury..." He trailed off, remembering the girl he'd lost ten years ago. "She couldn't take this life with me," he said quietly.

For the first time, I saw guilt in his memory. When he'd told me about Penny before, Eric had blamed her suicide on his family. It was because of their harassment that she'd slit her wrists, convinced she was worthless, to him or anyone.

But now...I couldn't quite say why, but something about that story didn't fit. I knew Eric's family now. I had spent countless hours with his cousin, his aunt, his mother, and his late grand-mother: the matriarchal quartet of a great New York dynasty. True, they weren't the warmest bunch in the world. Nina, Eric's cousin, was the nicest, and she was still basically an iceberg in training. Violet, her mother, and Heather, Eric's mom, each had the warmth of a freezer, while his grandmother, Celeste, had been a glacier.

But while I'd suffered my fair share of hazing upon my intro-duction, the worst had been from outsiders, not the de Vries family themselves. And not once had his grandmother ever suggested that Eric and I split up. From the second I'd walked into her perfect Park Avenue apartment, complete with rainbow-colored hair and my very weirdest clothes, she'd wasted no time inducting me into the family, even if it was paired with incessant criticism of my looks and harsh ribbing. And by the end, whether it was through the hours of wedding planning or the weekly trips to the Met, somehow, Celeste and I had become almost close. Bonded, maybe, by our mutual love of Eric.

Which was why it was hard for me to believe now that she would have ostracized a young woman to the point of death. Celeste would have seen an impressionable, and probably beau-tiful, young woman that her grandson loved...and she would have molded her. Not isolated her.

"Have you ever talked to Penny's parents? Since everything happened?"

Eric shook his head. "They were convinced it was my fault. They said she'd still be alive if she'd never met me." The three worry lines across his brow suddenly appeared. "They were right."

We walked silently down the long, narrow street, both of us lost in our thoughts. Occasionally a small car or someone on a moped would shove us back onto the "sidewalk" that was barely wide enough for one person, but for the most part, we had the cobbled street to ourselves. After checking his map a few more times (and making a couple of wrong turns), Eric eventually guided me up a large hill switch-backing up several wide, winding concrete staircases, until we found ourselves on top of the city.

"Look familiar?" he asked as we reached a large expanse of concrete surrounded by pillared stone railings.

I examined what looked like a glorified parking lot, dotted around the perimeter with a few cars and some closed stands. "Ah...should it?"

Eric smiled, then turned me around.

It was like looking at a postcard.

"Holy shit." I strode to the edge of one of the railings to look out.

It was Florence. But not the Florence I'd been staying in for the past week. It was the Florence of a million Instagram posts, of thousands of landscapes, of countless movies. Balancing my hands on the wide stone rail, I stared out at the cityscape, taking in the familiar muddy line of the Arno, the bridges I'd crossed so many times, the towering battlements of the Palazzo Vecchio, the massive cupola of the San Lorenzo Basilica, plus countless other landmarks I'd come to know.

On the other side of the piazza flowed Tuscany, now a bit browner than more popular photos would suggest, with leafless trees and fields left to rest for the winter. But beautiful nonetheless, dotted with villas and even larger buildings, and rows of tall cypresses guarding the hills. I sighed. Yes, this was worth the walk, for sure.

When I turned back around, I found Eric standing at the edge of the railing, staring out at the city too.

"Was this someone's castle once?" I asked.

He started as if he'd just realized I was there. "What? Oh, no. It was built in the nineteenth century, I think. As a meeting place, like a city center, and supposedly to showcase replicas of Michelangelo's work." He gestured toward a bronze statue that was indeed a replica of the David.

I looked back toward the city with him. "It seems like it would be a good place for a castle where a feudal lord could survey his holdings. The city in one direction, farmland in the other. You can see everything at once."

Eric looked down at me with a hint of a smile. "I don't think there was ever a king here, though. Florence was founded by the Roman empire. And then it was a mercantile city. Right?"

I shrugged. I wasn't exactly well-versed in Italian history. "My argument stands. Even if this wasn't a king's landing, it would have been a good one."

"Mmmm."

There it was again, that noncommittal shrug.

But it couldn't be denied, as I looked at him. Even with the bad dye job, Eric couldn't hide what he was any better than when he was in law school. He was kind. He was humble. But something else practically dripped off every inch of that strong, dignified posture. It was in the lines of his nose, cheekbones, the tip of his chin. Entitlement, some might have called it. But I saw something else: nobility.

"What?" he asked when he caught me looking at him. He smirked. "What are you thinking, pretty girl?"

But I wasn't in the mood to flirt.

I pushed a few strands of windblown hair out of my face. "I want to know when you're going to stop being such a damn chicken and really take what's yours."

All signs of amusement disappeared. "What?"

I licked my lips, trying to think. "You were a prince, Eric. And now you're a king. But you still act like a scared peasant."

His brow furrowed in confusion. "Jane, you don't know what—"

I stared at my hands. "I don't know? Okay, fine, I don't know. But I'm right next to you every night when you wake up shouting because of what Carson did. You've told me enough that I can imagine at least some of it. Ten days in a box having your balls swatted? And my picture flashed in front of you on a slideshow, right?"

Eric cast me a suspicious look. "Well...when you put it that way..."

I waved my hands in front of me. "I'm not trying to say it wasn't horrific. Traumatic. I'm just trying to say it didn't work"

He nodded slowly. "It didn't work?"

"Don't parrot me. You're not a circus animal. But no, it didn't. You said so yourself."

He crossed his arms. "I just said it didn't work with you. But like you said, I'm acting scared, just like he wants. Fuck, Jane, I *am* scared. That guy is capable of anything."

I turned, because the thought had only just occurred to me.

"It didn't work," I told him, "because you're here with me. All he wanted to do was make you hate me. Make you want to stay away. But you didn't. You couldn't, could you?"

Eric's hands fell to his sides, allowing me to put my hands in his pockets and pull him close.

"It didn't work," he repeated again, this time with a slight smile.

"No, my king," I said, only half playfully. "It did not."

"Your..." He shook his head again, confidence dashed. "Jane...

"Don't 'Jane' me. Not to get all *Lion King* on you, but in the words of Rafiki, 'it is time.' Mufasa's gone. Scar's on the loose, and he's trying to chase you back into the elephant graveyard. Except you're not a stupid lion cub, you're a full-grown man, and *you belong in New York.*"

"I didn't realize you were such a Disney fan, Lefferts."

"Don't change the subject. Time to take your place, Simba."

"Jane..."

"And don't take that tone either, like you feel sorry for me for not knowing your reality. Of the two of us, who's made the biggest effort to learn that *Gossip Girl* world?"

"What is it you think I've been doing every day at DVS?" he burst out. "Needle pointing?"

I snorted. "I'd actually like to see that."

"I've been working," Eric reiterated. "Doing my best to learn a company I never wanted in the first place."

"Never?" I countered. "Or just since you thought they killed Penny?"

"Thought?" Eric asked incredulously. "They *did*. They bullied her until she slit her wrists, Jane! I know you want to think my family isn't so bad, but their avarice and cruelty is the reason we are here alone right now. Meanwhile, half the stockholders at DVS think I'm just a trust fund brat there to fuck up their stock options, and the other half think I'm the devil himself."

"Are you really telling me there isn't any part of you that doesn't like it?" I demanded. "Or was that just an act, the way you would come home and chatter about your day? Tell me this and that about such-and-such deal before I traded the latest gossip from Nina? Was I imagining the way you enjoyed that give-and-take?"

His expression told me I wasn't. We both remembered those scant, beautiful days before the wedding. Before John "Titan" Carson. A few sweet months where things had seemed to gel.

"But it takes more than just a king to make things happen," I continued. "The good ones knew their entire courts. You were just getting to know yours, and now you've quit and run away."

Eric shook his head. "This isn't a monarchy, Jane. I'm not trying to maintain power."

"Well, maybe you should."

"What are you saying?"

I stepped up and pulled on his collar, looking for something to do with my hands. "I'm saying you were born for this. You're running away from the big bad guy like everyone else. But you're *not* everyone else. If you just take the time to really understand what is at your disposal—not just the company and the money, but the people, the businesses, the power brokers. John Carson spent plenty on courting politicians last year, but you know what? Your grandmother spent even more. You have thousands of people in your debt, Eric. Learn who, and you'll be just as big and bad as him."

Eric pulled me close and set his chin atop my head. It was a protective move, but also one that prevented me from watching that implacable face I was learning to read better and better.

"If I'm a king, does that make you my queen?" he asked finally.

I pulled back. His tone was light, but there was no laughter in his expression.

I pressed my lips together. "Well, that has yet to be decided, hasn't it?"

That marriage certificate felt like a ticking time bomb, but it wasn't fair to pressure him about it now. We had enough going on. I also couldn't blame him if he wasn't sure about it himself. But that didn't mean it didn't hurt.

"If I'm a king," he said quietly, a few minutes later, "it's because you make me one."

I snorted. "Right. I'm sure a half-breed bastard child of a trick-turning stewardess is super royal."

Eric pulled back to look down at me, but there was no joke in his eyes. "You know I don't like it when you talk about yourself like that."

"Is any of it untrue?" My words were unnecessarily sharp. Maybe it was because I hadn't quite come to terms with them myself. After all, I had liked being the daughter of a mild-mannered psychologist and an esthetician.

Be honest, Jane Brain. You never felt quite right in that life anyway.

I sighed. Dad was right even if he was a product of my imagination. I *had* always felt a little out of place in Chicago. Hell, everywhere. Maybe now I knew why.

"There are a lot of ways to command people," Eric said. He reached down and took my hand, then slowly pulled off my glove, one finger at a time. "You do it better than anyone I know. You sure as hell command me, gorgeous."

"Stop," I whispered. *Don't stop.*

"It's true," he murmured as his thumb brushed over my knuckles, lingering over my bare ring finger. "I might have the pedigree, Jane, but you're the one who's royal."

Then, before I could reply, his broad hands wrapped around my waist and lifted me suddenly to sit on the edge of the wall. They remained around the small of my back, keeping me from falling, strong and solid, as much a foundation as he claimed I was for him.

Maybe when we challenged each other, we made each other stronger. Maybe that was what Eric and I really did for one another.

But he didn't let me say it, instead kissing me. This time *he* commanded *me*, with strong lips, strong hands, the kind of kiss that whistles through the air right along with a brisk December wind. The kind that makes you forget that you're missing a glove on one hand and that no one else in their right mind is standing outside in this kind of chill. He kissed me long and hard and didn't release me until we were both breathless.

A sudden gust of wind sent a shiver down my spine, even under my thick wool coat. Eric held me close, shivering right along with me.

"I think," he said, "that maybe it's a little too cold for a picnic. Would you agree?"

I sighed, then nodded. We could always use our food from the market for dinner on the train.

"We passed a couple of good cafes on the way here," I said. "Why don't we get our fill of pasta while we can?"

Eric nodded, seemingly relieved that I was letting go of our previous topic of conversation. And I would, of course. But only for now.

TWENTY-FOUR

"Fuck. Me. Like, right in the ass."

"That could be arranged."

I nearly tripped on the porch steps of the tiny guesthouse we had rented outside of Engelberg, Switzerland.

"I think you took care of that a few nights ago," I replied dryly as I waited for Eric to unlock the door. I sagged against the cabin wall and dropped my snowshoes to the ground with a clatter.

Eric gave me a mischievous once-over that dropped slowly to the part of my body I'd just mentioned. "There's always room for improvement. I was enjoying myself, but you came too fast. We need to work on your endurance there too, I think."

I removed one of my new fleece mittens and swatted at him. He dodged easily, then chuckled as he shuttled me the rest of the way inside the warm, inviting little cabin. I had to give points to Switzerland for good cheap accommodations. What the country lacked in picturesque architecture, they made up for in basic, utilitarian comfort and, of course, mountains.

"Gaaahhhhh." I collapsed onto the bed in the middle of the

cabin, reveling in the rush of blood from my sorry, swollen feet back into the rest of my body. "I need to spend the next two days in a hot tub. Please tell me again: why did you think snow-shoeing for hours would be a good idea?"

"Because it's fun."

Eric unloaded the crash pad—essentially a giant foldable mattress he could fall on when rock climbing—onto the floor. He'd rented it from the owners of the tiny guesthouse along with a pair of climbing shoes he'd dismissed as "mediocre, but usable." We hadn't actually gone that far, just hiking maybe an hour until Eric found the particular three-story miniature mountain he was looking for that day.

I didn't know. They all looked like big rocks to me. But I enjoyed the solitude, sketching in my notebook, making tea on a Bunsen burner, and watching Eric play Spiderman until we were ready to make our way back to town.

I did wonder if he had taken me up here as much to distract from the fact that amidst all the snow, it was also Christmas Eve. The rest of the world was probably decorated up the wazoo, but our cabin only had a couple of pine boughs stuck on the fire-place. Maybe he thought up here, it would be easy to ignore the fact that we were spending the holiday alone and on the run instead of surrounded by family or friends.

"Lefferts."

I could barely prop my head up to see Eric squatting at the foot of the bed. "What is it, Petri dish? I'm too sore even for a decent comeback, so don't even think about tying me to this bed again."

The mention of what Eric had done the night before—a particularly creative episode that involved some of his climbing straps, snow, and a camisole re-appropriated as a blindfold—brought another sly smile to the man's face. But he remained where he was, untying my hiking boots.

"You just need to exercise more, gorgeous." One sleek brow arched. "Not that I'm complaining, to be clear. I just don't like to see you in pain." He popped over me for a moment and gave me a kiss. "Well, not unless it's the good kind."

I pulled him down to continue the kiss a bit longer, even as I flushed, thinking of the color of my breast the other night after he'd paid it some especially brutal attention. But even at that thought, I was too tired to respond. The man had simply worn me out.

I released him and flopped back onto the bed. "I street hike."

"Walking across Central Park is not hiking," Eric said as he pulled off my second boot.

"Sure it is. Through the concrete jungle, right? And I'll have you know that the Guggenheim and the Met are both multiple levels. Up and down those steps for an afternoon is basically like summiting the Matterhorn."

The smug bastard grinned from the foot of the bed, but his large hands closed over one foot and started to rub, so instead of continuing with another slick retort, I just moaned.

"Oh, *wow*, VD. You have the touch."

I jerked when he pinched my pinkie toe.

"What did I say about those names?"

"What is there to say?" I chided. "You earned it, you manwhore. Own your truth."

The hands on my feet paused. *Shit*. And for several seconds, no one moved.

When I finally propped myself up again, I found Eric watching me with a very intense expression. I froze, my entire chest tightening under the intensity of his dark gray, almost black gaze.

"You know it's just you, don't you?" His voice was soft, but almost a threat.

He scooted up the mattress to sit next to me. I sat up against the pillows.

"Jane," he said. "Tell me you understand that. Tell me you understand that the entire reason we're here is because of you. What you mean to me."

I couldn't help it. I melted. Like a fucking candle. "Is it?"

Eric's voice shook with emotion despite not rising one decibel. "*Yes.*"

I swallowed. I wanted to jump him, but my gaze landed on his empty ring finger. If that was the case, why hadn't he put it back on? Why hadn't I?

"What was it you said?" I murmured as I stared at his hand. "'Better single and poor than married to a whore?'" I hadn't ever admitted out loud how much those words stung. I could take that accusation from anyone but Eric. "It's catchy, you know. It almost rhymes."

"You know I said that to drive you away, don't you?" Eric took my chin, urging me to look at him. "Jane, the only thing I was thinking was that I needed you to get away from me. For your own good."

"And you thought calling me a whore would be just the key?"

He had the grace to look ashamed, but his ferocity didn't lessen. "I would have said anything in that moment to keep you safe."

But all I could do was shrug. This was our history—in moments of anger, we lobbed insults like Molotov cocktails. It wasn't like I didn't tease him incessantly about his sexual history. I had literally just called him a venereal disease, so I'd be a bit of a hypocrite if I couldn't take what I dished out on the regular.

Still, from Eric, in that moment, it had really, really hurt. Even if he believed it had been for my own good.

"I got you back with that slap," I finally said, shaking off his grip. "I think we're even." I offered a grim smile. "It's forgotten. See?"

Eric examined me for a moment. And then, before I could stop him, he tackled me onto the bed with another kiss that took my breath away.

"Stop it," he ordered.

For a moment, it was almost like we were wrestling, not cuddling. Despite my intense desire for him to subdue the doubt swimming in my stomach, I couldn't help but fight a little. Eric's hands wrapped around my wrists like handcuffs, pinning me to the bedding. I pushed back, sucked a little harder on his mouth, wrapped my legs around his stronger ones and bucked with my hips. Eric grunted with the effort to keep me in place, but still worked that much harder. We grappled on the mattress, enjoying a bit of cathartic combat that eventually gave way to surrender. On both sides.

No one loves to fight you like I do, he'd said. I sighed into his kiss. It was the truest thing I'd ever heard. And the truest thing I'd ever felt.

If only he could learn to fight like that for himself.

I pulled back, much to Eric's obvious disappointment. His chest rose and fell as he regained his breath, and his dilated eyes revealed how much he wanted to continue exactly what we were doing.

But I needed something sweeter.

"Tell me what you used to do for fun when you were small," I said as I rolled onto my back.

Eric's brow rose in surprise. He adjusted his pants. I did my best not to look—I'd be a goner if I did. "Are we going to reminisce about our childhoods now? I never took you for the banal conversation sort."

I just sighed. "I don't think it's banal. It's all part of knowing someone, isn't it?" Though my voice was light, I really did need some levity at the moment. For some reason, I felt like I was about to cry all over again. Maybe it was being on the run for this long, but something was really starting to take its toll.

Eric watched me for a few more seconds, then resigned himself to draping a long arm across my stomach.

"My childhood wasn't really what you'd call 'fun,'" he said. "I've told you that. It was a lot of classes and tutors, prep school and whatnot."

"Oh, come on," I prodded further. "You were a kid. All kids like to have some fun. What kinds of things did you enjoy doing with your parents? Maybe with your dad when he was alive?"

"Honestly, I still feel like I barely know my mother. She left most of the childcare to my nannies, and after my dad died, the majority of those parenting decisions went to Grandmother, not her."

Now he was the one looking away, muffling his voice in the pillow to avoid pity. I could imagine that life pretty clearly. The reality was that you didn't exactly see a brigade of mothers crowding around the schools of the Upper East Side—instead, it was a lot of women with darker skin than their charges' pale, WASPish features, or heavily accented English next to the kids' perfect, regionless diction. Women named Rosa, Khadijah, or Irina. Strong women. Kind women. Strict women.

In some ways, the real parents of the Upper East Side.

Eric blinked, perhaps remembering the same thing. "My dad was busy working most of the time, but sometimes he would take me to the park," he said quietly. "He liked baseball too. He used to take me to Yankees games—at one point, I think DVS had a box. But that was a long time ago."

"You miss him." It wasn't a question.

"I...I suppose," he said. "I was only ten when he died. It's hard to miss someone you didn't really know *that* well. I was still at the point in my life where I thought my dad was a superhero. The man I miss probably didn't really exist."

"You miss him," I said again.

My chest constricted as I remembered my own father—my *real* father, not the one who had apparently provided half my DNA. When I closed my eyes, I could see Carol Lefferts's kind, homely face. The nose that was a little too big and bulbous. The gray eyebrows Yu Na was always haranguing him to trim. The ready smile whenever he came home from work to be tackled by his overenergetic daughter.

"I miss home," I whispered.

Eric rolled over, then pulled me into him, pressing his nose into my hair so that the rhythms of our heartbeats blended together as one. The tip of his nose was still chilled from being outside, but the rest of him was a furnace. I closed my eyes, relishing the smell of linen, soap, and the salty residue of sweat. His cologne was back in New York, but I could almost smell it anyway.

"Can I call my mom?" I asked. "It's Christmas Eve. I just want to say hi. She probably thinks I'm mad at her again."

The look on Eric's face already told me the answer.

"I'm sorry, Jane," he said. "We just—Brandon's P.I. said he thinks she's being monitored. We can't risk it."

I pressed my lips together and tried not to cry again. I didn't know why I was getting so damn emotional. I knew this was the score when we'd taken flight, and I'd just left a message for her a few days ago from a payphone in Zurich. Maybe it was because it was Christmas Eve. Maybe it was because I'd been away from home—whatever that meant—for almost over four weeks with no end in sight. I felt shiftless, drifting. Sure, I was with Eric, but that didn't necessarily equal happiness. I needed my people. I needed my life.

After we lay there for a few minutes, he grabbed something off his nightstand.

"Here," he said as he showed me an iPad. "I borrowed it from the rental manager. We can't call your mom, but we can say hi to some other people."

I rolled onto my stomach with him as he propped the iPad up against the headboard. A few minutes later, he had dialed into an unfamiliar number on the Skype application, and a few seconds later, the faces of almost everyone I knew and loved popped up onto the screen.

"Merry Christmas!" they cried.

"Ahhh!" I exploded, hungry to see the faces of my closest friends. Jenny and Luis took up most of the screen with their round, pudgy faces, while Skylar and Brandon lingered in the back with Christoph and Annabelle. Behind them lurked the shadows of other people celebrating Christmas—their parents, Skylar's grandmother. Maybe Kieran and her partner, Pushpa.

I twisted a corner of the comforter in my hands. It was funny, when I lived in Chicago, I had gone months, of course, without seeing them, but now that I physically wasn't even allowed to talk to them for days at a time, I missed my friends dearly.

"How's the old country?" joked Brandon as he popped what looked like some kind of pastry into his mouth. Of course—it was late morning there. If Sarah was over, no doubt the entire kitchen was full of baked goods, starting with her famous blintz. "Are you guys having a good Christmas Eve?"

I nodded, overcome for a moment. "Yeah. Yeah, we are. Eric made me go snowshoeing again—"

"She's a little sore," Eric put in. "And not in a good way."

"Eric!" Skylar admonished him.

"Oh my God, Sky. Don't be such a prude," I said.

She grinned. I grinned back. It was good to talk to friends. Already I felt better.

"Any idea when you're coming home?" Skylar asked.

I shook my head, trying not to appear sad. "We've only been gone a month. To have a grand European tour, I'd say we need at least six. Maybe a year. What do you think, Petri?"

For that I was rewarded only with a smile and not even a smack on the ass, which told me I was still being humored.

"At least," Eric murmured. He turned to Skylar and continued to chat about the firm and its clients, about the kids, about everything else but the elephant in the virtual room—that we were talking like this because we were living like fugitives.

"Jane? Jane!"

I snapped back and found Skylar staring expectantly into the webcam.

"Oh, sorry. I kind of spaced out there."

"Yeah, I know," she said. "I just wanted to say I love you. And we miss you."

My heart sank again, and because I couldn't stop them, tears welled up and actually overflowed.

"Oh, Janey," Sky said. "Goddammit." She turned to Brandon. "Isn't there anything we can do? Has Zola said *anything* new lately?"

Brandon shook his head mutely, obviously not wanting to upset me.

I shook my head and swiped at my eyes. "I—shit, I'm sorry. It's okay. I know you guys are doing your best, and we are too. I'm—I think it's just because it's Christmas."

Eric took my hand and pressed kisses to my fingertips. The gentle gesture made me want to cry harder, so I focused on the ugly burgundy and blue pattern of the comforter until my breathing turned to normal.

"Okay," Skylar said doubtfully. "Well...maybe Nina can help. Hold on a second."

There was a bit of a shuffle as Skylar handed her phone to someone and we were apparently carried into another room, beyond the hubbub of the kitchen. Then, to our surprise, Nina's face appeared on the screen.

"Whoa," Eric scrambled to his seat and picked up the iPad for a better view. I turned around too, and we crowded together over the screen. "Nina? What are you doing there?"

"I...um...hi, Jane. Eric." Nina looked from side to side, her blonde hair swishing delicately around her face, like she was worried she would be overheard just saying hello.

Eric and I exchanged twin looks of confusion.

"I needed to talk to you," Nina said in hushed tones once she seemed satisfied no one was listening. "We've been trying to find you for weeks. Skylar had a feeling you might call here over the holidays, so she invited me and Olivia. So nice of them." She said it like she was surprised by the gesture.

"Where's Calvin?" Eric asked sharply.

Nina blinked seriously. "Not here."

"He didn't want to spend Christmas with his family?" I asked suspiciously.

Nina sighed. "Jane, I realize you don't know my husband well, but I shouldn't think it surprising that he doesn't prioritize free time with his daughter. Or me, for that matter." Her eyes were suddenly sharp. "Not everyone has that kind of marriage."

We were all quiet for a few awkward moments before Eric spoke again.

"Look, Nina, you knew I was leaving," he said. "I couldn't risk Calvin finding out and telling Carson where we were."

"Well, he figured it out—asking me to step in at board meetings wasn't exactly discreet, you know. And he said something about Florence last week—were you there?"

Eric's mouth pressed into a thin line. Carson must have had more spies than we thought. By some Herculean effort, I managed *not* to say "I told you so."

From what Eric had told me, Nina's pompous ass of a husband had been trying to work his way into the Janus society for years. It didn't matter that people were generally tapped while in the stages of some form of schooling, or that, from what we could tell, positions were generally reserved as one per family (if men were invited at all). As the de Vries member of Janus, Eric held that position—Calvin's efforts were in vain.

That obviously didn't stop him from trying to win Carson's attention, though.

"This isn't just a honeymoon, is it?" Nina asked pointedly.

Eric remained quiet. I just bit my lip.

"I thought so," Nina said. "Well, in that case, I've been asked to give you a message. If, you know, I just happened to speak to you." She rolled her eyes. She wasn't really aware of the stakes of what was happening, but she clearly thought all of this *The Spy Who Shagged Me* crap was dumb. I sort of agreed.

Eric frowned. "Who asked you to do that?"

We looked at each other.

"Calvin," Eric said.

"So the big bad wolf is coming to get us?" I asked.

"Jane," Eric said. "It's not funny."

Nina's mouth quivered, so I thought he was wrong about that one.

"Calvin told me to pass this on if I...if I could manage it." She looked almost ashamed to be doing so. "I hope you don't mind, but I read it. And Eric—look, we need you home. The board is wondering what the hell is going on, the stock took another dip, and the executor is starting to talk about breach of the will, even if you are on vacation. You need to come back and sort this out."

Eric wilted slightly. Over the last few weeks, I had enjoyed seeing his confidence rebloom a bit. But it still wasn't at the point where it had been when I'd met him. I was still waiting for that cocky bastard I loved and hated so much to return fully.

More and more, I had a feeling that would be tied indelibly to his willingness to stand up to Carson. My "father." That until he could walk around unafraid of the man, he wouldn't regain himself.

She unfolded a piece of paper and read a piece of poetry awkwardly aloud:

> *Indigently You feed*
> *Your majesty*
> *On proffered sacrifice*
> *And breathfuls of prayer.*
> *You would starve to naught*
> *If children and beggars*
> *Were not such fools full of hope.*

"And then it says, 'Hirschenplatz, eighteen hundred hours, December twenty-fifth.'" She looked up again. "Does that mean anything to you?"

Beside me, Eric was shaking his head. "Arrogant motherfucker."

"What?" I asked. "What is it?"

"It's a quote from Goethe, a poem about Prometheus," Eric said. "Carson thinks he's being witty."

"Refresh us, Professor," I said. "Who is Prometheus?"

Eric sighed. "Prometheus is one of the Greek titans. He was bound to a rock by Zeus for sharing fire with people. As part of his punishment, a bird would eat his liver daily. It would grow back to be eaten again."

I made a face. "That's brutal."

"He also never apologized for flouting the rules," Eric said. "Prometheus always presented himself as a lover of mankind."

"And that's what Carson thinks he is? Promethean?" Nina asked.

"It's supposed to be *ironic*," Eric said witheringly. "We're the ones on the run, but that asshole is making himself into a martyr." He pushed a hand over his head, causing his hair, which was looking truly awful now that his dark blond roots were starting to show, to muss up. "He's trying to get under my skin."

"It looks like it's working," Nina said pointedly. "If you let it, anyway."

I had to smile. I hadn't ever heard Nina challenge anyone in her family directly. I wondered if the death of her grandmother —with whom she had been quite close—had sparked some new growth in her as well. The de Vries family needed a new matriarch, after all. I doubted Violet was up to the task.

"He's letting us know he knows generally where we are." Eric turned to me. "Lucerne is only a half hour from Engelberg. There's a house there where Goethe stayed." He blinked. "We should probably leave. Get the hell out of Europe."

My heart sank. I didn't exactly want to talk to John Carson again, but a part of me doubted that running again was the way to go. If the investigators weren't finding anything, what did Eric want to do? Circle the globe for the rest of our lives?

"That's ridiculous," Nina said bluntly.

Eric frowned at the screen. Apparently, he was taken aback by her newfound candor as much as I was. "Nina—"

"Stop it," she said. "We could write off a month as an extended honeymoon for the two of you, but you can't act like a scared bunny forever. It's embarrassing."

Eric scowled. It was hardly the first time his family had called him such a thing, and I knew he didn't exactly take to it.

In fact, it made him more likely to do exactly what they *didn't* want.

"Eric," Nina said before he could argue. "You don't need to be scared of John Carson—yes, I know who he is. Brandon and Skylar told me all about him and this ridiculous society."

We blinked at each other. Brandon and Skylar must have had quite the discussion with Nina to trust her enough with that information.

"Nina," Eric said, "do you have any idea what he is capable of?"

"Do you have any idea what *you* are capable of, cousin?" she retorted. "Have you any real idea of the kinds of resources that are at your disposal?"

I didn't dare look at him. He hadn't really wanted to hear that exact argument from me again since Florence.

Eric shook his head. "I'm not going to misuse company funds that way. It's unethical. What do you think, the board is going to approve a family vendetta?"

"Good lord." Nina didn't even bother masking her irritation. "*This* is why you need to stop running off, if only to learn about your own actual life. I'm not talking about DVS, Eric. I'm talking about the family holdings. It's explicitly in the will, if you had just stayed to listen to it."

"Nina, my trust is not enough to scare off the likes of John Carson. He has half of Congress in his pocket."

"So does DVS!" Nina gave an exasperated sigh. "You *really* don't know your board, do you? Chariot is owned by one man, Eric, but we're a public company. Do you have any clue how many board members contribute to all of the super PACs we start? Do you have any idea how they all work together to further the interests of the company? If they thought for a moment that John Carson was trying to undermine the company, he would have earned the ire of twelve very powerful people. Chariot Industries might make weapons, but we control the ships and ports where they are delivered. *Nothing* works without trade, Eric. De Vries Shipping makes the world turn."

Eric glowered. Obviously, he didn't appreciate being lectured about a business he had been learning for the last six months. Or...maybe he knew she was right.

"That's the company, Nina," he said finally. "That's not me. And like I said, my trust alone won't compete with all of John Carson's power."

Nina just exhaled an exasperated breath. "Eric, that's just your allowance. If you had actually spoken more with the executor, you'd know that the majority of the family's personal holdings are in a separate account. Grandmother used it for things like this—security, investigations. You don't become the de Vries family without becoming targets. We protect ourselves. We always have."

"That fund..." Eric shook his head. "That's for the head of the family to manage."

"Eric!" Her voice blasted through the tinny speakers. Nina Gardner was demure, well-bred. Never one to raise her voice. But she wasn't stopping now. "You *are* the head of this family," she said evenly, but firmly. "Stand up and take your place!"

Eric opened his mouth several times, obviously considering a retort, but found he had none.

"Hey." I nudged his shoulder. "You're not alone in this."

He looked around the room, as if he were hoping one of the pieces of furniture would come to his defense. But, of course, nothing did.

"All right," he said finally. The defeat in his voice broke my heart. He reached out for my hand, and when I gave it, he gripped it so tightly that my fingertips turned white.

"You're going to Lucerne tomorrow?" Nina asked.

Eric nodded. "We'll go," he said. His voice dripped with dread. "Yeah. We'll go."

"I'll change and pack," I said, already standing up. "But I am *not* under any circumstances putting those boots back on. They can burn in hell for all I care."

TWENTY-FIVE

W e arrived in Lucerne the next morning under a haze of fog and snow.

"It's Christmas," Eric remarked, steering our rental car under a dizzying array of lights strung over one of the bridges.

"So it is." I looked at him queerly. "You didn't realize that?"

Eric blinked. "No, I knew."

But that was all he said, as if he were simply mentioning the day of the week. He drove on, feigning concentrating on the road, though the reason for his reticence was clear. He was scared.

Lucerne was a relatively small city, an odd juxtaposition of old and new buildings smashed together at the edge of a large lake nestled in the Swiss Alps. It was a bit jarring, really, to drive through loads of picturesque Swiss farmland, complete with fallow fields dotted with Brown Swiss cattle and the occasional tractor, and suddenly enter a city over which lorded a nine-teenth-century castle and a waterfront casino. Like a lot of European cities, the architecture spanned nearly a thousand years, but because of the city's density, medieval buildings ran into modern with the disorienting effect of time travel.

The city, however, was almost deserted as we rolled in—it was Christmas Day, of course, so most people were with their families. Nearly every shop was closed, and even the famous swans of the lake seemed to be hidden away.

We checked into our hotel, but almost immediately, Eric wanted to leave. As soon as we had deposited our things, he was up again, pacing the room.

"I can't just sit here like fish in a barrel, waiting to be shot," he said. "I need to move. Take a walk or something."

I didn't know what to say, so I sat on the bed.

Eric turned at the door. "Are you coming?"

"Do you...do you want me to come?"

Finally, his gaze softened. He walked across the room and knelt in front of me. "I always want you to come."

"Well, good," I said, trying unsuccessfully to appear nonchalant. "Because I don't want you to go anywhere alone right now."

Again, tears sprang to my eyes as I cupped his face. Lord, the intensity of this trip was really getting to me. I never cried like this. But sometimes I forgot just how beautiful he was. It wasn't a blinding beauty. Eric was more like a statue, carved and solid, but not necessarily ornate. His appeal was unwavering, something you wouldn't always notice, but when you took the time to look, made it hard to see straight.

His eyes, so often the color of a time-worn marble, blinked up at me, bright and full of love. I brushed my thumbs over his knife-edge cheekbones. His eyes shut, and his long lashes cast a light shadow over his fair skin.

He laid his head in my lap, and his arms encircled my waist. "Jesus *Christ*, Jane. You have no fucking clue how much I love you."

"Do you?" I wondered before I could even help it. Sometimes I honestly had a hard time remembering. Even after all this time. Even after a month. "Even after all I've cost you?"

"You've cost me?" Eric sounded genuinely confused.

"Well, if I wasn't John Carson's long-lost daughter, he would have left you alone, wouldn't he? We wouldn't be in this shitty situation."

He looked up with a somewhat amused expression. "The fact that you think any of this is your fault blows me away." He swallowed hard. "The more time I spend with you, the more I realize I'm nothing without you, Jane. Abso-fucking-lutely nothing."

"I don't like it when you talk about yourself like that."

I stroked his cheek again, and he closed his eyes, leaning into the light touch.

"Eric," I whispered. And then, because I couldn't think of anything else to say: "It's Christmas."

He offered a crooked smile. "So it is."

"Merry Christmas." Could I be any lamer? "Christmas is a time to be with the ones you love. Isn't that right?"

Eric deflated. He knew I missed my family, my friends. "Yeah. It is."

"Hey." I cupped his cheek, this time the one forcing *him* to look at *me*. "Then I'm in the right place."

That smile reappeared, complete with the dimple in his left cheek. "You think so, pretty girl?"

I smiled. I couldn't help it. But instead of shouting how much I loved him and tackling him onto the bed, I decided that now would be the best time to give him his present.

Eric watched curiously as I dug a small jewelry box out of my bag. It had been hard to buy without him knowing—Eric hardly ever wanted to spend time apart, considering how worried he was that we were being followed. But I'd managed to get this piece in one of the little old shops on the Ponte Vecchio one day when he was running.

He opened the box and pulled out the simple gold chain, at the bottom of which hung a small medallion, about the size of a nickel. Turning it back and forth in the light, he examined the engraving across the front and back of the hand-pounded disc. On the front was his father's full name: Jacob de Vries, followed by 1957-1996. On the back was Eric's full name, followed only by his date of birth.

Eric fingered the disc, remaining quiet.

"You originally wore the coin because it was your dad's, right?"

"Yeah."

He continued to examine the necklace while I grew nervous. His hand drifted up to the open collar of his shirt, to the empty space where the coin had hung before Brandon smashed it.

"I...he was about to become chairman too. When he died. I don't know. I guess I just thought it was a way of carrying his memory with me." Eric rubbed his face. "And then it became a clusterfuck. But yeah. I guess it was a way of taking him with me."

"I...if it's too morbid, I understand," I said. He was so still, so intense as he stared at the disc, that I wondered if I'd made a huge mistake. "I just thought—"

"It's great," he interrupted, his silver eyes meeting mine like a gust of wind. "Jane, it's *great*. Thank you." He pressed a kiss on my head.

I sat back a little awkwardly. It wasn't exactly the response I had been hoping for. "Ah, you're welcome."

He frowned, like he was wrestling with something. "I've been...I was alone for a long time. I mean, I had friends. I had Skylar and Brandon, other people I met at Harvard and around

Boston. But I...they...no one ever knew. They never knew who I was, you know?"

I nodded. I hadn't either, really.

"You know me better than anyone," he said. "Even before I told you anything, you always did."

He swallowed, and his eyes actually glistened. That, of course, was it for me in my current state of mind. My own tears started to overflow again, falling down my cheeks one at a time. I pulled off my glasses and swiped at my eyes. Eric smiled and used his thumb to brush away a few other tears.

"I...shit. Would you believe I don't have anything for you to open?" he said, wiping at his eyes too.

I giggled nervously. "It's okay. It's been kind of an odd Christmas. God, we're basically a Hallmark card anyway today, aren't we?"

"I did get you something, though." He pulled a card out of his wallet and handed it to me.

"*Tessuto Di Lorenzo,*" I read awkwardly, stumbling over the Italian. I looked up. "This is the fabric store I found in Milan. Their stuff was to die for!" On the day we had walked around Milan before taking the train north to Switzerland, I had spent a solid four hours in this shop, swimming in a sea of textiles.

Eric nodded. "I bought you, um, a few bolts of fabric. That's what they're called, right? Bolts?"

"Really?" I squealed. I had wanted to send some home, but had decided it was too much of a hassle, given the fact that I didn't actually know when we would be going there, if at all. "Oh my God, what did you get?"

Eric shrugged, like it was absolutely nothing. "Everything."

"*What?* You bought out an entire fabric shop? That's like thousands of yards of fabric!"

"Well, no," he said nonchalantly, "not the whole shop. Just the ones you liked."

My jaw practically hit the ground. I had mooned over at least twenty different fabrics in there. If Eric was keeping track... holy shit, I could literally design an entire fashion line, not just a few pieces here and there. If, of course, the idea wasn't absolutely ridiculous.

"You know what I love about you, Jane?" Eric said, interrupting my thoughts.

I stilled, though visions of boatneck shirts and paperbag waists were dancing through my head. "What's that?"

"Well, a lot of things," he said. "But even when we're fighting, even when I had to come home late and sleep in another fucking room right next to you...I'd still get to look into your room and see what you were making. I love the way you create, Jane. It's inspiring. *You*'re inspiring." Eric smiled, and this one wasn't cocky or knowing. It wasn't his "lady killer" smile either—the one he used to charm people, male and female alike. It was simple. Honest. "I just want to see what you'll make. I just want to see you happy."

We examined each other for a few more moments. Sometimes it was hard to realize that we were here. Amidst all the drama. All the games. All the fights. All the hurt. Somehow, we had come to a place where we could say plainly to each other those three simple words.

"I love you," I blurted out before I could think too hard about it.

Eric cocked his head. "I know, gorgeous."

"No, I mean I really fucking love you," I kept on. "Not because you're worth the earth. I—I did, Eric, I loved you so much way before I knew anything about your money or your family. It pisses me off, but I love the way you never let anything bother you. I love how you appreciate beauty, even something as small as a verse of poetry. I love how you're like this calm to my storm, how you forgive almost anyone and everything, how you really would do anything for people you love, even the ones who hurt you the most..."

Even people like me.

By the time I'd finished, all amusement on Eric's face had disappeared, leaving only an intense, watchful expression that made me feel pinned into place.

"Say it again," he said. "I want to hear you say it again."

"You just said it," I said. "I wanted to say it too."

"Goddammit, Jane, just say it again."

And then, like the emotion was too much for him to handle, Eric's face darkened, and he launched himself at me, steel hands wrapping around my arms, yanking me to him.

But he didn't kiss me. Not yet.

"Sometimes," he whispered, just a hair's breadth from my lips, "it's just too fucking much."

I stared at his mouth. And then I nodded. Sometimes it really was.

"Say it again," he ordered. "Please."

I dragged my gaze up to meet his and fought to hold it even. His own burned into me.

"I love you," I pronounced as clearly as I could. "I love you, you ridiculous, romantic, infuriatingly beautiful fucking man. I love you, and I always will."

I swear to God, I could hear our hearts beating wildly in time, like drums in the wind.

"I love you, too," Eric said. And then, finally, he kissed me.

It wasn't a gentle kiss. It was harsh and defensive, almost threatening. His lips practically warred with mine, and I fought right back, beating my fists into his chest while I took each tormented twist of his tongue again and again.

For some, love is sweet, but for Eric and me, it was a war—a war we were desperate to fight together. Not against each other. Against ourselves, maybe, because in our hearts, Eric and I were both people who were never quite comfortable with the world when it was sweet. We needed a little bit of fight to make our peace seem real. And if it wasn't there, we'd have to create it ourselves.

I gasped as his teeth scraped across my neck. Eric reached in front of my blouse, took both sides of the shirt, and ripped it clean apart. I stared at the buttons rolling across the carpet.

"Ah, I was wearing that," I said, though my sarcasm wasn't particularly heartfelt. I kind of wanted to fix the shirt just to see him tear it open again.

"If you try to keep *anything* between us right now, pretty girl," he growled, his teeth once again finding the lobe of my ear with a delightful pinch. "I will fucking demolish it."

His hands busied themselves with my jeans, and not to be overshadowed, I hurriedly undressed him too. Within moments, we were skin to skin. Maybe it was the meeting with Carson in a few hours' time. Maybe it was the fact that it was Christmas, and in that moment, we were all each other had. But for once, Eric and I were truly on the same wavelength. We needed each other. Maybe more than we had ever needed anything in our lives.

We tumbled back onto the bed. Spending the last month practically attached at the hip had somehow only made me crave the man more. His lean body buried me in the plush sheets, and he entered almost immediately.

"*Fuck*," he hissed as his cock found my slick, aching center. "You are so fucking ready for me."

I dug my fingers into his hips, wrapping my legs around his waist, eager to feel the powerful flex of muscles as he filled me again and again.

"Eric," I moaned. Lord, my nerves were on *fire*. I wasn't going to take long. I had thirty seconds, maybe a minute left before I was going to explode. This had to be some kind of record.

"Stay with me, gorgeous," he murmured as he pummeled forward. "Feel me. Goddammit, Jane, feel *us*."

And so I did. I clung to his flexed arms, his rippling chest, his strained neck like I was lost at sea, and he was the buoy. For the first time in my entire life, I gave myself completely to every unnamable sensation flowing through our joined bodies. Because it was him. It was Eric. Somewhere deep inside, beyond the constraints of body and mind, some part of me came alive when I was with him. And in giving myself up to it, I had ironically never felt stronger.

"Do you feel this?" His hips ground into me, driving a rhythm that was setting me alight. "Do you feel what we are?"

"Ummmm, *yes!*" I cried and arched my back, trying to open myself more.

And then, just as I was positive we were about to split apart together, Eric stopped.

I opened my eyes. "What?" My voice was shaky, hardly even coherent. My entire body throbbed. All I wanted was him.

Eric's eyes were bright, two stars in the dark of the room.

"Just listen," he said as he drifted kisses all over my face. "Right here. Right now. This is what you do for me, Jane."

"What?" I pleaded. "What do I do?"

"I never feel more powerful than right here," he said. "Right now. Inside you. Possessing you."

"Eric," I whimpered, knowing that it was true. He did possess me. I was his. A creature no longer myself, weak and strong all at once. Because of him.

"And all it makes me want," he said as he began to drive forward again, "is to give myself to you."

"Please," I whimpered, unable to wait any longer. I needed the release. I needed *him*.

"Take it, Jane," he ordered as his merciless pace drove even harder. "Take *me!*"

And I exploded. "ERIC!"

His name erupted from my chest, my soul, as I split into a million pieces and took him with me, just like he said. He collapsed over me, his beautiful body an effigy of passion, doused with sweat and heat. We spilled into each other, holding nothing back, until the lines between us were no longer clear. Until there were no boundaries between us at all.

———

SOME TIME LATER, we both floated back to reality. Outside, twilight was setting in as the afternoon drew to a close, with a few flakes of snow floating past the window and down to the dark waters of the lake.

I rolled onto my arms to watch the snowfall.

"I just want to stay here," I said as Eric joined me, wrapping his body over mine, a warm, muscular shelter. "I want to do that again and again for the rest of the night. Fuck Carson. Let him stand in the snow."

"Later," he whispered, drifting his lips across my bare shoulder. "Right now we have an appointment to keep."

I arched my brow. "We?"

Not that I was ever going to let him meet with Carson without me, but I had certainly been expecting a fight. When he had asked me before if I was coming, I had honestly thought he meant for a walk.

Eric nodded. "Where you go, I go, right? Well, it goes both ways, gorgeous."

And despite his fear, despite the fact that a terrible, horrible man who seemed hell-bent on ruining both of our lives was waiting for us only blocks away, I grinned. I absolutely beamed, because I knew that all I could ever need was right here in this room. And for once, he knew it, too.

TWENTY-SIX

We got ready silently, the air filled with an eerie heaviness, like we were getting ready to go to battle. We showered together, scrubbing each other's bodies nearly raw. Eric washed my hair, his skilled fingers weaving through my locks and massaging my scalp. He remained completely still while I helped him shave, his gray eyes glinting like steel the entire time.

When he made love to me again as the water cascaded down our bodies, it was with slow, deliberate movements akin to putting on armor. His teeth and fingers dug into my skin, memorizing the lines of my body with a new concentration I'd never really seen. When he found his release, it was with a furious shout that echoed off the tiled walls. It was almost like losing control that way allowed him to rebuild himself that much stronger.

We dressed silently for the cold. Him in a pair of tailored wool pants, sleek black boots, and a blue sweater that cast the same hue through his gray eyes; me in black jeans, knee-high black boots, and a chunky turtleneck with military-style buttons up one side. Eric worked product into his hair until it shone while he watched me apply makeup—a smoky eye and, of course, the bright red lipstick that was probably too garish for the holiday, but made sense tonight. After all, if anyone wanted to fuck with Eric, I was out for blood.

"I don't think I've seen you wear that since law school," he said as I took a moment to put in my nose stud.

I examined the tiny diamond in the mirror. "It was the first piercing I ever got. Did you know that?"

Eric shook his head as he continued messing with his hair.

"I was fifteen. And my mother *still* hadn't let me do anything I wanted with my face, my hair, anything. I hadn't even been allowed to pierce my ears yet."

He examined me with amusement. "It's hard to imagine you without all of that."

I nodded in agreement. "I know. I remember when I was finally allowed to wear makeup, I felt like I found my real face."

"You know I like the one underneath, don't you?"

I cast him an obvious look. "Well, yeah. I like it too. I just mean...the ability to change things. That was my face."

Eric smiled, and my stomach warmed. "I get it. You're a chameleon."

"I guess. Anyway, when I was in high school, I managed to pay off some seedy shop downtown with an extra fifty. I borrowed my friend's ID—these guys couldn't tell the difference between two Asian girls anyway—and got my nose pierced. When I showed up that night, Yu Na *flipped*. Like, grounded me for a month, no friends, no concerts, no *nothing*. But you know what? She told me when I graduated high school that she liked it."

"I always liked it too."

I shrugged. "She's always been funny like that. She holds on to things. And then she'll surprise you."

Eric left to find his coat, and I examined myself sadly in the mirror.

There was a pang in my chest when I thought of my mother. More than ever, I wanted to talk to her. Let her know I was okay. That, despite all of our differences, I loved her so much.

My eyes started to water again, and I sniffed back the tears furiously. I wasn't ruining my makeup right now. I could cry over Yu Na when this was over.

"Here." Eric handed me the burner phone. He looked at me knowingly. "Call her. Wish her a merry Christmas."

I took the phone. "Did you call yours?"

"No." He pressed a sweet kiss to my forehead. "But I will. Call your mother, Jane. It doesn't matter now. They've found us anyway."

So, I did. But unfortunately, she wasn't home. The call to her cell phone went to voicemail too, and after I left an awkward message wishing her a merry Christmas and asking to talk when she got home, I handed the phone back to Eric.

"She's probably at Ji-Yeon's for the holiday," I said. "I don't have that number memorized. I'll try again when we get back."

He took the phone and sat on the bed to wait while I finished braiding my hair into a severe fishtail and put on a pair of black cat-eyed frames.

"Jane."

I turned, and Eric beckoned to me. He held out the necklace I had given him for Christmas. "Help me put it on."

I crawled around him and clasped the chain, then lingered with my fingers dipping just below the starched blue collar of his shirt, feeling the line of his collarbone and the curve where his pectoral muscles lifted. Eric's hand covered mine, and I pressed my nose into his neck. He had watched me clip my rings around my neck again, though he hadn't put on his own. I didn't want to press it, ask what the hell we were doing. I figured after tonight, maybe we could talk about what had to happen within about a week. Or not.

"I love you," he said again.

I inhaled his scent—the musky hotel soap combined with the clean vibrance that only belonged to him.

"I know," I replied with closed eyes.

His phone buzzed on the nightstand. Keeping one hand over mine at his collarbone, Eric swiped open his messages, then quickly stowed the phone.

"That was Tony," he said. "It's time."

My stomach was in knots as we rode the elevator down, my palms sweaty in the pockets of my coat. I was so tense that I nearly jumped when we walked out to the street and were met by three large men in black coats. Their thick boots left deep prints in the thin layer of snow on the pavement.

"Mr. de Vries," Tony, Eric's bodyguard from New York, greeted us with a nod, then gestured to the two men standing behind him. "Mrs. de Vries."

Eric and I both stiffened, but neither of us corrected the name. Instead, he squeezed my hand tightly in his and nodded to Tony.

"This is Devon and James, colleagues of mine from London," Tony said. "Best I could find after you called, sir."

I looked curiously at Eric. "When did you..."

"When you were asleep last night," Eric replied. "He already knew we were going to be here. I'm not interested in being dragged to another fucking dungeon anytime soon. And it's like you and Nina said—Carson's not the only one with resources. It's time I trust some of mine."

Tony nodded in agreement. "Devon is former MI-6, and James served with the Queen's Guard. I trust them both with my life, sir. And, as you know, the Brits are no friends of Chariot."

Eric shook the new men's hands, and they both tipped imaginary hats at me.

I smiled again at Tony. I quite liked the fact that Eric had decided to trust his grandmother after all by keeping him in his service. Celeste would have enjoyed the fact that he had rehired her original picks.

"We scouted out the location," Tony was saying. "Devon watched the square all day. No one's been there. There's no sign of John Carson in Lucerne at all, although it's possible he arrived before we did."

Eric took a deep breath, then sighed. "He's here. He wouldn't pass this up." He turned to me. "Ready, pretty girl?"

For what? I wanted to ask. But instead, I just nodded. "Let's tell El Chapo where he can shove it and go home."

One side of Eric's mouth quirked, and he delivered another lightning-quick kiss. "Let's do it," he agreed.

We headed out into the snow.

———

IF LUCERNE HAD FELT quiet when we arrived this afternoon, now it was basically a cemetery. Though several churches were likely still open, nearly every one we passed had their heavy doors shut against the cold, their Masses held only in the morning. Most people were clearly home with their families to celebrate Christmas.

Led by Tony in front while the other two guards trailed us, Eric and I walked through the heart of the city, across the smaller of the two medieval foot bridges that crossed the river feeding into the lake. The interior of the covered bridge was striped by shadows and Christmas decorations, with garland and twinkling lights lining its interior everywhere. Below us, the famous swans of Lucerne floated in the water, heads tucked under their wings, seeking shelter from the snowfall.

Across the water, we climbed into the city, past the deserted shops and apartment buildings that were all uncharacteristically dark. Eric was silent, and so were the guards.

And then we reached the plaza. Tony, Devon, and James hung back in the perimeter shadows while Eric and I wandered to the center. Hirschenplatz was a small stone square surrounded by eighteenth- and nineteenth-century apartment buildings, several of them painted with charming old murals. Across one, deer dancing up and down the stucco sides (hence the name *"hirschen"*—German for "deer"). Snow stuck to the stone benches and the bricked ground; the city was swathed in a blanket of silence.

Eric looked around. The square was empty.

I checked my watch. "It's five-oh-five. We're right on time."

"Actually, you're late. I've been freezing my balls off for the last fifteen minutes waiting for you and your little pixie, Triton."

We swung around, finding a tall man who looked vaguely familiar to me stepping out of one of the far shadows. I didn't know his name, but he'd flanked Carson in the church when he'd interrupted our wedding. He'd watched Eric succumb to that strange call with something that, even in my desperate confusion, I understood as glee.

"You." The word, so innocuous, slipped out of Eric's mouth with pure vitriol. His generally unruffled demeanor had disappeared, instead replaced by such ugly, naked aggression that I almost didn't recognize him.

"Triton, Triton. You didn't really expect the *Caesar* to fly all the way to this backwoods town just to talk, did you?"

Eric and I both frowned. Lucerne wasn't exactly a hut in the middle of nowhere.

"What the fuck are you doing here, Jude?" Eric snapped. "Where's Carson?"

The man named Jude clicked his tongue. Yeah, that made me want to punch him in the face too.

"Language, Triton, language. Coarse words don't become a man of your station. A soon-to-be chairman, isn't that right? A little bird tells me the board will be voting next week. If, of course, you're brave enough to show your face."

Just like that, Eric's stony mask resumed its place. And for once, I was glad to see its arrival. I didn't want to give this bastard one iota of our emotions—it was clear that like most bullies, he was the type who got off on ruffling people's feathers.

"Jane and I are returning to New York tomorrow," Eric said.

I jerked. I certainly hadn't been aware of those plans.

He glanced at me with a spark of hope. "Together."

Jude, however, was not amused. "That's taking some chances, Triton. You might not like those odds."

"And why's that?" I asked.

Jude turned to me like he had just realized I was there. "You shouldn't be here, Cho-Cho-San."

My eyes narrowed. "Did you just call me Madame Butterfly?"

He cocked his head like he was watching a circus exposition. "Look at that. She reads too."

"Cut the shit, Jude," Eric snapped. "What are you doing here? Where's Carson?"

"First of all, Triton, let's use our terms of respect, shall we? You should refer to the *Caesar* as Titan, and I'd prefer if your girl here wasn't that familiar with my name either." He turned to me with a wink. "It's Hermes to you, my little courtesan."

It took everything I had not to gather a snowball and chuck it in this asshole's face. What in the fuck was it with people like him referring to me as a prostitute?

Jude—the *fuck* if I was going to think of him as a Greek deity—turned back to Eric with amusement. "You're to leave the girl in New York and continue to Los Angeles," he told Eric. "Tomorrow."

"No."

Jude sighed, like he was dealing with an errant child. "Need I remind you what happened the last time you disobeyed your *Caesar*'s orders, Eric? I can assure you that the next time, he won't be so lenient. In fact, he might not be lenient at all."

I blinked. Was that what I thought it was? This jackass was literally threatening Eric with death if he didn't run to a meeting?

Shoulder to shoulder with him, I thought I could feel a slight shudder through Eric's coat. But externally, he showed no sign of backing down.

"Carson—"

"Titan," Jude corrected.

"*John fucking Carson* wouldn't do that," Eric spat. "He acts like a kingpin, but he's no better than a common thug. A bully with a lot of big weapons who likes to swing his dick around. What you're trying to be, I suppose."

Jude narrowed his beady eyes. "I have a message for you, Triton, and you'd be wise to heed it: *deorum vocas*."

I froze, and not because of the snow. There they were again: those two odd words that Carson had spoken in the middle of St. John the Divine. They had echoed off the stone walls, and the minute he'd said them, Eric had apologized and, without another word, had followed him out.

This time, however, when Eric didn't move, Jude became visibly irritated. "Don't make me recite the entire thing," he said in a bored voice. "You know how much that annoys me. It annoys everyone."

"That's because it was a stupid verse to begin with," Eric returned. "He was too lazy to find one that actually fit. He just liked the sound of the footnoted version so much better that he just *had* to use it."

"That's not really the point, Triton."

"True. The point is that it doesn't fucking matter at all." Eric took my hand, his fingers gripping tightly around my glove. "You can recite Virgil until you're blue in the face. It's not a magic spell. I'm not coming."

"Virgil?" I repeated. "Is this for real? You guys just hop around the globe reciting Roman poetry to each other as summons?" I couldn't help but giggle. The whole thing was ridiculous, like something out of an Edgar Allen Poe poem. "Do you have a secret handshake too? Maybe some pointy hoods and matching canes?"

Ignoring me completely, Jude began to intone:

> *Medium video discedere coelum,*
> *Palantesque polo stellas. Sequar omina tanta,*
> *quiquis deorum vocas me in arma.*

I turned to Eric. "What is that?"

"Latin," Eric said quietly. "It's the verse from *The Aeneid*."

"Doesn't know her classics either?" Jude's voice boomed. "How terribly plebeian. This is what happens without a proper education, of course. Where did you attend school, Kanji State?"

I pressed opened my mouth, ready to tell him I went to the University of Fuck White Nationalism, but Eric cut in: "She attended Harvard, you racist dick. Before that, Northwestern. In Chicago, where she's from."

"And my mother's Korean," I added. "Not Japanese."

Jude rolled his eyes, like we were pointing out the differences between two shades of blue, not entire nationality differences. "Regardless, I'll have to enlighten her." His green eyes pierced, even through the twilight. "*Deorum vocas* is a calling. It refers to a loose translation as follows:

> "*I can see the cloud parting, the stars riding*
> *The arching skies. I follow a sign so clear,*
> *Whoever you are, the gods who call me into*
>   *action.*"

When he was finished, Jude looked triumphant, like he was a spelling bee contestant. "We're *all* supposed to know the *Caesar*'s call, Triton. Everyone picks their verse to call upon members' obedience. Just like your father did."

I blinked back and forth. "What's a *Caesar*? You keep saying that."

Jude turned to me, now visibly irritated. "It's a salad, Yoko. What do you think?"

I scowled, but before I could cut back at him, Eric gripped my wrist, pulling my attention to him.

"It means king," he clarified. "Like Julius Caesar. It's... someone who is voted in, but also remains in power until his death. It's how the leadership of the society works."

Realization dawned on me. "And your father..."

"Held the position, yes," he said. "As did my grandfather before him."

"Barely." Jude suddenly appeared next to us, apparently not wanting to be left out of the conversation. "Poseidon had what, six whole months before his little boat was smashed?" He chuckled. Eric's jaw tightened. "Pity, really. His death ruined your family's nearly spotless line of succession."

"Okay, I gotta ask," I interrupted. "What's with the names? Greek? Roman? Why not just use your real names all the time, since you obviously all know each other?"

"It's none of your business," Jude said, his smooth demeanor finally decomposing. He turned to Eric. "She shouldn't be here anyway, Triton. Carson might forgive it because she's his offspring, but considering he forbade this liaison to begin with, I sincerely doubt it. Just one more penance you'll have to serve."

"So, we're back to 'Carson'?" I mimed obnoxiously large finger quotes, enjoying the way my continued poking seemed to break Jude's smug exterior. "What happened to 'Titan'?"

"You would do well not to test my temper, chickie," he snapped. "I'm not very nice to people who do."

"*You* would do well not to threaten my wife, *Hermes*," Eric's voice cut through Jude's and my banter like a machete as he stood to his full six feet, two inches, nearly eye to eye with his adversary. "And I'll remind you right now that *your* contributions to the society don't happen without *my* family's ports. Hard to smuggle girls and drugs to meetings without customs looking the other way, isn't it?"

Jude examined Eric, looking very much like he wanted to throw something much worse than a few cutting phrases. But instead, he took a breath and turned his attention back to me.

"Wife?" he asked. "Have you made it official, then?" He looked down at my hand, which was, thankfully, covered by my glove. "We haven't seen any papers filed, Triton. And believe me, Titan has been watching *very* closely."

I had been holding my breath since Eric said the word, and now I waited for him to answer Jude's question. To say in no uncertain terms that we were on our way back to New York to do exactly that—sign the papers, file the contracts. Resume our *life*, this time married, just like we had wanted.

"We're on no one's timeline but our own, Jude," Eric said.

"And if you're going to tell Carson anything, it's that I officially abdicate my position in the Janus society. I want nothing to do with it. Ever."

"You can't just—"

"Watch me," Eric snapped. "He can cite all the idiotic Latin he wants. He can storm into board meetings. Kidnap me again. But I won't be making the same mistakes twice. Did you know he tracks us, Jude? He replaced all the coins we wear so now they record everything we do. The corrupt bastard is spying on us."

He pointed to the bracelet that was peeking out from under Jude's sleeve. From the man's suddenly blank face, I gathered he was unaware of this development.

"It's time for Carson to learn that he doesn't dictate the terms of my life or anyone else in this society," Eric continued. "And that includes marrying his daughter, whether he wants me to or not. *It's not his choice.*"

"Oh, Triton," Jude scoffed. "Don't you understand? He just doesn't want *you* to have her. It's your lesson in obedience. Carson doesn't care about this massage parlor refuse any more than he cares about what gets put out on the street for the trashman."

Eric threw a punch so quickly it was over before I blinked. His fist landed on Jude's nose with a sickening crunch, and a second later, Jude was lying on the ground after his head slammed against the brick.

"Try that again," Eric said, sounding like a man who had just shouted loud across the entire city for an hour. A lock of hair flopped onto his forehead while he shook out his hand. Flecks of blood landed in the snow, relics of a split knuckle. "Say one more fucking word about her—even think it—and I'll break a fuck lot more than your nose, you spoiled fucking prick."

"You'll regret this," Jude hissed as he pushed up from the

ground. From the way his nose was bleeding, I guessed it was actually broken. He clutched at the bridge, red-faced from blood and anger alike.

"Not as much as you'll regret disrespecting Jane," Eric snapped. "Carson wants me to remember who he is? You tell him to remember who *I* am. Eric Sebastian Franklin de Vries. Son of one of the oldest families in this country and every leader of the Janus society for the last hundred years. Carson wants to mess with me, he messes with a fucking dynasty."

Jude took a step forward, but before he could even think about launching a counterattack, Tony, James, and Devon appeared from the shadows, three looming figures forming a small fleet of muscle behind Eric's determined form. I just watched, slack-jawed. I'd never seen this side of him. Even though I'd practically begged it to come out, now that it had, I wasn't sure I knew what to do with it.

Jude sneered. "It's never been in the best interests of the de Vries men to put a woman before Janus, Eric."

Eric started, then stilled. "What in the fuck is that supposed to mean?"

Jude smirked. "I think you know."

"Penny." The word was a whisper, nearly carried away on the wind. But it came from Eric, and in that moment, his hand dropped mine. "You bastards. You didn't."

Jude smiled, a nasty red smile through which the whites of his teeth shone like a skeleton. "I guess we'll never know. But I'll say this: the poor girl was certainly an easy target. She never belonged in Dartmouth or anywhere near the likes of you. And deep down, I think she knew it."

Somewhere in the distance a bell rang. The gravity of the name slowly sank in as Jude spoke. Penny. Penelope Kostas. Eric's former fiancée. The girl he was convinced his family had bullied into suicide had died because of Jude. Carson. Janus.

The question was...why?

Unfortunately, Eric didn't have time to ask. He launched at Jude, moving with fury, if little grace, and running on enough surprise and adrenaline that he was able tackle the bigger man into the building behind him. Bits of painted stucco fell from their impact in a spray of pastel green that mixed with the bloody snow in a hideous parody of Christmas cheer.

"Do you know what the statute of limitations is on murder, you slimy little sociopath?" Eric shouted as he shoved Jude to the ground. "You're going to jail, asshole. You and the entire fucking society! You murdered an innocent girl, and—"

"Eric!"

Tony jumped forward and pulled Eric away, but not before he landed one last kick to Jude's ribs. I cowered back, my arms wrapped firmly around my waist. A few lights around the plaza actually went on. We needed to get out of there.

"You'll pay for that, Triton."

"The name is *Eric*, you entitled son of a bitch." Eric spat, the saliva landing perilously close to Jude's face. "I don't need to hide behind anonymity. I'm proud of who I am."

"That's right," I chimed in. "He doesn't like nicknames, Gatsby. The only one allowed to use them is me."

But it wasn't the time for laughs. Eric looked like he was two seconds from delivering another round of heat. Jude, however, cowered against the wall, above which a painting of Goethe, the poet, witnessed everything.

"You can tell Carson I'm no longer at his beck and call," Eric said, still held at bay, but just barely. "And if he has a problem with that, he can talk to me himself. Because the next time I see you or any of his little messengers near me or mine, I'll do a lot worse than break your fucking nose. I'll break your entire fucking life."

Before Jude could respond, Eric finally extricated himself

from Tony, shaking off his shoulders and head like a wet dog after jumping into a lake. When he had finally calmed, he turned to me with eyes like stone.

"Come on, Jane," he said, though he didn't extend a hand. "Let's go home."

INTERLUDE III

Police guided the cars from First Presbyterian to the old cemetery by St. Mark's. Eric sat in the back of the limo with Grandmother, watching the flashing lights of their motorcycles blinking red and blue so he wouldn't have to think about the contents of the car in front of them.

All the cars were black. Dad was in the first, weird-shaped one—Grandmother called it a hearse—followed by Eric and Grandmother's limo. His mother, Heather, rode in the second limo with Aunt Violet, Uncle Peter, and Nina. The rest of the family, all the extended cousins and so-and-so's, brothers or sisters-in-law, followed in their own cars or taxis. A strange, sad parade through New York.

He had heard people whispering in the church. It was boring, listening to the minister talk about his father like he wasn't there, like his body wasn't fully on display in the big brown box. Eric had focused on the giant photo next to the coffin, the one of his dad grinning in a suit. It wasn't how he remembered him, but it was better than the waxy body. Dad had liked to smile, sure, but his hair was always a little ruffled from the wind, not combed neatly like the picture. His shirts were always a little wrinkled—he loved bugging Grandmother by ruining them. And he never, ever wore a tie unless he was forced. Still, the twinkle in his eye that Eric had always known and loved was still there, and as Eric gazed at the picture, he could almost imagine that the people in the church weren't crying for his father. That his father wasn't actually dead.

They filed across the cemetery, following the coffin as it was carried by the men in suits—uncles, cousins, and unfamiliar friends—across the green field to the family plot. Eric had taken a seat in the front next to Grandmother while they waited for the ceremony to begin.

His mother sat behind them, wiping her eyes with a handker-chief. Eric didn't turn to her, and she had not offered to do anything for him either. When they had gotten the news about dad, she had been playing tennis at the club, and Eric had been home with Nina and Katarina, the current nanny. Katarina had offered all the hugs he needed, and Grandmother had arrived soon after with...well, not exactly words of encouragement. More like instructions. What they would do and when. Eric didn't have any other questions after that. And when he did cry, it was in his room, alone.

He stole a glance at the woman he was supposed to call Mother. At ten, Eric barely knew her anymore. Everyone kept asking him if he needed his mother. Told him they had to take care of each other now. But why would he want comfort from someone he barely knew?

A man approached and bent down next to Grandmother, the heels of his shiny shoes sinking into the dewy grass.

Grandmother frowned. "Garrett. What are you doing here?"

The old butler held out his hand. In it was a necklace. A gold chain, on which hung an oddly shiny, but old-looking gold coin. It was about the size of a quarter, but thicker, and had an odd picture of a man with two faces.

"It was on his body when it was recovered, ma'am," droned Garrett, as expressionless and haughty as ever. "The detectives delivered it at the church. I brought it here because"—he glanced at Eric—"I thought it might be wanted."

Celeste picked up the coin and examined it critically, turned it back and forth between her gloved fingers, then removed one glove and scratched the coin with her thumbnail.

"Terrible workmanship," she muttered to herself. "Two hundred years, and they couldn't do better than gold plating?"

Garrett wisely said nothing, but gave an almost imperceptible nod to let his mistress know he agreed.

Celeste handed back the coin. "Donate it. We have no use for it now."

"No!" Eric nearly shouted it, disrupting several of the people assembling around the gravesite.

Celeste turned, but Garrett paused.

"Eric," she said evenly, though her expression was deadly. "Do we shout?"

Behind her, Heather, Eric's mother, shrank, despite the fact that Celeste's wrath wasn't at all directed at her. Her deep brown eyes were reddened around the rims, and her bright blonde hair had a few strands out of place. All Eric could see was the flashing coin.

"It was Dad's," he whispered fiercely enough to attract a few glances from the people filing in for the final service.

"Eric—"

"I'm not shouting!" His voice was low, but so emphatic it was practically a hiss.

Celeste swallowed and patted her hair. Eric sensed that she didn't know what to say. It wouldn't do for the deceased's son to throw a tantrum in front of all these important people, but at the same time he also knew that later, he would pay dearly for his disobedience. But as he glanced at the coin, still shining in

Garrett's hand, Eric knew without a doubt that he would take any punishment she allocated to keep this one thing of his father's.

Celeste seemed to realize this fact. "Give it to him."

After Eric accepted the necklace from Garrett, he only wilted slightly when he saw his grandmother's ice-cold expression.

"There will be consequences for your misbehavior," she said quietly.

Eric just nodded, sticking his chin out slightly. "I understand, Grandmother."

She watched him for a moment, and then, almost like she approved of his willingness to take it on the chin, nodded back.

The ceremony started, but Eric didn't watch. He didn't listen as the minister said verses and prayers about the shadow of death. He didn't hear the moans of his mother as the coffin was lowered into the earth. He stood when he was told and sat when he was told, all the while focusing his attention on the shiny gold coin that flashed in the afternoon sun.

"No goodbyes," he whispered as people stepped forward to throw roses into the grave. For a moment, he considered throwing in the coin, but his fist wouldn't open when he stepped forward.

"Eric," Grandmother said as she stepped back from the grave.

She clutched a handkerchief, but her eyes were dry. The wrinkles at their corners looked deeper than usual.

Eric stepped away. He remembered now. They had to leave. More people were coming to the penthouse to pay their respects. Then, and only then, would he be able to escape back to his parents' apartment near the park, read his favorite Shel Silverstein books, and try to pretend that his dad was still on a sailing trip instead of just having died on one.

He followed them in a line: his mother, then his grandmother, then him. Past all the people who watched them and murmured how sad and sorry it all was.

Eric barely saw their faces until one in particular, a man

standing at the back of the crowd, found him with a deep gaze so dark Eric thought his eyes might have no color at all, just black like the sketch drawings in Where the Sidewalk Ends.

His mother stiffened as she passed the man, who reached out and touched her arm sympathetically.

"My condolences, Heather," he said.

"Th-thank you, John," she whispered. Then she dabbed at her eyes again and hurried on, her high heels kicked up dirt with each step, like she wanted to run, but couldn't.

As Eric filed behind Celeste, the man named John spied him, and his dark eyes flashed again. Up close, though, they weren't as dark as before. Hazel, actually. A cross between brown and green.

"Ah," he said. "The young heir. Eric, isn't it?"

Eric bit his lip, but knowing that he would be in a lot of trouble if he didn't answer—Grandmother did not abide rudeness —he simply nodded. "Yes, sir."

The man smiled. He reminded Eric of a shark. "Well-mannered, I see. Celeste, you've trained him well. Better than Jake, I hope."

"That's enough, John."

Eric looked up. Grandmother was glaring at the man. That in itself wasn't particularly strange; Grandmother glared at a lot of people. But something in her expression made Eric want to glare at the man too, though he didn't know why or what he had done.

He turned to find the man smiling at him again.

"What's that you have there, boy?"

Eric opened his hand halfway, but no more. There was some-thing about the man that made him think he might steal the necklace.

"A coin," said the man. "Well, well, well. Do you know who that is?"

Eric shook his head. "N-no, sir."

"That's Janus. The two-faced Roman god of beginnings and

endings. He has two faces, you see, because he looks to the future and the past."

Eric nodded, though he didn't really feel like he understood any of this. He just knew his dad wore the necklace, so he wanted it.

The man leaned forward, and Eric could smell a hint of alcohol on his breath. It was a little like the way his mother had been smelling for the past week, but the scent was heavier, somehow. Almost spicy.

"Janus reminds us that every time there is an ending, there is a new beginning," the man said. "Like now. Death might feel like an ending, but it's also a beginning."

Eric sensed the man's words were supposed to be encouraging, but for some reason, they made him feel worse. He closed his hand around the coin and shoved it into his pocket. When he looked back up, the man was watching him carefully.

"Triton," he murmured to himself. "Son of Poseidon. Yes, I'd say that fits."

"And I said that's enough." Grandmother jerked Eric's hand. "Come along, Eric." She glared at the man once more. "I will not expect you at the reception, John. I should hope that's clear."

The man held up his hands like he was surrendering to a policeman. "Of course, Celeste. Wouldn't dream of disturbing the family. Have to listen to the head of house now that de Vries and his son are gone, don't we?" He winked at Eric.

For a moment, Eric thought his grandmother might actually cry. Grandmother had stood next to him through the entire church service and while the coffin was lowered into the ground. But unlike his mother, his aunt, and so many of the other people in the church that day, her eyes had remained dry. Until now, when they glistened slightly, like sun shining off the East River, just a few blocks from the penthouse.

But then she straightened, and Eric noticed, not for the first time, Grandmother's unique ability to look and act much taller than her just over five feet. She looked the strange, sharkish man straight in the eye for a long time. And that man, Eric saw with a bit of triumph too, was the first to turn away.

"Yes," Celeste said definitively. "We do."

———

ERIC AWOKE WITH A START. Holy shit, how long had it been since he'd remembered that? His dreams about Penny, his father, both their deaths, had happened nightly since he and Jane left Switzerland. Had that exchange really happened? He remembered the coin. The moment Garrett had brought it to the burial. But had John Carson really been there too?

He honestly didn't know.

He waited for his heart rate to calm, but it was only when he turned to Jane, still asleep beside him, that it finally slowed. The sun creeping across the park cast a golden glow over her bare skin. Eric sighed. Just six or so weeks ago he was convinced he would never be here again with her. Now he was prepared to fight with everything he had to keep the privilege of mornings like these.

He and Jane had arrived three nights before and had slept for most of two, suffering badly from jet lag and the emotional stress of being on the run for a month. She had collapsed into their bed—fucking hell, it felt good to call it *their* bed again— nearly the second Eric brought her into the room. She had laughed when he insisted on carrying her across the threshold of the apartment. They weren't technically married, she'd argued, but he hadn't cared. It was just so damn good to be home. With her.

Jane snuffled and rolled onto her back, then sank into an even deeper sleep. She had been up late, still on European time, and so after tiring Eric out several times (he wasn't going to argue with it), had worked into the early hours of the morning on her sewing machine. There was muslin and cut patterns everywhere, but she was happy in the mess. Eric had gone to sleep to the hum of the machine and the occasional snip of scissors from her room.

"Hey," she said sleepily as he slid out of bed. Her hand dragged down his chest, tugging lightly on the necklace she'd given him. "It's early. Where are you going like a thief in the night?"

"The gym," he said. "I need to work off some nervous energy before the board meeting. Tony and Devon are coming with me, but James and the new guy will still be across the hall."

Jane blinked sleepily. Eric had to resist the urge to curl behind her and wrap her hair around his wrist. He could work off the energy another way, but he was pretty sure she was still sore from the night before. Even around her scalp—he'd pulled her hair pretty hard.

So instead he let her pull him down for a lazy goodbye kiss.

"Good luck," she said as her fingers stroked his cheek. "Call me when it's done."

"I will," Eric said. "I love you."

But Jane didn't answer. She had already fallen back asleep.

———

ERIC SPENT a solid two hours climbing nearly every route at Queensbridge Boulders until his shoulders ached, his forearms throbbed, and his fingertips were practically raw. Even then, as he put on his favorite gray Tom Ford suit and fixed his tie in the gym mirror, his heart was still racing as he contemplated what he was about to do.

Today, the board was going to vote on whether he was ready to assume leadership of the company built by his father, his

THE KISS PLOT   359

grandfather, and nearly six generations of de Vries men. Today, he would gain rights to the considerable resources and power that had always been promised to him, but which had been wielded by people who seemed more mythical than real for most of his life. Today, he was going to become the man he had been trained to be, and yet had fought so long.

If, of course, they would allow it.

At five minutes to eight o'clock, Eric stood in front of the large oak doors. For a moment, he paused, surveying the portraits of the previous chairmen, and the presidents before that, who lined the walls of the corridor. All ancestors, all named de Vries. Five different Johns or Jonathans. Three Jacobs, including his father, the penultimate chairman. The last portrait, however, was of his grandmother, the only woman, but just as fierce as any of them. Maybe fiercer.

He examined her, took note of the unforgiving line of her posture, the wry arch of her brow.

"You got your way, didn't you?" Eric murmured.

The portrait looked back, as if she were daring him to turn away now.

Eric turned, opened the double doors, and walked in without looking back, finally prepared to accept his destiny.

PART FOUR

ANAPHORA

On the day you left,
the sky was bright,
New York an open groan.
The sun, it shined,
the clouds, they laughed
as I stood there alone.
The pond, it gleamed,
the people sang,
their words a weary drone,
and books became
my resting place
as the ground became your home.

"On The Day You Left"
—from the journal of Eric de Vries

TWENTY-SEVEN

I combed through the rack of dresses from the stylist for what had to be the tenth time that morning. Sadie had sent them over a few days ago—all ready-to-wear since there really wasn't time for proper fittings. Originally, I'd wanted to make my own clothes for tonight; I'd come back from Europe with a sketchbook chock-full of ideas. But five days wasn't anywhere close to enough time to make something that I was comfortable with being splashed on the front page of every major paper. And this was arguably one of the biggest days of Eric's life. I needed to look perfect.

Despite his extended absence, the board unanimously voted him chairman, as well as voting through an addendum restoring larger fiscal powers to the position. In just a few minutes, Eric had assumed full leadership of his family's company as well as a higher position than even the CEO he had been shadowing for the last several months.

The board considered it a boon. Celeste had long been the face of DVS, appearing at public events, but she'd been stretching the truth when she'd promised Eric that the chairmanship was little more than a figurehead position. In fact, prior to her illness, Celeste had maintained quite a bit of power in the operations of DVS following her son's death. Once her illness had kept her from working, the CEO had apparently been doing the job of two people and so was more than happy for Eric to remedy that situation.

And so, the board and public relations team were thrilled that Eric was now the face of DVS. His own work experience combined with his general legacy seemed to assure shareholders of the company's future. Stocks had already gone up, and the announcement hadn't even been made official.

It also didn't hurt that the guy was handsome, I supposed. I'd get on a boat with him any day of the week.

The public announcement was tonight, at the company's annual New Year's Eve gala.

My only question was how, exactly, I was going to be presented. I glanced toward the back hall, where the office neither of us used contained our creased marriage certificate. I had locked it back in the second drawer after we arrived home. Eric hadn't mentioned it. I hadn't mentioned it. But I *was* keenly aware that in exactly two days, the certificate itself—and thus, our entire marriage—would be nulled under New York State law. It was, after all, a question on the New York Law Exam I'd taken on my computer just yesterday before filing for bar admission.

Yes, I knew the answer to that question. I just didn't know the answer to my own.

My iPad rang on my work table. Skylar, calling to check on our progress. My friend had been neurotically obsessed with calling after barely hearing from us for over a month. I didn't really mind. I missed her too.

"Hey," I greeted her once I opened the video chat. I returned to the rack, looking over my choices.

"Ready for the gala?"

"I will be after I make my choice. Are you guys staying in tonight?"

Skylar nodded. "We'll light some sparklers with the kids and watch the ball drop. I just want a night in. Has Yu Na called you back yet?"

I frowned, wishing away the sadness in the pit of my stomach. My mother still hadn't forgiven me for taking off like I did for a month. She'd barely returned any of my calls, and only with texts.

"No," I said. "She's pissed. I'm pretty sure it's going to take a trip to Chicago and some pretty serious groveling to earn back her trust again. But I think buying her a house might sweeten the pot. I don't know. How do you feel about bribery?"

Skylar shrugged. "It works on my five-year-old. Well, sometimes."

I sighed. I needed to make amends with my mother. This strange grudge match between us had gone on long enough.

"So, what are the dress choices?"

I raised a brow. "Since when do you care about fashion?"

"Since I couldn't talk to you for a month. Can we for once have a conversation that's *not* about our crazy families or the psychotic man spying on you?"

I relaxed. "Sure. And if he's listening, we can bore him to death talking about hemlines."

I turned the webcam to the rack of dresses against the wall and started pulling out my favorites, holding them up against my body and modeling them for my friend. "My makeup is done except for lip color. Which one should I choose?"

"You need to wear the red one," Skylar said immediately.

I pulled out the deep scarlet Valentino strapless column dress with a slit up to mid-thigh. "You don't think it's a little too on the nose? Eric's Asian bride all dressed up in red?"

"Well, I don't know about that," Skylar said. "But I know that color looks absolutely amazing on you. And this is your debut as a unit. You always tell me that red is a power color."

I looked down, considering. The truth was, I wasn't sure I wanted to stand out the way this dress would—it was Eric's night, after all. But at the same time, I did like the idea of showing a united front against all the haters.

We'd heard absolutely nothing from John Carson since we arrived in New York. Not a single word. No creepy messages. No snide messengers. Nada. Meanwhile, Eric had beefed up security. Gone were the days where I could take a spontaneous stroll through Central Park or meander around Soho for an afternoon. I mean, I could still do those things, but only with two giant bodyguards trailing me like oversized rottweilers. Eric, meanwhile, was escorted to and from his office, the gym, and anywhere else he had to be by an entire team of security headed by Tony. While I found it chafing, to everyone else, it seemed to make sense.

"Just try it on, Jane."

I rolled my eyes. "God, you're bossy."

"Takes one to know one. Just do it."

Without shame, I changed into the red dress and then stepped back in front of the webcam to model.

"Oh, Janey," Sky said, her voice now full of admiration. "You look amazing. Eric is going to freak, and in the best possible way."

"You think?" I stepped in front of the mirror and turned back and forth.

Immediately, I was struck by the sleek, flattering lines of my dress. Somehow, the combination of the classic silhouette and the loud color found an even mix of the different sides of my personality without clashing at all. I didn't just look nice. I looked perfect, but I also looked like me. For maybe the first time in my life.

The idea overwhelmed, and soon, I found myself reaching for a tissue on the table.

"Are you crying?" Skylar was incredulous.

"What? No." I dabbed at my eyes, careful not to smear my makeup. Hmmm. Maybe I needed to use the waterproof mascara. "What, can't a girl have a reasonable span of emotions? That's my right, Sky."

"Jane."

I turned to the webcam to find my friend watching me suspiciously. "What? I've sort of been through a lot recently."

"Jane," she said calmly, like she was talking to a crazed woman.

I narrowed my eyes. "Sky."

She leaned in. "When was the last time you had your period?"

I frowned. "What? Why?"

"You know why. How long has it been?"

I rolled my eyes. "Dude. I am not pregnant. To start, we use protection."

She did not look impressed.

"Second," I rattled on, "I've been irregular my entire life, so I honestly don't know when the last time was. I'm still not pregnant."

Skylar moved in closer, staring ominously into the webcam.

"You know that angle makes your forehead look about the size of Greenland," I remarked through a knot of tension that had just taken up residence in the pit of my stomach. Damn Skylar and her suspicious, practical mind.

My best friend didn't move, just blinked her big green eyes at me like a redheaded owl.

"Pregnancy usually manifests like PMS in the beginning,"

she said. "I know you know this. You're the one who handed me a test the first time *I* got pregnant. Your cousin, the OB-GYN, had nothing but bad news through *you*."

I cringed on her behalf. That definitely hadn't been the easiest time in her life. And Suejean did wonder why I was asking so many baby-related questions.

"Do you have any tests there?" she asked.

"What? No. I don't exactly keep them on ha—" I broke off quickly. As a woman who had had enough sex to have a few pregnancy scares, I did potentially have a pregnancy test somewhere in one of those boxes in the back room I still hadn't unpacked from Chicago.

Skylar watched knowingly. "Go do it."

I swallowed. "I can't. Eric's going to be here in about an hour, and we have to leave. I—"

"Just do it," Skylar ordered again. "It will take two minutes, and you won't think about anything else for the rest of the night anyway if you don't do it now."

"Yeah, but if I'm pregnant"—my entire body quaked at just the thought—"*if* I'm pregnant, I won't think of anything but that for the rest of the night anyway."

"Honestly. Sometimes you are such a baby."

I gaped. "I am *not*! I'm sorry, who was the one who literally smacked her husband three separate times for giving her gifts?"

"That was five years ago," Skylar countered. "We've grown up since then. We're not kids anymore, Jane. You're thirty years old. You're married—"

"Not officially—"

"You basically are," Skylar continued irritably. "But more than that, you and Eric are a family. A unit. Right?"

I opened my mouth, ready to argue, but found I couldn't. While I still worried that Eric and I might kill each other as often as we loved each other, Skylar was right. He wasn't going anywhere, and neither was I.

"If your family is growing, you need to know," Skylar said. "And take it from me, Janey. So does he. Don't hold that back from him."

My heart squeezed. She did know about the cost of secrets like that, more than most.

I sighed. "Okay. Wait here. I think I know where one is."

———

TEN MINUTES LATER, I returned to the room wrapped in a bathrobe, the small plastic stick pinched between two of my fingers. Skylar, bless her pushy, redheaded heart, had waited with me the entire time, so while I peed on the stick and waited for the results, I was listening to her fold laundry and chatter with Jenny about the latest *How to Train Your Dragon*.

"Jen, go find Daddy," Skylar shooed her daughter out when I reappeared in the frame.

"Bye, Aunt Janey!" cheered Jenny. "Don't say 'fuck' too much!"

"Jenny!"

But Jenny had scampered out of the room before she could receive her mother's wrath. Skylar clenched a dish towel and turned to me expectantly. "Well?"

"Oh my God," I whispered as I sat in front of the iPad. "Sky, I'm—"

"I know, Janey," she said. "I know."

"Holy shit. What am I going to do?"

"What do you mean, what are you going to do? Do you not want to keep it?"

My head jerked up. "What? *No!* Of course I want it!"

The speed with which the words flew from my mouth

surprised even me. It was funny. I had never considered the alternative. I had always considered myself *very* pro-choice, but anything other than having this baby wasn't even an option for me. It just wasn't.

I continued to stare at the two pink lines, unaware of the footsteps moving through the apartment on the other side of my work room's door. Until, of course, the door opened, and Eric swept in, still brushing snowflakes off his cashmere overcoat. He blew a few adorably off his face, looking a bit like an elephant. The movement made his hair, which had been cut quite short to get rid of the terrible dye job, wave slightly.

"Hi, gorgeous," he said with a grin. "Are you almost ready? Sorry I'm late."

"Get out!" I squawked, tumbling around the room in a hurry. I slammed the door in his face with unnecessary force, then wrapped the test up in a spare scrap of muslin from my work table.

"Jane?" Eric asked from behind the door.

"I don't want you to see me!" I screeched. "Stay out there!"

There was an audible chuckle. "We're not getting married again, Lefferts. Our relationship won't be doomed if I see you before midnight."

"Just *go*!" I bellowed.

There was a pause, like he wasn't sure whether I really wanted him to obey me or not. Then I heard the sound of Eric's footsteps receding down the hall to our bedroom.

"I'm going to let you get ready," Skylar said.

"Don't you dare desert me right now, Sky," I snapped, whirling back to the iPad.

But it was too late.

"Put your big girl pants on and face your shit, Janey," she said and blew me a kiss. "Tell me how he freaks out later, okay?"

She grinned, as if the thought of Eric's horror brought her genuine joy.

Under normal circumstances, I might have felt the same way. But this...this wasn't the same at all.

I sank to my knees in front of the tablet. "Sky. What if...what if he..." I couldn't bring myself to ask the question that already made my heart sink. *What if he doesn't want it?*

Eric and I had never talked about a family. I honestly hadn't ever thought about kids myself, although in this moment, I knew without a doubt that I wanted this one. Maybe it would be a boy, tall with Eric's gray eyes and my dark, wavy hair. Or maybe it would be a girl, a sweet blonde child with almond-shaped eyes a little too dark for the rest of her features. Maybe I'd push a stroller to the Met like all the other Central Park moms, sew baby clothes for the next nine months, and eventually do my best to raise a human who wasn't a complete asshole.

It wasn't a future I'd ever imagined for myself. But right now, it was the only one I wanted.

Skylar's features softened as she leaned close again.

"Oh, my friend," she said kindly. "I wish I could jump into this screen and give you a giant hug."

Tears welled all over again. Oh, holy shit. I really was pregnant, wasn't I?

"He's going to want it, Janey," she said. "He's going to want it because that man only wants you and anything that comes from you. I have literally never heard him say a bad word about you. The only thing he has ever wanted was to make you happy. And I am one hundred percent positive that will extend to your baby."

I considered her words and found I couldn't argue.

There was a tentative knock on the door. I cringed. Eric, who had just had the door shut in his face.

"Jane?" he asked. "Are you okay? I'm sorry I'm late, but we really have to get going. It's almost eight."

Skylar waved at me sympathetically. I stared at her, practically begging the screen to magically transport her through it, just like we wanted.

"Good luck," she said. "It's going to be fine."

TWENTY-EIGHT

I tried to tell him. I really did.

I mouthed the words to myself in the mirror as I put on the diamond drop earrings Eric had gifted me upon our return to New York. Apparently the twenty bolts of fabric weren't an adequate Christmas present.

And the words were on the tip of my tongue when I walked out in the red dress and a pair of sky-high Giuseppe Zanotti heels, my hair pinned up in a mass of shiny black coils. Unfortunately, one look at Eric's face told me I needed to take the dress off immediately or find a new one. Skylar was right about the Valentino—I did look fabulous in it. So off it went, along with the rest of our clothes for the next twenty minutes. The shoes, however, stayed on.

And then I tried again when I had to redo my hair and makeup next to him in the master bathroom, but the smell of him was too distracting, and this time *he* was the one who was shoved against the sink while I fell to my knees, right before he turned me around and fell to his too.

An hour later, we were standing next to each other for the

second time in the bathroom, trying not to make eye contact lest we miss the party completely.

"It's nice to have you back," Eric murmured with a sly grin that I only caught out of the corner of my eye as I carefully lined my lips with a deep red that matched my dress.

I rolled my eyes. Apparently, pregnancy hormones made me a cross between a Lifetime tearjerker and Pornhub's hall of fame. There was no in-between. I was such a cliché, and I couldn't have cared less.

"Is it, Petri dish?" I asked as I pulled the makeup brush out of my cosmetics drawer.

He narrowed his eyes playfully at me through the mirror as he fixed his bow tie for the third time, and then, without warning landed a sharp swat to my backside.

"Oh my God!" I yelped. "I'm going to look like a clown if you do that when I'm putting on makeup."

"You know there's a consequence for using that name, pretty girl. I'm not above dispensing it in the middle of a party."

A shiver ran down my spine. *Promise?* I wanted to say. Except I didn't, because my eyes drifted down to the still-flat expanse of my stomach. Was I imagining that it had grown already?

"Hey," Eric said. "What is it?"

I opened my mouth, but before I could get it out, there was a brisk knock on the front door. Eric and I both jumped. We didn't really get unannounced visitors before, and we certainly never got them now—not since Tony and his security squad had been installed in a newly empty apartment downstairs precisely to monitor situations like this.

We crept out of the bathroom and peered at each other for a moment.

"You don't think it's…"

Eric shook his head. "I don't know." He stared at the door like he expected a herd of cattle to come charging through it.

"You want me to get it?" I asked. "He might be kinder to his own flesh and blood."

Eric swallowed, pulled at his collar, and set his jaw. Then, as he pulled on his jacket, he strode to the door and peered through the peephole.

"Oh," he said with surprise and an odd note of tension. "It's Zola."

He opened the door, and indeed, there stood Matthew Zola, looking pretty damn tired, a little bit wet from the snow, and very cold.

"Hey," he greeted me with chattering teeth after Eric invited him in. He took in our formal wear with a bit of surprise. "Bad time?"

Eric glanced between him and me. "Well, it is New Year's Eve. And yeah, DVS is holding an event. There's an announcement I have to be present for."

"Eric was unanimously voted chairman!" I bragged, unable to help myself.

"Oh, shit. Hey, that's great." Zola shook Eric's hand, though he seemed a bit dazed.

"Would you like to come with us?" I offered, ignoring Eric's sharp look. He got along with Zola now that he was helping us investigate John Carson, but that didn't mean he liked him. I wasn't going to lie. I still kind of enjoyed poking that bear.

"Ah, no," Zola said. "That's all right. I've got a stack of police reports and a bottle of grappa at home to help me ring in the New Year."

I nodded sympathetically. Even though I was still planning to start working again in the spring, I did not particularly miss bringing my work home with me every night of the week.

"Besides," Zola said. "I have a feeling I'd be underdressed."

"Probably," Eric agreed, earning an elbow in the gut from me. He lifted his shoulders, as if to say "What?"

"That's, uh, some dress, Jane," Zola said, to the point where I wondered if he did it just to get back at Eric, who was now glowering openly.

I ignored him and turned back to Zola. "Thanks. So, what's up?" I asked. "You're the first DA I've met who makes house calls. Do you want something to drink or anything?"

But Zola just hovered around the door, keeping his coat on and his hands shoved in the pockets.

"I...well, first I wanted to tell you what I know that my boss does not yet. But he will, because he's very good at his job."

I leaned against the breakfast bar while Eric crossed his arms to listen.

"What is it?" Eric demanded a little too sharply.

But Zola met his gaze, his dark brown eyes shining almost as much as his sleek dark hair. He wasn't a billionaire, but this was a guy who had been going after the worst of New York for a long time. He wasn't scared of Eric or anyone. I respected that.

"I looked into John Carson. Found stuff you probably did too. Places of birth, things like that."

I nodded. I had a whole file from friends in Chicago to go through that had been compiled while we were away, along with some extra stuff from the investigator.

"But I also, uh, took it upon myself to take his New York assistant out for a drink one night," Zola said, looking really uncomfortable.

"Oh?" I asked playfully. "Was she cute?"

Zola just looked mildly disgusted with himself. "She was, ah, lonely. And kind of a lightweight. But also had a lot of information on her computer that would probably not be permissible in court."

Carson's assistant, as it happened, had access to his travel records since they had been stored on computers—which, since his company was in the tech business, meant since the early eighties. All of the company's records were in the process of being moved to the cloud, and by some oversight of its IT department, not all of it had been encrypted yet.

"He was in Seoul around 1989, Jane," Zola said, somewhat regrettably. "And he did fly on your mother's airline. It looks like his and your mother's stories pan out, for what it's worth. I'd still request a paternity test though, if he really wants to claim you're his daughter."

Eric snorted. One of my hands drifted to my stomach before I realized what I was doing and sat on it.

"I, um, yeah. Probably not going to happen," I said.

"It was odd, though," Zola said. "He hasn't been back since. The South Koreans really do not like him. At all. And I don't know why. Maybe they know what he did to your mom."

No one laughed. It was a bad joke. Eric folded his mouth into a tight line.

"No one cared about my mother," I said, guilty once again that she still hadn't wanted to talk since I'd come home. "That's why she married my *actual* dad. He was the only one who did."

There was an awkward silence between the three of us. Zola eventually tugged at his collar and cleared his throat. "Ah. Sorry."

"So that's why you came all the way up here on New Year's Eve?" Eric asked sharply. "To verify Jane's paternity?"

Zola looked even more uncomfortable. "Ah, no," he said. "There have been some other...developments. And I'm not really supposed to talk about them with you. I just thought you would want to know."

Eric frowned. "That there are developments you can't tell us? Why would we care about that?"

My stomach dropped as Zola's warning clicked. "Because we're objects of an investigation." I shook my head. "Fuck."

"We're *what*?"

Zola held up his hands in mock-ignorance. "I didn't say anything about it. Literally."

"No," I assured him. "You didn't. You're obviously not here either...right?"

Zola nodded and turned to the door. "As far as I know, I'm already halfway to Sheepshead Bay by now, dog-tired after working all night." He sighed. He knew he'd just dropped a bomb on us, and there was nothing he could do to help us clear it up.

"Any..." I chose my words carefully. "Any idea why the DA would be particularly frustrated by us knowing this information?"

I prayed he would say no. I prayed he wouldn't say the thing I had a feeling was the case—that Zola had come all the way here on December 31st because something terrible was going to happen almost immediately. Someone was getting arrested. Someone was going down.

He just shrugged. "I really don't know the answer to that. I'm...well, I'll put it this way. I'm definitely *not* telling you every-thing I know."

I sighed, but tried to be understanding, though I was just as confused as before. He was already risking his job—hell, his license—to be here and tell us any of this. Why not just go all the way and give us a head start?

But instead, Zola turned to leave.

"Happy New Year," he said. "And, Jane?"

I turned back. "Yeah?"

"For what it's worth, the DA isn't particularly happy with the other investigator that Skylar and Brandon hired. He said he was going to ruin the discovery process today before it even got started. I was surprised, honestly, that he didn't say I had to keep that fact to myself."

I swallowed. Well, then. Message received, loud and clear.

Zola looked meaningfully at both Eric and me. "I'll, um, well, I probably *won't* be seeing you. At least not for a while."

I bit my lip and nodded again. "Thanks, Zola."

He opened the door. "Bye, Jane. Eric."

The door closed, and after a few beats, Eric whirled to me.

"What in the hell was all of that?"

I waited until Zola's footsteps had receded completely down the stairs before I sank back to my stool. "It was a warning."

"About what?"

I looked up. "Has the last six months knocked out every bit of lawyering sense from your brain? What do you *think* he meant?"

Eric opened his mouth as if to argue, then shut it again. "Do me a favor. You seem to speak his shady cop language better than I do—"

"That's because I was a prosecutor too, you goon."

"I *know*," Eric said tightly. "So lay it out for me, will you?"

I took a deep breath. "He was telling us we're under investigation for something related to John Carson. Either both of us, or you. Which means he can't talk about it at all."

"Yeah, I picked up on that part," Eric said.

"Any idea what it might be?"

I might have imagined the pause before he said, "None at all. I've been here the whole time with you."

"Except when you were disappearing into graveyards."

"Jane."

"All right, all right, all right." I waved his silent protests away with one hand. "Sorry."

"What did he mean about the other investigator? Why would he be ruining a discovery tonight?"

"Something's going on." I crossed to the living room, where I picked up my laptop from the coffee table and opened my email. "The investigator found something they don't want us to know they know. Something they are trying to verify themselves, but that our investigator apparently discovered as well."

Sure enough, in my inbox there was a link from Skylar to an encrypted file. I opened it, entered the password we had agreed upon, and started paging through the documents that had been submitted this evening by the P.I.

"This is weird," I said as I scanned through the report.

"What's that?" Eric pointed at a few pictures from his seat next to me on the couch.

"The street where I grew up," I said. "That's in Evanston. My house is that one on the right."

I squinted. The blurry surveillance photos weren't focused on the old house, but instead on the curb in front, where a simple black sedan was parked. There were two figures in the back seat of the sedan, and I thought I could make out John Carson's long, slightly hooked nose. But the other was too short to see anything notable. Why they were sitting in my old neighborhood was a completely different question.

"Huh," I said as I scrolled down to the notes below. "There's nothing that explains this. Maybe the investigator will upload something else tomorrow or on the second. I'll call then."

I kept going, looking through the various bit of biographical information the P.I. had collected on John Carson. Some I'd already found on my own. Other stuff, like his collection of known residences or liaisons, was interesting, though not urgent.

"We should go through this after the party," I said, looking at the clock. "It's already past ten o'clock. They are probably waiting for you so they can announce the appointment."

"Wait," Eric said. "What the hell is that?"

He continued scrolling down in a hurry to a list of transactions that had been noted. Stock movement between companies. Specifically the transfer of quite a few shares of DVS stock to an LLC called "Horse and Chariot Ventures." Which, with a bit of more careful prodding, appeared to be a foreign business attached to the same account used personally by one John Carson.

"Jesus," I murmured. "This guy is good. I wonder what kind of Swiss dick he had to suck to get these numbers."

Eric, however, was already incensed. "That son of a bitch. He's been buying more DVS stock. A lot more than he said."

"He has," I agreed. "Why?"

But before I could prod more, Eric had whipped out his phone and called his assistant.

"Bridget," he said as he started pacing the room. "Yeah, get me Thomas Clark on the phone. And conference in Nina in about five minutes. "

Thomas J. Clark. The family's estate attorney and financial consultant.

"Hey, Tom," Eric said once his call had been connected. "I just need to know...how much liquid cash do I have access to right now? No, I don't mean after the will takes effect. I mean now. As of tonight."

Tom's voice was indistinct on the other side of the line, but whatever he said made Eric scowl.

"Okay," he said after. "Okay, thanks."

He hung up and dialed another number immediately.

"What are you—" I started to ask, but was cut off when Eric started talking.

"Hey, Greg, it's Eric de Vries. Yeah, Happy New Year to you, too. Listen, I was wondering if you could give me an estimate for this idea I had."

I frowned. He was maneuvering a stock deal on New Year's Eve? The market wouldn't even open for two days.

"How much would it take to up the family's share to a full sixty percent?"

Apparently, the answer was not a good one, because Eric swore profusely under his breath.

"Fine," he replied once he was done. "How much could we purchase with our current liquid assets?"

Again, the broker's voice was inaudible.

"All right," Eric said irritably. "When the market opens, buy as much as we can afford. Fifty-two is better if we can get there. Do whatever you need to make sure the family owns fifty-one by the first board meeting next week, all right?"

I waited a few more minutes while Eric accepted the conference call he'd requested and instructed Nina to purchase as much stock as she could too.

"What did you just do?" I asked when he was finished.

"What was necessary," Eric replied. He glanced at the clock again. "Shit. We really have to go."

"Oh, now you care about making a grand entrance?"

"I need to be the face of this company more than ever," Eric said. "Because if John Carson is trying to oust me from DVS, I need to make sure the stockholders who are currently invested in the company stay that way instead of selling to him."

TWENTY-NINE

We arrived at the party at ten past ten, after Eric had spent nearly the entire drive through a snowy Manhattan (filled with New Year's traffic) on the phone, trying to convince his other family members to buy up as much DVS stock as they possibly could. It wasn't an easy sell (oddly), because the family was already the majority stockholder by far at forty-nine percent of the company. But Eric seemed to think it was necessary to hold as much as possible—fifty-one percent or higher—and by the time we reached the party, he had convinced Violet and a few other relatives to direct their brokers to purchases smaller chunks.

By the time he was finished, victory practically radiated off the man. And I couldn't lie. Watching Eric get his Gordon Gekko on was doing serious things for my apparently unquenchable libido. Unfortunately, there was nothing I could do about it, because at that moment, we arrived at the gala.

Calling the DVS New Year's Eve event a "party" would have been a huge misnomer. This wasn't some frat house kegger, nor was it a tasteful garden soiree. This was a Great Gatsby-level bash like I had never seen before.

It helped that the space itself was gorgeous. Entering DVS was actually its own adventure, as the lobby was sunken a solid thirty steps below the sidewalk, over which thick glass walls arched inward before the main offices soared to the sky. The effect was that once you were inside, it genuinely seemed like you were completely ensconced in glass while streetlamps, passing cars, and other random lights from outside blinked off nearly all the surfaces in a remarkably celestial pattern. Now that the entire place was bedazzled with twinkling lights, silvery streamers, and fizzing champagne, it was like walking into the middle of Van Gogh's *The Starry Night*.

As we descended the stairs, which had been covered by a midnight-blue carpet for the occasion, Eric and I took a moment to survey the scene. The lobby was packed—other than the usual craze in Times Square, the DVS party was obviously the hottest ticket in town for tonight. A full band wailed swing standards in front of a crowded dance floor, there were at least four open bars, and the entire party was bubbling over with champagne, hors d'oeuvres, and raucous conversation.

The guests themselves were just as stunning as the decor. Dior, Siriano, Rodriguez, de la Renta. It was like watching the pages of Vogue come to life. I recognized several faces from our wedding, though none of whom I'd been able to meet personally, considering the reception had never actually happened.

Was this what it would have been like, in the ballroom of the Waldorf Astoria? Was I even enough to compete with this kind of splendor?

"Is it always like this?" I wondered as Eric escorted me inside.

He turned and smiled. Not for the first time, I appreciated how completely dashing he looked. His tux was a custom

Armani he'd commissioned a few months ago for tonight, with a navy and black embroidered cummerbund and a matching bow tie. He was stylish without looking like a dandy—that line between sophisticated and gaudy that Eric walked so well. His gray eyes shone, glinting like the bouncing lights around us.

"I don't know," he admitted. "I haven't been to one of these in a long time. But I remember looking forward to New Year's Eve every year when I was a kid—maybe even more than Christmas. It was the one day of the year everyone in my family let loose. Nina and I could get into as much trouble as we wanted so long as we stayed in the building and I kept my tails clean."

I hid a smile. It wasn't hard to see Eric and Nina as the only two kids at a party like this, sunshine-headed imps ducking around ballgowns. Eric, with natural charm, would have been the obvious instigator of whatever mischief they got into.

When he removed my coat to check, I heard a tight hiss of breath behind my ear. Eric's fingers brushed over my bare shoulders, lingering just a bit too long around the diamond pendant that matched my earrings.

I twisted around. "You can't be serious. You've been staring at me in this thing for hours now. You know what it looks like."

"Not this close," he murmured. His gaze burned over my bare shoulders. "If I didn't make it clear before, you look incredible tonight."

"Eric! Jane!"

We turned to where Nina was pushing through the crowds, looking impossibly gorgeous and tall in a white silk gown that shimmered like snow. She traded air kisses with both of us, but still looked genuinely happy to see us both.

"We've been waiting for you for hours," she said. "Gerald Post got into the punch early, so Uncle Rufus has been trying to talk him off the stage ever since. Calvin disappeared forever ago, and I've been fielding questions from reporters. Everyone is waiting for the announcement."

Eric waved at a few people who had already spotted him eagerly. "We'll make it soon," he said. "I just need to help Jane with her dress. She, uh, tore a seam getting out of the limo."

"Well, don't be long. Everyone wants to congratulate you. Considering I'm about to sink half my trust back into this company, I insist you make a good impression." She tugged on his sleeve.

"I'll be right there," Eric said, shooing her away. Then he turned to me with a decidedly darker expression. "Go to the bathroom on the second floor." His lips brushed against my earlobe, setting my skin alight as he gestured up the three flights of glass stairs above us. "Take off your underwear. Then bring them back to me. For good luck."

I blinked as coquettishly as I could manage. It seemed to work—Eric glanced around and adjusted his pants with a lightning touch.

"What if I told you I decided to forgo undergarments tonight?" I asked.

"Are you serious?"

I pursed my lips, making Eric's gaze beeline right to them. It was hard not to smirk. "Well, yes. Panty lines don't really go with couture. Plus, you removed them at home...and I never put them back on."

His gaze seared down my dress all over again, and I was thankful for the structured bodice—otherwise everything I was thinking would be evident across my chest.

"Then I think," he said as he lifted my hand to his lips. "You need to go into the bathroom and wait for me there." He lifted one brow. "That's all."

I bit my lower lip. "Right away? Won't people be a little suspicious if we just disappear like that?"

Eric offered a positively wicked half grin. "It's my party. I'll fuck my wife if I want to."

And just like that, all flirtation vanished. My mood, a complete and total roller coaster, took a nosedive all over again. Right into a pool of ice water.

Wife, he said. Except I wasn't. Not really. He didn't wear a wedding ring, and neither did I. Last I saw them, they were sitting in an acrylic tray at home, right next to my favorite magnolia-scented soap and Eric's cologne on the bathroom counter. Doing absolutely nothing. Just like the certificate in the office.

"Jane."

I looked up, blinking furiously. I would not cry, I would not cry, I would. Not. Cry.

Eric's expression, thankfully, was heated enough to evaporate any tears that threatened. Ah, and there was my libido again.

"You have five minutes," I said. "Otherwise I'm leaving, and you'll have to wait for as long as *I* want."

Eric grinned. "Game on, gorgeous."

————

THE SECOND-FLOOR BATHROOM was empty as promised, so when I stood in front of the marble countertops, it didn't take long for my thoughts, which had been pinballing all evening, to jump right back to the revelations I'd already had that night.

Pregnant. Holy shit, I was pregnant. I was...people were going to wonder already, I realized. They were going to see me do things like *not* drink champagne and get extraordinarily tired for no reason. They were going to see me cry at the drop of a hat and wonder if I'd gotten a sudden boob job.

I grabbed one of my breasts. Was it bigger? More sensitive? Honestly, I couldn't tell. Maybe that was going to happen later. How far along was I, anyway?

Would Eric want to know? Would he want to know now?

Tears mounted again as I also realized this couldn't be happening at a worse time. True, I was thirty—if I was going to have a kid, it was better now than later. But at the same time, we had a sycophantic madman after us who was obsessed with not "sullying his bloodline" with the de Vries genes. He already nursed a nasty vendetta against Eric. What would he do if he knew I was carrying his enemy's baby?

Behind me, the bathroom door swung open, and Eric strode in, already unbuttoning his jacket in anticipation.

"Hands on the sink, pretty girl," he ordered, but stopped immediately when he got a good look at me trying and failing not to have a nervous breakdown. "Whoa. Jane, are you okay?"

"I'm fine." I coughed and turned to the sinks, just like he had told me to. But now I had absolutely no desire to get busy. I just wanted to be left alone so I could calm the hell down.

"Liar."

I looked up, my temper flaring. "*I'm* a liar? Who just told everyone I had a faulty dress, huh? How do you think that makes me look when they all know I design clothes? They already like to laugh about it."

"Hey, hey." Eric stepped back, holding his hands up. "It was just a joke, gorgeous. No one cares if you have a torn seam."

"Don't call me that."

He frowned. "I always call you gorgeous. What the hell is wrong with you?"

"Wrong with *me*? Just because I'm not interested in playing one of your stupid games right now? Did it ever occur to you that I don't always want to be your weird arm candy doll?" Good God. The hormones were messing with my comebacks too.

"What in the hell. Where is all this coming from?"

Eric's eyes widened, like he was witnessing an animal going suddenly berserk in a zoo. He walked around the bathroom to my other side, giving me a wide berth. The mask was in place, and all I wanted to do was tear it down.

"Fuck," I muttered toward the sink. "*Fuck.*"

"Jane."

I stood up and faced him, suddenly livid. "What? What do you want?"

"I want to know why you're acting like a goddamn maniac, to start," Eric snapped back. "Two seconds ago we were ready to tear each other's clothes off, and now I'm a pariah. What the hell happened on the way upstairs?" He started as something occurred to him. "Shit, Caitlyn's not here, is she?"

"No," I sneered. "Do you wish she were? Caitlyn and her magical red panties? Maybe you could stuff those in your pocket. Or, you know, in our bed."

I scowled at my dress, suddenly hating its bright red color, though not as much as I hated the words coming out of my mouth. Good fucking God, if this was what pregnancy did to a woman, I already hated it.

Eric glared at me. "This again? Sometimes you are really a fucking headcase, Jane, you know that?"

"Don't gaslight me, asshole—"

"It's not gaslighting if it's true."

"That's *exactly* what a man would say to make a woman feel crazy!"

"Come on, really?" Eric protested. "I'm only trying to help. I just want to know what the hell is wrong with my wife, and she won't fucking tell me!"

"Stop calling me that!" I shouted, suddenly feeling like my mind was outside of my body.

Eric scowled, but crossed his arms and remained silent. I

waited for him to say something, but he didn't. He just looked cold. Cruel. Like he wanted to be done with me.

A hot tear slid down my cheek. I couldn't tell if it was out of anger or sadness.

"Is this some game to you?" I demanded as I swiped at it. "Some fucked-up game where you toy with my emotions? How do you think it feels when you call me that in front of people, knowing it's not really true?"

"Call you what?"

"Your *wife*."

"What are you talking about, it's not true?" he demanded. "I call you that because you *are* my wife."

"NO, I'M NOT!" I shrieked. "How many times did you say that? As soon as you got back after the wedding, again and again and again! You made it absolutely clear that we are not married. In any fucking way!"

Eric sucked in a harsh, impatient breath. "Jane, you know it killed me to say that. I thought we were past this. We just ran away together for a month. We're here *together*. I'm about to announce that I am chairman of my family's company with *you* by my side!"

"And for how long, huh?" The tears were rivers now. It was going to take forever for me to redo this makeup, even if it was only to look normal as I walked out the doors.

"What is that supposed to mean?"

I shook my head, trying in vain to suck back my tears. I sounded like a dust buster. Super-hot. "Nothing. It means nothing."

"Jesus Christ, I can't keep up with you!" Eric exploded. "Hot and cold, hot and cold. You're practically quicksilver, you're so unstable!"

"*I'm* unstable?" I choked. "Wh-wh-who treated m-me like a g-ghost for w-weeks! You're giving m-me whiplash!"

"I was doing it to protect *you*!"

"It still hurt!"

"Oh, for fuck's sake." He turned toward the door, rubbing his brow like he was exhausted. "This is ridiculous."

"Is it?" I asked. "Is it? Two days, Eric. Two days, and you'll be rid of me. This marriage will be nulled. You want to tell me you're not basically counting the minutes until you can leave me, this company, everything. Get rid of your crazy 'wife' who's basically good for one thing? I'm just the town whore—you said so yourself."

Eric's mouth dropped like he couldn't believe what he was hearing. A part of me couldn't blame him. I couldn't really believe I was saying it.

"Is that what you think?" he asked finally, his voice low.

I swallowed painfully. "I—what else am I supposed to think? You're playing me like a damn drum."

He watched me for a long time. And then, to my complete and utter shock, he reached into his pocket and pulled out a folded piece of paper, whipping it open and smacking it onto the countertop between us.

"Here," he said. "You want me to sign it? I was going to ask you to do it at midnight, but let's do it now, Lefferts. No regrets. No doubts."

I stared at the marriage license—the one that had been sitting in the desk. Then I stared at him. And then I turned into a fucking fountain.

"What the..." Eric pulled me into him immediately, apparently caring nothing for tear stains marring his immaculate tux.

"I'm pregnant!" I sobbed into his shoulder. "Oh...oh...oh my...I can't—Eric, I can't b-breathe—"

Eric looked like he'd been smacked across the head by a two-by-four. I just wailed harder, clutching around my middle and collapsing into the granite. My sobs physically hurt, and when I choked on one, it seemed to snap Eric out of his stupor. In less than a second, he picked me up and set me on the bathroom sink, then gathered me close.

The bathroom door opened—a woman stepped inside and immediately stopped when she caught sight of us.

"Get out," Eric snapped, sending the woman running. He cupped my cheek. "Are you going to be okay for one second?"

Still weeping too hard to speak, I nodded. He looked at me doubtfully, then swiftly crossed the bathroom, locked the door, and returned. I collapsed into his chest, and his strong arms enveloped me completely, one at my waist, the other reaching around so he could splay a large hand over my bare back and rock me gently.

"All right," he said in a calm voice once my sobs eventually turned to sniffles. "Do you think you're calm enough to repeat what you just told me?"

I sniffed again, accepting a paper towel to dab under my eyes—I probably looked like a raccoon that made out with a clown. Eric watched me unblinking, but it wasn't until my eyes had cleared completely that I realized he was shaking a bit too.

Fuck. Oh, *fuck.*

Eric exhaled slowly. "So...you're pregnant?"

"I'm sorry," I whispered.

"And you're upset," he continued. "Because we aren't legally married."

We both eyed the license beside us. Just a piece of paper, really. But in that moment, it meant everything.

I gulped. I didn't know what to say. Why did it bother me so much? We didn't have to get married. And I had never wanted to get married before now. It shouldn't have mattered, baby or not.

And yet it did matter. It really, really did.

Eric released me as if to examine the license, but instead

braced his hands against the sink's edge, rocking back and forth for a second like he was wrestling with something deep inside.

"I didn't sign it," he said finally, "because I didn't think you wanted to." He stood up, and his gaze was an arrow. "I forced you into this. The terms changed. You didn't have to do it anymore. I didn't—God, Jane, I thought this was what you wanted. Freedom. To be with me or not, but of your own accord."

"Then why do you keep calling me your wife?"

"I guess I thought I should take advantage of it while I could." One side of his mouth lifted in a sheepish half smile, and for a moment, Eric almost looked like the brash young twentysomething I had met on that first day on the Harvard lawn. "I really liked calling you my wife, pretty girl. Even if it wasn't going to last."

He shoved a hand over his face and forehead, knocking a few perfect strands of hair out of place. I fought the urge to fix them. I wanted to touch him. I wanted to know he was real.

"I thought if you really wanted it, you would have said something too," he admitted finally, with a yearning in his eyes that almost broke my heart. "I gave you my vows, Jane. But you...you never gave me yours."

Dread settled in my stomach like a stone. He was right. I hadn't really consecrated how I felt. Not like he had.

God, I was so, so stupid.

"Eric?" I ventured, watching his heartbroken form wrestle with his vulnerability.

He looked up. "What, Jane?" The fatigue in his gray eyes said he thought I still wanted out. I was still crying. It was still painful. But not as painful as the idea of not being together.

"You said...you once said you wouldn't have asked me to marry you if you didn't love me," I said. "Was that true?"

Eric nodded. "Yeah," he said. "It was."

I nodded. My heart lifted, though I had to dab at a few more tears. "Well, I wouldn't have said yes if I didn't love you too."

Eric watched me carefully. "What are you saying?"

"I'm saying..."

Another several streams of tears fell when I saw them mirrored on Eric's face. His gaze dropped to my stomach. I took a deep breath and held it for a moment.

"I'm saying I don't want it to end." The words were choked, caught in a mess of tears lodged in my throat. Tears that had been waiting years to be let loose. "I'm saying I want it to be real. I promise to be yours. Now. Forever. Until death do us part. P-please. I'm saying stay. Stay...stay with me. Us. Be my husband. Let me be...let me be your wife. Not just now, but for always. Marry me, Eric."

He didn't brush away his own tears, just watched me steadily with silvery eyes that seemed to have no limits, as deep as the ocean, but so much warmer.

"Jane," he said finally, reaching out for my hand. "You ridiculous woman. I already did."

I watched in awe as he reached into his other pocket and pulled out our rings. Both of them. His and mine.

"What are you doing with these?" I asked.

He offered yet another charmingly lopsided smile. "I took them with me tonight...sort of a good luck charm, I guess. Just in case you said yes at midnight."

He held out my engagement ring with its deep black stone and the matching diamond band alongside the simple ring of platinum we had chosen for him.

"If I stay, I'm not fighting about this again," he said. "I'm tired of having to prove over and over again that I love you. Every time you push me away, it's like I leave some part of me behind." He took my hand and pressed it over his heart. "There are only so many times you can walk away from the other fucking half of your soul, Jane. Even when she's the one pushing."

"I don't want to push you away." I stared at the place my hand covered. It took everything I had not to kiss him right there, above his heart, tuxedo and all.

God, how cheesy was I?

"Come here," Eric ordered quietly, taking my hand and pulling me off the counter so I stood in front of him. He slid on my engagement ring and kissed it tenderly.

"Eric," I said. "I'm not the Pope. I want you to take my hand in marriage, not kiss it."

He shook his head with a crooked smile. "Well," he said, holding out the other band. "Will you take me?"

I grinned so wide I thought my face might split in half. "Over and over again, you idiot."

With glee, I watched as he slid my wedding ring next to the diamond.

I took his ring and asked him the same question. "Will you take me? Basket case and all?"

"Always, pretty girl."

I slid his ring on and admired it for a full five seconds. Then I looked up, and his lips found mine with the kiss I hadn't known I'd needed since that terrible day at the church. Sweet and full, it assured me that no matter what, we really did belong together. That neither of us had to be alone ever again.

"Come here, you beautiful, crazy, stubborn, gorgeous woman. You're pregnant?"

I could barely grin under all the kisses that covered my face.

"And you want to...God, Jane, do you want to—" Eric shook his head. "You know, I'm almost afraid to ask."

I grabbed his chin and forced him to look at me. "You goon. Of course I want to keep it. Why in the hell do you think I'm so upset about this? I want my baby to know its dad."

Eric's smile didn't just shine. It fucking lit up the entire room.

"I need a pen!" he erupted, checking his pockets in vain and jumping around the bathroom like a bean. "Fucking hell, where is a fucking pen?"

I giggled uncontrollably while I searched my clutch—his sudden mania was contagious. When I managed to find one, Eric swooped down on the document and signed his name with violent flourish. But when he handed it to me, he was tentative.

"Last out, pretty girl," he said, though there was no threat in his voice.

I took the pen and grinned. Hot and cold indeed. Suddenly, I felt like the sun was beaming through me.

I bent down and signed the document, taking a moment to admire our signatures, side by side.

"There it is," Eric murmured from over my shoulder. "Now we're officially Mr. and Mrs. de Vries. Or we will be on Tuesday when we file it."

"Ah, that's Ms. Lefferts to you," I said. "I like my name very much, thanks."

"I don't care what you call yourself. As long as you call yourself mine."

I grinned into the mirror. We really were ridiculously cheesy, but I couldn't love it more.

"Come on," Eric said. "As much as I'd love to consummate this marriage fully right here like we planned, right now, I just want a first dance with my wife."

I beamed at our reflection. A marriage of opposites that somehow matched perfectly.

"Let's do it," I said as his hands spread over the life inside me. "Let's go toast to new beginnings and the New Year."

THIRTY

"The board of directors for De Vries Shipping Industries is proud to announce that we have unanimously elected Eric de Vries, the son of the late Jacob de Vries and grandson of the late Celeste de Vries, as chairman of the board. The board has total faith in Eric's ability to continue his family's legacy of guiding DVS toward new horizons of innovation and success. Congratulations, Eric, and welcome."

Photography flashes of the several press agents who had been invited to the party went off like fireworks, and the crowd assembled in front of the mainstage erupted with applause as the announcing board member finished his short speech. Eric tipped his glass toward the ceiling, and I just did my best to smile and not cry again. While his eyes sparked with clear pride, the shadow of a smile at his lips whispered of a bashfulness I found utterly endearing. Pride sung through me at this man that I could finally call my own.

He took my hand and raised it to his mouth while he smiled around, then finally looked at me and truly beamed. I couldn't help but beam back.

"Can I tell them?" he murmured through the shouts in front of us.

I didn't have to ask about what. His eyes flickered to my stomach, which seemed to flutter in response to how crazy proud the man obviously was of the fact that we were going to have a baby.

Holy shit. Eric de Vries and Jane Lefferts. Polar Opposites. Married couple. Now expecting?

I should have been freaking out, but right then, I couldn't have been happier.

Celeste must have been crowing in her grave.

Still, I shook my head. "It's a little early, yet, don't you think?"

A part of me wanted to keep our secret to ourselves. You know, at least until we got used to the idea.

Eric shrugged as the hubbub died down, and we exited the stage as the band started playing again. It was only a few minutes to midnight, and it still felt like the party had just begun.

After accepting congratulatory handshakes of at least twenty people, Eric swept me into an easy two step.

"I've had at least five separate people ask me tonight why you aren't drinking champagne, Lefferts," he said. "Honestly, I should have already figured it out. I don't think you'll be able to hide it long."

"Tell them I'm a recovering alcoholic," I suggested. "There are enough of them here. New York's upper class is lousy with drunks."

Eric snorted, but he couldn't stop smiling either. Our joy was infectious.

"Fine," he said, pulling me closer. "But I'm not keeping this to myself forever, Mrs. de Vries."

His smirk told me he was trying to get under my skin with the name. But it didn't work. Instead I tipped my head up for a kiss, allowing him to be as public with his affection as he wanted about our news. He kissed me for a few beats longer than strictly necessary, ignoring the flashes of cameras.

"I wish Celeste could see this," I thought out loud.

Eric looked surprised for a moment, then nodded. "She would have been very, very satisfied," he said, chuckling. "But you know, I think maybe she died knowing she was going to get what she wanted anyway."

"I think what she wanted was to make you happy," I replied.

Before we could ruminate too long on Celeste, we were interrupted by several other people wishing Eric good tidings and best of luck on his new position. The announcement wasn't a surprise for anyone, but I got the feeling that most people probably thought Eric would be more of a figurehead than an active member, or else wouldn't assume the position until the beginning of the next fiscal year.

"Congratulations, Triton."

At the sound of the familiar voice, Eric paused mid-conversation with an investor from Connecticut. He rearranged his smile, bid the man good night, then slowly turned around.

His eyes narrowed. "You've seriously got a death wish, Jude."

The man otherwise known as "Hermes" stood in front of us wearing a nose brace that covered most of his face. He looked like he wanted to be anywhere but here at the moment, and I couldn't help but notice that he kept a solid three feet between himself and Eric.

Eric's hand sought mine, and he pulled me securely into his side.

Jude's eyes roved over my body. "Your little China doll cleans up well. She's almost unrecognizable in that finery."

"Careful." Eric's voice was steel.

"What are you doing here?" I snapped. I wasn't nearly so

circumspect. "If it's not obvious, you're not fucking welcome, you neutered GI-Joe."

Eric snorted, but the squeeze of his hand told me he wanted me to be quiet as people glanced at us curiously.

"I was invited," Jude said as he bared his teeth in an ugly parody of a smile. "A plus-one, as it were, since Triton—sorry, *Eric*, since we're using our given names now—couldn't be bothered to send his brothers proper invitations. My date...let's see, where is that little imp...she's an old family friend. Ah, there she is."

He pointed across the hall, and Eric and I followed his gaze to a woman watching us from her spot at one of the tables. The sight of those honey-brown tresses and the twinkling, tasteful jewelry that delicately accented her ice-blue dress made me want to scream.

Eric stiffened.

Caitlyn fucking Calvert.

"I believe you know Catie," Jude said. "So many of us do, don't we? She's a regular Becky Sharp, isn't she? Even more than this one."

I frowned, recognizing the reference to the social climbing heroine of *Vanity Fair*. "What is he talking about?"

"Caitlyn is originally from Paterson, New Jersey," Eric clarified to me. "She was a scholarship student in school with us when she was younger, and at one point, Violet took her in for a while. Celeste sponsored half her education."

"Ohhhh." So much made sense now about that conniving little bitch's behavior. Her strange obsession with the de Vrieses. Her almost maniacal desire to shove me out of the way. She had wanted nothing more than to become one of them herself, at nearly any cost.

And that included infiltrating, whether knowingly or not, one of the most illustrious societies at its heart.

"I think you should return to your date," Eric said. "I won't kick you out, but you should know that Jane's right. You're not welcome. Neither of you are."

Jude shook his head. "I really came to see if you had changed your mind since our last...altercation." He cocked his head. "On Titan's orders. He's really so much more generous with you than I would be." His green eyes gleamed with even the possibility of vengeance, but instead he pulled a chain out of a coat pocket and dangled a necklace in front of Eric. One bearing a familiar gold coin.

"Your choice, Triton. But it's your last chance."

Eric took the coin, fingering it gently. Then he clenched it in his fist and tossed it roughly back at Jude.

"You can tell John Carson that he needs to stay away from me and mine. And that includes my company. Or else he's going to suffer consequences too, and he has not yet experienced how creative *I* can be with my vengeance. Can you deliver that message...*Hermes*?"

Jude's eyes narrowed, but after a moment he held his hands up in surrender. "You're an idiot, Triton," he said. "I always thought so. Carson gave you more credit than you deserve." He stepped backward into the crowd. "Still. I'm going to enjoy this."

"What's that?" I asked.

But the big man just turned and walked away.

Eric turned to me, and for a moment his hands hovered protectively around my waist.

"Should we call Tony?" I asked.

He shook his head. "I'm not scared of that asshole. Let's just enjoy the party. I want to dance some more with my wife."

I grinned. But something else was bothering me.

"I want to call my mom first," I said, already maneuvering through the crowd to find a place where I could actually hear. Eric followed, giving polite nods and waves as we went.

"Will she be up?" he wondered after we found a relatively quiet corner.

"Chicago is an hour behind us," I said. "And it's New Year's. She's probably at her cousin's guzzling *soju*. She'll be up."

Eric nodded and was pulled into a nearby conversation, keeping an eye on me as I swiped over my mother's number.

"Please answer, please answer," I repeated as I listened to it ring.

I gazed down at my left hand. The rings looked good there. Felt right. In two days, Eric and I could file the papers before our deadline passed and be officially married in the eyes of the state of New York. My mother had been begging me for grandchildren for years. I wasn't in a hurry to announce it to the party, but this was just the thing to put our drama to bed.

But, to my utter disappointment, the call went to voicemail. I tried again, and the third time, finally left a message.

"*Eomma*," I said, my voice uncharacteristically small. Once again, I was battling tears—Lord, this pregnancy was going to be an emotional nightmare, I could already tell. I figured I should just name the kid Catharsis and be done with it.

I turned toward the corner, smiling weakly at some curious onlookers. For a lot of people, this was the first time Eric and I had been seen in public since the wedding.

"*Eomma*, I'm *sorry*," I whispered emphatically. "But I think this has gone on long enough, don't you think? I'm so sorry we missed Christmas...but I have things to tell you. We need to make this right." I sighed and worried my lips, contemplating. "Look, I'm going to come to Chicago. This week, okay? I just...Eric and I have to take care of something on the second, but after that, I'll be on the first flight there. *Eomma*, I love you."

My voice cracked on the last statement. My mother and I hardly ever said I love you, so it felt cheap somehow to be saying it to a machine. But for some reason, right now, I needed her to know it more than ever.

"I just want to make sure you're all right," I said just before hanging up. And then I stared at the dark screen of my phone for a long time.

"Everything all right?" Eric unwittingly repeated my last phrase, approaching with a worried look.

"You know," I said. "I don't think it is."

Before he could ask why, I was overcome with sudden urgency.

"I need to go to Chicago," I said as a strange, chilly sensation crept up my spine. "Something's happened. Something is wrong." I looked up. "Eric, I haven't heard from my mother for almost six weeks. No voicemails. Just texts. She hates to text, I..." I shook my head. "Something happened. I know it."

He examined me for a moment, but my concerns must have been written all over my face. The car. The house in Evanston. Her ongoing lack of communication. I didn't know what was going on, but I had absolutely no doubt that John Carson had something to do with it.

This was why we had felt so blissfully unbothered for the past month. We weren't the ones he was bothering. My mother was.

"I'll get the jet," Eric said immediately.

I blinked. "The jet?"

He nodded, no sign of a smirk. "Chairman of the board comes with certain privileges. Like use of the company plane."

Ten minutes ago, I might have had a sharp comeback about *Lifestyles of the Rich and Famous*, but right now, I was just grateful we had the resources.

"I need to go home and change," I said, suddenly moving around awkwardly in my gown. "I'm not going to look for my mother in Jessica Rabbit cosplay."

Eric nodded. "I'll tell Tony to bring the car around."

But before we could do anything, a sudden commotion disturbed the party. People scattered as a horde of police officers flooded down the stairs, fronted by several men in black suits who looked, if Hollywood was correct, an awful lot like federal agents.

They plowed through the crowds, and the band stopped playing. A hum of voices remained, but otherwise, most people stopped talking to watch the squad make their way to us.

"Eric de Vries?" A tall man with a barrel chest addressed Eric with an utterly no-nonsense tone.

Eric frowned. "Yes. Is there a problem?" He glanced around. "Can't be disturbance of the peace. I own the building, and it's New Year's Eve. The entire city is up right now."

The man pulled out a badge—just as I suspected, he was a bona fide G-Man.

"Charles Dryden, FBI. Mr. de Vries, you are under arrest for conspiracy to commit securities fraud."

Eric's jaw dropped. "Insider trading? Are you kidding me?"

"This has to be a misunderstanding," I said, stepping in front of him. "Eric would never do something like that."

But Eric took my arm and pulled me to the side. Dryden raised a hand, and a rush of officers came forward to grab Eric by the arms.

"Easy!" Eric protested. "Do I look like I'm resisting here?"

They ignored him, wrenching his arms behind his back in order to handcuff him roughly while Dryden proceeded:

"Eric de Vries, you have the right to remain silent. If you give up that right, anything you say can and will be used against you in a court of law. You have a right to an attorney and to have an attorney present during questioning. If you cannot afford an attorney, one will be appointed at no cost."

"Jane." Eric's eyes zeroed in on mine, begging me to watch

him. "Jane, call Skylar. Find Nina, and call Skylar and Brandon. Take Tony with you anywhere you go, and do not trust anyone else, do you understand? *No one else.*"

I nodded, my lower lip trembling as I walked alongside while they escorted my husband to the street. I fumbled with my phone, unable to make my fingers work as the icy wind caused shivers to sprint violently all over me.

"I'll be out tomorrow," Eric called over the gusts screaming from the Hudson Bay.

I nodded, unable to speak. This was crazy. I needed to call Zola. Find out what the hell had been happening. Was *this* what he was trying to tell us?

We should have run, I thought, over and over again. We should have kept running and never stopped.

"Jane!" Eric's voice rang out over the din as he stood in front of the waiting car.

Our eyes met—brown to gray, earth to steel. His flashed like the stars hidden by the city's aura.

"I love you," he shouted. "The both of you! Don't forget it."

I nodded frantically, but my voice was stuck.

"I love you too," I called back, fighting over the crowds and the drum of my own heart to get the words out. The words I desperately wanted him to know, beyond the shadow of a doubt.

But it was too late. The cars pulled away, a caravan of police.

Eric de Vries.

My lover.

Fighter.

Husband.

Father-to-be.

Was already gone.

POSTLUDE

Cold steel teeth that close.
A box of gray,
an icy sky.
The only thing that saves me is her skin,
waiting for me
out there.

"Cube"
—from the journal of Eric de Vries

The angry buzzer sounded as the guard let Eric through the heavy doors that led to one of the visitors' rooms of Rikers Island correctional facility.

It was January fourth. Eric had been sitting in this shithole for the last five days. Two while they waited for his arraignment on the second, and three more while he counted down to the trial. Almost an entire two weeks he had to be here, only because Carson, that bastard, had pulled enough strings in the judiciary to have him labeled a flight risk. After all, argued the prosecutor, hadn't Eric already fled the country once?

Bullshit. All of it. The newspapers were having a field day—the de Vries heir, the golden prince of New York, rotting in prison not hours after he'd just been crowned king. Fucking fantastic.

Jane was sitting in one of the clusters of chairs on the other side of the communal visitation room, hands folded at the edge of the wobbly table. She was dressed completely in black, the only color her bright red lips and the twin shade of her thick cat-eye glasses.

"Don't cross your legs," barked the guard as he led Eric to the table.

Jane started, but obediently uncrossed her legs. It was all Eric could do not to glare at the guy.

Still, her face lit up when Eric reached her, and she practically bounded into his arms for the short embrace they were allowed. He even snuck a bit of tongue into his kiss for good measure, but he was too scared to do more after the warning he'd been given before coming in here.

They retook their seats amid the clamor of the room, and when she looked at him, Eric felt something deep inside him relax.

"Hey," she said quietly. Too quiet for her.

"Hey, gorgeous," he said.

She blinked rapidly. Pregnancy hormones, she said, but Eric couldn't say he didn't love seeing all those emotions swimming across her beautiful face. He just wished he wasn't the one making her cry.

He slid a hand across the table. Hers approached as well, fingertips touching fingertips.

"No touching!" barked the guard.

Eric sucked in a deep breath. Being in here was not good for his state of mind. He wanted to throttle anyone and everything keeping him from being with his wife and growing child, but he needed to get out. Anything but the best behavior would kill his chances.

"Lloyd called this morning," Jane said, referring to Eric's defense attorney. "He said the preliminary hearing was moved up to next week. Apparently, several of the board members called in personal favors with the judge. They said it's bullshit that you're being held without bail."

"That's because it is bullshit. I'm chairman of the biggest shipping company in the United States, and my wife is pregnant. I'm not a fucking flight risk."

"I know. Of course you're not." But there was something in her voice. Some kind of strange hesitancy.

"What?" Eric asked a little more sharply than he intended. "What is it?"

She worried those plump lips enough that suddenly he wanted to jump over the table just to suck on them. Fuck the guards. Fuck their stupid tasers. Fucking *hell* it was hard being away from her, even just for a few days.

"I was reading the indictment," she said. When her hazel eyes met his, they pierced. "Eric, I need to know something. Michael Faber. Jude LeTour. Kyle Madison." She counted the names off with her fingers and looked up. "Is that the same Jude who..."

Eric nodded. "They're all in the society. Funny. I never knew Faber's first name until today."

Jane worried her lips again. "Is it...is any of it true? Did you pass information on to these men about DVS stock?"

He couldn't lie. He was disappointed she even asked. But at the same time, he also understood. He had lied to her about Janus. Lied about his past. About all of it. She had every reason to wonder what else he had kept from her.

But this…this wasn't one of those things.

"I didn't. Do. Anything," he said, doing his best to convey his innocence with every cell in his body. "I swear to God, Jane. I didn't. You heard Jude in Lucerne. I gave bad information. For exactly this reason."

"And the other charges. They are naming the transactions you requested on New Year's and the recommendations you made to the board members and your family. They must have tapped your phone, didn't they?"

Eric bit his lip. "It wasn't insider trading. We are a family interested in purchasing a full majority. There were no laws broken."

She examined him for a second, and then relaxed. "Okay. I believe you."

"But Carson and Jude…they did try," Eric continued, wincing when Jane tensed again. "It was part of the requirement of being in the society, or so they said. Everyone had to bring things…to offer. At one point, Jude suggested I provide trade tips about DVS in exchange for Carson leaving us alone."

"That's extortion," she said nastily. "That motherfucker."

"Which is why I provided false tips," Eric replied as he massaged his knuckles. They were sore. More than once he'd gotten upset enough to go to town on his mattress. The shitty piece of foam didn't protect much.

"But you didn't do anything else besides that?" Jane asked.

Eric grimaced. "I thought about it. I really did. But then I realized that if I did do it, I'd just be giving him one more thing to hold over me. One more bit of leverage." He shrugged. "Maybe I should have. Maybe that's why I'm here."

But Jane just shook her head. "He wouldn't have cared. Sociopaths never do."

They sat there a moment, just watching each other. Unsure of what else to say. It was impossible not to hug her, kiss her.

Vaguely, Eric wondered how much it would cost to arrange for a conjugal visit. The state prisons in New York allowed them, but he didn't know about the city jails.

"The license?" he asked softly. He was almost afraid to ask. But just like her, he had to know.

"It's filed," Jane said, scooting her chair closer with a nervous look toward the guards. "I dropped it off myself and stayed until the clerk actually entered that shit into the system. The certificate is in a safety deposit box at the bank. We're not fucking around with spousal privilege."

Eric sighed with relief. Not just because now Jane wouldn't have to serve as a witness if this bullshit actually went to trial, but because one of the few things that kept his mind sane in this place was knowing she was in his corner. There was always the chance she could have decided against it in the end. That it wasn't worth her time to be trapped with a jailbird. She still had time to get out.

But, to his utter relief, it seemed she didn't want to.

She was now really and truly his.

"That jumpsuit is really working for you," she remarked, and the light in her eyes told him that he wasn't the only one hard up. "They didn't let you keep your tux, though? I thought you could wear your own clothes when you were just remanded."

Eric thought back to the party, or really just before, when she practically couldn't keep her hands off him. Some women felt like shit when they were pregnant, but Jane seemed to have morphed into even more of a nymphomaniac than ever. And he. Was. Missing. It.

Fuck.

"They gave it to me because I was getting harassed for wearing a tuxedo. They said my clothes were 'distracting the other inmates.'" He looked down, disgusted by the coarse prison wear. "I look like a highlighter."

Jane grinned. "You look like a badass. And pretty damn fuckable, if I do say so myself. We might need to rotate escaped prisoner into the bedroom when you're out, *Papillon*."

For that, she received a withering glare that might have made her laugh if they hadn't been in these shitty circumstances. Instead, Jane bit her lip, and Eric had to adjust himself as stealthily as he could.

"I brought a change of clothes anyway," she said. "All synthetic. No ironing needed."

Eric nodded gratefully. "Good. Thank you."

"I don't know why you don't just let me represent you," Jane said as she examined her rings. "I'm probably ten times better than your lawyer anyway."

"Lloyd Bennett is the best defense attorney in the city."

"Hey, Folsom Prison, I'll have you know that I was a damn good prosecutor. I had more convictions than any other ADA in their first five years."

"Maybe you'd land me in jail then."

"Eric..."

"What about Zola?" he interrupted. "Any news there?"

Jane shook her head, causing the black waves to jostle around her face. "No contact. He told Skylar he couldn't because of the open investigation. The FBI are apparently working in conjunction with all of the New York City DAs." She didn't sound terribly surprised. "He was risking a lot in the first place telling us anything."

Eric sighed. It wasn't unexpected news, but it wasn't great either. "What about Nina?"

"Nina and Olivia have been staying with me, actually."

Eric perked. "What?"

"She wants to help, and she doesn't like that I'm alone. I hope you don't mind, but I told her about the baby. I also wonder if she's been having some issues with Calvin because of all of this. It sounds like he's been feeding information to Carson for a while."

Eric contemplated that. Calvin had always been a conniving little shit, but he seemed loyal to the family. At least, until Eric returned. Now Eric wondered just how long he'd been the family's Benedict Arnold.

"How are you feeling?" he asked, suddenly wanting to change the subject to anything but these shitty circumstances. "Are you sick at all? Skylar was a wreck when she was pregnant with Jenny."

"Don't remind me. I don't want to jinx it. So far, the only side effects I've been experiencing are mood swings, bigger tits, and wanting to get it on with my husband at all hours of the day. Pretty inconvenient, since he's locked up at the moment."

"I want you to stay out of this, Jane," Eric said even more abruptly. No room for jokes. Certainly not denial. "Absolutely out. Leave it to the lawyers, all right? You need to stay safe. You and the baby."

She shrugged, a noncommittal movement that was so incredibly unlike her that Eric sat up straight immediately.

"Jane," he said. "Promise me. You'll stay out."

Her eyes locked with his, glinting gold, like the crazy eyeliner she was wearing. "I can't do that."

"Jane—"

"I said *no*," she repeated. "I'm not going to just sit around and let you rot in here or go through some bullshit trial. Honestly, Lloyd will probably get the whole thing dismissed if there's no evidence. But in the meantime, I'm not interested in letting the shark go without so much as tossing out a net."

Eric frowned. "What the hell does that mean?"

She removed a photo from her back pocket and pushed it across the table. Eric examined the picture of a car outside a small house in what looked like a field. An Asian woman stood by the door.

"What is this?"

"The investigator finally found something," she said. "They found my mother."

Eric looked again. "That's Yu Na?"

Jane nodded. "In Hwaseong, Korea. It's the town where she grew up. And that's a car that was rented to someone named Jonathan Carr." She rolled her eyes. "Some people have no imagination."

Eric frowned. Something about that name sounded familiar, but he didn't know what. "He took her back to Korea?"

"Looks that way."

"Why?"

"I don't know." Jane wasn't quite able to keep her voice from quavering. "But I'm going to find out."

Eric swallowed. "What are you going to do? What does that mean?"

"It means," she said, "that Carson doesn't understand who he's fucking with. He thinks he had some idiot bastard child who would be scared of him no matter what."

She sat perfectly still, and in that moment, Eric had never felt so terrified or turned on.

"He forgot something critical." Jane leaned in, close enough that Eric could see nearly every succulent ripple on her puckered red lips. "He gave his daughter away to a smart man and the most tenacious Korean lady this side of the Pacific. And that daughter...took down bad guys in one of the most crime-ridden cities on the planet."

Eric blinked. His skin prickled all over. "Jane, you can't be serious."

"I spent five years putting much worse motherfuckers than him behind bars, Eric. John Carson doesn't scare me. If anything, I should scare him. And the fact that I don't gives *us* the advantage."

"Jane, I'm serious. *Stay out of it.*"

She didn't answer, just covered her stomach—which was still completely flat—with her hand. Her nails were painted black with tiny diamond studs at the ends. Eric smiled to himself at the sight of them. Even in a shithole like this, Jane was a damn beacon of beauty and badassery, as she might say. And in that moment, Eric knew there wasn't anything he could do to stop her from trying to help.

Shit. Now he *really* needed to get out of here.

"How was the appointment?" Eric asked, suddenly eager to change the subject.

Jane adjusted her glasses. "It was fine."

"Fine?"

She sighed. "What do you want me to say?"

"I want you to tell me what happened," Eric retorted. "Is it something bad? Did something happen to the baby?" The possibility that it was a false alarm shot through his mind, and his chest froze.

"Calm down," Jane said. "It was fine. Look." She reached into her back pockets and pulled out another photograph, which she set on the table. "They said I could show that to you."

Eric picked up the paper like he was touching a priceless artifact. He stared at it for a really long time.

"You...okay there?" Jane asked.

His brow furrowed, making the spider-thin lines over his eyebrows come into high contrast. "I feel like an asshole. But...I can't see it." He pushed the paper back to her.

Jane just giggled and pointed to a tiny speck that resembled a piece of packing popcorn.

"I couldn't see it either until the ultrasound tech printed it out and did the same thing," she said. "Right there. They said I'm a little over six weeks."

Eric looked up. "Thanksgiving?"

Jane blushed under the heat of his stare, and Eric found he *really* liked the way it looked. More, even than the pink of her flesh when he smacked her ass. He swallowed hard. All she could do was nod, her breath stunted.

Eric grinned, but his smile faded when he realized again where he was. Grappling all over again with the fact that his family was out there, literally growing, while he was stuck in here. Even worse, that he couldn't touch his own damn wife now that she actually *was* his wife.

So he focused on the picture. "Hey there, peanut."

Eric was surprised Jane didn't tease him for the name.

"My dad used to call me peanut," she said, almost dreamily.

He put the photo down. "Jane."

She swallowed hard. "Don't. Not...not until we get you out. You don't understand, I'm pretty much on fire under all these layers, and it's not because of the wool. You making googly eyes at our little cluster of cells isn't helping matters either."

Eric quirked a brow. "Is that right?"

She rolled her eyes. "Don't get too excited, Petri dish. It's the hormones, like I said."

He cocked his head. "You know you're going to pay for that as soon as I'm out of here, right?"

Jane bit her lip again, then looked quickly around before she reached out a timid hand and stroked a finger over his knuckles. The rings he'd bought her, the ones that marked her as his, caught in the light and gleamed. Just like the one on his left hand.

"Oh, Mr. de Vries," she said in a low, husky voice that managed to mock and love all at once. "I'm counting on it."

———

To Be Continued...

September 2019 in The Love Trap

Preorder the final book in Eric and Jane's saga now before the price goes up: books2read.com/thelovetrap

In the meantime, you can **read the first chapter here**: bit.ly/TLTChapters

To receive a first-alert about the next book of Jane and Eric's story, subscribe to Nicole's newsletter at bit.ly/NicoleFrench-Newsletter

While you wait...see how Jane and Eric met in the Spitfire Series, Brandon and Skylar's story. Book I is FREE here: https://www.nicolefrenchromance.com/spitfire

ACKNOWLEDGMENTS

Second books in a trilogy are never easy. It's the zenith of the story's arc. They are basically conflict the whole way through—to a writer, sometimes they can feel a little like walking through mud.

Which is why I have to thank my readers first. I can't even tell you how your comments really did push me during this writing process this time around. Every time I would post an excerpt, every time I was unsure of a scene, your enthusiasm buoyed me. Thank you for falling in love with Jane and Eric. Thank you for voicing your adoration for them on my social media pages, in my Facebook reader group, in response to my newsletter. Your voices mean the world. I love you all.

To my alpha and beta readers—Patricia, Danielle, Rebecca, Grahame, and Talia. Your alternating kind words and structural advice helped polish this book in endless ways. Talia, I'm sorry I didn't keep the correct pluralization. To Justin, thanks for all the legalese, and just for talking through the "sassy girl's" story sometimes.

To my lovely editor, Emily Hainsworth, for catching all the

inevitable errors and goofs and reminding me about Rikers Island. And to Judy Zweifel, whose eagle eye is the fastest in the land. I couldn't do this without you.

To my other friends in the author world, of which there are maybe too many to count. I have had the privilege of meeting so many of you in the last few months, and I am grateful to call you my friends. Jane, Harloe, Kim, and Laura—what, oh, WHAT would I do without your humor and advice? To the ladies of the Port Townsend retreat, I honestly don't think I would have finished this book without you. To every beautiful author I met at TalkBooks this year, I love ALL your faces. Thank you for your support.

And of course, to my husband, kids, and family. The Dude is in all of my books, but this time he actually provided a few choice lines for me. How else would I know what a nano acoustic transducer array is? (Spoiler: I don't, but he does, and thank God for that). My three kids are endless founts of inspiration, especially the little one, who is now "making books too." And to the women in my family who are so daringly reading my books, thanks for taking a chance. I love and cherish you all.

ABOUT THE AUTHOR

Nicole French is a lifelong dreamer, Springsteen fanatic, and total bookworm. When not writing fiction or teaching composition classes, she is hanging out with her family or going on dates with her husband. In her spare time, she likes to go running or practice the piano, but never seems to do either one of these things as much as she should.

For more information about Nicole French and to keep informed about upcoming releases, please:

Visit her website at www.nicolefrenchromance.com/.

Check out Nicole's Goodreads page: www.goodreads.com/authornicolefrench

Want to hook up with other Nicole French readers or interact with the author? Join Nicole's reader group, La Merde.

www.ingramcontent.com/pod-product-compliance
Lightning Source LLC
Chambersburg PA
CBHW020504260626
47156CB00006B/1853